Also by Lucy Gilmore

Ruff and Tumble

Forever Home

Puppy Love

Puppy Christmas

Puppy Kisses

I HATE YOU MORE

LUCY GILMORE

sourcebooks casablanca

Published by Sourcebooks Casablanca, an imprint of Sourcebooks
P.O. Box 4410, Naperville, Illinois 60567-4410
(630) 961-3900
sourcebooks.com

Library of Congress Cataloging-in-Publication Data

Names: Gilmore, Lucy, author.
Title: I hate you more / Lucy Gilmore.
Description: Naperville, Illinois : Sourcebooks Casablanca, [2021] |
Summary: "Ruby Taylor thought her days of high-stakes competition were over, until she joins the dog show circuit to get lazy golden retriever Wheezy into shape...and falls head over heels for a handsome veterinarian who won't stop getting under her skin"-- Provided by publisher.
Identifiers: LCCN 2021015755 (print) | LCCN 2021015756 (ebook) |
Subjects: GSAFD: Love stories.
Classification: LCC PS3607.I45258 I3 2021 (print) | LCC PS3607.I45258 (ebook) | DDC 813/.6--dc23
LC record available at https://lccn.loc.gov/2021015755
LC ebook record available at https://lccn.loc.gov/2021015756

Printed and bound in the United States of America.
KP 10 9 8 7 6 5

Chapter 1

"THAT IS, WITHOUT QUESTION, THE MOST BEAUTIFUL CREATURE I'VE ever seen."

Ruby gave a start of surprise at the unexpected voice so close behind her and jerked the leash in her hand. Predictably, the dog on the other end—a poodle shaved and trimmed into a series of white puffs like a Q-tip—didn't move. Ruby had been holding on to her for over five minutes, and she had yet to see the dog do anything but blink. Her owner had commanded her to stay, so stay was what she intended to do.

"I shouldn't say that," the voice continued in a low, flirtatious rumble. Its owner, a tall, well-built stranger with shoulders like a linebacker, smiled as he stepped close. "I'm not supposed to play favorites, but you've obviously put a lot of time and effort into this dog. What's his name?"

"Her," she said. "It's a girl dog."

"Well, she's got something special, that's for sure." The man extended a hand, his eyes smiling down into hers. They were gorgeous eyes, so dark they were almost black and ringed with the kind of long, curling eyelashes that Ruby had regularly pasted on when she was kid. "I'm Spencer Wilson, by the way. In case you can't tell, I'm one of the judges."

In studded jeans and a faded T-shirt that stretched a little too tight for Ruby's tastes, he didn't *look* like much of a dog-show judge, but she knew better than to be deceived by appearances.

"Ruby," she said, shaking his hand. "Ruby Taylor. Only there's been a mistake. I'm not—"

At the sound of her voice, the only other dog in the room sent up a howl of dismay. They were in a hallway of sorts, waiting to submit their entry to the West Coast Canine Classic, and the golden retriever wasn't happy with the delay. He wasn't happy about *anything*, especially the fact that Ruby was giving all her attention to the perfectly poised poodle that had been left in her care. The poodle's owner had forgotten some papers in the car and dashed out to grab them, begging Ruby to keep an eye on her precious darling in the meantime.

Unfortunately, Wheezy wasn't a dog who shared. Wheezy wasn't a dog who did much of anything except make Ruby's life difficult.

"Yikes," the man—Spencer—said as he took in Ruby's *actual* charge. It didn't help that Wheezy had met with an accident on the way in, which mostly involved the discovery of a mud puddle and a determined effort to reach the bottom of it. "What happened to him?"

"It rained this morning," Ruby said, feeling defensive. Okay, so Wheezy didn't look his best right *now*, but the competition hadn't technically started. They were just here to drop off their paperwork and pay the entrance fee. There were still a good two months until the actual dog show. "There are puddles all over the parking lot."

"And yet you managed to get your dog inside without falling into any." Spencer grinned at her. It was a *good* grin, the kind that started in his eyes and crinkled into laugh lines around his mouth, but something about it felt off. Probably because the man was mocking poor Wheezy before they'd even managed to get a foot in the door. That didn't seem like very professional dog-show-judge behavior to her. "I'm sure I don't have to tell you how many of these we get every year."

"How many *whats* you get?" Ruby asked, suspicious.

He heaved a mock sigh. "Everyone with a beloved family pet seems to think they can just roll up here and enter the show. No training, no grooming, no pedigree… I mean, come on. Would *you* bring an animal like that to the most prestigious dog show on this side of the country? To compete against a gorgeous girl like this one?"

Spencer placed a reverential hand on the poodle's head, but his gaze wasn't focused on the dog. Instead, his wide, obvious smile took Ruby in from top to bottom.

She pretended not to understand him.

"He's not *that* bad," she said with a nod at Wheezy, who'd given up howling to scratch at an itch on his neck. Enthusiastic flecks of mud splattered all over the white linoleum. "A little rough around the edges, maybe, but he has something this poodle doesn't."

"Fleas?" Spencer suggested with a laugh.

Ruby wasn't impressed. "I was thinking more along the lines of personality."

To be fair, the man wasn't entirely wrong. Wheezy—a golden retriever of questionable parentage, zero formal training, and the personality of a slug—was the last animal on earth who should be entering *any* dog show, let alone the West Coast Canine Classic.

Yet here they were, doing it anyway.

"Why, dear—don't you think you can help Wheezy win?" Wheezy's owner had asked. Mrs. Orson, who weighed all of a hundred pounds soaking wet, had been in bed at the time, which was Ruby's excuse for giving in so easily. Mrs. Orson always looked her frailest while she was lying down. And she knew it, too, the old sneak. Of all the residents at the retirement community where Ruby worked as a nursing assistant, Mrs. Orson was the wiliest. *"I was so sure you could manage, with all your experience in pageants… No matter. It's only a dying woman's last wish. I'll ask Harry if he can do this one small thing for me instead."*

Harry, who'd never set foot on a pageant stage in his life. *Harry*, who'd once thrown Mrs. Dewan's Maltese into the community pool after Ruby had spent two painstaking hours combing the tangles out of its hair. *Harry*, who'd gladly let Ruby do every bit of work around the retirement community and then proceed to take credit for it.

If Ruby had stopped to think for five seconds, she'd have seen Mrs. Orson's tactics for what they were. The older woman had been threatening to die for as long as Ruby had known her and always rallied the moment she got her way. But Ruby, with her pride on the line and the image of Harry Gunderson in her stead, had ruffled up, hotly defended her ability to claim any crown no matter the odds, and accepted the task set before her: to bring home a dog-show trophy for the world's most useless animal.

In theory, putting Ruby in charge of a golden retriever's show-dog debut was a sound plan. For the first eighteen years of her life, she'd been a show dog herself. Okay, she'd technically been a show *human*, but the idea was the same. She'd been primped and curled and trained to jump through the right hoops. She'd spent hours every day on grooming and deportment. She'd gazed longingly out the window at the other children chasing balls and going for walks.

She'd won, too. Her childhood bedroom—untouched by time or her mother's hands—was a testament to all she'd once been and would ever be. The walls were lined with obscenely large tiaras, stacked and organized by size and weight. Should the Big Quake ever hit Seattle and raze it to the ground, no one standing inside that room would survive. They'd be buried under a mountain of Ruby's gilded—and wasted—potential.

"Where's his owner, anyway?" Spencer asked with a glance at his watch. "It's past ten. The show's probably closed to new entries by now."

"*Probably*?" Ruby echoed. "Shouldn't you know? I thought you were one of the judges."

"I am," Spencer was quick to say—almost too quick, if you asked her. "Which is why you're in luck. For the small price of dinner with me, I'd be willing to fudge the time stamp in your favor."

Every part of Ruby recoiled. Like most women who'd grown up on the stage, she was well aware of the image she presented to the world. Her hair was a tangle of golden-blond curls that she tamed into submission every morning, her eyes a rich brown that she made the most of with carefully winged eyeliner. Add her mother's fantastic bone structure and years of good skin care into the bargain, and Ruby had all the traditional Eurocentric beauty standards checked.

None of that made interactions like these more palatable. Getting chatted up by strangers was nothing new, but she didn't take well to such heavy-handed tactics. It was nice when a man at least pretended to be attracted to her personality first.

Before she could tell Spencer what she thought of his methods, the poodle's owner appeared in the doorway, breathless but holding the requisite forms. As Ruby knew from the stack in her own bag, there were *a lot* of them. You could buy a house with less.

"Thank goodness," the woman said. "I hope I'm not too late. Muffin would be devastated to miss the deadline."

Muffin looked as though she'd never suffered a disappointment in her life, much less a devastation, but the poodle sniffed happily as her owner drew near.

"Muffin?" Spencer asked with a laugh. "Did you name him that because he ate too many of them?"

Ruby stiffened. While there was no denying the golden retriever was somewhat…portly, she didn't appreciate jokes being made at Wheezy's expense. It was hardly his fault that he was carrying a few extra pounds around the middle. Life as the pampered darling of a dozen elderly ladies would do that to a dog.

"Oh dear." The woman took the leash from Ruby's hand and cast an anxious eye over her poodle. "Do you think she's put on too much weight? We switched to organic chicken breast recently, but I didn't think—"

"Wait." Spencer reared back with a start. He glanced back and forth between the two women and then the two dogs, confusion lowering his brow. "This poodle belongs to *you*?"

"We've been looking forward to this all year, haven't we, Muffin?" the woman cooed. She swelled with maternal pride. "Muffin comes from a long line of show dogs. Her mother took Best of Breed at the National Dog Show three years ago."

"Come, Wheezy," Ruby said, hoping to put Spencer in his place. It didn't work. Wheezy showed as little interest in her as he did the air around him. He heaved a sigh and dropped to his belly instead.

"We're still working on that one," she explained. They were still working on *all* of them, but she wasn't about to admit that out loud.

The poodle owner spoke up. "We're not too late to enter, are we? We were both here in plenty of time, I promise. It was only that I left the silly papers in the car, and this woman very nicely offered to wait for me before heading in."

"Weren't you just saying you'd be willing to change the time stamp for me?" Ruby asked, sensing an opportunity. "It's only fair that you'd offer the same to my friend and her poodle."

Hope lit Spencer's eyes. "Does that mean you'll go out with me?"

"Of course not. But I'm sure the AKC would love to hear about how you use dog-show extortion to trap women into dating you."

For the longest moment, Ruby was afraid she'd pushed too far. It was obvious that this Spencer guy was used to getting his way—and even more obvious that he felt no remorse at breaking the rules to do it—but she'd stopped using her physical charms to win pageant judges' approval years ago.

Ten years ago, in fact. And she wasn't about to change that now.

With a good-natured laugh, Spencer threw his hands up in the air. "Fine. You win. I can't resist a gorgeous woman making threats. Welcome, both of you, to the West Coast Canine Classic."

The poodle owner let out a long, relieved sigh, but Ruby wasn't buying it. "Don't you need to look over our applications first?"

"Caleb!" A sharp male voice interrupted before the man could answer. "What are you doing here?"

Ruby turned to find herself facing another version of Spencer. A *literal* version of Spencer that made her swivel her head in a double take. Instead of facing one finely sculpted paragon of masculinity with eyelashes painted by the hands of a master, she was facing two of them. The newcomer was built just as powerfully as the first, but he was dressed more formally in a button-down shirt and well-pressed slacks. He wore his dark hair neater and cropped closer to the head, and his movements were more rigidly controlled, but they were otherwise as identical as, well, twins.

"Spencer!" Spencer said—only…wait. That couldn't be right. "Just the man to help us out of this fix."

The newcomer strode forward, his mouth set in a firm line. "Caleb, I don't know what you're doing or how you got here, but you need to get home." He glanced at a clock on the wall and added, "*Now.*"

"Don't worry," the man said. "I have a half hour until the next bus comes, so I thought I'd pop in and see how things are going."

By this time, the poodle owner looked as perplexed as Ruby felt. "I'm sorry…" She glanced back and forth between the two men. "Which one of you should I turn the application in to? Muffin and I are anxious to get everything squared away."

Muffin didn't look the least bit anxious, but Wheezy was starting to show serious signs of *something*. He strained and pulled in an attempt to get closer to the newcomer, a low whine escaping his lips. In all the time Ruby had known this dog, she'd only ever seen him this animated about pork products.

"To neither of us, I'm afraid," the newcomer said. He stabbed a finger at the wall. "The entry cutoff was at ten. You missed it."

At this, Wheezy let out a bark of protest. Ruby wasn't slow to follow. "But this man—Spencer, Caleb, whatever—said we could still enter."

"*I'm* Spencer," the newcomer said. "And I'm in charge of the dog show. I don't know what my brother told you, but rules are rules."

Wheezy showed exactly what he thought about that. With a yelp, he flung himself at the real Spencer and did his best imitation of a dog who'd never known the comfort of a human's touch. To his credit, Spencer immediately squatted down to Wheezy's level and extended a calming hand. Instead of accepting it, Wheezy began enthusiastically licking the man's face.

"I don't understand," the poodle owner said.

Ruby did. She cast a sideways look at the first brother—Caleb—at which he promptly winked. "Can you blame me?" he asked, laughing. "I'd have lied and pretended to be Prince Harry if it meant I'd get a chance to talk to you."

"Prince Harry would never do anything so underhanded," Ruby retorted. "Prince Harry is a *gentleman*."

By now, the rest of the party had caught up on the lie. The poodle owner looked flustered, Caleb looked amused, and Spencer looked extremely displeased.

Ruby could hardly blame him for it. She was leaning that way herself.

"Let's try this again, shall we?" Ruby said, forcing her irritation down. "My name is Ruby Taylor. I'm here to enter this golden retriever in the dog show." She turned to Spencer. "And you must be the *real* judge. Where would you like us to drop off the forms?"

Instead of softening the man, her comment seemed to increase his displeasure. "I'm sorry, but I can't allow you to enter." He glanced at the poodle owner with a touch of actual regret. "It sounds harsh, I know, but we have to stick to strict guidelines. In the name of fairness."

At that, Ruby's competitive instincts sat up and took notice. It seemed this new Spencer wasn't going to be nearly as easy as the first.

"If it's *fairness* we're talking about, then you should let both these dogs in," she said. "Your brother already said we could enter. It's only right that you honor his promise."

"But Caleb isn't—" Spencer drew a deep breath and tried again. "Despite what he may have told you, my brother doesn't have anything to do with the show. Not officially. He's a dog trainer, not a judge."

"And yet promises were made. How are this woman and I to know which of you is which? Is it our fault we were misled about your identity?"

"It's not—" Spencer was cut off as Caleb released a low chuckle.

"I think you should give in," Caleb said. "I already tried to get the better of her, and it didn't work."

A spark of something combative flashed in Spencer's eyes. All at once, Ruby was struck with how much better that spark suited those long lashes than Caleb's insouciance. Eyes like that were meant to be taken seriously. Eyes like that were meant to carry fire.

"Fine." Spencer stood up and took a step back. "Show him to me."

"Um…" Ruby waved her hand in Wheezy's general direction. "He's right there."

"No, I mean *show* him. Put him through his paces. Let me see what he can do."

Ruby hesitated as she ran through her list of options. It wasn't a long one. Wheezy's skills included very little outside of eating and napping. Putting him in the spotlight—and with that dratted poodle looking on—wasn't going to end well for any of them.

Except maybe the poodle.

"Wheezy, sit," she said.

Wheezy didn't sit.

She went for an easier one. "Wheezy, stay."

In a move of pure perversity, the golden retriever started wandering down the hallway. A sound halfway between a laugh and a snort escaped Spencer's mouth. That did more to set Ruby's hackles up than all the rest combined. No man laugh-snorted at her and got away with it. At least, not unless she *wanted* him to.

"Wheezy, you stubborn beast, make us both look like fools," she said.

This time, Wheezy happily complied. Discovering a half-open garbage can, he got up on his hind legs and started to explore its contents.

"Oh, for the love of Pete." Ruby took off after the dog. She grabbed hold of his collar and tugged, but it was no use. It took a lot to get Wheezy animated, but once you did, he was a force to be reckoned with. Wheezy had discovered something delicious inside the garbage and had every intention of digging his way through until he found it.

To her surprise, a solid male form came up behind her. She didn't need to look to know it was Spencer. The ease with which he extracted the golden retriever from the garbage can was clear proof of that.

"You can't seriously plan to enter this dog in the West Coast Canine Classic," he said. The hand he laid on Wheezy's head was gentle even as he squared off against Ruby.

"Oh, I don't," Ruby replied, turning to meet him head on.

Relief started to touch Spencer's lips, but Ruby stopped it short. "Wheezy isn't just going to *enter* the dog show. He's going to win. Can't you tell a pedigree champion when you're looking at one?"

Apparently, he could. "This dog is overweight."

"Don't be rude. Beauty comes in all shapes and sizes."

"He isn't properly trained."

"That's not true," Ruby protested. "He knows all the commands. He just doesn't always feel like listening to them."

"He doesn't look like a purebred."

Ruby had no response for that one. Mrs. Orson swore up and down that Wheezy was as much a pedigreed golden retriever as his papers claimed, but Ruby was pretty sure she'd had them forged. For such a sweet old lady, Mrs. Orson had some pretty shady connections.

"I have his paperwork." Ruby crossed her arms defensively. "And the full entrance fee. He deserves his chance as much as any other dog."

"Let me see his papers."

Ruby blinked. Spencer might be in charge, but she'd never responded well to demands—particularly when they were uttered by people in positions of authority. Police officers, bosses, teachers...the more power they had to shape her life, the less likely she was to fall in line.

She was a lot like Wheezy that way. She knew all the commands. She just didn't always feel like doing them.

"Why?" she asked. "What are you going to do?"

She'd never know the answer to that question. The poodle owner walked up, looking a lot less worried about her chances now that she'd seen Wheezy in action.

"Is it Muffin's turn now?" the poodle owner asked. "She's ready to show you what she can do."

Ruby felt a smug smile cross her face. It was beneath her, she knew, and alienating one of the judges of the dog show she was trying to enter was hardly a strategic move, but she couldn't help it. If this man wanted to keep Wheezy from entering the dog show, then he'd have to refuse that gorgeous poodle, too.

And men could never resist a pretty face. Goodness knows her mother had taught her that, if nothing else.

"Sure." He shot a look of annoyance at Ruby, which she absorbed like it was a blast of sunshine. It was obvious this man *hated* that she'd put him in this position but equally obvious that he'd abide by the rules no matter what it cost him.

They all watched, unsurprised, as the poodle bowed and pranced and otherwise acted the way a show dog was supposed to in front of an audience. At the end of it, the woman triumphantly handed Spencer the dog's papers. Ruby slipped Wheezy's in a few seconds later.

"In case you have questions about his legitimacy," she said, unable to stop a laugh from escaping. "It should all be there."

Spencer rifled through the papers with a sigh, but Ruby could tell that the decision had already been made.

"Thank you," he said as he tucked the application under his arm. "Muffin has been cleared for entry."

Ruby waited for the same courtesy to be extended to her. "Well?"

Spencer drew closer. His lips were pressed in a tight line, but Ruby recognized the glimmer in his eyes. That particular glimmer—of determination and drive, of *daring*—was one she knew well. He might not like having Wheezy in his precious dog show, but the die had been cast.

And now he had to play.

"This dog needs to be put on a healthier diet or he'll be disqualified before the first competition," he said in a stern voice that Ruby found much more appealing than all his brother's schmoozing charm. "No table scraps and lots of long, brisk walks. If he doesn't show signs of improvement, I won't hesitate to forfeit your entry. Understood?"

Ruby nodded. "Absolutely. Deprivation and exercise. I know them well."

His glance was suspicious, but he kept going. "You'll also need to get him some training. And not just a few hoops in your backyard. I mean *real* training from a professional. We can't allow dogs who will disrupt or distract the others, and this animal, I'm sorry to say, will do both."

She hesitated. "You mean a pageant coach?"

"Is that going to be a problem?"

It was, but not for the reasons he suspected. "I, uh, haven't always had the greatest experience with pageant coaches," she admitted.

"That's probably because you never had the right one," Caleb said. She'd been so busy trying to stare down Spencer that she hadn't even noticed his brother joining them.

"No," Ruby agreed, but without feeling. There was no way she could explain her complicated relationship with her pageant coach to these two—especially considering her pageant coach was and always had been her mother. "I suppose not. I'll have to see if I can find one."

"Oh, there's no need for that," Caleb said, grinning. "It just so happens that I know the perfect person for the job. He's qualified. He's cheap. And best of all—he's handsome."

That last one caught Ruby by surprise. "He's *handsome*?"

"Caleb, don't even think about it," Spencer said, but Caleb ignored him as he slipped a business card into Ruby's hand.

"You won't regret hiring me, Ms. Taylor," he said with a wink. "If there's one man in the world who knows how to beat Spencer at his own game, it's me."

Chapter 2

"WELL, MRS. ORSON, IT'S DONE." RUBY LET GO OF WHEEZY'S LEASH and watched as the animal waddled up the walkway to where his mistress sat on her front porch. Mrs. Orson was reading a romance novel with a picture of a fleshy, naked couple embracing on the cover. Ruby had recently started a book club in hopes of sharing her affinity for sweet, small-town love stories with the residents of Parkwood Manor, but it had taken the group all of two months to take it over.

They now read straight erotica. If there wasn't at least one act of pegging between the covers, the book was immediately vetoed.

"Of course it is. I didn't doubt you for a minute." Mrs. Orson traded her book for a cookie, which she dangled between her fingers as an incentive. Wheezy saw it the same time as Ruby, so she had to pounce quickly to beat him to it.

"Oh no, you don't." Ruby whisked the cookie away and shoved it in her mouth before either the dog or his owner could protest. The dry, cloying taste of cloves and molasses had her regretting her impulse about two seconds later.

Mrs. Orson saw her expression and laughed. "That's what you get for stealing Wheezy's snack. Darla brought over a whole plate of these earlier. I wish someone would take her oven away. She's threatened a tea cake for tomorrow."

Ruby suppressed a shudder. Darla Templecombe was a dashing widow who'd spent the majority of her life dining in five-star restaurants. Retirement had brought with it a fervor—but not the technique—for baking.

"I hate to be the one to break it to you, but you're going to have to find another way to get rid of the cake," Ruby said. Wheezy, deprived of his treat, whined once, heaved twice, and plopped himself at Mrs. Orson's feet. "From now until the West Coast Canine Classic, Wheezy is officially on a diet."

Mrs. Orson looked as outraged as Ruby had felt when Spencer had outlined the rules for Wheezy's late-stage entry into the contest.

"You can't mean to starve my poor darling!" Mrs. Orson cried.

Her poor darling, sensing that his life was about to be turned on its side, uttered a mournful groan. He'd been uttering them nonstop over the past hour—first to protest stopping at Ruby's apartment so she could change into her uniform, then because he objected to the traffic on I-5, and finally because she'd had to park half a mile away. Parkwood Manor, a huge, sprawling retirement community that offered private detached residences, assisted living apartments, and a long-term care facility, was perennially short of parking spaces.

Ruby was ready to start groaning herself. Wheezy wasn't the only one who objected to trudging along in the heat, but at least the dog didn't have an eight-hour shift ahead of him. Mrs. Orson had one of the nicer private residences. There was nothing but relaxation and pampering in *his* future.

"He won't starve," Ruby promised, though not without first crossing her fingers. She'd spent far too many years of her life not starving to know that it was one thing to set a daily caloric budget and quite another to stick to it. "One of the judges recommended a few dog-food brands and a long walk every day. That won't be so hard, will it?"

Mrs. Orson lifted a shaky hand to her brow. Ruby could have sworn it wasn't shaking when she'd been holding her book, but that was Mrs. Orson all over.

"I'm sure I can manage. I'll just get my walker and take a few pain pills first. My ankles should hold out for a few more weeks. Or maybe Harry—"

Ruby held up her hand, unable to stop a laugh from escaping. "Save the theatrics for another day. I meant *I'll* walk him. I have to take him to deportment lessons with some fancy dog trainer, so I can do it then."

"Deportment lessons?"

Ruby held back a grimace. The lessons were as awful as they sounded, but it wouldn't do to let either Mrs. Orson or Wheezy know how much. Ruby used to spend hours sitting with her legs crossed just so, her spine elongated, and an increasingly heavy set of books on her head. At the time, it had felt like literal torture, but there was no denying that her posture was still on point. Her core strength went a long way in helping her lift the residents who needed more care than the Mrs. Orsons and Darla Templecombes of this world.

In fact, if she didn't get into the long-term care facility soon, she was going to be late for work.

"You're going to be late for work," a voice called from behind her.

Ruby sighed, refusing to turn around until she recalled a few more of those deportment lessons. *Breathe in and out. Maintain a ladylike calm at all times. Never allow your true feelings to show.*

"That makes—what—the third time this week? For shame. What would the boss say?" Harry Gunderson laughed. Only after Ruby absorbed this laugh, chewing it and swallowing it like one of Darla's bone-dry gingersnaps, did she turn around. Harry took one look at her serene expression and said, "Just kidding. The boss'll go ahead and let this one slide. I'm feeling generous today."

It was a lie. Harry never felt generous. He was obnoxious and wheedling and an ever-present pain in Ruby's side.

He was also, as he liked to remind her daily, her boss. They'd both applied for the floor supervisor position that had opened up six months ago, but Ruby hadn't even come close to landing it. It didn't seem to matter that both she and Harry had been working as nursing assistants at Parkwood Manor for the same amount of time or that Ruby wasn't a narcissistic weasel who stole the residents' pain meds and sold them to his friends as a side hustle.

You're a good worker, Ruby, and the residents like you, but you aren't really management material.

There's a lot of paperwork that goes along with a job like this one. We're not convinced a desk is the best place for you.

Are you sure this is what you want out of life? Someone with your... strengths must have other options.

Her strengths. Right. Smiling and looking pretty—exactly what every woman needed for a long and fulfilling medical career.

"I was just returning Mrs. Orson's dog to her before I start my shift," Ruby said in as sweet a tone as she could muster. She'd learned a long time ago that the best way to get around Harry was to ooze docility and then turn around and do exactly as she pleased. "No need to worry—I don't plan to put in for overtime. I'm happy to do these little extra errands for the residents."

Harry gave her an appraising look. Although his personality was decidedly rodential, he looked like a walrus. This was due mostly to his mustache, which was bristly and patchy in the most unattractive possible way.

"What did you do to the dog?" he demanded. "He looks the same as he always does."

"Wheezy is dying," Mrs. Orson announced in much the same manner that she regularly foretold her own demise. "He has six months left to live, and Ruby here is doing her best to ensure that his final days are happy ones."

"Mrs. Orson—" Ruby began, but she was quickly cut off.

"We'll go to our graves together, Wheezy and I," Mrs. Orson announced. She allowed her hand to start trembling again and held it to her chest. "Speaking of, I can feel a spasm coming on. Be a dear, Harry, and fetch my heart pills from the medicine cabinet, won't you?"

Harry's mustache gave an excited twitch. "Of course, Mrs. Orson. Anything you say, Mrs. Orson."

Ruby waited only until he'd ducked inside the small house before speaking. "You know he's going to steal half your pain medication while he's in there, right? You shouldn't let him wander around without supervision. None of you should."

Mrs. Orson laughed. It was always such a delight to hear that robust sound coming from such a tiny body. "Oh, honey. You think we don't know what he's up to? We may be old, but we're not dead."

Ruby could only stare at her.

"Sugar pills and baby aspirin, that's all he'll find in our cabinets. The real stuff—the *good* stuff—is hidden with the cleaning supplies. No man is ever going to look twice at a box of scrub brushes. You can quote me on that."

"Mrs. Orson! If you have proof, you should report him. I've tried to do it a dozen times, but no one believes me. They think I'm after attention."

Mrs. Orson's answer was a gentle but mocking smile. It was a look Ruby got a lot, but it didn't bother her as much coming from the residents. She liked to think of them as the fleet of loving grandparents she'd never had.

"It's not right," Ruby insisted. "He shouldn't get away with it."

"He doesn't, dear."

Harry emerged with two white pills in his hand. He rattled them around the same way a gambler would a pair of dice, and Ruby couldn't help but imagine his pockets overflowing with baby aspirin with the A's scraped off.

She shook her head as Mrs. Orson accepted the pills and carelessly kicked them back. Ruby could work here for the rest of her life and never run out of ways to be surprised. Every day was an education.

"Five minutes," Harry warned as he took himself off. He pointed a finger at Ruby. "Then you need to be scrubbed in and on the clock, understood? I don't care how many dogs are dying around here."

Ruby was superstitious enough to reach down and pet Wheezy as soon as Harry rounded the corner. "He didn't mean that," she said, running her fingers through the tangled curls of his ears. The golden retriever did no more than stir, so she turned to glance up at Mrs. Orson. "And *please* stop threatening death every time you don't get your way. Think of how bad you'd feel if something happened to Wheezy."

This admonishment had about as much effect on the older woman as the revelation that Harry was stealing her medication. Mrs. Orson blinked at her for a moment before picking up her book once again.

"But you said yourself that he's in perfect health," she pointed out. "You had that nice man from the dog show check him out."

"I said he gave me diet food recommendations," Ruby corrected her. "And he wasn't nice. He insulted poor Wheezy."

"Did he now?"

"Several times, actually. He also tried to bar him from entering the contest just because we were a few minutes late."

"Then it was good of him to change his mind. You must have been very convincing."

Ruby hesitated. *Convincing* wouldn't be the word she'd have chosen to describe her interaction with Spencer Wilson. She'd used logic, yes, and persuasion, and maybe even a little bit of cunning, but he clearly hadn't been won over—not by Wheezy and definitely not by her.

Holding her place in the book with one gel-tipped fingernail, Mrs. Orson glanced up. "Ruby, honey, if doing all this extra work for Wheezy is too much, I won't hold you to your promise—and I won't ask Harry to take your place either, so there's no need to look at me like I just ran over your favorite bicycle. It's only a dog show."

"Only a dog show," she echoed. She'd spent her morning literally dragging Wheezy across the city, facing down a grumpy dog-show judge, and promising to reform an unreformable animal, and Mrs. Orson wanted to quit? Already?

"I thought it would be a fun project for you, that's all. It doesn't seem like you spend much time with people your own age. You're always hanging around here after work when you should be off enjoying your youth." She nodded once. "I'll tell you what... Forget I ever mentioned wanting Wheezy to enter the dog show. You can go to a movie or something instead."

"Oh no, you don't," Ruby said. "You're not doing this to me."

"Doing what, dear?"

"Ending things before I even have a chance to get started. *You* already paid the fee, and *I* already negotiated the terms of Wheezy's admission. There's no way we can back out now."

"One can always back out of an unpleasant duty."

That wasn't even a little bit true. Ninety percent of Ruby's life was an unpleasant duty. She worked and she took care of her mother and she ran errands for a pack of residents who obviously didn't appreciate the lengths to which she went for them.

"Besides, you said yourself that the dog-show judge insulted you and Wheezy," Mrs. Orson added. "I understand if you'd rather not face him again."

Ruby got the impression that she was once again being played. This felt like reverse psychology or Stockholm syndrome or some weird combination of the two where she was trapped into doing Mrs. Orson's bidding and not-bidding depending on the hour of day. Unfortunately, even equipped with that knowledge—aware that Mrs. Orson was manipulating her—Ruby couldn't stop what came next.

"I'm *not* afraid of the dog-show judge," she said.

"If you say so."

"He has no idea what I'm capable of."

"I'm sure he doesn't."

"I'll follow his stupid rules. I'll get his stupid deportment lessons. And then I'll win."

"You mean Wheezy will win," Mrs. Orson pointed out.

"Of course that's what I mean," Ruby said quickly, but she wasn't fooling either of them. She'd no more back out of this plan now than she'd rummage underneath the sink and steal Mrs. Orson's *real* medication. All she had to do was conjure up an image of Spencer Wilson, his eyelashes fluttering as he tried to bar her from his precious dog show, and she felt the kind of burning passion she thought she'd buried when she left the pageant circuit. It was a more dangerous sensation than Mrs. Orson could know.

The day Ruby had stood in front of her mother and announced that she would never again set foot on a pageant stage had been the best—and worst—of her life. It had been like stepping out of prison after a decade behind bars, crawling out from a hole in the ground and feeling the sunlight on her skin for the first time. She'd been *free*—to make her own choices, to carve her own path, to go through life without a panel of judges commenting on everything she ate and wore and said.

She'd also quickly realized that without the pressure of competition to sustain her—without the drive to win, to succeed—she was about as useful a creature as Wheezy. It had been almost a decade since she hung up her tiara, and what had she done with her life since then?

The answer was easy: nothing.

But that didn't mean she was *completely* useless. Especially when it came to pageantry. If this Spencer Wilson thought a condescending glare was all it took to stop her, he was about to learn the lesson of a lifetime.

Mrs. Orson must have picked up on some of Ruby's thoughts because she let out a laugh. "I knew I chose the right woman for the job." She turned her attention back to her book. "Now get to work before Harry comes back to look for you. I've had just about enough of his face for one day."

So had Ruby, but there were eight more hours of it to get through. And then eight hours after that. And eight hours after that…

She suppressed a sigh and leaned down to drop a kiss on Mrs. Orson's papery cheek. If nothing else, at least this dog show would give her something—and someone—else to focus her energies on. She might not be able to beat Harry Gunderson at his own game, but she could give Spencer a run for his money. Of that she was sure.

"I'll do this for you, Mrs. Orson, but I should warn you ahead of time that pageantry isn't all it's cracked up to be. It can be awfully cruel sometimes."

"So can life, dear." Mrs. Orson didn't bother looking up from her book. "Yet here we both are, living it anyway."

Chapter 3

SPENCER PULLED HIS TRUCK AROUND THE BACK OF HIS HOUSE, THE vehicle jostling up and down over a path that was growing increasingly rutted as time went by. There was a perfectly good driveway a few feet away, leading up to a perfectly good garage, but Spencer hadn't touched either of them in months.

He came to a stop and hopped out of the cab, careful to ensure his emergency veterinary bag was secure in the back. House visits weren't as common nowadays as they used to be, thanks in large part to the offices that had started cropping up to offer twenty-four-hour vet services, but his practice still got the occasional late-night call. A dog-show judge might be able to get away with regular hours, but he'd always be a veterinarian first and foremost.

As Spencer walked up the dirt path toward the back door, he caught a flash of movement out of the corner of his eye. The white-and-brown blur drew closer until it stopped a few feet away. There it transformed into a bulldog—ancient, patient, and with his oversized tongue dripping so far out of the side of his mouth that it almost touched the ground.

"Caesar, for the last time, you don't have to wait for permission." Spencer patted his leg. "Come on, boy. Come say hello."

At this cue, Caesar bounced up and ambled closer. His greeting was an enthusiastic—if wet—one, and Spencer might have allowed himself a moment to enjoy it if not for the sharp whistle that sounded from the other side of the house. The *garage* side.

"Some help you're turning out to be, Caesar. You're supposed to help me adjust the height of the tire jump, not wander off the moment my back is turned." Caleb appeared beside the garage. He had a wrench in his hand and a whistle on his lips, both of which fell a few inches when he saw Spencer. "Ah. I didn't hear you drive up."

"I see you got yourself home okay," Spencer said in as level a tone as he could muster. "You weren't late getting back?"

Caleb reached down and patted his ankle. "Not by so much as a second. Sorry to disappoint you."

Spencer felt his jaw grow tight. Contrary to what his brother thought, he wasn't disappointed to find Caleb back home where he belonged. If anything, he felt nothing but deep, abiding relief. Even though it wasn't *his* job to ensure that his brother followed the conditions of his house arrest—that was what his parole officer and ankle monitor were for—he still felt responsible.

"That was a pretty big risk you took, stopping by like that today," Spencer said.

"You know me. Always living on the edge."

"You're supposed to go straight to the parole office and come straight home. No detours."

"Stopping by to help my brother with his dog show isn't a detour," Caleb said, showing no sign of remorse. He grinned. "Especially since you needed all the help you could get. Have you ever *seen* a woman as beautiful as that one?"

No. Never. Not once in the entire thirty years Spencer had been living on this planet.

"I didn't notice anything out of the ordinary," he lied.

Caleb didn't fall for it. "Bullshit. You were knocked just as far sideways as I was. That's the only explanation for why you were so mean to her." He sighed and held a hand to his chest. "Now, if it were *my* dog show and a woman like that came sauntering in…"

"If it were your dog show, you'd have done the exact same thing," Spencer protested. "There are certain rules we have to follow, and she was in violation of at least half of them. You know that as well as I do."

"Some rules were made to be broken. Especially with a prize like *that* waiting at the end. Did you read her application all the way through? She used to be a beauty pageant queen. I've never dated one of those before."

Spencer clamped his mouth shut against the retort that sprang to his lips. What he *wanted* to say—that breaking rules was what had gotten them into this mess in the first place—would only set Caleb's back up. And what he *should* say—that no human being, however gorgeous, was a prize to be won—stuck in his throat.

The truth was, Ruby *was* the most beautiful woman he'd ever seen. She was a terrible dog handler, obviously, and he was pretty sure she was going to end up being a huge pain in his ass, but there was no denying her allure.

Considering Spencer was an expert on the subject of clinically objective beauty, that was saying something.

Before he could come up with something safe to reply, Caleb gave a short whistle that caught Caesar's attention. With an apologetic glance at Spencer, the dog trotted over to Caleb and planted himself at his feet. If Spencer hadn't already been feeling uncharitable toward his brother, that would have cemented it. Caesar was *his* dog. He'd raised that bulldog from a puppy—loved him, sheltered him, and cared for him every day of his life.

In the three months that Caleb had been living with Spencer, however, the dog had decided he preferred the company of the second Wilson twin.

Just like everyone else.

"And before you yell at me for pretending to be you, remember that it's been three months since I've seen any woman except Next-Door Nancy." Caleb sighed and shook his head. "These are desperate times, and I, brother dear, am desperate."

"What have you been doing to Nancy?" Spencer demanded.

"For shame, Spencer." Caleb winked. "A gentleman never tells."

Considering that Nancy was a sixty-five-year-old retiree with a penchant for gardening and automotive repair, Spencer was pretty sure Caleb was messing with him. Which made sense. That was what Caleb did best, pushing every button Spencer had before he'd even set foot inside the door.

Still…

"Dammit, Caleb. We talked about this. You can stay here until your house arrest is up, but you can't go around alienating my neighbors."

Caleb held up his hands and took a step back, a laugh hanging from his lips. "'Alienating' isn't the word I'd use to describe what we're doing."

"Just do your six months, keep your head down, and stay out of my business. That's the deal."

"I didn't realize you considered Nancy your business." Caleb laughed louder, his hands still up as if warding off an incoming attack. He continued backing up, each step a little slower than the last. "Message received. I'll step aside and clear the field. She's all yours. I'm sure you'll be very happy together."

That wasn't even remotely what Spencer meant, and they both knew it.

"We just chatted about property values, I swear," Caleb added. His expression grew suddenly serious, a flash of sobriety on a face that was almost always the exact opposite. It was like looking in a mirror, but not in a way that gave Spencer any satisfaction. He didn't want to be the twin who looked like he'd just eaten a box of cardboard, who scowled and grumbled and stomped around like a giant in his castle in the clouds.

For once in his life, it would have been nice to just be Spencer Wilson, veterinarian and dog-show judge, a little stiff upon first meeting but not a bad guy once you got to know him.

"Thank you for not saying anything when I gave Ruby my business card," Caleb said. "I mean it. It's nice to have a project to work on again."

Mentioning the project—dog training, Wheezy, *Ruby*—didn't help matters any. Neither did Caleb's next words.

"In fact, I'm so grateful I won't mention that you've crossed over onto my side of the yard." His brother nodded down at the ground. Sure enough, all of Caleb's backing up had carried Spencer over a faint white line on the grass. The line had been applied with a can of aerosol stripe paint that continued inside the house with more durable duct tape.

Spencer jumped back as though he'd just lost a game of Floor Lava—which, in a way, was exactly what he'd done. "That doesn't count," he protested. "You lured me over."

"Maybe I *will* mention it. Cash or crunches? We're up to a hundred and thirty."

"I'm not paying you a dime. You deliberately stepped backward so I'd either have to follow you or shout from across the yard."

"Payout or push-ups?" Caleb asked. The serious look on his face was wiped out by now, replaced with his much more customary smirk. "Bucks or burpees? The choice is yours, but I could really use the money."

"I'm not giving you a hundred and thirty dollars," Spencer repeated. He'd already covered all Caleb's legal fees and was paying a ridiculous amount every day for that ankle monitor—not to mention his brother's food, utilities, and the literal roof over his head. He had yet to receive so much as a thanks for any of it.

"Then you'd better choose an exercise," Caleb said. "You made me do a hundred and twenty crunches last week when one of my socks barely touched your side. Fair's fair."

Spencer threw up his hands. "Fine. I'll do the push-ups."

"Excellent choice." Caleb lowered himself to the grass and wrapped a casual arm around Caesar. The bulldog settled in to watch the spectacle with his favorite Wilson brother. "I'll keep count. On your mark, get set, go!"

Spencer didn't go on his brother's command. He didn't even go in the next twenty seconds. He took a moment to undo the top few buttons of his shirt and roll up his sleeves, not to mention kick off his shoes. He always dressed comfortably for his veterinary work, but not *that* comfortably. He wasn't going to ruin his favorite brogues just because Caleb was a cheating bastard.

It was a stupid game, and he was even stupider for playing it, but rules were rules. The only way the two of them could coexist inside a house was by dividing it in half—in *literal* half—and strictly enforcing the boundary. They could each stay on their side of the house and the yard, but there was no crossing over the line.

Spencer got into position and started in on his one hundred and thirty push-ups. After ten, he fell into a fairly good rhythm. Twenty, and the familiar strain of exertion started creeping in. Thirty, and he let himself follow the pattern of Caleb's counting.

He'd never admit it to his brother, but it felt good—the monotony of the exercise and the cadence of Caleb's voice, this game they'd been playing in some form or another since they were kids. It had started out innocently enough, a system of retribution for when one of them lost a dare or a game of Monopoly. The loser had a choice: pay a quarter or do five push-ups. At age six, both of those had seemed unsurmountable feats, especially since they increased with each subsequent loss. Two quarters or ten push-ups. A dollar or twenty push-ups.

As they'd gotten older, the stakes had changed—mostly in terms of monetary compensation, since there was a limit to how many repetitive exercises a body could feasibly do. A few more weeks of living like this, and there was a good chance one of them would either end up ripped as all get-out or broke.

His brother's counting fell away around eighty, but Spencer forced himself to keep going. Caleb had probably gotten distracted by something shinier and more entertaining. Follow-through had never been his strong suit. Spencer kept count under his breath and was rounding a hundred when he heard a female cry in the distance.

Something that sounded suspiciously like "Wheezy, no!" rose up just as he was hit in the side by a bag of rocks—a heaving, hairy bag of rocks that began lapping at his face with an exuberance that seemed excessive, given the length of their acquaintance.

"Did I forget to mention that we're getting started on the dog training tonight?" Caleb asked from somewhere above his head. "Oops. My mistake."

Spencer tried to roll out from underneath the golden retriever's bulk, but there was no hope for it. Caesar took one look at the dog pile in progress and decided that he couldn't allow it to continue without him. He heaved his massive body on top of Wheezy and began a game of sniff-and-wrestle that Spencer was powerless to stop.

In other words, he was pinned to the ground, half-dressed, covered in dogs, and making a fool out of himself in front of the most beautiful woman in the world. And just as he'd been unable to prevent her from entering the dog show in the first place, there was nothing he could do about it now.

Chapter 4

RUBY WASN'T NORMALLY A WOMAN WHO STARED. AS A FORMER beauty pageant star, she'd seen literally everything the female body had to offer; as a nursing assistant, she'd seen the same when it came to the bodies of the elderly.

And as for men, well, she'd seen her fair share of those too. Dressed and undressed, big and small, handsome and not so handsome, there were only so many ways a collection of body parts could be put together. Once you'd seen the apex of one pair of thighs, you'd basically seen them all.

But nothing—and she meant nothing—could have prepared her for the sight of Spencer Wilson doing barefoot push-ups with his forearms fully revealed.

Or for the sight of Wheezy pouncing on him before Spencer noticed their arrival.

Her "Wheezy, no!" might as well have stayed unuttered for all the attention the dog paid. It had taken twenty minutes and the threat of untold tortures to get Wheezy in the car in the first place, but the moment he caught sight of Spencer, he was as eager as if the dratted man were a piece of raw steak.

"You were right to hire me." Caleb found his way next to her. He pushed his hair out of his eyes and offered her a lopsided grin. "That dog needs some serious work."

Ruby turned her attention to the second Wilson twin, grateful for the opportunity to gain her bearings. She didn't *love* the idea of spending the next two months with Caleb, but she didn't have any other choice. Dog trainers didn't grow on trees—especially ones who knew the West Coast Canine Classic as intimately as this man did.

If she was going to win—and she was—she needed to pull out all the stops.

"I know he needs work," she said. "That's why we're here."

"Does he attack everyone he finds on the ground, or just the ones who judge him for a living?" Caleb asked.

"He's not *attacking* him," Ruby protested, watching as Spencer struggled to free himself from underneath the squirming mass of dogs. To be honest, she was happy to find that the grumpy-looking bulldog appeared to be as poorly behaved as Wheezy, though she could hardly blame either one of them. Wrestling with a half-dressed Spencer Wilson didn't look like a bad way to spend an evening.

It was a *terrible* way to spend the evening, obviously, but… She tilted her head and watched as Spencer gave in and allowed himself to be buried under all that canine affection. Not bad. Not bad at all.

"He's excited about his training," she lied. "And from being cooped up in the car." Louder, she added, "I'm so sorry about this. Wheezy! Wheezy, you promised to be on your best behavior."

Wheezy paid no more attention to her than he had any other time she tried to command his attention. It was almost enough to make her wish she was back at work, toiling under Harry's mocking stare.

Almost.

"Shouldn't you go over there and help?" she asked. "I'd try to save your brother myself, but Wheezy delights in doing the exact opposite of what I say. I'd only end up making things worse."

"Can't," Caleb said with a half shrug. "It's not my side of the yard."

"Your side of the yard?" she asked, but Caleb didn't answer. He emitted a sharp whistle instead. It had the effect of bringing the elderly bulldog to attention. The animal gave up on his playful attack and lumbered happily across the grass to park himself at Caleb's feet, his tongue so heavy with exertion that it dripped out the side of his mouth.

Wheezy didn't go so far as to *obey* the summons, but he did tilt his head in interest—and stopped trying to dig himself into Spencer's lap, which was the most important thing.

"There. I saved him for you," Caleb said. "What's my reward?"

"Your reward?" she echoed again.

Caleb flashed her a smile. "Don't worry. I'm sure we'll think of something before our session is through. I can be a very good boy when I put my mind to it."

From experience, Ruby knew that the best way to deflate a man with an ego as big as Caleb's was to ignore him.

"I'm so sorry," she repeated, turning her attention to Spencer this time. She extended a hand to help him up, but he didn't accept the olive branch. He took his time getting to his feet instead, pausing to unroll his sleeves and button the cuffs at his wrists. This act of rebuttoning, of closing himself off from her view, did more to set her pulse alight than any amount of Caleb's flattery ever could. "If it helps, Wheezy only reacts that way when he's happy."

When Spencer *still* didn't reply, she added, "I didn't know you lived with your brother, or I'd have tied the dog down before I opened the car door. Either that or dosed him with sleeping pills. That's a joke, by the way. I only tranquilize people. Never animals."

Caleb chuckled obligingly, but Spencer only stared. "You do nothing of the kind."

"Actually, I do. Can't you tell?" She glanced down at her attire, which could only be described as *nursing assistant chic*. No one looked good in scrubs, but she did her best by wearing ones in bright colors. This turquoise set went really well with her squeaky white tennis shoes.

"You're a *doctor*?" Spencer asked, and with such a note of disbelief in his voice that Ruby felt all her earlier annoyance come roaring back. He didn't have to act so surprised. She might not be a doctor, but she was technically a member of the medical profession. It wasn't *that* far out of the realm of possibility.

"Most days, I work long and erratic hours, so I had to come straight here," she said. She salved her conscience with the thought that it wasn't strictly a lie. Harry made the schedule, so she always got the worst possible shifts. "I hope that's not going to be a problem?"

Caleb tsked playfully before his brother could come up with a suitable retort. "A doctor *and* a beauty pageant queen? Be still, my beating heart."

Ruby saw her chance to change the subject and pounced. "How do you know I used to do beauty pageants?"

"It was on your dog-show application," Spencer said irritably.

His brother didn't seem to share those feelings. "I knew it from the moment I laid eyes on you." Caleb allowed his gaze to trail up and down her body. It left her feeling just as cold as all his other attempts at flirtation, but there was something about the mulish set to Spencer's mouth that made her more open to it. At least *some* people didn't look at her and immediately assume the worst. "Is this an attempt to regain your former glory? Your big return to the stage?"

"Oh, this isn't about me. It's about Wheezy."

"Yeah, Caleb," Spencer said. "It's a dog show, not a beauty contest. We care about a lot more than…"

The *than*, in this instance, was a vague wave of Spencer's hand in her direction. Ruby interpreted it as she was sure it was intended—which was to say, the total summation of her exterior parts, everything she was and, in the eyes of the world, all she'd ever be.

The last of her self-restraint, never her greatest asset in the first place, gave way. Okay, so she might not have done much with her life *yet*, but this old dog had a few tricks left in her.

"For your information, beauty pageants are about a lot more than *this*." She made a similar gesture over herself. "They're hard work, incredibly competitive, and neither of you would last five minutes on one of those stages. It takes more stamina and drive than you can imagine—years of training, rigorous travel schedules, tens of thousands of dollars, and that's just at the amateur level. The women who compete professionally would crush you—literally. If they didn't tear you to pieces verbally within five minutes, they could put you between their rock-hard thighs and squeeze until you begged for release."

Spencer's mouth fell slightly open, but she wasn't done yet. It was one thing for Caleb to look at her and assume she was a piece of meat to be picked up; it was quite another for Spencer to look at her and assume she was a piece of meat to be picked *apart*. Both brothers were deeply, categorically wrong, but only one of them was insulting the very essence of her being.

"Now. In case either of you has forgotten, I'm here as a paying client." She nodded at Caleb. "I have a dog in need of training and a check in my purse for your full fee. Are you prepared to start acting like a professional pageant coach, or am I going to have to find someone else to take your place? Because I can tell you right now that I know what a pageant coach should be able to do. And you, my friend, are not living up to expectation."

Caleb's response was a deep, rumbling laugh. "Oh, this is going to be good," he said with a shake of his head and a grin at his brother. "We're only ten minutes in, and it's already the most fun I've had in months."

There were serious disadvantages to sharing a house with a man who took up as much space—physically and metaphorically—as Caleb. Caleb was messy. Caleb was loud. He blended frozen margaritas at two o'clock in the morning and snored on the couch louder than any human being had a right to. He never did his laundry and was happy to go days without taking a shower. It was like living with a man-sized toddler deep in the throes of his terrible twos.

Then again, it wasn't always so bad.

"Wait… I'm confused. You mean you literally can't cross over this line?" Ruby stood in the middle of the living room, her legs straddling the duct tape that divided Spencer's one-bedroom home in half. It had taken quite a bit of argument and mediation before they'd been able to agree on a division of assets, but the result was an equitable one. Outside, Caleb had the garage and driveway, while Spencer had to make do with the back deck and a small space to park his truck. Inside, Caleb was sole possessor of the kitchen and most of the living room, but Spencer had access to his bedroom and the bathroom.

As far as Spencer was concerned, he had the better bargain—life without a bathroom and regular access to the washer and dryer was inhuman. From the way Ruby's nose wrinkled as she took in the sight of Caleb's dirty clothes strewn about, most of which were hanging from various pieces of furniture, Spencer assumed she agreed.

"You do this on purpose? Every single day?" She glanced back and forth between them. Spencer would have gnawed off his own arm rather than admit it, but she looked really good in scrubs. She also looked as tired as he felt, her hair in a loose ponytail and her eyeliner starting to smudge. Caleb might have spent the better part of his day playing video games on the couch, but he and Ruby had both worked full shifts like the functional adults they were.

It went a long way in making him regret that earlier remark about her being a doctor. He hadn't meant to sound so judgmental, but it was too late to back down now. Besides, he wasn't sure he wanted to. Things were better this way.

If that woman had *any* idea what kind of power she had, this dog show would be over before it began. Ships had been launched for a face like that. Entire kingdoms lost. Add in the fact that she was a doctor with a laugh like honey and a tongue like a sword, and Spencer didn't stand a chance.

And if the expression on his brother's face was anything to go by, neither did he.

"Well, I don't know that I'd say I live this way on *purpose*, but yes." For once in his life, Caleb seemed ashamed of his lifestyle. He started sweeping up his clothes and shoving them into the black plastic bag in one corner that served as his dresser and laundry hamper all in one. "Sorry it's such a mess. Spencer has all the closet space."

Considering that Caleb had the kitchen cupboards and the coat closet, this wasn't even a little bit true, but Spencer wasn't going to squabble. He was going to go to his room and leave these two to their business. He might have allowed Caleb to pick up Ruby as a client, but that was where all affiliations stopped. The dog training had nothing to do with him. He was just Caleb's roommate, an unfortunate bystander, a—

"What happens if one of you crosses over?" Ruby turned in a circle, her movements slow and deliberate. "Do you immediately implode or something?"

"Ask Spencer," Caleb said. "He was in the middle of his payment when you pulled up. Speaking of, I think you still owe me about thirty push-ups."

Against his better judgment, Spencer allowed himself to be pulled into the conversation. If he left Caleb to tell the story unchecked, there was a good chance Ruby would dislike him even more than she already did.

Which, to be fair, was his own fault, but what else could he do? Instead of accepting Ruby's payment and getting to work like a normal human being, Caleb had insisted that the dogs needed half an hour alone in the backyard to get to know each other—and then invited her in for a drink. Spencer had enough of a handle on himself to accept Ruby as a client of Caleb's, to catch the occasional glimpse of them putting Wheezy through his paces in the backyard, but he could not, would not, *dare* not be drawn into more than that.

He wasn't going to be part of some twisted triangle involving his brother. He already knew how that story would end.

"Our system is basically a monetary one," Spencer explained. "Anyone who crosses over the line has to pay the other one off, kind of like putting money in a swear jar. Except we have the option to do physical tasks instead of payouts."

"Physical tasks? You mean like push-ups? That's what you were doing out there? Payout push-ups?"

Spencer felt himself starting to grow hot around the ears. When put into words like that—or at all—it sounded ridiculous, but they had to have some kind of system in place. Otherwise, his brother would take over everything.

The house, the yard, his *dog*. For as long as Spencer could remember, everything he loved eventually found its way into Caleb's hands. When he'd spent a year as an exchange student living abroad, Caleb had shown up with a backpack and a forged passport to accompany him. When he'd announced his intention of starting a dog show, Caleb had taken up professional dog-show training.

And he wasn't even going to *think* about what happened when Caleb had been arrested for running an online gambling website and used his one phone call to beg Spencer to bail him out. The evidence of that was clear.

"I know how it looks, but it's not what you think," Spencer said.

"Well, don't let me stop you." Ruby made a gesture toward Spencer's feet. He was standing in his half of living room, which was more of a walkway than an actual living space, but there was plenty of room for an impromptu workout. "If you have a debt of honor outstanding, I think you should pay it."

"Yeah, Spencer," Caleb chimed in. "You should always pay your debts."

He shouldn't let himself get goaded into it, Spencer knew, but there was something about Caleb's expression that got under his skin. It was the satisfied smirk of a man who was *certain* Spencer wouldn't do it. Of the two of them, Spencer was the responsible one, the boring one, the one who knew better than to show off in front of a woman who was the walking definition of trouble.

He was all those things, it was true, but he was still flesh and blood.

And that blood burned *hot*.

"Fine." He didn't bother rolling up his sleeves or removing his shoes this time. "Thirty more? Go ahead and start counting."

This time, the push-ups didn't come easily or make him feel relaxed. He was too aware of Ruby's presence, of how fixedly she stared at him as he went through the motions.

Thirty push-ups wasn't a huge strain on his physical resources, so it was over with fairly quickly. He sprang back up to his feet to find that while his brother had moved on to more interesting things, Ruby was still staring.

He expected something caustic to come out of her mouth, but she tilted her head and asked, "How many can you guys do? Like, how high does the number get before you have to give up?"

"I don't know," Spencer said honestly. "It was one thirty today, which means it'll be one forty the next time. I've never done more than that."

"So there's no forfeiture rule? Like, you have to pay double the money if you fail, or the duct tape line gets moved over a few feet?"

Spencer groaned. "Please don't give Caleb any ideas—"

It was too late. Caleb already had them. "A forfeiture rule? That's genius! You're a genius!"

Ruby started to murmur a protest, but Caleb swooped close and pulled her to his side of the living room. It was such a Caleb thing to do, this impulsive and easy burst of affection, that Spencer wasn't the least bit surprised when his brother whirled Ruby in a circle and planted a kiss on her parted lips.

"If one of us can't do the exercise, it's double the money or the line moves six inches, agreed?" Caleb said as soon he released his hold on Ruby. She looked a little bemused but was otherwise silent.

Which made sense. Caleb had that effect on people. He dazed them, *dazzled* them. The only thing Spencer had ever dazzled was a black Lab's fingernails when she was under anesthesia for a tumor removal.

Caleb extended his hand over the line toward Spencer. It had been so long since Spencer had voluntarily touched his brother that he didn't immediately reach back.

"Come on." Caleb wiggled his fingers. "I won't bite you, and we need a little something to spice up the routine. It's the perfect solution. I've had my eye on that bathroom for weeks."

Spencer couldn't think of a way to refuse without looking like a bad sport. Maybe if they didn't have an audience, if Ruby wasn't watching to see what he would do... Who was he kidding? He'd have given in anyway. Even after everything Caleb had done, everything he was *still* doing, Spencer was unable to resist the magnetic pull of him.

He had just slipped his palm against Caleb's when Ruby interrupted.

"Wait. You don't have access to the bathroom?" She turned to Caleb with a look of horror. "As in, *any* bathroom? Ever? Where do you...?"

She followed the line of Caleb's gaze to the kitchen where, unfortunately, Spencer had caught him using the oversized farm sink as a urinal on more than one occasion. When Caleb's house arrest was over and he finally moved out, Spencer was going to have to haul out his surgical sterilizer and put every item in that kitchen through it. There was a portable bathroom in the garage, but most days, Caleb was too lazy to go out there.

"Uh, I've decided to pass on that drink, thanks." Ruby shook her head and started inching toward the back door. "We should get started on the dog training."

Spencer couldn't help but laugh. At the sound of his deep chuckle, Ruby glanced over. When she'd first come inside, her eyes had seemed to hold all the light in the room. Now that they'd fixed on him, he could feel the air leaving his lungs to join it.

"You're the one who hired the first dog trainer you could find," he said, forcing the words out despite the sudden tightness in his chest. "Don't be mad at me if you get what you pay for."

With that, he turned on his heel to leave them to their work—or play, if Caleb had anything to say about it.

Which he usually did.

Chapter 5

"Oh, thank goodness, darling. You're just in time." Ruby's mom popped her head out from the kitchen, a beige phone receiver in her hand. "Will you please talk to these people about the electric bill? They keep saying they're going to cut the power off and plunge me into darkness. It's inhuman, the things they'll do to make a buck. Down with capitalism! Eat the rich!"

As these last two remarks were shouted into the phone, Ruby wasn't surprised to find an incredibly annoyed woman on the other end.

"Yes, ma'am, I am aware that you make minimum wage. No, ma'am, I don't think it's effective to shout at customer-service workers." Ruby stuck her tongue out at her mother, but not until she was sure her mother's back was turned. Sticking out a tongue was right up there with nail-biting, fidgeting, and blinking too much—all things that marked a pageant score down and were therefore banned under this roof.

Even with her back turned, her mother was a sight to behold. She'd had Ruby at a young age, so she was only forty-six to Ruby's twenty-eight, but she could easily pass for a decade less. In fact, she *did* pass for a decade less. One of her favorite pastimes was to visit bars with her daughter in tow, telling everyone who'd listen that her younger sister had come for a visit. Her hair was a more brittle platinum than Ruby's honey-tipped curls, and her figure more carefully honed by celery sticks and regular visits to the gym, but no one who saw them standing side by side doubted the sincerity of this claim.

"I'll swing by the office this afternoon with the payment in full," Ruby promised. She lowered her voice and added, "And in the future, it'll be better if you call my number instead of this one. You might as well forward the bills to me while you're at it. They aren't going to get paid otherwise."

She rattled off her phone number and her address, unsurprised when the woman didn't protest this unorthodox billing method. Over the years, Ruby had learned that most companies didn't care who did the paying, as long as the check didn't bounce.

It took some careful budgeting and more overtime than she cared for, but Ruby's checks never bounced.

"That feels better, doesn't it?" Her mother smiled brightly before pressing a kiss on both of Ruby's cheeks. Ruby could feel the print of her signature rose lipstick leaving a mark and was oddly comforted by it. Some things would never change—and her mother, no matter how frustrating she could be, was one of them. "Bless you, love, for taking care of your poor old mom. Would you like some iced tea?"

"Yes, but only if you put sugar in it. You know I can't stand it unsweetened."

Her mom shuddered but didn't protest, which said a lot about the current state of their relationship. Like Ruby only sticking her tongue out when she couldn't be seen, her mom did her best not to comment on Ruby's eating habits. It had taken ten long years to reach this precarious balance, not to mention Ruby threatening not to pick up the tab when her mother inevitably fell behind on her bills, but they'd reached it.

To Laurel Taylor, Ruby was and always would be the daughter who could have reached the top…but didn't. Instead of the famous actress/model/arm candy for some rich millionaire that her mother had hoped she'd be, she was a nursing assistant whose BMI fell smack-dab in the middle of average. It was hard to tell which of those offenses hurt her mom the most.

"I'll put two teaspoons in, but I can't bring myself to sully it any more than that," her mother warned as she moved efficiently through the kitchen. When she wasn't working on marrying her own millionaire, her mother made ends meet by waitressing. It showed in how neatly she worked—and how lithe her form was. Nothing, she said, burned calories like waiting hand and foot on ungrateful customers. Unless it was waiting on ungrateful men. "Ruby Maynard Taylor, why is there a dog standing behind you?"

"Probably because I told him to stay put." Ruby turned to glare at Wheezy, who stood panting and pleased with himself in the doorway to the kitchen. She had no idea how he'd managed to shrug his way out of his collar and leash, but he'd done it. "I'm sorry, Mom. I know how you feel about animals in the house. I tied him up under the tree in the front yard, but he always does the exact opposite of what I want. Watch. Come, Wheezy."

Wheezy promptly slumped himself to the linoleum floor.

"Stay, Wheezy."

He groaned himself back to a standing position and took a few tentative steps into the kitchen. Even her mother's warning hiss didn't stop him.

"I'll give you a cookie, Wheezy. All you have to do is come closer."

He narrowed his eyes in suspicion, sniffed the air, and called her bluff. Without paying either of them the least heed, he wandered into the living room and hefted himself into a comfortable spot in the corner of one of her mother's black velvet couches.

"He'll shed all over everything!" her mom cried. "Ruby, how could you? You don't have the time or the space for a dog. I hope you're not planning on leaving him here."

Ruby shook her head in a strong negative. Wheezy was a nuisance and a menace, but she wouldn't subject her worst enemy to life under her mother's roof—especially once her mom found out Wheezy had started pageant training.

It wasn't that her mother wouldn't care about the dog; it was that she *would*. She'd take over Wheezy's diet and lifestyle and free time and every waking thought. Nothing drove that woman like a golden trophy looming on the horizon. Ruby had come by her competitive impulses honestly. No one liked winning as much as her mom.

"Don't worry, Mom. He's not mine. I'm taking care of him for one of the residents at Parkwood Manor."

That got her mom to perk up. "Oh? A resident? Have I heard of him?"

Ruby couldn't help but laugh at how quickly her mother changed face. Laurel had cried the day her daughter landed a job taking care of the elderly. According to her, it was a waste of Ruby's youth and beauty. She'd disappear into an old persons' home, she said, smelling of antiseptic and lavender perfume and never seeing anyone who mattered.

Unfortunately for them both, her mom had come across a magazine article a few days later. It told the story of a young woman who took care of the old man who lived next door to her, only to discover that he was a rich miser sitting on millions of dollars and without any next of kin to spend it. A whirlwind romance, an elaborate wedding ceremony, and six months of wedded bliss later, that young woman had become an incredibly wealthy widow.

"Just like Anna Nicole!" Ruby's mother had cried. "Only without all that messy legal nonsense afterward."

Since that time, her mother refused to believe that Ruby worked at Parkwood Manor because she genuinely liked the residents there or because it felt good to contribute her meager bit to society. To hear her mother tell the tale—which she did to an embarrassingly exaggerated degree—Ruby was on the hunt for a rich husband with at least one foot in the grave.

"It's a her, Mom, and no, you haven't met."

Her mother was nothing if not resilient. "Does she have a son?"

"Not to my knowledge, no."

"A nephew? A grandson? A brother?"

"I'm going to stop you before you start asking whether her father is still with us." Ruby held up a hand. "She's a sweet old lady who doesn't get many visitors. I like her and promised to help. That's all."

"Help her with what?"

Ruby sighed and toyed with her glass of tea. It wasn't nearly sweet enough to be palatable, but she took a sip anyway.

"Help her with what, Ruby?"

"You still have all my pageant stuff in storage, don't you?" She couldn't quite meet her mother's eyes. "There are a few things I'd like to pull out, if you don't mind."

A strong hand drove into her shoulder and pushed her to the nearest chair. Ruby fell with a plop, spilling tea on herself in the process. She'd known it would be a risk, coming over here and saying "pageant" out loud to her mother, but she needed all the help she could get. So far, she and Caleb hadn't done much except introduce Wheezy to the agility course equipment—the rings and tunnels and posts that would prove him to be a dog in peak physical condition—but that had been enough. Mostly because all Wheezy had done was chew off one end of the tunnel.

"You stay right there," her mother commanded. "I'll get the key to the pod."

"No, Mom. I don't need you to dig out the entire museum. I only meant—"

It didn't matter what she'd meant because Laurel Taylor was a woman on a mission.

"What do you want? The gowns? The shoes?" Her mom sucked in a sharp breath, her joy almost palpable as she swung a glittering pink key ring around her finger. "*The harp*?"

Ruby groaned, but it was no use. It had been too long since her mom had a project—or a hope. There was no easy way out of this.

"No, Mom. The harp isn't going to do the dog a bit of good." She paused and reconsidered. "Well, he can't be any worse at it than I was, but since I can't even get him to sit on command, I'm not ready to tackle musical scales."

"The dog?" her mom echoed, the key ring coming to a sudden halt. "Why would you want the dog to play the harp?"

"The only thing I want him to play is fetch. I thought I'd start with that old baton-twirling kit of mine. The spangled hula hoops might come in handy, and I was also thinking maybe I could take that stage platform you had Stepfather Deux build for me. You remember the one with the rigging and the lights?"

Not unsurprisingly, her mother didn't take well to this request. Of all her stepfathers—and there had been three of them—the second had been Ruby's favorite. Laurel's, too, though nothing could prevail upon her to own it. The day he'd left—on foot, because Laurel had sold his truck to finance a pageant down in Texas—had been a blow to them both.

She tossed her head. "I'm not sure I still have all that nonsense."

Ruby snorted. "You're a terrible liar. You kept every bead and scrap of lace from my pageant days. I know you've been hoarding it all in hopes I'll return to that world someday, but I have something even more important in mind."

Despite herself, her mom's interest was caught.

"Dog pageantry," Ruby announced with a nod toward the living room. "Wheezy over there is going to win the West Coast Canine Classic."

Of all her mother's qualities, one of the best ones—and the one that had caught her so many husbands—was her laugh. She was frustratingly driven, competitive to the point of obsession, and as vain as a fairy-tale villain, but when that sound escaped her lips, it was impossible not to fall in love with her.

"I know," Ruby said, unable to help herself from chuckling along. "It looks hopeless. And if you'd seen him when we tried to get him to jump through a hoop, you'd feel even worse. But I'm determined to help him win."

"Oh, Ruby. Whatever for?"

It was a more difficult question than her mother realized. The quick answer—that Mrs. Orson had conned her into it—was no longer accurate. Mrs. Orson may have sparked this whole thing, but sometime in the past week, the older woman's happiness had taken a back seat to a much stronger and much more attractive motivation.

"Because a man told me I couldn't," she said.

Her mom nodded as though that made perfect sense. "They usually do."

"He's also really good-looking," Ruby felt compelled to add.

"They usually are."

"And he thinks I'm an idiot."

Not even this confession—probably the strongest motivator of the lot—had the power to move her mother. Without so much as a flutter of her eyelashes, Laurel sighed and said, "Then let's go get you the platform. Though I don't see what good it's going to do that dog. Unless you plan on hiding him underneath it?"

Ruby threw her arms around her mother's neck. Say what she might about a vain, fanatically competitive woman who treated marriage like a newly leased Lexus, there was no denying that her mother had always been there for her. Granted, she'd usually been holding a jeweled scepter like a cattle prod at the time, but it still counted.

"The platform is just a theory I have," Ruby said as the pair of them headed out the back door toward the temporary storage pod that had been sitting in the backyard for more years than Ruby could remember. "Wheezy is the laziest dog in the world, and he refuses to do anything I tell him, but he has a flair for drama. I'm hoping a stage will motivate him, give him a little oomph."

Her mom stopped the key in the middle of the lock. "Where on earth are you going to put it? Not here, I hope. Ruby, I don't have room and—"

Ruby shook her head before her mother went down a rabbit hole of unnecessary excuses. "It'll go up at the dog trainer's house. Caleb said I could bring anything I wanted."

"Caleb?" her mom asked in the least nonchalant voice possible. She turned the key and pulled open the storage door to reveal a treasure trove of pageant paraphernalia. Every color of the rainbow glittered and gleamed; it was like peering up a unicorn's ass. "Is that the man who…?"

Ruby shook her head, grateful that she'd worn her hair down so the curls fell over her face. The last thing she needed was for her mother to realize just how deeply Spencer had affected her. All those things she'd said about him were true—he *had* tried to keep her out of the competition, he *was* good-looking, and he *did* seem to think there was no way

Ruby could be a doctor—but those qualities didn't turn her off. On the contrary, she found herself able to think of little else.

"Caleb is the dog trainer. A nice enough guy, but not my type." Ruby lifted a finger in warning. "Before you tell me that it never hurts to try something new, I should also point out that he lives with his brother and doesn't have a bathroom. I don't think dog-show trainers make very much money."

"He doesn't have a *bathroom*?"

"Don't ask. It only gets weirder from there." Ruby hoisted herself into the pod, her cell phone on flashlight mode as she searched for the equipment in question. The hula hoops and baton kit were easy enough to find, but the handmade stage was larger than the rest of the gear. It was shoved all the way in the back, buried behind racks of dresses and more shoes than any human being should own. She'd once pointed out to her mother, on a day when both of their bank accounts were running low, that they could sell their hoard and clear five figures, but she might as well have suggested they sell their internal organs.

"I hope you haven't hit the gym yet today," Ruby said as she appraised the monumental task before them. "Because we're about to get a workout."

A workout was precisely what they got. Unfortunately, her mother was in such phenomenal shape that the exercise barely winded her. She whiled away the time with questions that Ruby, trapped inside a storage pod with no exits, had no choice but to answer.

"What's the name of the man you like?" her mom asked as they wheeled out the third rack of bagged and tagged gowns. They were organized by color and cut, each rack growing heavier as the number of beaded crystals increased.

"His name is Spencer, and I don't like him. I'm *attracted* to him, but there's definitely no liking."

"I felt the same way about Stepfather Trois. What a pain in my ass that man was. Amazing in bed, though."

"Mom!"

"What do you get if this dog wins the show?" her mom asked as soon as they managed to wrangle the platform out of the pod. "Is there a cash prize?"

"It's not about money. It's about the glory."

"You can't live off glory, honey. Believe me—I've tried."

The final question came as they were securing the platform to the roof of Ruby's car. It had taken some doing to get it up there. This entire enterprise would have been easier if they'd had help, but Ruby would rather die under a cascade of her old gowns than ask Spencer, and Caleb had been strangely loath to accompany her.

Which was just as she figured. A man who peed in a sink and lied about who he was to pick up a woman wasn't the type you could count on to help you move.

"What happens if the dog loses the show?" her mom asked. This question was so unlike her that Ruby almost lost her grip on the edge of the wooden platform she was holding up. "Don't look at me like that… I'm just curious. If you're putting all this time and work into the competition, it's important to have a backup plan in case things don't go the way you want. I always did."

This was news to Ruby. For years, the word *lose* had been banned from her vocabulary. Runner-up was synonymous with failure, and second runner-up was practically a death sentence.

"Don't you remember that year I took you to Disneyland after you lost the Little Miss Missy Pageant to that redhead with the gap tooth? You were so devastated, you wouldn't even take a picture with Mickey Mouse."

Ruby could only stare at her mother as she secured the final rope.

"I had to bribe you with churros to leave the hotel," her mom added with a shudder. "Nothing but carbs and sugar in every bite."

"That wasn't Disneyland, Mom. It was a roadside carnival that later got shut down for reckless endangerment. And the churros made me sick for three days."

"A carnival, Disneyland… What does it matter? You were too young to know the difference."

"I was old enough to know better than to ride that death trap of a roller coaster."

Her mother's signature laugh rang out. "You always were a smart little thing."

The introduction of ye olde pageant days was as good a signal as any that it was time for Ruby to head out. With her mother, short doses were always best.

"I'm just saying that you might want to book yourself a spa vacation where you can take this Spencer character in case you and the dog don't win," her mother said as she accepted Ruby's parting kiss. "You'll need the distraction. You never did take losing well."

Ruby wasn't sure whether it was the insinuation that she could afford a spa vacation after paying her mother's electric bill or the idea of whisking Spencer Wilson away for a romantic weekend that upset her most, but there was no denying her sudden swell of annoyance.

"I have no problem with losing," she said. She whistled for Wheezy, knowing full well that the animal wouldn't come but determined to try anyway. "I lose things all the time. Control, my keys, promotions..."

Her mom only smiled. It was such a typical mom expression—that worldly, matronly knowing—that Ruby almost forgave her for it. *Almost.*

"Of course you don't, honey. That's why you work at a nursing home."

Ruby whirled on her. "What's that supposed to mean? I work there because I like it. It has nothing to do with winning or losing."

"Forget I mentioned it."

"Even if I didn't, it's not as if I had a strong scholastic foundation to build on. I missed more school as a kid than all the rest of the students combined. What other choice do I have?"

"Very true. I've always been a terrible mother."

"Mom!" Ruby released a sound somewhere between a laugh and a cry. "That's not what I meant, and you know it. I'm *happy* with my life—I really am. It's not the glory you wanted for me, but I get by."

Her mom might have had more to say, but the landline inside the house started ringing just then. Wheezy took immediate exception to the sound and started barking with all his might. And his might—with his ninety-five pounds of heft to back it up—was considerable.

"That's probably another bill collector. You'd better get it while I try to wrangle this dog of yours into the car. Unless you'd rather switch…?"

The idea of tackling Wheezy was much more daunting than the possibility of hundreds of dollars in unpaid bills. With only a slight sigh, Ruby left to answer the phone.

Which just went to show, didn't it? She couldn't even win an argument with her mother. These days, losing was the one thing in the world Ruby did best.

Chapter 6

"HELLO, EVERYONE, AND WELCOME TO THE INAUGURAL WEST COAST Canine Classic meet and greet."

A female voice rang out loud and clear over the high school gym, which held about a hundred dogs and twice as many of the humans attached to them. It spoke well of this year's candidates that Spencer's co-judge and vet partner, Eva Johnson, didn't have to resort to shouting or a microphone. The dogs were so well trained that they immediately hushed when she spoke.

"We'd like to take this opportunity to welcome everyone and remind you that neither you nor your animals are being judged today. This is about getting to know the other dog-show entrants to share tips, tricks, and, if either you or your animals are single, phone numbers." The diminutive brunette laughed, which meant the entire room laughed with her. She was that kind of person. "My two fellow judges and I are here to observe and answers questions, but don't feel like you need to show off. We won't bite. Hopefully, none of your little darlings will either—and if they do, we claim no liability for the damages."

That earned Eva another laugh. Spencer would've liked to point out that she was serious, and that any dog caught misbehaving or acting aggressively would be immediately banned from this and all future events, but Eva didn't give him an opportunity. Which was just as well, since he was already the least favorite of the three judges. *Everyone* adored Eva, who was one of the friendliest people Spencer had ever known, and Lawson, a large-animal vet who'd been at school with them, was equally beloved. He was almost as big as the horses he took care of and had the personality to match.

Spencer, however, was the judge who'd memorized the rulebook. Color, coat, conformity...he knew them all by heart. He even carried a ruler in his pocket to check the fur length on certain breeds. As soon as people saw him whip it out, they were known to run screaming from the room.

Lawson rubbed his hands together and cast a glance around the high school gym where the meet and greet was being held. It was the same location they'd used for the registration, but there was a lot more activity this time around. Not everyone participated in these informal events, but they were always well attended. Dog-show people loved nothing more than an opportunity to show their dogs.

"Where should I start?" Lawson asked. "The hounds? The terriers? Who am I kidding? We all know I'm heading straight for the toys."

It was a well-known joke among them that Lawson only had eyes for tiny dogs. He and his husband owned three rescue Chihuahuas. Every year, their Christmas card featured the dogs dressed up in some outlandish costume. Last year had seen them turned into tiny reindeer hooked up to an even tinier red sleigh.

"Ooh, I'll come with you," Eva said. "There's a King Charles spaniel over there who's been giving me the eye since I came in. I assume you're off to ogle the working dogs, Spencer?"

He was about to answer in the affirmative—give him a big, strong Alaskan malamute over a teacup poodle any day—but a commotion at the door drew their attention.

Commotion was the only word Spencer could think of to describe it. In addition to once again arriving late, Ruby had been forced to resort to underhanded tactics to get Wheezy through the door. She entered the room backward, a cheeseburger in her hand and a coaxing note in her voice.

"Come on, Wheezy. Just a few more steps. You can do it." She gave the burger an enticing waggle. Had it been any other woman bribing a dog through the doorway with a piece of meat, she might have gone unnoticed, but she gave her ass an equally enticing waggle. She was clad comfortably and casually in a pair of loose green overalls over a black tank top, but as far as Spencer was concerned, she might as well have been standing up for the swimsuit competition. It was impossible to look at her and not be aware of every part of her body. Hair and lips and shoulders and waist and—

"She can't give that dog a cheeseburger," Spencer announced before his list—or his imagination—moved any further downward. "Did she listen to nothing I said? He needs a healthy diet and exercise."

"Oh dear." Eva muffled a giggle. "Is that the woman Caleb was telling me about?"

Spencer glanced over, his gaze sharp. "You talked to Caleb?"

Instead of answering, Eva sighed. "He wasn't kidding, was he? She's *gorgeous*. Do you think she wants to be my friend?"

"Eva, please don't—" Spencer began, but he didn't know why he bothered. Once Eva decided to like a person, it was already done.

"I was wondering why Caleb was so excited to get a new client, but it makes total sense now. Didn't the first training session go well?"

Spencer pinched the bridge of his nose. He'd known this would happen from the moment that woman first thrust her dog's papers into his hands. He was trying to give her *less* space in his life, not more. The last thing he needed was for Eva to roll out the full welcome-wagon routine.

"Of course the first training session didn't go well," he said. "We're talking about Caleb. He spent nine-tenths of his time flirting."

"I don't blame him. I'm tempted to leave Maury and take a stab at her myself. Then again, she seems more your type than mine."

Spencer groaned. If Eva had any idea…

"You'd better go help her," Eva said, laughing at his distress. "I don't trust the way that dog of hers is eyeing his competition."

It was a ruse, of course. Even from his position across the gym, Spencer could tell that Wheezy wasn't eyeing his competition. Wheezy didn't even know there *were* other dogs around. His whole world had diminished to the cheeseburger in front of him. His golden retriever instincts followed it like he was tracking the movements of a duck.

Aware that Eva was watching him much more closely than he cared for, Spencer strode toward the door.

"Don't come any nearer," Ruby said before Spencer made it all the way over. "I mean it. You'll distract him, and we're so close."

"Close to what?" Spencer asked. There was no finish line that he could see, no pot of gold at the end of the rainbow. Just endless encounters like this one. "Maybe I didn't make myself clear before, but a cheeseburger isn't on a heart-healthy dog diet."

"Don't listen to him, Wheezy. This bacon-cheddar masterpiece has your name written all over it. Look at how it oozes. See how it glistens." Although she had yet to turn toward Spencer, she nodded at the doors they'd come through. "Pretty please will you slam and bar those doors? I don't know how much longer this is going to work."

Spencer would have liked to dig in his heels and refuse to play along—with this or any of Ruby's outrageous schemes—but there were a hundred dogs and just as many people watching in the background. Besides, he was curious to see how this would play out. What did she think would happen to Wheezy once he was trapped inside the gym?

No sooner had Spencer clicked the doors shut than he heard a whoop of triumph.

"Ha! I got you, sucker! Take *that*."

At first, he assumed *he* was the sucker and that he'd just fallen for some elaborate trick plotted at his brother's hands, but he turned around to find Ruby taking a triumphant bite out of the burger.

"You didn't actually think you were going to get any of this after what you put me through, did you?" she asked with her mouth full. She took another bite before she'd swallowed the first. "Let that be a lesson to you. Rule number one: Your pageant coach isn't your friend. They'll find ways to ruin your life that you didn't even know existed."

Spencer found himself unable to look away. There was nothing delicate or ladylike about the way Ruby was attacking that cheeseburger, but it was still like watching an exquisite painting come to life.

Girl with a Double Patty. La Demoiselle de Meat.

He managed to shake himself off just in time. "I'm sorry… Did you just double-cross a *dog*?"

Her golden laugh rang out. "Yes. Caleb said reward-based training is the best way to get results. All I have to do is find the thing that motivates Wheezy and use it to get what I want." She paused and smirked. "Apparently, dogs and men are exactly the same. Who knew?"

Even though Spencer supported rewards-based training in all forms, he couldn't help but feel outraged on the dog's behalf. And his own. It took a lot more than a waggling cheeseburger—or a nicely formed ass—to motivate him.

"I don't know what Caleb has told you about rewarding canine behaviors, but it only works if you actually *reward* Wheezy," he said. "All you're doing right now is teaching him not to trust you."

"Oh, don't worry. I've got that covered." She reached into her front bib pocket and extracted an oversized carrot. "What a good boy you are, Wheezy. Thank you for walking with me. You're a prince among dogs."

Wheezy took one look at the vegetable being held out to him and howled.

"You don't even know what it is," Ruby coaxed. "Maybe you love carrots. Maybe they're your favorite thing. They're crisp and refreshing, and they make you see in the dark. Don't you want night vision like all the other dogs?"

"No dogs have night vision," Spencer said, feeling irritable. He might have prescribed the diet in the first place, but giving Wheezy a carrot as a consolation prize for a cheeseburger was just plain cruel. "They have more retina rods than humans, but not nearly as many as cats."

"That shows what you know. The best pageant coaches can gaslight you into believing anything. Mine convinced me that eating chocolate caused freckles—a belief I held until I was well into my teen years. Imagine my embarrassment when I finally learned about UV rays."

He stared at her. "That can't possibly be true."

"I also thought every kid had to do an hour of articulation exercises before they were allowed to go to school in the morning. I was the only one who treated the Pledge of Allegiance like it was an audition for Broadway."

"Good God. Who was your pageant coach?"

"My mom. The night-vision carrots were another of her stories that I bought into much longer than I should have. I wasn't a very bright child."

Something about the wistful way she spoke made Spencer think there was more to the story, but he didn't dare ask what it was. Getting to know her—allowing himself to be lulled by friendliness—would only lead to his cheeseburger being taken away.

Nodding at the dog by her feet, she added, "And even though the carrots were a lie, I still ate them. Come on, Wheezy. Don't you even want to try it? Think of all the crumbs you'll be able to find in the dark."

Apparently, Wheezy wasn't as trusting as a young Ruby Taylor. The animal sniffed once, grumbled twice, and flounced away. Spencer had spent the majority of his life surrounded by canines of all varieties, but he wasn't sure he'd seen a dog flounce before. Wheezy's nose was in the air and everything.

"It's all you're getting until breakfast tomorrow, so you might as well eat it," she called as the animal waddled over to a corner and sat himself in it. He wore such a look of dejection, of utter betrayal, that Spencer took pity on him.

"Come here, buddy," he called with a snap of his fingers. "We'll see if we can do better than a root vegetable."

"I just spent the past three hours removing everything even remotely delicious from his owner's kitchen so she won't be able to sneak him treats when my back is turned. If you give him anything with more than forty calories, I'll—"

Spencer didn't have an opportunity to hear what kind of vengeance Ruby had planned. She stopped herself as soon as she realized Wheezy had seen the hand Spencer was holding out to him and lifted an interested ear. When Spencer didn't do anything more than continue standing there, his summons clear, Wheezy hefted himself to his feet and grumblingly came forward.

"That's a good boy." He found a spot behind Wheezy's right ear and scratched it. The dog, pleased with this turn of events, sat down and thumped his leg on the sleek gym floor. Spencer nodded down at him. "For future reference, you might want to consider rewards other than food. As you can see, affection works just as well."

Ruby snorted. "Not from me, it doesn't. Watch." She tossed the rest of her burger and the neglected carrot in a nearby garbage before reaching down to scratch Wheezy's other ear. Even though her movements were as gentle as Spencer's, the animal gave such a loud yelp that several nearby dogs barked in sympathy.

"See?" she demanded. "He's immune to my charms. Nothing I do or say appeals to him."

Spencer couldn't resist. "First time that's ever happened to you?"

"No, actually. It happens more often than you'd think. Try as I might, I can't seem to win some dogs—or people—over."

"I wonder why that is?"

"My fierce competitive streak, probably." She caught his gaze and held it. "I don't know if you've noticed, but when I do a thing, I do it all the way."

There was no need for her to tell him that. He'd only known Ruby for a little while, but she'd more than proven her commitment to this dog show. He'd have admired it if he wasn't so irritated by it. Not once did she question her right to be in this gym even though her dog was the worst-behaved by a vast margin. It also didn't occur to her that insulting a judge and coordinator of the dog show might not be the best way to go about winning a trophy. She'd determined on a course of action—in this case, taking over the West Coast Canine Classic—and that was the end of it.

Determination and drive were qualities he liked just fine when it wasn't *his* dog show on the line.

Or, he was forced to admit, his pride.

Before he made the mistake of voicing any of this out loud, Eva came bounding up with Lawson in tow. "You must be the infamous Ruby Taylor," she said with a wink for Spencer.

Spencer watched as Eva wrapped the other woman in a warm—and surprise—hug. Ruby's eyes flew to Spencer's as she accepted the embrace, but all he did was shrug. Letting people witness Eva in action was much easier than trying to explain her.

"I'm so glad to finally meet you," Eva said. "When I didn't see your name on the sign-in sheet, I was afraid Spencer had scared you away for good."

"Is there a sign-in sheet?" Ruby pulled herself away and cast a quick glance around the gym. "Oops. I didn't realize."

"No worries. I jotted your name down for you." Eva tugged on Lawson's sleeve to draw him closer. "But since we didn't get to meet you at registration, I thought we should go through the formalities now."

"About that." A look almost like guilt crept over Ruby's features. The fact that she felt guilty around Eva and *not* around him wasn't lost on Spencer. "Sorry about my late entry. I'm not sure if Spencer explained it, but—"

Eva held up a hand. "No explanations needed. We're happy to have you."

Spencer wasn't sure about *that*, but there was no denying he felt… something at having Ruby near.

Eva tugged on Lawson's sleeve. "This is Lawson Dawes. He's our third judge, but it's no use trying to get on his good side because he only does the toy and terrier categories. Well, that and Best in Show, but if you manage to get that dog of yours anywhere near the finals, I'll eat my shoes."

That caused Ruby to poker up. "Wheezy has as good a chance as anyone else here."

Eva looked down at the dog in question and laughed. She slapped a hand over her mouth in an attempt to keep the sound back, but it was too late. "Oops. That was unprofessional of me. Of course he has a chance. Such a good boy. So handsome. So stately."

As Wheezy had at that moment discovered an itch near his genitals that required his immediate and intense attention, not even Ruby could maintain a straight face.

"Mind your manners," she said, nudging the dog with her foot. He treated this the same way he did most of Ruby's requests: he ignored it. "Sorry. He's not used to such refined company, but that's why we're here. I brought him hoping all the good manners would rub off on him. Caleb said dogs learn a lot of their behaviors from other animals."

"Caleb?" Lawson quirked one of his bushy eyebrows at Spencer. "How interesting. I didn't realize you were working with him."

Spencer shook his head in warning, but Lawson pretended not to see.

"Did he come with you?" Lawson glanced around the gym even though he already had the answer. If Caleb had been here, Lawson would have known it. *Everyone* would know it. Like Ruby, Spencer's brother knew how to make an entrance. "Trainers are always welcome at these events. In fact, we encourage it. It's nice to know who's working the dogs."

Ruby wrinkled her nose. "I asked him, but he said he had plans."

"Plans?" Eva shot Spencer a questioning glance. "What kind of plans?"

Spencer bit back a sigh. Although both Eva and Lawson knew about his tumultuous relationship with his brother—and their bizarre living arrangement—they didn't know the reason behind it. No one did. That was the one thing Caleb had insisted on as soon as the judge issued his sentence. He didn't mind if people thought he was an unemployed squatter with a strange reluctance to go out, just so long as they didn't know the truth about what he'd done.

He wanted to look good rather than be good, play the hero instead of behaving like one.

"I'm not my brother's keeper," he said tightly. "What he does in his free time is of no interest to me."

"That means he has a hot date," Eva told Ruby. Spencer didn't want to be interested in Ruby's opinion of Caleb—and wanted even less to show it—but he couldn't help watching to see how she reacted. If she was dismayed by the prospect of his brother wooing another woman, she was phenomenal at hiding it.

"Come on," Eva added with a nudge of her elbow. "I'll introduce you to a few of the other golden retriever owners. Maybe they'll have some ideas about how you can whip Wheezy into shape."

Ruby perked up. “You think?”

Eva eyed the animal in question. “No, I don’t. But you might make a few friends in the process.”

Lawson waited only until the two women dragged Wheezy toward a row of docile golden retrievers before pouncing. “So,” he said, a laugh rumbling low in his voice. “We’re letting any old mixed breed into the dog show now, are we? How interesting.”

Spencer felt his ears grow hot. It was the same thought he’d had the first time he’d laid eyes on the dog, but that wasn’t the point. *He* wasn’t the one bending the rules for Ruby’s sake. *He’d* wanted to put his foot down from the start.

“Wheezy has all the right paperwork,” he said stiffly. “I checked it myself.”

“Staking our reputation for the sake of a few golden curls?”

“I made stipulations. He has to lose some weight and meet the basic training requirements first. I can veto his placement at any time.”

The rumbling laugh turned into an outright guffaw. Lawson clapped a heavy hand on Spencer’s shoulder, using so much force that it almost caused him to choke. The problem working with people like Lawson and Eva was that they knew him too well. Sometimes, a man just wanted to sit alone with his lies.

“I wasn’t talking about the *dog’s* curls,” Lawson said.

“If you were a real friend, you’d steal a sample of that dog’s saliva and get his breed tested for me,” Spencer grumbled, only half-joking. “I’d ask Eva to do it, but she has all the stealth of a militarized wombat.”

“Probably less,” Lawson agreed.

Spencer assumed his friend would issue more jokes along these same lines—look at Spencer relaxing his rules for a pretty face, watch as Spencer lost all his scruples—but he sobered instead.

That was another problem working with people like Lawson and Eva. They also cared too much for their own good.

“Everything okay with Caleb, by the way?” he asked. “He’s never missed one of these things before. He’s the first to arrive and the last to leave, and always with a smile on his face. I hate to say it, but the West Coast Canine Classic doesn't feel the same without him."

Spencer wasn't sure whether this was intended as an insult, but it certainly felt like one. His brother had nothing to do with this event. He used it as an opportunity to peddle his training services and ingratiate himself with Spencer's friends, yes, but that was where the overlap ended. Their parents bred border collies, so they'd grown up around pedigrees, but it wasn't until Spencer had taken things one step further and started the West Coast Canine Classic that Caleb had shown any real interest in show dogs.

"He's fine," Spencer said. "He has his own stuff going on right now, that's all."

"Fine. Don't tell me. I'll get the story out of him eventually."

"I'm serious. We're not joined at the hip. He has his own life, and I have mine."

That made Lawson laugh and slap him on the shoulder all over again. This time, it was hard enough to make Spencer wince. "Sure thing, Spencer. You're just two brothers who can totally function independently of one another. I've known it all along."

As far as dog-based social events went, the meet and greet was a success, mostly because no dog attacked one of its peers. No human did, either, and that was saying something when you were talking about a competition at this level. There was no cash prize for winning the West Coast Canine Classic, but since all three of the judges were qualified by the AKC, their scores counted toward an animal's overall show points and champion status. These could be used for access to other, more grandiose shows and were therefore highly coveted.

With so much on the line, most people treated the meet and greet exactly like what it was: an opportunity for breeders to meet other breeders, for handlers to chat about the latest in training techniques, and a chance for dogs to sniff and frolic and preen.

And for Wheezy, apparently, to take a nap.

"Just tell him about the exciting plans you have for tonight. That should get him to budge." Ruby stood several feet away, a cell phone pressed against her ear, supremely unconcerned that everyone else had exited the gym a good ten minutes earlier. Being alone with Ruby wasn't how Spencer would have chosen to end the evening, especially since he'd done a decent job of avoiding her for most of it, but both Eva and Lawson had families to get home to. They'd agreed a long time ago that Spencer's single state meant that it was his privilege to clean up and clear out the stragglers.

In this case, stragglers meant Wheezy, who looked as though nothing short of a natural disaster would move him.

"What's today?" Ruby asked with a tap of her fingernail against her teeth. "Wednesday? That means bingo and Jell-O at the rec center. Tell him about that."

Spencer was standing a few paces back, well out of Ruby's line of vision, but he didn't miss the sound of a loud female voice coming through the phone receiver.

"Well, no," Ruby replied when the voice had finished. "I don't know that I'd get excited for bingo either, but it's not like he knows the difference. Make something up."

He watched as Ruby proceeded to hold the phone against Wheezy's ear. The female voice on the other end coaxed and cooed, but it was no use. Wheezy slumbered on.

Without second-guessing the wisdom of his actions, Spencer strode forward and plucked the phone from Ruby's hand. He had a strong desire to speak to the owner of this particular dog—and not just because she was a friend of Ruby's. Anyone who woke up next to that animal every day and thought, *This is an award-winning golden retriever if I've ever seen one*, was seriously deluded.

"Do I have the honor of addressing Wheezy's owner?" he asked. Ruby made a grab to take the phone from him, but he warded her off with one upheld hand. Since it seemed highly likely that the dog would only be exiting this building if Spencer picked him up and carried him out, this phone call seemed the least she could do in return.

"Who is this?" the voice demanded.

"My name is Spencer Wilson. I'm one of the judges of the West Coast Canine Classic."

"Is that so? What are your qualifications?"

He was taken aback but didn't hesitate to answer. "I'm a licensed veterinarian with over five years of experience running this dog show. What are yours?"

The woman didn't hesitate either. "I don't have any, but if that's something you care about, Ruby is as pedigreed as they come."

He didn't dare look over at the woman in question. Ruby's pedigree had never been in question. All it took was a glance to realize *that*.

"Be that as it may, this is a competition that judges dogs, not humans."

"Is that so?" she retorted. "Then why do you have me paying out the nose for a trainer to whip Wheezy into shape? Seems to me that a person's capabilities have a little something to do with it."

The woman had him there—especially since it was his own brother getting the payout. "It's true," he admitted. "But Caleb has been around dogs as long as I have, so you don't have to worry about not getting what you paid for. I can personally vouch for him—in fact, I do."

There was a humming sound on the other end of the phone, as though the woman wasn't sure whether to believe him. She had no need to worry. Caleb might be the least responsible person Spencer knew, but dogs were the one thing he never failed at. Spencer was good at providing them with medical care and judging their behaviors, but Caleb was the one they turned to when they wanted anything more.

"The password is 'mayonnaise.'"

Spencer blinked at this sudden change of subject. Unable to help himself, he cast a questioning look at Ruby. She stood with her arms crossed, one brow arched as she watched the conversation unfold.

"You're the one who wanted to talk to her," she said in a voice too low for the woman to overhear. "By all means, continue."

"I'm not sure I understand," he said. "What password?"

"It's Wheezy's green light," the woman said.

"His green light to what?"

"To continue. You know—like a danger word."

That didn't clarify things in the slightest. "A danger word?"

Ruby choked on a sudden laugh.

"I'm afraid I'm not familiar with that term," Spencer said carefully, mistrusting that laugh. He *liked* it, obviously, but that was the problem. He liked a lot more about Ruby than he wanted to.

"You're not? What a pity. The good men never are." The woman on the other end of the phone released a short sigh. "I don't see what more I can possibly do to help out. He's only a dog. How hard can it be to walk him out a door?"

She hung up without saying anything more. Spencer stared at the phone for a second, sure he'd missed a step somewhere.

"I could have told you how that would go," Ruby said as she took her phone back. "Mrs. Orson is a lot like her dog. She doesn't make anything easy."

"Neither do you," he pointed out. "You should have brought a second cheeseburger to lure him out again."

"I'll remember that for next time," she said. "What was that about, by the way? Why did you want to talk to her?"

Rampant curiosity and a desire to know Ruby better seemed like the wrong answers, so he countered with "What's a danger word? And why do only bad men know what it is?"

The half-choked gurgle of laughter escaped her again. "Oh dear. How to explain this delicately? You see, when mommies and daddies love each other very much—"

Every part of his being balked—reared up, pulled the brakes, and refused to go one step further. "Never mind. I think I just figured it out."

"—and when those mommies and daddies are feeling a little bored in the bedroom—"

"You can stop now. I get it." He might not be the most sexually savvy man in the world, but he could put the pieces together. Danger word/safe word. Green light/red light. They were talking full-on sexcapades here—a topic fraught with danger and red lights on all sides. He would *not* allow himself to discuss mommies, daddies, or any of the things they got up to with Ruby.

Mostly because he wouldn't mind discussing them with her at all.

"Who *is* that woman?" he asked, finding it best to change course.

This time, Ruby's laugh was a full, glorious peal. "The bane of my existence and one of my favorite people in the whole world. She lives at the retirement community where I work."

"She's your patient?"

Ruby's eyes shifted down to her feet. "Something like that. She's the reason I'm doing all this in the first place." She rolled her shoulder in a half shrug. "She sort of roped me into it against my will. Wheezy winning the West Coast Canine Classic is her dying wish."

Spencer cast a look of alarm down at the dog. Wheezy was *technically* qualified to participate in the competition, and Caleb was as good a dog-show trainer as you could get last-minute, but that dog wouldn't get anywhere near the final trophy unless he sat on it.

"Dying wish?" he echoed. "I don't think—"

"Oh, don't worry. She's not actually dying. She uses that line to force me into doing things I'd rather not." She laughed again. "She's also an avid reader of erotica, if that bit about the danger word didn't tip you off. We have a book club."

He didn't want to ask. He wouldn't say the words out loud.

He did anyway. "You read *erotica* together?"

She nodded. "And then we discuss it. At length. And girth, if you want to get specific. Why? Would you like to join us?"

No, he decidedly would not. Especially not if Ruby was going to look at him like that while he did it. "If a danger word is what I suspect it is—"

Her smile widened. "It's basically the opposite of a safe word. It means full steam ahead, all engines are a go, pistons ready. It was in the last book we read—it was kind of cute, actually. The couple would text each other the word *porcupine*, and then meet up at the nearest seedy motel without asking any questions. Of course, they were also exhibitionists who left the curtains wide open for everyone staying at the motel to see, but it takes all kinds."

This conversation had taken a dangerous turn, but Spencer didn't know how to extricate himself without making things worse. What he'd have liked to do was offer an easy reply—be more like Caleb, who could discuss porcupines and voyeurism with a gorgeous woman as if it meant nothing—but he couldn't.

It didn't mean nothing. Not to him, at least. It never had. That was the whole problem. His brother could meet a woman like Ruby and enjoy a brief, playful flirtation—the kind of flirtation that a dog-show judge and contestant *might* be able get away with, assuming they kept things discreet—but not Spencer. Within seconds of meeting this woman, he'd known himself to be way in over his head.

And instead of heading up for air, he just seemed to be diving deeper and deeper.

"The dog's danger word is 'mayonnaise,'" he blurted out.

She blinked. "What?"

He didn't have to explain himself. As soon as the word crossed his lips, Wheezy lifted his head, his eyes wide open and his nose twitching.

"Is that how it works, Wheezy?" he asked, eager to latch on to anything other than the topic at hand. "You like mayonnaise?"

As if on cue, the golden retriever extended both paws out in front of him and executed a bow. It wasn't an unusual position for a show dog. It was, however, an unusual position for a dog who balked at every command thrown his way.

Instead of being impressed by this sudden show of docility, Ruby drew closer, her eyes narrowed. "I wouldn't trust it," she warned. "He's up to something."

"He's a dog. He's hardly plotting a bank heist. Watch." He snapped his fingers to draw Wheezy's attention. "Mayonnaise, Wheezy. May-o-nnaise."

Once again, Wheezy proved himself a paragon of show-dogmanship by twirling in a circle. He also grinned up at Spencer in a way that proved he was fully aware of his actions. It was the expression of a dog who knew he was being a Very Good Boy and who wanted to be acknowledged for it.

Spencer had always been a sucker for oversized brown eyes. "That's right, Wheezy," he said, patting him gently on the head. "What a good dog you are. What lovely manners."

"I'm still not buying it," Ruby said. She put up a hand to nudge Spencer a few steps back. The touch on his chest was light and impersonal, but he felt the imprint of it long after her hand fell away. "Wheezy, it's high time we mayonnaised out of here and headed home."

The dog blinked up at her.

"You can even ride in the front mayonnaise, if you want."

His eyes started drooping.

"I'll open the mayonnaise and you can hang your head out the whole way."

He started to lower himself to the floor once again.

"Dammit, Wheezy!" Ruby swooped down to prevent him from lying down. "Help me, Spencer. If he hits the floor, I'll never get him back up again."

Spencer did as he was asked—and *not* because of the pleading note in Ruby's voice or the look she cast up at him, as if he alone was capable of coming to her rescue. It was just that he had to be out of here by eight o'clock, and Wheezy was already on his feet. That was half the battle right there.

It worked, too. With only a negligible amount of coaxing and references to his favorite condiment, Wheezy allowed himself to be led across the gym and out a side door. In true Seattle fashion, the evening had grown rainy and overcast, but even the sharp tang of ozone and a twenty-degree drop in temperature didn't send the golden retriever running back indoors.

"Someone's trained this animal," Spencer said as the dog parked himself obligingly at his feet. "This performance isn't random. Wheezy is responding to commands." He thought of the way Wheezy had dropped at the sound of Ruby's voice and amended, "He's responding to *my* commands, anyway."

"Yes, well, that's how danger words work, isn't it?"

Spencer wasn't so entrenched in the world of erotic literature that he could make the immediate connection. Ruby was quick to enlighten him.

"It's not the word that gets the engine running," she explained. "It's the person saying it. A porcupine is just a porcupine until it crosses the right lips. *Your* lips, in this instance."

Spencer's mouth went dry, but he refused to allow himself to read anything into the remark. He didn't have any magical powers over the dog, and he *definitely* didn't have any over the woman.

"Try it and see what happens," she said. When he could do no more than stand there goggling at her, she added, "Or do you need me to show you how it's done?"

Spencer tried to shake his head, but he was having a hard time remembering how his muscles worked.

"That's a lovely porcupine you have there, Spencer," she cooed. The smile that played about her lips was full of danger—and temptation. Temptation most of all.

He cleared his throat. "I don't think that's the correct context."

"So big and ferocious."

He put on his best stern-veterinarian voice and tried again. "Porcupines are quite docile as a species. It's a common misconception. They only attack when they feel threatened."

His best stern-veterinarian voice didn't work. Ruby clucked her tongue and jutted out one deliciously rounded hip. "Do you feel threatened by me, Spencer? You shouldn't be. I promise I'm also quite docile—until I feel threatened, that is."

His throat constricted. He couldn't tell if she was flirting with him or taunting him, but it didn't matter. Under no circumstances was he taking this woman to a seedy motel. If he was going to sneak off with her for a night worthy of an erotic novel, he'd take her somewhere private. *Very* private.

That thought almost floored him—and made him feel thoroughly ashamed of himself. If given an opportunity, he'd do exactly that. Forget his position. Forget his dog show. Forget his brother. All this woman had to do was say the word, and he'd happily toss every other consideration aside.

And, oh, how he'd enjoy himself in the process.

When he only stood there staring at her, doing his best *not* to imagine Ruby in connection with a motel—seedy or otherwise—she dropped the sultry pose.

"See what I mean?" she said. "You're exactly like Wheezy. In the book, all the woman has to do is murmur the word and get an immediate response. But when *I* say it, nothing happens."

On the contrary, there was plenty happening. Spencer felt her presence in ways that reverberated in every part of his body. Their practice didn't get a lot of calls for the care of porcupines, but he'd never be able to go anywhere near one of them again without feeling this tight coil of desire and frustration. He wanted to throw caution to the wind, to accept the overture she was offering and whisk her into his arms, but he didn't dare. She was only testing his boundaries, seeing how far she could push him before he cracked.

She didn't know it, but he had the answer ready to go. *This far.* This was as far as she could push. The longer she stood there, holding herself just out of reach, the closer he was to breaking.

Fortunately for his state of self-preservation, she decided to end the challenge as quickly as it had begun.

"It's too bad I can't hire you to help me train Wheezy instead of your brother," she said, turning both herself and Wheezy away. "You have all the makings of a great pageant coach."

Considering how bitterly she'd discussed her own experiences with pageantry, he knew better than to take this as a compliment.

"I don't train dogs," he said, his mouth so dry the words felt stuck. "I only judge them."

"And what do you do with women?" she asked. With a sigh, she shook her head and didn't wait for his response. "Never mind. I already know the answer to that. You judge them, too."

Chapter 7

THIS WOULD GO A LOT FASTER IF YOU GRABBED A HAMMER AND helped me set up the stage." Ruby pointed at the box of tools located a few feet from Caleb's head. He was sprawled on the grass next to the two dogs—Caesar slumbering sonorously on one side, Wheezy chewing on a tree root on the other. "Many hands make light work."

"I could, but then I wouldn't have such a lovely view," he said. Since his eyes were pretty much trained on her ass as she did all the manual labor associated with erecting a six-foot platform, she had a good idea which view he was referring to.

"I can tell you right now that it's never going to happen," she said. "No offense, but you're not my type."

He sighed and sat up, a grin splitting his face. "I know, but I had to try anyway. What is it? My hair? My personality? My inability to do anything with this useless lump of a dog?"

She was forced into a laugh. Caleb had just spent the past hour trying to trim Wheezy's unruly curls into a semblance of order, and the golden retriever had howled as though he was being stabbed with the scissors instead of getting a nice haircut.

"You should have told me that he's useless before you cashed the check," she pointed out.

"Probably," Caleb agreed. "But I needed the work."

It was on the tip of her tongue to point out that there was plenty of work to be done in setting up the stage, but he turned his attention toward the dog. With the same neat efficiency she'd seen Spencer display toward animals, he ran his hand over Wheezy's muzzle.

"In this handsome guy's defense, he has all the makings of a winner. He doesn't totally conform to the breed, but there's good width to his skull and he has a nice broad face. Gorgeous eyes." He tugged one of Wheezy's ears forward and clicked his tongue in satisfaction. Ruby had done enough research on showing golden retrievers to recognize his actions as those of a judge examining a contestant. For all his apparent laziness, Caleb—like Wheezy—was capable of a lot more. "Other than the excess weight around his middle and a slight bow to his gait, he's not a bad specimen. And if you fix the first, you may very well fix the second. Whoever earmarked this dog for competition-level shows knew what he was doing."

She paused in the act of nailing one of the boards down. This was the first time she'd heard anyone other than Mrs. Orson utter a word of praise about Wheezy. "So you're saying we have a chance?" she asked.

"Nope. Not even a little. Spencer would never allow it."

The way he spoke—as if Spencer was the judge, jury, and executioner all in one—had her tightening her grip on the hammer to a dangerous degree. Tool safety was one of the few lessons Stepfather Deux had managed to squeeze in before her mother had squeezed him out, but she couldn't help herself.

Yes, Spencer was attractive. Sure, he lit a fire inside her in more ways than one. And, okay, she wouldn't have said no if he'd taken her up on that porcupine offer, but that wasn't her main goal in provoking him the way she had.

Once upon a time, Ruby had been the sort of girl who'd let nothing stand in her way—who'd looked upon each challenge as an opportunity to strap on a tall pair of heels and crush it to oblivion. There was a lot about pageantry she had no desire to return to, but there was no denying that she hadn't seen that girl in an awfully long time. Now that she was showing signs of returning to life, Ruby realized how much she'd missed her.

And it was something about Spencer that was drawing her out again.

"We'll just see about that, won't we?" She swung the hammer, pounding the nail through the wood and almost losing a finger in the process. "There's more than one way to win a trophy."

Caleb chuckled. "It'll never work—not even for a woman as beautiful as you. Spencer's not the type."

It was a good thing Ruby's face was turned toward the stage because there was nothing beautiful about it right now. She knew what Caleb was insinuating—that if she *really* wanted a shortcut to Wheezy's success, she could use the assets that God and her mother had given her—but that was beyond insulting. When Wheezy won Best in Show, it would be because Spencer had no other choice but to give in.

And when Spencer finally realized she was more than a pain in his uptight, gorgeous backside, it would be for the exact same reason.

She was about to say as much to Caleb—and with words that would have caused her mother to wash her mouth out with soap—but the sound of a truck pulling around the side of the house prevented her. Glancing up, she found that Spencer had barely managed to park before the passenger door swung open and his friend Eva bounded out. The topaz-skinned brunette was already halfway across the yard by the time Ruby had put the hammer down.

"I don't know why you're here or why Caleb has you swinging a hammer, but I can't tell you how happy I am to see you." As was the case at the meet and greet, Eva wrapped her arms around Ruby and squeezed. Ruby wasn't normally the sort to hug virtual strangers, but she was starting to see the appeal. She'd met this woman all of twice, and she was already well on her way to adoring her. Anyone who ran roughshod over Spencer the way she had was worth getting to know. "What are you building, and why does Wheezy look as though someone took a pair of garden shears to his coat?"

"Oh no." Ruby cast an anxious glance at the golden retriever. "Is it bad? Caleb was trying to groom Wheezy, but he didn't like it. He howled."

"Men always do." Eva clucked her tongue. "You should see what happens when I try to give the boys a haircut. Speaking of, my husband will be here any minute with the pack of them. Spencer invited us over for a barbecue. Will you stay? Please stay you'll stay."

Ruby did her best not to watch for Spencer's reaction as this invitation was offered, but she was acutely aware of him as he drew close. He stopped short of the white-painted line in the yard, his eyes dark and his expression unreadable.

"Of course she's staying," Caleb said. His brother's arrival seemed to have sparked some life into him. Like the two dogs, he was suddenly restless and excited, eager for attention. He didn't have a tail, but the spirit of it wagged within him. "Whatever Eva wants, Eva gets."

"If that's the case, then Ruby is coming to any and all gatherings until one of you brings home a girlfriend." Eva rolled her eyes in Ruby's direction. "You have no idea what it's like to be the only female at these things. It's penises everywhere I turn. No, don't laugh—I'm serious. The little ones will whip it out any chance they get, and as for the big ones, well, I'm sure I don't have to tell *you* the lengths they'll go to show it off. You probably get more dick pics than a syphilis hotline."

"Some of us are able to control ourselves in public, thanks," Spencer said tightly. "No matter what the provocation." He nodded toward the stage platform. "What's all this about?"

Just like that, Ruby decided to stay. She wasn't sure if it was the reference to Spencer's iron will that did it or if it was the way he glared at the stage as though it had personally offended him, but there was no way she was going to bow out and give him the field.

She was a paying customer. Wheezy needed training. And since the platform was on Caleb's side of the yard, she was well within her rights. If anything, *he* was the one getting in the way of *her* opportunity to transform Wheezy into a star.

"I'm improvising." She cocked her head at him. "Why? Don't you like it?"

"What is it?" he asked, diplomatically choosing not to answer.

"This is how Ruby and I are going to get Wheezy his championship title," Caleb said. "It's a stage."

Spencer sighed and scrubbed a hand along his jaw. "Yes, I can see that. What I meant was, for what purpose? You know as well as I do that the dogs don't appear on a stage—they show in the ring. You'll only confuse the poor animal if you make him prance around on this thing."

"Wheezy is a highly intelligent animal and a natural showman," Ruby retorted, feeling nettled. The stage wasn't for *prancing*. It was for performing. "He only needs the right setting—a little something extra to light his theatrical fire."

Considering that the dog in question was trying to bury his tree root underneath his own body right now, her theory was a hard sell.

"I didn't give permission for this to go up in my backyard," Spencer said.

"But it's not technically in your backyard, is it?" Ruby glanced at the line separating them. Since now seemed as good a time as any to show how far they'd come in the training, she released a sharp whistle. The sound had the effect of causing Caesar to waddle obediently up, but Wheezy didn't lift his head.

Because *of course* he didn't.

She was about to make excuses for him—the trauma of the haircut, the deliciousness of the tree root, all that hammering sending his senses into disorder—but Spencer beat her to it. With his usual air of command, he said, "Wheezy, come."

When the dog didn't do more than twitch one of his curly golden ears, Spencer snapped his fingers and added, "*Now.*"

With only a mild grumble at being thus summoned, the golden retriever got to his feet and trotted over to his side.

"Wheezy!" Ruby cried. "You're making us look bad!"

"Spencer does that at the office, too," Eva said. "All he has to do is clap his hands one time, and the dogs just line up."

"Don't get too excited" was Caleb's contribution. "There's probably roast beef in his pocket."

Whatever magic Spencer kept inside his pants remained a mystery. After offering some low-voiced praise to the animal at his feet, he turned his attention to Ruby. "You're more than welcome to stay for the barbecue," he said, sounding surprisingly like he meant it. "Caleb doesn't seem to be doing much with your dog, so the least we can do is feed you."

Since the alternative—to take Wheezy back to Mrs. Orson, still untrained and now boasting a lopsided haircut—wasn't very appealing, Ruby decided to take him up on the offer. Besides, the ease with which Spencer got Wheezy to comply with his orders was giving her an idea. There was more than one Wilson man in this world capable of issuing orders.

"I'd love that, thanks," she said. Eva jumped and clapped her hands, which sealed the deal. "But someone had better grab a hammer and help me finish this stage. I know just how we're going to get Wheezy to start acting like a show dog."

"Unless the answer is hard work, years of training, and carefully curated breeding, there's no point," Spencer warned.

Her only reply was to hoist the hammer and return her attention to the stage. She'd been curated since the day she was born, and hard work and training were in her blood.

Along with a spark that delighted her as much as it burned.

"Mayonnaise, Wheezy," Caleb said from the opposite end of the yard. He was doing his best Spencer impersonation, which meant he'd screwed up his face into a grimace and kept all inflection out of his voice.

The whole thing was starting to seriously irk Spencer. He inflected. He inflected all the time.

"Sandwich spread." Caleb tried again. "Condiment. Aioli."

"I don't think pulling out a thesaurus is going to make a difference." Ruby pursed her lips thoughtfully. "Try to go a little deeper and sterner next time. You need to sound more like the kind of guy who'll whip your knuckles if you don't follow the rules."

"You guys know I can hear every word you're saying, right?" Spencer asked.

They ignored him as Caleb made another attempt at Spencer's voice. As kids, they'd been so good at imitating each other that they could even fool their parents, but those days were long gone. Somewhere along the way, Spencer had apparently developed the voice of an old-timey schoolteacher.

"No, that's not it," Eva said. Like the other two, she was seated in a lounge chair—Spencer's—that had been dragged over and set up on Caleb's side of the yard around Wheezy. The golden retriever, exhausted with the labors of stealing not one, not two, but three of Eva's kids' hot dogs, was sleeping off his extra calories. "It needs to be sexier. Like maybe you wouldn't mind the whipping every now and then."

"You guys know I can also hear every word you're saying, right?" Maury, Eva's husband and the only person Spencer currently considered his ally, cast Spencer a supportive grimace.

Maury was a short man, balding and with a slight paunch to his gut, his disposition as cheerful and easygoing as Eva's. The fact that all three of his kids—Julio, Xavier, and toddling little Max—were currently holding an unsupervised pirate sword fight on the stage was proof of that.

"You're the sexiest man I know and the only person I want to spank me," Eva obediently replied. She ruined it by adding, "But I'm not wrong, am I, Ruby?"

"No, you're not. In fact, I think you might be onto something. Okay, Caleb. Picture yourself decked out from head to toe in skintight black leather and try again."

Spencer refused to look at her, but he didn't need his eyes to tell him what she looked like right now. She'd be wearing that same expression as when she'd discussed danger words at the meet and greet, with a laugh on her lips and that challenging gleam in her eye. He hadn't been able to track down the book about porcupines yet, but he'd done enough internet research to realize that the world of erotic literature ran deep.

And, he was forced to admit, *girthy*. If that was the sort of thing Ruby enjoyed, then it was a good thing he'd decided to have nothing to do with her. Some of the things he'd read about seemed downright painful.

"Mayonnaise," Caleb said in a voice that sounded less like Spencer and more like Tom Jones in the middle of murder spree. Wheezy must have agreed because he didn't stir. "Goddammit, Spencer! What's the trick? You must have been doing something else at the time."

At a shout from the three small boys—and a look of reproach from Eva—Caleb coughed.

"I mean, poppycock," he amended. "Balderdash. Fiddlesticks."

Spencer held back a snort. Which one of them was the old-timey schoolteacher now?

"I'm not going to do your job for you," he said. "If you can't train that dog, then it'll be better for all of us if you admit it and issue Ruby a refund."

From the shouts of protest on the other side of the backyard, it was obvious that wasn't going to happen.

Maury confirmed it with a sigh. "You might as well tell them your secret and save us both a lot of trouble," he said to Spencer. "Eva won't stop until that dog is transformed. She's emotionally invested now."

"I don't have a secret," Spencer protested. "Just like I don't have anything but an ordinary voice. Ruby is only saying all that to wind me up."

"Oh, so you *are* aware that I'm doing it?"

Spencer glanced up to find Ruby standing above him, her head tilted to block the setting sun. She was a vision against the streaks of pink and yellow. If he hadn't known it to be impossible, he'd have said that she'd convinced the sky to be her own personal lighting crew.

He scowled. "It doesn't matter because it won't work. That dog will never be anything but a waste of space. A *cute* waste of space, but still."

A retort formed on Ruby's lips, but Maury hoisted himself out of his seat before she had a chance to utter it. "As much as I'd love to sit here all night, eating smoked meats and watching that dog fail at everything, it's getting late and the boys need baths before bed."

"Late?" Spencer echoed with a glance at his watch. It wasn't late—not by any standards but those belonging to parents of young children—but it *was* ten minutes past the hour. "Oh shit."

"Balderdash," Ruby reminded him.

He ignored her and released a short whistle. For once, it wasn't to call Caesar or Wheezy to attention. "Hey, Caleb? I don't suppose you noticed the time, did you?"

Caleb, who was regaling Eva with a story that was making her laugh so hard she was crying, glanced up. "What? No, why?"

Spencer didn't say anything. He didn't need to—nor did he particularly want to. He'd sworn time and time again that he wasn't his brother's keeper and that Caleb needed to be responsible for his own life, but it always came down to this.

"Ugh." Caleb frowned as realization sank in. "Are you really going to make me pick up your dry cleaning? *Now?*"

Spencer felt his jaw grow tight. Trust Caleb to turn the tables so that *Spencer* was the one who looked like the bad guy. The truth—that Caleb was late for his weekly court-mandated gambling addiction meeting—was unpalatable and therefore covered up.

"You know me," Spencer said. "Always a stickler for the rules."

"You can go one week without your dry cleaning. It won't be the end of the world."

Spencer hunched his shoulder in a half shrug. "Suit yourself. You're capable of making your own decisions."

Understandably, this exchange caught the interest of the rest of the adults gathered around. Eva and Maury had witnessed enough hostility between the brothers to treat it as an everyday occurrence, so they set about carrying dishes inside and gathering up their brood. Ruby, however, watched them both with narrow-eyed interest.

"Wouldn't it have made more sense to pick up your dry cleaning on the way home from work?" she asked Spencer.

Caleb answered for him. "He needs a special shirt. It wasn't ready until now."

"Then can't he pick it up on the way *to* work tomorrow?"

"He wants to wear it tonight. It's a special shirt." Caleb was physically restricted by the line in the yard, but he managed to sidle as close to Ruby as he could while still falling within the boundary. "I didn't want to say anything while Eva and Maury were listening, but it's made of skintight black leather."

Ruby laughed. "There's no way that's true. Now I *know* you're hiding something."

Caleb was no more immune to the sound of Ruby's laughter than Spencer was. Since Caleb couldn't swoop her into his arms without stepping over the line, he grabbed her hand and held it to his chest with mock reverence instead. "You're right. I can't hold it in anymore. You, Ruby Taylor, are a goddess among women. A paragon of femininity. A vision of loveliness—"

"Not about *that*," she said, cutting him short. She snatched her hand back in a way that made Spencer feel warm all over. He wasn't sure he'd ever seen a woman less interested in his brother. "You two give the appearance of being upstanding citizens who love well-behaved dogs and obedience more than is good for you, but there's something else going on here. I can feel it."

"We *are* upstanding citizens who love well-behaved dogs," Spencer said. He would have been more than happy to let the subject drop there, but Caleb had never been good at knowing when to stop. He eyed Spencer as though seeing him for the first time.

"You know, the people at the laundry service would never be able to tell if *you* picked up the dry cleaning instead of me," he said.

Spencer couldn't pretend to misunderstand him. What his brother was hinting at—and what he was asking—was for Spencer to take his place at the meeting. It would be an easy enough thing to do. Although Caleb couldn't emulate Spencer's voice well enough to trick a dog, Spencer was more than capable of pretending to be his brother.

"I'll do no such thing."

"They don't really care who comes to get it, just so long as they get a signature. And you've been able to forge my handwriting for years."

"Caleb, I'm not doing that. You need to get the dry cleaning for yourself. You know it as well as I do."

Even though Spencer was vaguely aware of Ruby standing and watching the entire interaction, she'd become only a secondary consideration. Caleb *did* need to get the dry cleaning for himself, and he *did* know it. Not because a judge had told him to, but because Caleb's gambling addiction was a very real and destructive thing. All you had to do was look at their current living situation to realize it.

They both had a competitive streak, it was true. What hadn't been implanted at birth had been forged by a boyhood spent in a constant game of one-upmanship. It wasn't just the push-ups and quarters, either. They'd constantly tried to see who could jump farther, climb higher, push harder—a good-natured rivalry that had given their parents many a visit to the emergency room.

By the time they reached puberty, Spencer had started to apply that drive to his education. The same resolution that had made it possible for him to hold his breath underwater one more second had helped him rise to the top of the class and stay there. Caleb, however, had found less productive ways of channeling his talents.

Spencer couldn't understand it. His brother was smart. He was good with animals and even better at people. When he applied himself—*really* applied himself—there was very little he couldn't accomplish. In fact, until his gambling website had been flagged by the federal government for breaking about twelve laws, it had been an undeniable success.

"It's just a few shirts, Spencer," Caleb said. "Let it go."

"It's never just a few shirts," Spencer returned. "I can't."

He had no idea how long the pair of them might have stood there, trapped in a stalemate that neither one of them was willing to give up, but it was probably hours. That was the problem with sharing your DNA with another human being. His brother was part of his blood, the other half of his soul. Whatever it was that drove Caleb to recklessly push his luck was the same thing that drove Spencer to rescue him at the first sign of trouble.

"Well, I give up," Ruby said, unlocking their horns without even being aware of it. "I don't know what you two are talking about or why you're getting all hot and bothered over laundry, but I have to get up early for work tomorrow. Thank you, Caleb, for letting me set up the stage on your half of the backyard. And thank you, Spencer, for dinner. I'd offer to stay and help with the dishes, but I refuse to go anywhere near that sink."

"Oh, we don't put the dishes in the sink," Eva said as she came up to bid them farewell. Maury was in the middle of packing his kids into their minivan, so all he could offer was a harassed wave. "There's a plastic tub in the front where Spencer puts everything. He washes them with the sprinkler."

"It's not a sprinkler," he said, but his protest was a feeble one. He might not use a sprinkler, but he did use the hose. Living in only half a house was a lot more difficult than most people realized. "It's a custom open-air sanitation process."

Ruby laughed. "How fancy. Next, you'll be telling me that your living arrangement is a unique lifestyle modification instead of some weird brother rivalry."

"And you'll be telling me that Wheezy is a highly prized experimental breed instead of a golden retriever." He paused and glanced down at the dog in question. "Actually, that one's probably true. Except for the highly prized part."

Somehow, he and Ruby had drawn closer during their conversation. They were still surrounded by the others, their every interaction being watched with interest, but for what was probably the first time, Spencer didn't feel self-conscious about it. He was too busy trying not to fall under her spell. Ruby was fun and funny and had made everyone's evening better because of it, but she wasn't going to win. Not his dog show and not this battle of wills between them.

From the expression on her face, her lips curling in a self-satisfied smile, she didn't agree. Probably because his hands were balled in fists at his sides. It was the only way he could keep himself from reaching out and kissing her.

And she knew it. Damn the woman. She *knew* it.

"I'll carry Wheezy to your car," Caleb offered before Spencer could do something drastic like unclench his fists and give in. "I doubt you'll get him out of here any other way, and it seems as though I've got some errands to run whether I like it or not."

Spencer was too relieved to hear that his brother was planning on going to his meeting to care that Ruby had once again gotten the better of him. He was also relieved to see that Wheezy put up a fight, rolling around like a dropped pencil in an attempt to prevent himself from being carried away.

That wasn't a dog who was going to ruin his dog show. He couldn't participate if no one could even manage to get him in the door.

Eva stood next to Spencer and watched the struggle take place. "Your brother seems to be enjoying himself," she said as Caleb started listing all the words he could think of that rhymed with mayonnaise: paraphrase, Chevrolets, Bolognese. Only that last one seemed to interest the dog—which, considering how much he loved to eat, made sense. Wheezy was a lot more intelligent than he wanted them all to think. "You have to admit his offer to train with Ruby is working out well."

Since Wheezy chose that moment to leap into the driver's seat of Ruby's ancient, faded Volkswagen, *well* was a generous term. She could hardly drive out of here with that dog in her lap.

"I was starting to worry about Caleb, to be honest," Eva continued. Spencer could feel her looking at him, but he didn't turn his head. Eva was emotionally intuitive—and nosy—enough to see exactly what Spencer was thinking. "He never seems to want to leave the house anymore. I even offered to set him up with a friend of mine, but he said he had plans. When has Caleb ever turned down a date?"

Never. Not once. If there was one thing Caleb loved more than gambling, it was women.

"He's never going to make anything of that animal, but at least he's taking an interest in *something*. And he's showering again, thank God."

Spencer was forced into a laugh. It hadn't been a shower so much as a sink bath that left little to the imagination, but Eva was right. His brother had even started to make an attempt to clean up his side of the living room. There were now *two* black garbage bags full of his clothes.

"This Ruby thing seems to be working out pretty well, doesn't it?" Eva persisted.

Spencer pressed his lips together and watched as Caleb and Ruby worked together to get Wheezy secured in the back of her car. As soon as the door was slammed shut, they high-fived as though they'd known each for years instead of days.

"That depends," he said, turning to look at Eva. "What exactly is the Ruby thing again?"

Eva's answer was a light, teasing laugh. "To help a woman train her dog for our show, obviously. Why? Did you have something else in mind?"

Chapter 8

Be a love and make my bed for me while you're in there, would you?" Mrs. Orson popped her head into her bedroom and smiled beatifically at Ruby. "My strength isn't what it used to be, and you do such a good job on the corners. You must have been a soldier in a past life."

Ruby sighed as she wriggled out from the closet, where she'd been doing her best to lure Wheezy out for his daily walk. Things had come to such a pass that all she had to do was step inside Mrs. Orson's front door and he ran straight for hiding.

"I wasn't a soldier. I was one of those mall kiosk people who spray perfume on you without asking. That's why I'm being punished now." She gestured to where Wheezy had burrowed himself, his head resting on a pair of Gucci flats that probably cost more than Ruby earned in a month. "Can't you tie him up or something before I arrive? I'll never get him out now."

"Then you might as well make the bed," Mrs. Orson said brightly. "Since you came all this way."

Ruby gave in with another sigh. After an eight-hour shift that Harry had eked out to nine, her feet hurt and she wanted nothing more than to head home, but she was determined to make some headway with the golden retriever. Hanging out with Spencer and his friends at the barbecue last week had been more enlightening than she'd expected—and not just because she'd been pretty sure, for a moment there, he was going to kiss her. She'd also noticed that even though Spencer hadn't done anything to help her train Wheezy, he hadn't done anything to stop her, either.

"I'll make your bed, but only if I can tell my mother that you're an obscenely wealthy widow whose favor I'm courting in hopes of getting in your will," Ruby said. She pointed a warning finger at Mrs. Orson. "If she calls you—and don't be surprised if she does—you have to swear to back up my claim."

Mrs. Orson blinked up at her, not the least bit offended. "Would you like all my money when I'm gone, Ruby? You can have it."

Ruby's whole body gave a jerk. "What? No—*no*, Mrs. Orson. It was a joke. I would never ask you to do that."

"I'd always intended to leave it to the big hospital that takes care of the kids with cancer, but if you need it more than them, it's only a quick call to my lawyer."

"Mrs. Orson, *please* don't change your will." Ruby gave up on both Wheezy and the bed to turn her full attention on the older woman. She looked so tiny and frail, her five-foot frame swathed in a fringed shawl that swept the floor, that Ruby's heart gave a lurch. "Not for me, and not for anyone. It doesn't matter how much they say they need it or what they offer you in return. Promise me you won't make any changes without talking to someone first."

"There's no need to yell at me, dear. It's not as if I can take my savings with me."

Ruby hadn't been yelling, but the prospect of Mrs. Orson allowing herself to be taken financial advantage of was enough to get her started. There were too many unscrupulous people in this world—and on the retirement community's payroll—for her to be comfortable leaving things where they were.

"Don't you have someone who can advise you about these things?" she asked. "A niece or nephew, maybe, or a trusted family friend?"

Mrs. Orson stared at her for a long moment before sighing and shaking her head. "You sound just like my husband. He always used to worry about me, too."

Although Ruby had known this woman for over a year, references to her life before Parkwood Manor were rare. "It sounds like he might have had a good reason," Ruby said. She would have added more, but she caught sight of a small smile hooking the corner of Mrs. Orson's mouth. It was the same smile Mrs. Orson had worn the day Harry had been sniffing out prescription painkillers.

"What is it?" she demanded. "What aren't you telling me?"

"Wheezy was his dog. Did I ever tell you that?"

"No, you didn't."

"He adored that animal. Spoiled him rotten, which is why you're having such a hard time with him now. It was always his wish that Wheezy win the West Coast Canine Classic."

Ruby's heart gave a pang for the older woman, but she knew better than to let it show. Mrs. Orson wouldn't appreciate the sentimental outburst. Unlike many of the widows' homes around here, hers had no pictures of her husband, no reminders of the life they'd once shared.

"Is that why it's so important to you that he win?" Ruby asked in as neutral a tone as she could manage. "Because it was what your husband wanted?"

Mrs. Orson nodded.

Another thought occurred to Ruby. "Wait—is that also why Wheezy responds so well to Spencer's command but not to anyone else's? Because the dog was trained by your husband? Because he only recognizes a specific man's voice?"

"Well, your veterinarian friend doesn't *sound* like Norbert—not literally, you understand—but there's something about him that feels familiar. His forcefulness, perhaps, or his sense of command. Is your Spencer a tall man?"

Ruby didn't see what Spencer's height had to do with anything, but she answered anyway. "Yes. He's not *my* Spencer, though. Or a friend. He's more of a..."

Mrs. Orson cocked her head like an expectant bird as Ruby sought the right term to describe her relationship with Spencer Wilson. He infuriated her. He goaded her. He made her want to dig her heels in and throw things at his head until he was forced to recognize her as his equal. But he also fluttered his long, dark lashes and looked at her as if he wasn't as averse to the idea of skintight black leather as he let on.

From the way her body suddenly contracted in on itself, she wasn't averse to that idea herself.

Taking a deep breath, she forced herself to focus on the more immediate problem of Mrs. Orson and her willingness to give her money to the first friendly stranger who held out a hand. "It doesn't matter what Spencer is. He's the man who stands between Wheezy and your husband's final legacy, and that's all you need to know."

"Could he be paid off, do you think? Maybe I should offer to leave *him* my money instead." Mrs. Orson took one look at Ruby's face and laughed. "I'm not serious, dear. If you don't want it, it'll have to be the cancer kids."

"I want the kids to have it," Ruby replied without hesitation. With equal determination, she added, "I love a good romance. I wish you'd tell me about him."

"Who? Norbert?" Mrs. Orson shook her head. Ruby thought she detected a note of sadness in the gesture, but the older woman pasted on a smile and refused to let it show. "Maybe another time, dear. All that's important right now is that nothing would make me happier than to see Wheezy make his dog-show debut. And to have a nicely made bed for when I go to sleep tonight, but do what you feel is best."

Ruby gave in and started to tug at the sheets. She wanted to know more about the person who'd once captured Mrs. Orson's heart, but she knew better than to push.

Sometimes, when a woman didn't want to talk about a man, it was for a good reason.

"I'll give you twenty. No, fifty. No, a *hundred*." Ruby sat across the table from Eva, doing quick mental calculations to figure out where she was going to find an extra hundred dollars lying around. She could always tell Mrs. Orson that it was a dog-show expense—which, technically, it was—but she felt bad enough about how much of the older woman's money she'd already spent. Between the entrance fee and Caleb's training costs, it was starting to add up.

Before Eva could respond to the offer, an earsplitting shriek rent the air, followed almost immediately by a thump and a bump. Then silence.

Eva, sublimely unfazed by either the scream or the ominous nothing that followed, grabbed the bottle of pinot grigio at her elbow and filled her glass to the top. Ruby had stopped by Eva's house straight from making up Mrs. Orson's bed, so it was still early, but Eva seemed to adhere to the "It's five o'clock somewhere" rule of drinking.

"Um…" Ruby peered over her shoulder toward the next room, where they'd left Eva's children playing a game of what looked like a mix of hide-and-seek and murder. Between the swords they'd been trying to stab each other with at the barbecue and today's game, which seemed to involve sitting on the head of the boy nearest you, she was starting to feel seriously alarmed. "Shouldn't we go see—?"

"No."

"But don't you think they might have—?"

"It's entirely possible."

"Then aren't you worried—?"

Eva didn't put the bottle down. Instead, she tilted it toward Ruby's glass and poured out every last remaining dreg. "Maury is in charge of the playroom for the next thirty-three minutes. Then and only then will I cross the threshold to assess damages." She took a long drink from her glass, her gaze never leaving Ruby's. "If you've ever wondered what the secret to a successful marriage is, it's this right here."

"An ungodly amount of wine?"

Eva's laugh rang out loud and clear. "I meant a clear and equitable division of labor, but sure. Ungodly wine works, too."

Sounds of life were starting to pick up in the next room, so Ruby allowed herself to relax against her chair. She also realized what she'd have to do to get her way—and without spending a cent of either her or Mrs. Orson's money in the bargain.

She should have been ashamed of herself for coming over here with the intention of making a devil's bargain, but desperate times called for desperate measures. If Wheezy refused to give in to the allure of her pageant stage—which he showed every sign of doing—and if Caleb remained unable to match the exact pitch and timber of Spencer's voice—which he also showed every sign of doing—then she wasn't left with much choice. Mrs. Orson's long-lost romance with Norbert demanded it.

"I'll babysit," Ruby said.

Eva paused in the middle of bringing the glass to her lips once again. "I'm listening."

"One free night of babysitting." As yet another piercing scream sounded from the next room, Ruby pushed her qualms aside and amended, "Two free nights. Of your choosing. Including holidays and special occasions."

Eva still hadn't moved—not even to blink. "Do you mean two separate nights, or are we talking two of them in succession? As in a weekend? A *whole* weekend?"

An entire weekend of trying to keep three boys alive wasn't what Ruby had meant, but if there was one thing she knew how to do, it was how to say what was expected of her. She stretched her brightest, pageantiest smile. "Absolutely," she said. "It'd be my pleasure."

Eva thrust her hand across the table so fast that Ruby almost spilled her wine. "No takesie-backsies. Once you shake on it, it's a done deal and there's nothing you can do or say to reverse it."

Ruby was startled enough by this to hesitate, but she caught sight of Eva's expression and relented. Dealing babysitting favors might not have been her intention in coming over here, but it would have been the height of cruelty to deny the excitement on Eva's face. She looked like a woman who hadn't had a weekend away in, well, ever.

"Sure thing. As long as you get me what I need, I'll give you any weekend you want—except, of course, the West Coast Canine Classic."

"Agreed." Eva yanked Ruby's hand into her own and shook it. The deal thus made, Eva sighed, kicked off her shoes, and yanked out the pen that had been holding up the long, dark waves of her hair.

Ruby couldn't help feeling wistful at how happy and comfortable Eva looked, like an old pair of jeans that fit just right. It was something she'd always envied about other women. Eva was the sort who would only get better with time, who would let the silver streaks come naturally into her hair and look amazing doing it, whose energy and bright spirits would keep her young well into her retirement years.

Ruby, on the other hand, was the pair of jeans bought for clubbing one night and regretted every day since—low-rise and far too tight, but so expensive that you couldn't bring yourself to throw them away.

"I can't remember the last time I felt this relaxed," Eva said, smiling at her from across the table. A deep dimple formed in one cheek. "Is this the part where I confess that I would have done it for free?"

Ruby sat up straight in her chair. "You *what*?"

"In fact, I'm looking downright forward to it. I'm already starting to plot all the ways I can make it happen." She reached down and fished in her purse until she extracted a dragon-themed coloring book and a twelve-pack of jumbo crayons. Tearing out a page that had been liberally scribbled on, she pushed it across the table at Ruby. "Here. Make a list of those words for me. I want to make sure I remember them all."

Despite the fact that she'd once again allowed a much wiser, much wilier woman to manipulate her, Ruby plucked a purple crayon from the pack and obeyed.

Her plan was a simple one, planted there by Mrs. Orson herself. Food bribes were obviously a no-go, especially since Wheezy was too smart to fall for a bait-and-switch carrot again. The stage platform had done little more than give the golden retriever a new place to nap, and nothing Caleb did to his voice made Wheezy sit up and listen.

As much as she hated to admit it, the only thing that seemed to work with any regularity was "her" Spencer. It was just as Mrs. Orson had said—there was something commanding about him, something forceful—that neither she nor Wheezy seemed able to deny. The only way Ruby was going to get anywhere was with his help, but she'd have rather died than ask for it.

Which left her with this. She needed a recording of Spencer's voice saying everything needed to train a dog for showmanship, and Eva was just the person to get it for her. With any luck, Eva could follow him around at work long enough to get her "sit" and "stay," "roll over" and "present." Most of all, she needed "mayonnaise," and as events were proving, she'd stop at nothing to get it.

She was debating whether to include a few compliments in the wish list—"good boy" or "yes, Ruby, I do think you're a capable and highly intelligent human being"—when Eva cleared her throat.

"So," she said, her voice and expression so transparent that Ruby's heart sank. "Those Wilson twins are something else, aren't they?"

As a twenty-eight-year-old single woman whose mother had been trying to marry her off to the highest bidder for years, Ruby knew exactly where this conversation was headed.

"Don't you dare," Ruby warned. "Caleb pees in a sink, and Spencer is doing his best to keep me and Wheezy out of his precious dog show. I'm not interested in either of them."

Eva laughed. "If it helps, Caleb wasn't always like this. This feud with his brother is doing weird things to him. To both of them, actually. Spencer wasn't always like this, either."

"Like what?" Ruby couldn't help asking.

Eva pursed her lips and gave the question careful consideration. There were several adjectives Ruby could have supplied her with—annoying, condescending, *attractive*—but Eva's eventual response took her by surprise.

"I don't know. They both seem a little sad."

"Sad?" Ruby echoed. She had yet to see Caleb do anything but smile and laugh and play, and Spencer… Well. He was Spencer. He was hardly the kind of guy you'd consider the life of the party, but that was what intrigued her. His smile was rare and his laugh even rarer, but when they came, it was like catching a glimpse into his soul. Ruby had seen—and shown—far too many false smiles to feel anything but admiration for someone who refused to play that particular game.

"'Sad' is the only way I can think of to describe it. They've always been wildly competitive, but something changed about three months ago. Before that, they were always playing in rec sports leagues or hanging out at breweries together—inseparable in every sense of the word. Then Caleb moved in, and it all stopped. Everything. They don't go anywhere together, and their little competitions aren't fun anymore. Every time I try to ask one of them about it, they just zip right up." She made the motion of a zipper cutting through the air. "I tried to convince Maury to see what he can find out, but he refuses to get involved. He says they'll work it out, but I don't know. I've been friends with Spencer a long time. Something's not right."

Ruby had a hard time imagining a Spencer and Caleb who drank casual microbrews together, but she didn't doubt that Eva knew what she was talking about. After all, she'd seen the evidence with her own two eyes. That whole conversation about dry cleaning had been about something deeper than dirty laundry.

"Well, the good news is, if anyone can shake some sense into those two men, it's you," Eva said brightly. "I have every hope that you'll have things sorted out in no time."

"Me?" Ruby echoed. "I barely know them. What can I do?"

Eva's laughter filled the kitchen. "Are you kidding me? With that face and those legs and the way they both look at you?"

Ruby could only shake her head. If there was one thing she'd learned in this life, it was the adages were true. *Beauty is only skin deep. It's what's on the inside that matters. Pretty is as pretty does.* A face and a pair of legs like hers might get her through a lot of doors, but those doors rarely stayed open for long. One look at her mother's life—and her own—made that abundantly clear. As much as they had to offer on the outside, their insides weren't anything worth writing home about.

"You have no idea what effect you have when you walk into a room, do you?" Eva asked as though reading her mind. She clucked her tongue. "And I'm not just talking about how beautiful you are, so don't poker up at me. There's something about you… I don't know how to explain it, but you make everyone want to sit up a little straighter."

Ruby had long ago learned to control her blushing—reddened skin never photographed well under the lights of a stage—but she could feel herself warming all over. "You're just saying that because I promised to take your kids for a weekend."

Eva's laugh rang out like a pinging bell, and she squeezed Ruby's hand before letting go. "Well, yes—but that's exactly what I mean. If you really wanted Spencer to say these things for a recording, all you'd have to do is bat your eyes and ask him. He'd do it for you in a hot second."

This was veering dangerously close to what Caleb had insinuated the other day, but Eva wasn't done.

"Between you and me, you could probably get a lot more than that out of him, but you won't, will you? Not the easy way, I mean. You're going to earn Wheezy a spot just like everyone else—by putting in the time and doing the work." Her smile deepened. "Spencer hates that about you. I mean, he *likes* it, obviously, but he also really, really hates it."

"T minus five minutes!" came a shout from the next room. It was followed by the cheerfully bald-pated head of Eva's husband popping through the doorway. Maury looked harassed but happy, especially once he caught sight of his wife. "You'd better down the last of that wine fast, my love. They've just discovered the box of finger paints we were hiding in the back of the coat closet."

"Maury, you wretch! I told you to bury them under something heavy."

"I did, but they're like heat-seeking missiles. They can't be stopped." Maury turned his smile toward Ruby. "Hullo, Ruby. Sorry to cut your chat short, but a deal's a deal. If I spend any more time with these three, I'm going to lose my hair. What's left of it, anyway."

He and Eva were so good-naturedly relaxed about everything that Ruby couldn't help but return his smile. Someday, she wanted a house like this one. No one under this roof cared about appearances or trophies or how many calories were in that bottle of pinot grigio. They were so busy trying to keep everyone happy—and alive—that they didn't have time for anything else.

"I'd argue for a few more minutes of girl time, but we should get Ruby out the door as fast as possible." Eva slid out of her chair and took Ruby's glass. With a wink, she tipped back the contents. "The longer she spends around the kids, the greater the chance she fakes her own death to get out of our bargain. You won't believe it, Maury, but she's offered to take the boys for a weekend. A *whole* weekend."

Maury, who'd been about to drop a kiss on his wife's forehead, paused in the middle of this comfortably romantic gesture. "What? Are you serious?"

"As a heart attack."

The speed with which Maury moved belonged to a much younger man. "You must have dozens of things to do. Here, let me help you." He pulled Ruby's chair out, yanked her to her feet, and pushed her toward the door—and all without giving the impression of being anything but her best friend. "Drive safe, and don't forget to look twice at the stop sign at the end of the street. It's a tricky one."

Ruby laughingly allowed herself to be thrown out of the house. There was no need for such haste, and she wouldn't have minded saying goodbye to the boys, but she was still reeling from everything Eva had said about Spencer.

That all Ruby had to do was bat her eyes at him to get her way.

That he *liked* her.

"Why is she smiling?" Maury asked his wife as the pair of them blockaded the doorway and waved a cheerful farewell. He spoke loud enough for Ruby to hear, which she felt sure was the entire point. "She just promised us forty-eight hours all to ourselves. Doesn't she know what she's in for?"

"Not a clue, poor thing. I can hardly wait."

Chapter 9

WHAT WOULD YOU LIKE ON YOUR SANDWICH?"

Eva poked her head into the exam room, where Spencer stood gently prodding the edges of a fatty lump on a dachshund's abdomen. The dachshund, Jujubee, was prone to such lipomas. Since his body mass dragged so close to the ground, he regularly had to have them removed.

"That's a good boy," he said as he gave the dog a treat and rubbed his head. "The usual, please."

Eva gave a small jump. "Wait… Could you say that again?"

"What? The usual?"

"No, before that. When you were talking to Jujubee."

Spencer waited until he placed the dog on the floor and clipped on his leash before speaking. Eva had been acting strange all day, skulking around his office and asking a bunch of questions she already knew the answers to. In addition to a highly suspicious query about a cat who showed signs of being anemic, she'd asked him to consult on a leg fracture for an older sheepdog—both of which she could have easily handled on her own.

"I can't get him to… What's the word, again?" she'd asked as the sheepdog had stood on the table, his right foreleg held aloft. "I need him to relax and get comfortable so I can perform the exam but he won't…?"

"Sit?" Spencer had suggested.

"Yes!" Eva had beamed as though she'd just been handed a million dollars. "That's exactly it. What a help you've been."

This whole poking her head in to ask about lunch was another sign that something was off. First of all, the receptionist always put in the lunch order for the office. Secondly, he'd ordered the same thing every day for the past four years. Turkey sandwich on rye, no cheese, extra pickles, light mayonnaise…

His heart gave a heavy thud. She wouldn't.

"I said 'good boy,'" he said, emphasizing the words. "Good. Boy."

Eva's eyes lit up with so much excitement that he knew his suspicions were correct.

"And about the lunch order," she added in the same voice her kids used whenever they were up to no good. "Tell me what your usual is, again? Isra's busy with the appointment book and asked me to put today's call in, but I can't for the life of me remember what you like on your sandwich."

"I like mayonnaise," he said with painstaking care. "Lots and lots of mayonnaise."

"Oh dear." A giggle escaped before Eva could stop it. She slapped a hand over her mouth. The sound had the effect of startling Jujubee, who was already showing signs of being nervous at his continued presence in the exam room.

Spencer could only shake his head in wonder. It was exactly as he'd told Lawson. Eva had all the stealth of a militarized wombat. He passed the leash to her with one hand and held the other out in command.

"Give it to me."

Although Eva had been caught tape-recorder-handed, she showed no signs of remorse. "Sorry, Spencer. I can't."

"You can and you will. Where is it?"

"You don't want to know. I suspected something like this would happen and took precautions." She dropped her voice to a theatrical whisper and added, "It's in my pants."

"Eva, you traitor. How could you?"

She giggled again. She also showed no sign of reaching into whatever mysterious part of her body where she'd hidden her phone, which wasn't a good sign. "I was just trying to help my new friend," she said.

"You'd have done it if you'd been there, too. She begged. She pleaded. She offered to watch my kids for a weekend."

That last one caused him to start. "She *what*?"

"I know, right?" With a cluck of her tongue, Eva shook her head and added, "I think you should just man up and face the truth. You're going to have to let Wheezy in the show. Anyone willing to go that far to get what she wants is an unstoppable force. For all we know, Ruby has a backup plan in case this doesn't work. Her next step is probably to have your house bugged to get a recording—and you *know* Caleb would go along with it. He'd think it was hilarious."

Eva wasn't wrong. Anything that might cause Spencer annoyance or embarrassment was something Caleb would embrace with both hands. The only way to prevent something like that happening was to confront it head on.

And to confront *Ruby* head on.

The idea wasn't as unpleasant as it might have been a few weeks ago. He still wasn't sure why Ruby was so determined to get Wheezy into the dog show—or why she'd decided that the only way to accomplish it was to declare Spencer her personal enemy—but he was starting to enjoy this game.

Especially since he had the upper hand for the first time since she and Wheezy had tumbled into his life. He might not be able to control what his brother or Ruby did, and he'd never been able to predict which way the winds would take Eva, but dogs he knew. Dogs he understood.

"You know what?" he said. "You can go ahead and toss that recording out. I'll make a better one and give it to Ruby myself."

"You will?" Eva was instantly suspicious. It had been so long since Spencer had allowed himself to play *anything*, let alone a twisted game of one-upmanship with a woman he couldn't get out of his mind, that Eva's suspicions were justified. "Why? What are you going to do?"

He shrugged. "It's like you said. She's going to fight her way into the dog show no matter what. I might as well do my part to avoid a disaster."

Jujubee gave a sudden whimper. Spencer soothed him with some nonsense about how much better he'd feel after his surgery. He *would* feel better, but not right away. Like most things in life, it took time, patience, and hard work before things started to really improve. Everyone always seemed to want a shortcut in life.

Everyone except Ruby Taylor, that was.

He wasn't ashamed to admit that he'd been wrong that first day, when he'd assumed she coasted along on her good looks. It would have been easy for her to use her charm to get her way, twisting Spencer and Caleb around in knots, capitalizing on Eva's admiration, and begging favors from dog-show strangers, but she didn't. She was a sneaky, stubborn cheat, yes, but she had grit.

He liked that about her. He *respected* it.

"Fine," Eva capitulated. "But you'd better not jeopardize my free babysitting weekend, or I'll never forgive you. Maury and I haven't gone away in ages. We're looking forward to this more than we did our wedding."

He felt oddly hurt by this. "You could have asked me to take them. I'm always willing to help out."

Her laughter as she pushed open the door and led Jujubee out didn't do much to make him feel better. "And risk our friendship forever? Yeah, right. No offense, Spencer, but as good as you are with animals, my kids would eat you for breakfast."

"I brought you a gift."

Ruby gave a startled jump and dropped the book she was holding, losing her place in the process. It *wasn't* the erotic novel she was supposed to be reading for the book club, but that didn't stop her from feeling guilty at being caught.

Mostly because she was sitting inside Spencer's house. Alone.

"Caleb said I could stay here while he went back to the dry cleaners." She pointed toward the door to the patio, where Caesar and Wheezy's slobbery enthusiasm was painting streaks across the glass. "We were in the middle of dog training when he suddenly remembered a pair of pants that needed to be dropped off."

Spencer accepted this excuse—and her presence in his house—without so much as a blink. She was *technically* on Caleb's side of the living room, so it wasn't as if she was trespassing, but he was well within his rights to put up a protest.

"Don't you want to know what the gift is?" he asked.

She did, but nothing would make her admit it. Not when Spencer was watching her with so much intensity. He must have come straight from work, because he was dressed in what she recognized as his "veterinary wear." Any other person who worked with animals all day would dress in easily washable cottons and dark colors that hid stains. Spencer, however, was every inch the dog-show judge, his buttons securely fastened, his clothes as crisp and fresh as if they'd come straight from the cleaners.

It was enough to make her think that maybe Caleb really did pick up the dry cleaning that much. It had to take a lot of starch for Spencer to maintain that aesthetic.

"If I'm in the way, I can take Wheezy for a run or something until Caleb gets back," she said by way of answer. "I weighed him this morning, and he's actually put on three pounds since this whole thing started. Maybe I can drop him off in a field in the middle of nowhere and make him find his own way home. That'll slim him down."

Spencer had yet to move from where he stood, his feet carefully positioned on his side of the duct-tape line. At her words, he allowed himself to unbend enough to drop his shoulders. Like the intense stare, it did upsetting things to her equilibrium.

"Is that another pageant tip from your mother?" he asked. "The survivalist's diet?"

"No, thank goodness. She never went that far. She *did* sometimes make me reach milestones on the treadmill before I could have dessert, though."

His posture tensed again. "That sounds awful, Ruby. I'm sorry."

If her equilibrium had been unbalanced by his smile, his ready sympathy flipped it upside down.

"It's not as bad as it sounds," she was quick to say, feeling flushed. "She always made herself do the exercises with me so I never ran alone. Everything she pushed me to do, she pushed herself just as hard."

"You're a lot like her." He didn't phrase it as a question. He also didn't phrase it as a negative—a thing that startled as much as it pleased her. Most of the time, discussing her contentious relationship with her mother resulted in sympathy and outrage, as though no one else could imagine a childhood with such a woman.

It had been difficult, yes, and the pressure to succeed had been more than a lot of people could bear, but Laurel was still her mom. For all her flaws, she was—and always had been—a force to be reckoned with.

"More than I want to be sometimes," she admitted.

Instead of replying, Spencer reached into his pocket and extracted his cell phone. "What's your phone number?"

There was enough of her mother in her to cause Ruby to reveal a sultry smile. "Why, Spencer Wilson. Are you hitting on me?"

He glanced up just long enough to lock his piercing gaze with hers. It wasn't an answer, but it wasn't not one either. Gifts, kindness, phone numbers…if she didn't know any better, she'd say they were making progress.

"I could always get it from your application," he warned.

"There's no need to resort to such tactics. If you want my number, I already told you that all you have to do is say the word."

He couldn't pretend not to know what word they were talking about. "Do you want the gift or not?" he demanded.

She gave him her phone number, watching carefully to see how he reacted, but in this, as in most things, he didn't make it easy.

Her phone chimed with an incoming message. Had it been any other man offering to send her mysterious gifts via text, she'd have assumed she was about to be the recipient of an unsolicited dick pic. Where Spencer was concerned, she had no such fears. She doubted he'd send one even if she expressly asked for it.

"An audio clip?" she asked as soon as she opened up her phone. "Is this one of those dog whistle apps? Because I tried that, and it doesn't work. Wheezy just whines and covers his ears."

"It's not a dog whistle app" was his unhelpful reply.

Curious, she pressed the play button. Much to her surprise, his voice came through loud and clear.

"Mayonnaise. Mayonnaise."

She darted a quick glance at him, but he was as impassive as always.

"Sit. Sit. Stay. Stay. Heel. Heel."

The stern and careful repetition of these commands continued for the length of the recording. It was much better than anything Ruby had hoped Eva would be able to get for her, but that was what alarmed her. What had Eva told him to get him to give in so easily?

When the recording was finished, however, he didn't look like a man who'd heard anything unpleasant. He rubbed a hand along the back of his neck instead. "I'm supposed to tell you that this in no way cancels your deal with Eva—and if it does, then I'm supposed to forcibly take the phone from you so she can renegotiate. I think she's really looking forward to her weekend away."

Ruby laughed, surprised to find that it wobbled around the edges. "She told you?"

His answer was a rueful smile. It was lopsided, one side of his mouth twisted higher than the other, and the sight of it made her heart lurch. Everything about this man was so carefully protected, as though he'd been born inside a metal shell.

But when he smiled… When he laughed…

Gah. It was like getting a glimpse of what lay beneath. Ruby was sure there was something soft and squishy in there—something worth uncovering.

"Let's just say you didn't choose the best spy for the job," he said. "Eva is great at a lot of things, but subtlety isn't one of them. She popped around the corner at work every couple of minutes to ask me questions that she's known the answer to since she was three."

Ruby couldn't help but make a comparison to her own workplace dynamic. Harry had a tendency to pop up, too, but usually because he had a snide comment to make or he wanted her to mop up bodily fluids. "It must be a riot to work alongside her every day," she said wistfully.

Spencer gave a start of surprise. "It is, actually. I can't imagine doing any of this without her. She has a way of making everything ten times better than it would be by myself." He hesitated before adding, "I don't know what it is, but you have that ability, too. These past few weeks have been…fun."

Ruby couldn't have been more shocked if Spencer had confessed to be a time traveler sent through the eons to right the wrongs of the future. *She'd* been having a good time trying to beat him at his own game, it was true, but this was the first sign Spencer had shown of feeling the same.

As if there was nothing more to be said on the subject, he nodded toward the sliding glass door. "Did you want to let them in so we can test the recording? I'd open the door myself, but it's on Caleb's side."

"He's not home. I told you. He went on another one of those mysterious dry-cleaning errands."

"I know, but it's his side regardless of whether he's here. We have a code."

Ruby wasn't sure whether to tell Spencer the truth: his brother's code was a lot more relaxed than he let on. In the past few weeks, they'd held several dog-training sessions while Spencer was at work, and Caleb had shown no such qualms about stepping over the line. He'd furnished her with drinks and snacks from Spencer's mini fridge. He'd run around the entire house with the dogs and snooped through Spencer's drawers. He'd even used the bathroom like a decent human being.

"What he doesn't know won't hurt him," Caleb had laughingly said. "He spends so much time at work and getting ready for the dog show that I practically live here by myself."

She glanced down at the duct-tape line separating her from Spencer. At most, there were three feet between them, which was a reasonable distance for a conversation like this one. From the way Spencer was careful not to draw too close to the line, however, they might as well have been miles apart.

With a lurch, she realized that any distance from Spencer was too much. A smart woman would approach Spencer as one would a baited bear. Cautiously, carefully, and in full protective gear.

As had already been established, Ruby was not that woman. And Spencer, she suspected, was not that man.

"You really won't come over here?" she asked as she took a wide step back. "Under any circumstances?"

"No." He shook his head. "Caleb and I have an agreement. That agreement exists regardless of whether he's here to witness it."

It was such a Spencer thing to say that Ruby couldn't help feeling irritated. What happened to the man who was finally starting to unbend? "What if I was choking?" she asked.

"You're not."

"What if I keeled over and had a heart attack sometime in the next five minutes?"

"Then I'd help you, but only if I was sure you weren't faking it. Medical emergencies are the exception to the rule, but it *is* still a rule."

She took another step back. "Spencer."

He didn't move. "Ruby."

"It's a pretend line."

"It's a *symbolic* line," he countered. "Just like stoplights are symbolic traffic signals. They only mean something because we believe in them. If everyone decided one day not to recognize them anymore, there'd be chaos."

He wasn't wrong, but that didn't make Ruby feel any more charitable toward him. If anything, it only made her more annoyed. She was having a moment here—an actual human moment fraught with emotion and desire and all those things that made life worth living. And *still* he wouldn't admit that he was having it, too.

"So unless I'm having a medical emergency, you won't come over here," she said, stating it more as fact than a question.

"No."

"No matter what I say or do."

"You already know the answer to that."

"Okay," she said and reached for the bottom of her tank top. "Suit yourself."

She had her shirt whipped off before Spencer even realized what was happening. She could tell because she watched as the implication sank in. The moment her skin hit the air, his eyes widened and he went perfectly immobile, like a deer caught in the lights of a strip club.

"What are you doing?" he asked, his voice rough. Ruby *hoped* it sounded like that because he was pleased by what he saw, but she wasn't as sure of herself as she'd have liked to be. Removing clothing in front of a grumpy, reluctant man wasn't as easy as it seemed.

It helped that she was wearing a cute neon-pink bra today—and that nature had enabled her to fill it. She no longer had the taut, carefully honed body of an eighteen-year-old beauty pageant contestant, but she'd never had any complaints, either. She dipped where men liked a woman to dip and swelled where they preferred a little padding.

"Whatever you're trying, it won't work," he said, not moving. He was staring, though, which was the most important thing.

She jutted her hip to give her dips and swells more emphasis. If nothing else came of her long tenure on the stage, at least she knew how to position her body so it looked its best. Spencer's eyes never left her, and he licked his lips with a slow, meaningful deliberation that did much to boost her confidence. She *knew* she couldn't be alone in this attraction or that the push and pull between them hadn't left him just as shaken and exhilarated as it left her.

"I think it might be working a little," she countered.

He shook his head. "I'm not the man you think I am, Ruby. I know what you're trying to do, but I can't. I'm not built that way. I'm not like—"

He didn't finish his comparison. Now that Ruby's tank top was tossed unceremoniously to the floor, she reached for the top button of her favorite high-waisted jeans. She didn't intend to remove *all* her clothes and had decided on nothing more than a teasing show of the top line of her panties, but Spencer decided he'd had enough. With a jolt that reminded her of Wheezy chasing after a piece of bacon, he dashed forward.

Across the line. Over his principles. Past his better judgment.

His hand touched on top of hers. No other part of his body came into contact with her, his whole frame held in deliberate abeyance, but that didn't seem to make any difference. His fingers caressing hers, preventing her from removing her pants—*begging* her not to—set off something wild inside her.

"You don't really mean it," he said, his voice hoarse. His gaze was no longer trailing over her naked upper half; it had locked on hers with a desperation that caught in her throat. "You're only doing this to me because you can."

On the contrary, she was doing this because she was no longer capable of pretending she had any self-restraint. She knew it was the contrarian in her who needed to see such a precise, intellectual man come undone and that there was no way he'd ever look at her with the respect she yearned for, but none of that seemed to matter right now. While they were alone in this living room, both of them breathing as hot and heavily as if they'd run several miles to get here, there didn't seem to be any chance of escape.

"It looks like you crossed a line, Spencer Wilson," she said. Her own voice sounded raspier than usual. "So much for those rules you love so much."

"You don't really mean it," he repeated. "Not with me."

This time, she read in it a question—a *plea*. It would have been so easy to reassure him, to tell him that she'd never wanted anything as much as she wanted him right now, but she wasn't sure that was the answer he was after. From the expectant way he was watching her and the tightening clasp of his hand over hers, it was almost as though he was begging her to say no.

There was only one way to handle a situation like this, and it just so happened that it was one of the few things she knew how to do.

Challenge. Compete. *Win.*

"One hundred and forty, right?" She took a deep breath and backed away. The distance between them increased but the heat remained. "That's where you left off, right? You and Caleb?"

His eyes flashed a warning. "*That's* what this is about?"

"No, but it's what I'm going to make it about." She nodded toward the line behind Spencer. "You said you weren't sure you could make it that high, so we're about to find out."

"You want me to do push-ups right now? While you stand there without a shirt on?" He glanced down at himself, where the clean lines of his slacks were starting to show serious signs of strain. "Do you have any idea how impossible that is?"

She released a shaky laugh. Physical exertion would be equally difficult for her, even if the evidence wasn't on display. Her insides were rapidly turning liquid. "I'm not that cruel. I was thinking more along the line of strokes."

His breath hitched. "*Strokes*?"

The way he said the word—with just as much interest as incredulity—brought a smile to her lips. Whatever else she might say about this man, his competitive instincts matched her own.

"Unless you don't think you can?" she said. "It's asking a lot, I know. You can always forfeit."

He took two steps backward, refusing to speak until he was safely ensconced on his half of the living room. "You did that on purpose. You wanted me to cross to the other side. You wanted to punish me."

"It doesn't have to be a punishment, Spencer. In fact, if we do things right, it can be the exact opposite."

Without him there to stop her, she flicked open the buttons of her jeans one by one, tugging them lower each time. She didn't stop until her jeans were low enough to reveal the top band of her panties. It wasn't her sexiest pair by a large margin—comfortable cotton with rainbow elastic across the top—but that didn't seem to make a difference. Spencer took one look at the soft skin of her lower belly and immediately forced his gaze back up.

With a sinking heart, she realized it wasn't going to work. Even after all this time together, even with his recording on her phone and *that* glint in his eyes, he was still uninterested in taking things to the next level. She'd called the bluff on his attraction, and that was the end of it for him. He'd done what so many men had done before—taken one look at her and decided he knew exactly what kind of woman she was. Only this time, it hurt a lot more.

To Spencer, she was and always would be Ruby Taylor, former beauty queen and current waste of space. Nothing she did—or exposed—was going to change that.

"One hundred and forty?" Spencer said. Ruby was so startled by the sound of his voice that she didn't register what was happening right away. It took him tugging the bottom of his shirt out of his slacks for that. "Fine. Easy. I can do that with one hand tied behind my back."

A squeak of surprise and delight escaped her. He was going to do it. He was going to meet her on this battleground—this sexually charged, bizarre battleground—and he was going to do it as her equal.

"I imagine most men only need one hand," she pointed out, too entranced by the sight of him slipping out of his shoes and shrugging off his jacket to do more than that. So far, he'd exposed no more skin than she'd seen before, but there was something about the systematic way he was loosening all his bindings that made her mouth go dry. "Do you want me to take the rest of my clothes off, too? I'm more than happy to if you think it'll...help."

He paused in the act of unbuckling his belt. "Leave your clothes exactly where they are. This is going to be hard enough as it is." A low chuckle escaped him as he added, "I guess I should admit that it already is."

Ruby almost combusted on the spot. Spencer was making jokes. Spencer was making jokes about his erection. Spencer was making jokes about his erection mere seconds before he was going to pull it out for her.

A whimper escaped before she could stop it. Spencer heard it and pointed a warning finger at her.

"You can't make those sounds, either. It's not sportsmanlike."

"I'm not sure I'll be able to help myself," she confessed. "What's the forfeiture rule, by the way? If you, ah, don't make it all the way?"

His mouth firmed in a hard line. "I'll make it."

"You don't know that. One hundred and forty is an awful lot of stroking. And rubbing. And pumping. And—"

"Stop it. You're making that sound again."

It was true. She *was* making that sound again. She was also starting to feel a little faint. She'd wanted this—wanted him—from almost the moment of their first meeting, but she'd expected to be a more active participant. *She* wanted to be the one rubbing and stroking and pumping and—

"How about this?" Spencer asked before her whimper had a chance to devolve into an out-and-out moan this time. "If I don't make it, then you can come over here and I'll stroke *you* a hundred and forty times instead."

The liquid heat that had been building up inside her turned into a deep, tugging pang. If she'd wanted to win this challenge before—and she had—she'd stop at nothing now. The thought of Spencer's hand between her legs, of him punishing himself by putting his fingers inside her, was making her whole body take flight.

"Oh, you foolish man." Ruby squared her stance so that she had a complete, unadulterated view of him. "You shouldn't have said that."

"Why?" His hand hovered over his fly. "What are you going to do?"

"I won't make a sound," she promised. "And I'll keep the exact same amount of clothing as I have on now. But that's all I can guarantee. Everything else is fair game."

She half expected him to argue, but as she lifted her hand to the lip of her bra, tracing the line where fabric met the soft swell of skin, all he seemed capable of was licking his lips.

"I can agree to those rules," he said.

Ruby had spent the majority of her adult life escaping the rigidity and discipline of rules. Rules and competitions had stolen her childhood. They'd prepared her for a lifetime of disappointment and failure. They'd turned her mother into someone who could throw away a marriage to a nice, decent man.

But right now, looking into the eyes of a man whose life was shaped by rules of every variety, she could only remember the excitement. The anticipation. *The joy.*

"Then you'd better get started," Ruby said with a nod toward his lower half. "May the best man win."

It took all Ruby's concentration not to make a sound as Spencer tugged at the fly of his slacks to reveal the flat planes of his lower abdomen. Caleb had made it a point to remove his shirt several times during training, so Ruby already knew that the Wilson genes were good ones. This ridiculous game they played—all those push-ups and crunches and burpees—only enhanced what nature had given them. They were lean without being thin, strong without being sculpted, muscular without making a show of it. But while Caleb preened and pranced and did everything he could to draw attention to himself, Spencer was content to focus on the task at hand.

The task at *literal* hand.

No matter how many times or how strenuously she echoed the words *thigh apex* inside her head, she could only marvel at the vision before her. Spencer was a tall, well-built man with all the parts to match—and even better, he was weirdly unconcerned with it. After the amount of effort it had taken her to get to this point, she expected him to face his back toward her or at least be more furtive in his movements. There was nothing boastful about the way he handled himself, but there was nothing bashful about it, either.

It had been her intention to win this challenge as quickly as possible. There were all manner of tricks she could pull that didn't involve making sounds or removing clothing. She had lips to bite and breasts to touch, eyelashes to bat and hips to undulate. In her experience, it didn't take much to move a man to completion—especially when he was obviously *up* for anything.

She hadn't been counting on Spencer Wilson.

"One," he said, and moved his hand so slowly that she could see his erection being revealed to her inch by painstaking inch.

He took a deep breath and did it again—even slower this time, though how such a thing was possible, she didn't know. "Two."

She glanced at the clock on the wall behind her. "Um, I don't know what kind of relationship you have with your brother, but he won't be running errands forever. I doubt you're going to want him walking in on this."

Spencer didn't comment on the fact that she'd made a sound—several of them, in fact—but smiled and shook his head instead. "I have plenty of time. He won't be home for another forty-five minutes. I'll use every single one of them if I have to."

Forty-five minutes of this? Ruby didn't think she'd make it.

"What if he gets done picking up the dry cleaning quickly? What if he forgot something and has to come back to get it?"

"He won't."

The confidence with which he uttered this rivaled the confidence with which he continued his penance. Three. Four. Five. Six. Each stroke seemed to come slower than the last, as if Spencer wanted to eke this moment out as long as humanly possible.

Seven.

Eight.

Nine.

"That's not how you're supposed to do it," she said. The whimper was back again, though she managed to keep it contained. "A *real* stroke is fast and hard and—"

This time, he did put up a protest. "You're not allowed to make any sounds. And I don't need your advice on how to get myself off, thanks. I think I've got the mechanics worked out by now."

"This doesn't count."

"Ten," he said and stroked.

"You're not doing it right."

"Eleven," he said. "Twelve."

It occurred to her with a start that he was doing this on purpose—presenting himself like a god, showing how much control he had. It was the same thing he did whenever getting Wheezy to do what he wanted. He made the rules. He was in charge. He was the master.

Even if it had been *her* hand sliding up and down his length, even if she was on top of him and had that beautiful erection inside her, he wouldn't hurry things. He wouldn't stop until he finished what he came to do.

He wouldn't come until she did.

That thought—of Spencer taking his time with her, of his beautiful voice dictating what she could and couldn't do, of her doing what she damn well pleased anyway—was Ruby's undoing.

"Thirteen," he said, adding a flourish to his tip this time. *Showing off.* "Fourteen. Fifteen. I can do this all day. Can you?"

"I'm not sure," she said, since it was no more than the truth. This particular kind of competition had never come her way before, but she was nothing if not willing. "Let's see what happens if I give it a go."

She had the satisfaction of watching Spencer lose his concentration—and his count—as she walked her fingers down her belly toward her open fly. He didn't move again until she'd worked her hand inside her panties.

"What are you doing?" he demanded.

With her free hand, she made the motion of a zipper over her lips. No sound was made, and every article of clothing stayed exactly where it was. All that changed was that she pressed her palm flat against her mons and slid her fingers into the damp folds of her own body. She was breaking no rules—only playing the game.

"It won't work," he warned, though the hoarse note in his voice indicated that it was working just fine. "You can't force me to go any faster than I want to."

She knew she couldn't, so she didn't try. Giving herself over to pleasure instead, she started doing some stroking of her own.

Like Spencer, she was something of an expert when it came to her own body, so it didn't take long to work herself up to a state of slick enjoyment. She would have preferred to have fewer clothes on, and it would have been a lot more fun if Spencer could watch closely as she ran her finger in circles around the outside of her clit, but she could only work with what she'd been given.

"Sixteen," he said, almost defiant as he resumed his strokes. "Seventeen-eighteen-nineteen."

These last three came faster than before—which was good, because there was no way she was making it anywhere near a hundred and forty. Not when Spencer couldn't tear his eyes from her. Not when his hand started moving with a force that had been lacking before.

Now was the time to pull out all the stops. Ruby took her lower lip between her teeth and arched her back so that her breasts jutted out, allowing her hips to take over the rhythmic pressure instead of her hand. As she'd hoped, Spencer noticed her movements in a very big, very rough way. She had the satisfaction of hearing him utter a deep groan before saying, "Twenty, twenty-one, twenty-two. This isn't fair, and you know it. Twenty-three, twenty-four, twenty-five. You aren't even trying to hold back."

It was true. She'd long since given up on outlasting Spencer. The waves of pleasure between her thighs were building up too quickly for that. The entire room seemed to be dwindling to two features: the hot, unyielding tug deep inside her belly and the magnetism of Spencer Wilson. His gaze locked on hers with so much intensity that she thought she might be able to come on the power of it alone.

In fact, if she didn't do something soon, that was exactly what was going to happen.

The words—*I give up, you win, screw the imaginary line and come screw me*—were starting to form on her lips when Spencer gave up on counting altogether.

"Goddammit, Ruby," he swore, losing track. "You're making those sounds again."

She'd been unaware of anything except the way Spencer was looking at her, but she was in no position to defend herself. Any moans or sighs escaping her right now were entirely out of her power. She was nothing but heat and sensation, desire and need.

Either her movements were timed to Spencer's or his were to hers, because she could almost swear that it was her hand on his erection and his hand between her thighs. If she closed her eyes, she could probably conjure up an image of just such a scenario, but she didn't dare. She wanted to watch as Spencer struggled with himself. She wanted to see the expression on his face as he finally gave in.

"You're free to quit at any time," she said as she took her lower lip between her teeth. "But I'm going to have to finish one way or another. You have no idea how good this feels."

He must have had *some* idea, because that was the end of the line. He uttered a deep, guttural groan and managed to say "sixty-four" before finally giving himself over to release.

Ruby had never been so grateful for a man's ejaculation in her life. She'd lost this game long before it had begun, and there was no use pretending otherwise. Without waiting to see if Spencer was paying attention, she jerked against her hand and cried out before sinking gratefully to her knees.

She could only assume Spencer was having a similarly difficult time resuming a normal pattern of breathing, of *existing*, because he uttered a gruff, "Don't move," and "I'll be right back," before turning away.

She used the moment to close her eyes and savor the satisfaction of what had to be one of the hottest and most bizarre sexual experiences of her life. The only touch she and Spencer had shared the entire time was the brief clasp of his hand on top of hers. They hadn't hugged, hadn't kissed, hadn't even held hands for an appreciable amount of time. There'd been no embracing and no bodily fluids exchanged.

Yet she was *spent*.

When Spencer returned to the living room, he'd changed into a clean pair of slacks and was drying his hands on a towel. He looked as cool and as in command of himself as he'd been when they'd first met, and Ruby felt herself responding to it the exact same way as before—with every single one of her lady parts.

Apparently, she wasn't as spent as she'd thought.

"I'm not sure if we can determine a clear winner from that," Spencer said in a voice that was a little too neutral to be believable. "I didn't get even remotely close to one hundred and forty, but you broke just about every rule we had to make sure of it."

She laughed and reached for her shirt—not because she was feeling particularly modest but because she needed to get herself under wraps before she forced him over the line again. "Maybe you should ask the dogs what they think." She nodded toward the sliding glass door, where two pairs of expectant eyes were watching them. Neither Caesar nor Wheezy looked particularly impressed. "They witnessed the whole thing."

Spencer laughed—a deep, rumbling sound that made her glad her shirt was on and her jeans buttoned back up.

"What?" she asked. "Why is that so funny?"

"We're not in a seedy motel, but I think that counts as exhibitionism, don't you? This was my very first porcupine."

Ruby's mouth fell open. He was doing it. He was saying the word.

"Say that again."

"What?" He quirked a smile. "Porcupine?"

She leaped to her feet and drew closer. For reasons she didn't entirely understand, she was careful not to step over the line that separated the two sides of the room. "One more time."

He shook his head—and, for the first time since he'd walked into the house, appeared slightly abashed. "I don't think I can right now."

"Right now?" she echoed. That phrase implied that he *could* another time—that this experience between them was the start of something more. What that something might be, she had no idea, but her every limb quaked at the thought. "Does that mean you want me to be on call for the next time you say it?"

Both his smile and his sheepishness deepened. Ruby was having a difficult time telling which of those two responses was affecting her more, but she was leaning toward the sheepishness. It was such a charming, natural, *human* response to what they'd just shared.

"That won't be anything new for you, will it?" he asked.

She halted, suddenly unsure what he was getting at—or, worse, *exactly* aware of what he was getting at—when he clarified with one disastrous sentence.

"I always thought that being on call was tough for a veterinarian, but it's probably nothing on what you have to put up with."

Her heart gave a lurch before settling somewhere near the pit of her stomach. *On call.* Right. Because as far as Spencer knew, she was a geriatric doctor working around the clock at a nursing home—a woman with an advanced degree and all the financial perks that came with it. And the worst part was, she had no one to blame for that but herself. She'd been so annoyed at him assuming she couldn't go to medical school that she'd never made any attempt to set the record straight.

"I don't understand it, to be honest," he said, shaking his head at her. "You're the most beautiful woman I've ever met—not to mention intelligent, driven, and successful. How are you still single?"

Ruby tried to answer him; she really did. The words were hovering right there, and all she had to do was utter them. *I'm not intelligent. I'm not driven. I'm not successful. I'm hovering one financial emergency away from bankruptcy, unskilled and unequipped for life in the real world. I'm not trained to do anything but smile and look pretty, and even that doesn't carry nearly as much weight as it used to.*

But her mouth went dry, her tongue cleaved to the roof of her mouth. The moment she said those words out loud—admitted to Spencer that the only thing she had to offer was what he was looking at—she knew that anything between them would come to an end.

So she did what she always fell back on when faced with a difficult situation. She turned it into a game.

"I could ask the same thing of you. You're a successful veterinarian and dog-show judge. You're hot as hell. And having just caught a firsthand glimpse of the way you handle yourself, I'm willing to bet you know your way around the bedroom."

As she'd hoped, mentioning Spencer's ability to *handle* himself had the effect of wiping all other thoughts from his mind. He went white all over and then pink, the tips of his ears taking the brunt of the color. She expected him to give her back her own again, as was their custom, but when he spoke, it was with a serious tone that snagged at her heart.

"I should think it was pretty obvious," he said. "You've met my brother."

"Yeah, I've met him. And I took his measure in the first twenty seconds." She narrowed her eyes, unable to believe what she was hearing. Did Spencer really think that when it came to the two of them, he was the *less* attractive twin? "You're worth two dozen of him, Spencer. Easily. Any woman who sees the two of you side by side and can't immediately tell the difference is an idiot."

Spencer's entire body went still. He looked like a man who'd been struck by lightning—and who wasn't sure he enjoyed the experience.

"You mean that," he said, no hint of a question in his voice. "You're being serious."

She couldn't help laughing a little. A reassuring hug would have been a more appropriate response—no man looked as though he needed one more—but that wasn't the nature of their relationship.

Yet.

"Of course I'm serious. I know you think you're the expert when it comes to judging people, but believe me, I've had plenty of practice. When it comes to dogs and men, I know what I like."

At the mention of dogs, Spencer once again glanced over to the sliding glass door. Caesar was still sitting with the patience and calm of a well-trained animal, but Wheezy had discovered some kind of residue on the glass and was licking it in slow, repetitive circles.

Spencer was forced into a chuckle. "Why do I get the feeling that wasn't a compliment?"

She had the answer ready—and even more importantly, she meant it.

"Because you haven't seen the magic inside that animal," she said. She waited until he looked back at her, his expression sharp, before adding, "But don't worry, I have. Other people might not think he's worth the effort, but I know better."

From the way he swallowed, it was obvious he knew exactly what she meant: that the dog's potential was nothing compared to his own. Spencer was just as recalcitrant as Wheezy and twice as frustrating, but as her initial instincts had proven, there was a lot more lurking underneath that pair of dark, brooding eyes.

Her instincts also warned her that now was a good time to make her exit. With any luck, Spencer would be so busy digesting this new information that he'd fail to realize that although he'd readily answered her question about his single state, she hadn't dared to touch his.

"Tell your brother I decided to finish the session at home, will you?" she said. "Now that I have access to your voice anytime I want, nothing can stop me."

Since Spencer was still standing there looking as though he'd been hit with a lightning bolt, she braved a step forward. Crossing the line, she lifted a hand to his cheek. His skin was surprisingly soft, and she was startled enough by the feel of it—and of him—that she allowed her thumb to stray to his lips. The scent of her desire still clung to her fingertips, but that didn't stop him from touching his tongue to her skin. Instead, it seemed to encourage him, and he only stopped himself from taking her thumb all the way into his mouth by forcing a deep, shuddering breath.

"Thank you for the recording, Spencer," she said. "And for one of the best orgasms of my life."

"But I didn't even touch you," he managed to say.

"I know," she agreed. "It makes me wonder what will happen once you finally do."

Chapter 10

"OH, SPENCER! SPENCY-BOY! I SAW YOUR TRUCK, SO I KNOW YOU'RE home. You can't hide in your room forever."

Spencer glanced up from the romance novel he was reading—something called *To Hook a Star*. In all the bustle of getting Wheezy hooked up to his leash and dragging him away, Ruby had left her book behind. Since it had been well ensconced on Caleb's side of the living room, Spencer had been forced to break his own rule to go grab it, but that hadn't bothered him as much as it might have a few weeks ago.

While he still believed in the *theory* of symbolic rules as a way of keeping order, there was no denying that it had felt good to step over that line.

Really good.

"What do you want?" He got to his feet and poked his head out his bedroom door, the book still in hand. *To Hook a Star* wasn't nearly as graphic as the erotic novel that sat half-read on his nightstand, but he liked it. More to the point, he liked that Ruby liked it. It hinted at a softer side he was only just starting to see. "I'm busy."

"No, you're not. You're brooding alone in your room like you always do." Caleb drew up to the edge of the line and made a big show of looking around the living room. "Where's Ruby? She was supposed to wait for me."

"She wanted me to tell you she's going to finish the training session at home."

"Goddammit, Spencer. What did you say to run her off? I was only gone an hour."

He ignored this. To divulge any of the details of his interaction with Ruby would be to divulge all of them. How she looked as she'd removed her shirt, daring him to do something about it. The way her eyes had widened in shock when he'd accepted the challenge. The sound of her moans. The gyrations of her hips. The—

He cleared his throat and forced himself to think of expressing anal glands and removing embedded maggots instead. He had to go to the darkest side of veterinary care; Caleb would see through him otherwise. He'd never been able to lie to his brother.

"Maybe she has better things to do than sit around waiting for you," he said as soon as he had a better handle on himself. The maggots helped. "You forget that most of us have responsibilities."

Caleb laughed. "Don't worry. Living with you is a constant reminder of the weight of responsibility. Am I allowed to ask why you're holding a book with a pink cover, or is it better not to know?"

Spencer didn't make an attempt to hide it. "It's research. And I'm serious. Has that animal improved in the slightest since you took this job?"

"Of course he hasn't. I assume that was why you allowed me to take her on as a client in the first place. You know damn well Wheezy is untrainable." Caleb paused just long enough to take a breath. "Aren't you going to ask me how it went with my parole officer?"

Spencer sighed. For once in his life, he wanted to talk about something other than his brother's legal problems. He wanted to discuss what they were going to do about Wheezy. He wanted to talk about his feelings for Ruby. He wanted to rip that tape up off the floor and sit in his own living room so they could have a conversation face-to-face.

Shit. What he really wanted was a friend—*his* friend, his twin brother, the companion of his youth. Not the roommate who lived to thwart him or the reckless competitor who would do anything to win.

Once upon a time, being around Caleb had been easy. His brother had always laughed and loved large, as his obscenely high number of friends could attest. All that laughing and loving got him into trouble sometimes, but that was Caleb all over. He never let anything bring him down. Not the guidelines and conventions that were Spencer's bread and butter, and definitely not the idea that an arbitrary set of rules could dictate his life.

He admired that about Caleb. He always had.

"Caleb, I—" he began, but his brother interrupted before he could figure out what he wanted to say.

"Hang on a sec, would you?" Caleb asked. "Caesar wants to be let in."

Spencer heard the sounds of the sliding door opening and the bulldog bouncing exuberantly inside. Even though he'd gone out to play with and feed the dog after Ruby had left, Caesar had declined the invitation to accompany him inside afterward. The arrival of Caleb, however, was a cause for celebration.

"Yes, boy. I see you. Yes, I've missed you. I would've brought you with me, but you know you get carsick."

Spencer watched as his dog and his brother enjoyed a reunion fit for a separation of a year instead of a few hours. Caesar licked every inch of skin he could reach before jumping up and tackling Caleb to the ground. There, the pair wrestled and laughed and generally acted the way man and his best friend were supposed to.

"He likes you better than he likes me," Spencer said as Caleb pulled off one of his socks, balled it up, and tossed it like a chew toy.

For the first time in his life, the words didn't cause him a pang. After the things Ruby had said to him—the things she'd *done* to him—he wasn't sure they could.

"Everyone likes me better than you" came Caleb's easy reply. "But you don't have to look so sour about it. I'll be out of your hair sooner than we thought. I'm up for early release next week."

"Wait." Spencer almost dropped the book in his hand. "What?"

"You don't have to look so surprised. I've been a good boy, remember? I've attended all my meetings and followed all the rules. You made sure of that."

Spencer's first feeling was one of unadulterated delight on his brother's behalf. He knew how much being tied to this house chafed him, how hard this whole thing was on an extrovert who thrived on other people's attention.

His second feeling was of deep foreboding. No matter how much more charitable Spencer might be feeling toward him, Caleb wasn't ready to be foisted back on the world yet. Nothing about him had changed—he'd shown no regret over his actions, altered nothing about his habits. Other than this training gig, he had no plans for long-term work, and Spencer didn't see that changing anytime soon. Throwing him back out in the world without any rehabilitation would only result in the same outcome as before.

And the worst part was, Caleb knew it. It was Dog Training 101. Until you addressed the underlying cause of the behaviors, they would always remain.

"Just think—a few more days, and then freedom will be mine. I can practically taste it. The first thing I'm going to do is ask Ruby out. Somewhere with drinking and music and very little clothing."

"I don't think that's the sort of thing she'll enjoy," Spencer said doubtfully.

Caleb laughed. "What you mean is, it's not the sort of thing *you'd* enjoy. I hate to break it to you, but you're not an eighty-year-old recluse—and neither, I might add, is Ruby. A woman like that wants to be taken out and treated like a queen."

Spencer shook his head. That wasn't the Ruby he was coming to know—the one who spent every minute of her free time training a dog that wasn't her own and for no reason he could tell other than her determination to prove him wrong. The one who was strong without being showy, sweet without being shy.

"You'd be better off taking her to a dog park for extra training," he said. "Or treating Wheezy to a fancy grooming session somewhere. The only thing she wants is for that animal to win the West Coast Canine Classic."

Caleb's laugh was both loud and long enough to bring the heat rushing to Spencer's ears. "And this is why you're still lonely and single at the ripe old age of thirty," he said with a shake of his head. "Women don't want to be taken to the dog park, Spencer. They crave romance and passion. They want excitement."

The dog park *was* exciting. One look at Caesar's face anytime they pulled up was all the proof Spencer needed of that.

"You're single, too," he pointed out. "And why are you so sure she's going to say yes, anyway? Maybe she prefers men who are more... serious-minded."

It was a dangerous thing to do—to show his hand like this, to admit that Caleb wasn't the only one attracted to Ruby—but it was too late to back down now. He held his breath as he waited for his brother's inevitable reaction—the laughter and mockery, the assurance that of the two of them, Spencer was the less likely to win her regard.

Caleb didn't disappoint. "Well, I'll be," he said, grinning like the Cheshire cat. "You *like* her."

"I didn't say that."

"You think she's hot."

"This isn't about appearances."

"You want to kiss her."

"I didn't say that either."

"With tongue."

"Now you're just being juvenile."

Caleb threw himself onto the couch, his hands behind his head as he settled in and got comfortable. Not by even a fraction of an inch did his smile recede. "Out with it. When did these feelings develop, and what have you done so far to woo her?" He nodded at the book in Spencer's hand. "I'm assuming your newfound love of romance novels has something to do with it? Trust you to go about *reading* instead of doing something."

Spencer could only blink across the room.

"I can probably convince her that another few training sessions every week are necessary, but we'll need to make sure she can schedule for a time when you're home." Caleb tapped his front teeth with his forefinger.

"And as soon as I get this stupid monitor off my ankle, I can come up with some kind of excuse to leave you alone together. Fuck, I'll be glad to see the last of this thing."

"Wait… Are you serious? You want to help me?"

"God knows you need it," Caleb said. "No offense, but from the way you treat that poor woman, you'd think she was single-handedly trying to run your dog show into the ground."

"She *is* single-handedly trying to run my dog show into the ground."

"She'll do it, too, if you're not careful." Caleb laughed and rubbed his hands together. "Now. What have you done so far to get on her good side? No, don't answer that. It'll only depress me. So far, all I've seen you do is scowl."

Despite his better judgment, Spencer found himself being pulled further into the living room—and into this conversation. "I thought you were planning on asking her out for yourself?"

Caleb shrugged an indifferent shoulder. When he spoke, however, it was with a sincerity that Spencer had rarely heard from him. "She's already told me eight times that I'm not her type. I think she might mean it. But if *you* like her—"

Spencer allowed himself to say the words out loud for the first time. "I do like her."

The spreading grin started to return to Caleb's face. Spencer didn't trust it, but not for the reasons he'd have expected a few minutes ago. That wasn't the grin of a brother who planned on swooping in and sabotaging his relationship with Ruby. That was the grin of a brother who planned on doing his utmost to facilitate it.

"Then let's get to work—starting with whatever is happening with your shirt. Do you always *have* to button it up to the top?"

Spencer ignored this slight. As much as he relished this unprecedented show of support and camaraderie, he couldn't help but feel there was a lot more to be said between them. "Caleb, about your parole and about us sharing the house—"

"You mean, about the fact that you're standing on my side again?"

Spencer glanced down with a start. Sure enough, he'd once again made his way over the duct-tape line and into enemy territory. And he couldn't even blame someone else for luring him over this time. He'd walked on his own two feet.

"Goddammit. Not again!"

Caleb laughed. "You must be getting soft in your old age. What'll it be this time? More push-ups? We're up to a hundred and forty now. I'm not sure you can make it."

Spencer thought of the challenge issued him less than an hour ago in this exact spot and shook his head. After the agony of feeling his own weight in his hand, of watching Ruby watch him as he stroked himself, push-ups seemed like child's play.

"Oh, I can make it," he vowed as he started to loosen his shirt cuffs and get in position. "I could probably even do it with one hand behind my back."

Chapter 11

"SIT."

At the sound of Spencer's low, stern voice, Wheezy sat.

So did Ruby.

So did Julio, Xavier, and Max.

"Roll over," the voice said. This time, the three small boys were the first to respond. Of all the commands on the recording, *roll over* was their favorite. It usually ended up with them halfway across the backyard in a pile that was composed of equal parts giggling and brotherly wrangling.

This time was no exception. As soon as Wheezy had maneuvered himself into rolling position, Eva's kids were already squirming their way through the grass.

"Ruby, you're not rolling!" cried the oldest of the boys. Julio, who was six years old and the self-designated spokesman of the lot, took after his mother in the best of ways. Ruby didn't think he'd stopped chattering since she'd arrived. "You hafta do it or Wheezy will get mad."

This comment wasn't as ridiculous as it sounded. Ruby had thought it a stroke of genius to bring Wheezy to spend the weekend at Eva and Maury's house. Two full days of dog training and a built-in distraction for the boys seemed like the perfect plan. Unfortunately, she hadn't accounted for just how fixated small children could get. When they'd heard that Ruby was training Wheezy to be a show dog, they wholeheartedly jumped on the plan. When they'd realized that Wheezy preferred to have company while he followed commands, they'd taken to sitting and shaking and rolling over with an obedience that would have done a military school proud.

When they'd realized that Wheezy would get personally offended if Ruby didn't *also* participate, well, this was the result. She'd been rolling all over the yard for hours.

"I can't, you guys. I'm old. My bones can't take much more of this."

"Ru-by!"

"Ruby!"

"Roooo!"

This last protest was uttered by Max, the youngest of the lot. At just two years of age, he was the one Ruby was most concerned about keeping alive, but he seemed to be composed of a combination of bulletproof glass and hard rubber. Nothing slowed him down.

When it came to slowing *her* down, however…

She rolled onto her back and closed her eyes. Thanks to the long hours spent on her feet at work, she was in good physical condition, but that didn't mean anything when compared to the energy levels and capabilities of Eva's kids. This was going to be a long weekend.

"Have they killed you already?"

Ruby's eyes flew open. It took a moment for her pupils to adjust, so all she saw at first was a dark shadow looming overhead. She felt no fear at that shadow, suffered no nervous qualms. As she took in the outline of Spencer's familiar shape and absorbed the soothing tones of his voice, all she could feel was the pitter-patter of her heart.

"I'm not dead," she said. "I'm resting my eyes."

By this time, Eva's brood had noticed the new arrival and launched themselves at him full speed. Amid shrieks of joy and Wheezy's whining excitement, Spencer allowed himself to be embraced from every side. The boys clung to his legs like they were preparing to climb a tree, all three talking at once.

"What have you done to these poor kids?" Spencer asked with a quirk of his brow. "They're never this happy to see me."

"Uncle Spencer, we're training to be show dogs," Julio informed him.

"Dogs!" chimed in Max.

Xavier, who was the quietest of the three and therefore Ruby's favorite, merely nodded his solemn agreement.

"Want to see?" Julio asked. "Ruby's been making us practice all day. We can't have a treat until Wheezy does five things in a row, but he's not very good yet. He can only do three. Well, two and a half. Ruby promised us ice cream."

"Ice cream!" echoed Max.

Xavier's stomach growled its agreement.

"Don't look at me like that," Ruby said as Spencer's brow went even higher. "I have a low-calorie frozen yogurt cup for Wheezy. He won't know the difference."

She'd had time to stand up and brush herself off by now, but it wasn't doing her any favors. Five hours of babysitting might not sound like a lot to someone who'd never met Eva and Maury's children, but Ruby felt as though she'd been run over by a car, hosed off with napalm, and hung up to dry. Spencer, however, looked as impeccably cool as always.

"Low-calorie frozen yogurt sounds delicious," he said.

"And the boys are getting sugar-free Popsicles laced with sedatives."

He chuckled. "I'm going to assume you're kidding about that one. Can I see?"

She was still so rattled by Spencer's sudden appearance that it took her a moment to realize what he was asking. Her initial thought, that he wanted to see and approve Wheezy's snack, was quashed only when the golden retriever gave an expectant whine.

"Can I do it?" Julio asked. Without waiting for an answer, he took the phone from Ruby's hand and pressed a button on the screen.

"Sit," Spencer's voice said through the speaker. Wheezy seemed a little alarmed to find Spencer's voice coming from a source that wasn't his face, but these past few hours hadn't been spent in vain. He obligingly set his butt onto the grass.

So did the children.

"Speak," Spencer's recorded voice said. As this was another favorite command of all three boys, a loud cacophony of human and canine barks filled the air.

"That's good," Ruby said, hoping to forestall the next step. "Let's put that away and—"

"Roll over," came the next command. There was no stopping the boys after that. All three boys started rolling and giggling anew, but Wheezy, who had reached his two-and-a-half limit, found a patch of shade and stretched himself out in it.

"We're still working on a few things," Ruby said, feeling defensive. "He's made considerable progress the past few days."

"He'll be a show dog in no time," Spencer agreed blandly.

"We still have three weeks to go," she added. "There's no saying what could happen between now and then."

"You two will be the stars of the event."

"You'll end up having to eat your words… See if you don't. He's lost a pound since you last saw him. Once I take him to the groomer and they clear out some of his undercoat, he'll have lost twice as much."

"He's never looked better."

All this calm acquiescence was starting to alarm her. She turned to face Spencer, arms akimbo and much of her energy restored. "Okay, who are you, and what have you done with Spencer?"

Instead of taking offense, he laughed. "I'm determined not to let you get to me today. Nothing you say or do will move me."

The idea of Spencer being docile and good-humored was intriguing enough to pique her interest, but not so intriguing that she was willing to accept it at face value. Spencer didn't make *anything* easy. It was a large part of his charm.

"Nothing?" she countered. "Those are bold words coming from a man who…rises so willingly to a challenge."

"Nice try, but it won't work this time." He nodded across the yard to where the boys were attempting to roll circles around Wheezy. "And since you can hardly start taking off your clothes while you're watching those three, I figure that gives me twenty-four hours of safety.

Thirty-six, if I know Eva. She's going to stretch this weekend out as long as she can."

The prospect of being abandoned to the mercy of those high-adrenaline children for that long didn't, as it might have a few minutes earlier, daunt Ruby. Thirty-six hours in Spencer's company—thirty-six hours in which to chip away at his resolve one innuendo at a time—was enough to make her wish Eva and Maury would never return.

"They have to sleep sometime," she pointed out.

Spencer laughed. "Is that what you think? Oh, my sweet summer child."

"You have to sleep sometime, too." She paused as the full implication of thirty-six hours sank in. "Wait… Are you staying here? With me? For the whole weekend?"

A tinge of pink touched his ears. "I won't if you don't want me to, but I thought I'd make the offer. Eva and Maury usually tag-team, and they still end up looking like something the dog dragged in by the end of the day." He hesitated. "It's not a commentary on your ability to babysit, I swear. I just thought you might like the company."

It was such a sweet offer—and such an unexpected one—that Ruby could only blink at him. Spencer Wilson seemed like the last person on earth who would willingly indulge in domesticity. Especially the messy, rambunctious, chaotic kind found under this roof.

Then again, he was closer to Eva than he was to anyone. You could tell a lot about a man from the company he kept. Caleb, for example, didn't seem to see anyone but his own reflection in the mirror. Harry, for another example, hung out with drug addicts who didn't balk at stealing from the elderly and vulnerable.

Spencer was friends with a chatty, oversharing mother of three and a large-animal vet who was obsessed with tiny dogs. That meant something.

"Thank you," Ruby said. She got up on her tiptoes and planted a kiss on his cheek. He smelled of soap and a freshly mown lawn, but that might have just been because the scent of grass was all over her hair and clothes. "The extra hands will be nice."

"Ewwww!"

"She kissed you!"

"Girls have cooties!"

Ruby laughed as she pulled away. She laughed even harder when Spencer swallowed so loudly she could hear his throat working up and down. He clearly hadn't been expecting her easy acceptance of his offer—or the touch of her lips on his skin.

"Are you still sure nothing I do will move you?" she asked. "I hate to break it to you, but there's a lot more where that came from. A cheek isn't the only thing I know how to kiss."

His eyelashes fluttered with interest, but he still didn't move. "I'm sure," he said. "A dog-show judge is immune to bribery of all kinds. It's in our blood."

"Then it's only fair to admit that I don't just kiss," she said with something almost like a purr. "In the right mood, I also lick and nibble and wrap my tongue around—"

A screech filled the air before she could finish making her threat. She whirled and found that in the five minutes she and Spencer had been talking, Julio had managed to get all the way up an oak tree that stood stately and dangerous in the middle of the yard. He was fine, as were the two little boys egging him on from the ground. The cat he appeared to be chasing up the branches, however, strongly resented the interference.

Instead of reprimanding the boys or running to the rescue, Spencer laughed. It was an amazing sound—a deep, low rumbling that made her feel like nothing in the world could be terrible as long as he was in it. No more did she feel anxious about the future, and gone was the fear that Spencer would discover her lie about being a doctor and look at her the way he had that first day.

In this moment, with that laugh, she felt nothing but happy.

"Oh, I'm not worried," he said, watching as Julio swung himself from branch to branch as though he'd been born in that very tree. "By the end of today, you won't even have the ability to blink, let alone wrap your tongue around anything."

It was her turn to laugh. "There are only three of them, Spencer. Spend an evening with twenty elderly residents doing keg stands with their walkers, and then we'll talk."

"Where are we going, and why does it look like the sort of place you'd abandon a woman and three children you want to conveniently dispose of?"

Spencer shook his head as he turned Eva and Maury's minivan down a dirt lane that rumbled and kicked up a wake of debris behind them. "I could tell you, but then I'd have to conveniently dispose of you."

Even though his eyes were trained on the road, he could feel Ruby's soft laughter shaking in the passenger seat. If he was being honest, he could feel every single movement she'd made for the past hour. Each soft breath that escaped her lips, each twist of her body, each strand of hair she tucked behind her ear… After the challenge she'd uttered back at Eva and Maury's house, he defied any man to sit within ten feet of her and not feel the strain.

"You wouldn't get away with it," she said. "The second I didn't show up for a shift, the residents at the retirement community would call the CIA, FBI, *and* Homeland Security. They're kind of obsessed with me."

He didn't find anything odd about this statement. As someone who was becoming rather obsessed with her himself, he could understand the motivation.

"You must take really good care of them," he said and held out his hand. To his delight, Ruby accepted his hand and squeezed it. She didn't let go, either, content to slip her fingers through his and hold them there.

It was one of the first real touches they'd shared, this holding of hands while zipping down a highway with three kids fighting in the back seat. In the grand scheme of romantic gestures, it was barely a blip, but Spencer's chest started to contract all the same. Like Eva handing out hugs as though they were lollipops, Ruby made this feel so normal, so *good.*

"I *try* to be good to them." She squeezed again. "Although it rarely ends up well for me. No matter how hard I fight it, I fall in love with each and every one of them. Some of the independent residents like Mrs. Orson live there for years and years, but the ones I physically take care of—the nursing-home patients—come in with a clock ticking over their heads. Even though I know it's going to hurt and that I could do my work so much better if I didn't get attached, it happens anyway."

"I keep forgetting how similar our jobs are. I feel the same way about every animal I take care of."

She laughed but there was a brittle quality to it. "That's right. You and I are just two highly trained medical professionals making our way in the world. Nothing special to see here."

"What made you choose geriatric medicine as your specialty, if you don't mind me asking?" Spencer felt himself to be on dangerous ground, but he didn't know where it had come from. "It can't be easy, only seeing your patients in the end stages of their lives. I couldn't be a vet if it only included late-stage care."

Her hand slipped out of his as easily as it had slipped in.

"What is it?" he asked, risking a sideways glance. "What did I say?"

Her only answer was a shake of her head. Her curls, which refused to stay contained in a ponytail at the nape of her neck, covered her face and masked her expression, but he didn't need to see her to know that he'd struck a nerve.

"I have to pee," Julio called suddenly from the back seat. "And so does Xavier."

Ruby twisted in her seat to look at the kids. Spencer couldn't say for sure, but she seemed relieved at the interruption. "I'm sure we'll be there any minute now. How about you, Max? Can you hold it until we get there?"

Max giggled. "Too late!"

She groaned, but it was a good-natured groan rather than an exasperated one. "I knew I shouldn't have given you guys all that apple juice. What's our ETA, Captain?"

Spencer caught sight of the familiar sign off the highway and clicked the blinker. "Five minutes, tops. And I'm sorry I didn't plan for a pit stop. I'll take care of Max."

"Oh, it's not a problem. Believe me, cleaning up a two-year-old's mess is nothing compared to a ninety-year-old's."

This confession took Spencer by surprise. Although he wiped away his fair share of animal accidents, they usually had vet techs to help with the more grueling day-to-day details. It was on the tip of his tongue to ask how much she had to do with the routine care of her patients, but he wasn't about to risk another misstep.

"Well, it's a pretty place to die, I'll give you that," Ruby said as they pulled up to a sprawling ranch house set against the emerald green of western Washington. In the spring, the fields behind them were covered in a blanket of colorful tulips, but they boasted nothing but leafy greens and shorn heads right now. "What *is* this place?"

"You'll see," he said as he hopped out and began extracting the boys from the back seat. True to her word, Ruby reached for both Max and the bag containing his change of clothes. From the way she took it all in stride, it was clear she hadn't been making an idle boast. She was as casually unconcerned with bodily fluids as she was with everything else he'd seen thrown her way.

It was the strangest sensation. He'd witnessed this woman, so flawlessly beautiful that heads literally turned when she walked into a room, spend hours trying to train an untrainable animal, single-handedly build a pageant stage in his backyard, and roll around on the grass with three rambunctious children. She refused to let anything he said or did deter her from her goals, and she tackled every challenge that came her way with a smile. She had terrible taste in show dogs, it was true, but even that fit the intoxicating mixture of beauty and tenacity that characterized her.

She was magnificent in every meaning of the word, and for reasons he couldn't even begin to understand, she seemed to want to share that magnificence with him.

"You're going to have to get Wheezy out of the back for me," Ruby called over her shoulder. "I don't think you included a 'Get your stubborn behind out of this car' in the recording."

"I'll put it in the next batch," he promised, but there was no need for Spencer to say anything to the animal. As soon as he lifted the hatchback, Wheezy lumbered to his feet, sighed, and jumped out.

"I know how you feel, buddy," he said, running his fingers over the silken curls of the dog's ears. "But there's not much else you can do, is there? The moment she walked into your life, you didn't stand a chance."

And neither did I.

By the time Spencer encouraged Wheezy up the walkway, Eva's boys had recognized their surroundings. There were shouts of joy and laughter, followed almost immediately by the slamming of a screen door. His father appeared on the front porch of the sprawling farmhouse with a puppy in one hand and a bottle in another. It was such a familiar sight—that tall, stately man cradling the runt of the litter—that Spencer could feel the last of his tension ebbing away.

He'd needed this. A weekend with kids and puppies, the comforts of home. *Ruby.* The only thing that was missing was his brother, but there was no chance of Caleb getting anywhere near this place until his sentence was lifted—and even then, he wouldn't come willingly.

"It's about time you came out to see us," his dad said as the two older Johnson boys ran up the steps and embraced his legs. "There's nine in this batch. Can you believe it? *Nine.* Tilly is exhausted. So is your mother, but don't tell her I said that."

"I want to see the puppies!" Julio cried. "Ruby, this is where the puppies live. *All* the puppies. Can I take Wheezy to say hello?"

"I think your first stop should be to the restroom," she reminded him. He looked as though he'd like to argue, but at a nod from Spencer, he took Xavier's hand and led his brother into the house.

The sight—of such easy brotherly affection and care—caused another of those reminiscent pangs, but there was no time to reflect on it. Before Spencer could introduce the adults to one another, Ruby stepped into the fray. Shifting her position so Max was cradled on her hip, she extended a hand out toward his father and smiled brightly. "There's no need to tell me who *you* are. I'd have known you for Spencer and Caleb's father anywhere. They look exactly like you."

His father chuckled and accepted the handshake. "And you must be Ruby," he countered. "Spencer's told us so much about you. He said you were going to be the professional ruin of him, but you don't look like you'd hurt a fly."

Spencer did his best not to blush, but he could feel the tips of his ears growing warm. He'd had *one* conversation with his parents about Ruby, and he couldn't remember saying anything of the sort. He'd mentioned Wheezy and Ruby's pageant history and how determined she was to get the better of him in literally everything, but…*huh*. Maybe he hadn't been as discreet as he thought.

"Don't tell anyone, but he's much more likely to be the ruin of *me*. I've never known anyone who handles dogs the way he does. Or people, come to think of it." She gave the child on her hip a waggle. "I hate to be rude, but do you mind if I take this little one in and clean him up? It was a bit of a drive."

"Of course." His dad stepped aside to allow her to pass. "The other two will be in the guest bathroom, but there's another one just off Spencer and Caleb's old room. Down the hall and second door on the right."

Spencer wanted to utter a protest at this invasion into the privacy of his former bedroom, but there was no chance. Not only did Ruby saunter through the front door as though she'd been born here, but he was still reeling from that casual reference to how well he handled people. Being friendly and approachable had always been Caleb's thing, not his.

His dad, however, only chuckled. "Well, I like her."

He gently transferred the puppy to Spencer's arms. Wheezy took exception to this with a brush of his paw against Spencer's leg, but his dad hadn't bred border collies for the past forty years for nothing. With a stern command not to make a nuisance of himself and to come closer so he could take a good look at him, his dad managed to get Wheezy into something approaching docility.

"Don't show Ruby how good you are with him," Spencer warned as he watched the pair of them interact. "She'll recruit you to help train him and then start showing up on your doorstep every single day until the West Coast Canine Classic is over."

"*This* animal?" His dad's chuckle deepened. "Oh dear. She's got an uphill battle ahead of her."

It was true. She did. But while Wheezy had to be dragged up that hill, kicking and howling the entire time, Ruby showed no signs of flagging.

Since his dad had a handle on the golden retriever, Spencer turned his attention to the black-and-white bundle of fur in his arms. Gently prodding the puppy's mouth open and finding that only the top two canine teeth had come in, he estimated his age at around three weeks.

"See if you can get him to take the rest of that, will you?" His dad handed him the feeding bottle and turned to go inside the house. "You always had a way with the reluctant ones."

Spencer followed his father, gently coaxing the nipple into the puppy's mouth while he did. The animal's short, sleek fur and still-rounded head made it difficult to tell what he would look like when he was fully grown, but Spencer didn't doubt that he'd be something special. *All* his parents' dogs were. He'd lost track of the number of them that had gone on to work farms, gotten placed in service training positions, and won dog shows.

Not *his* dog shows, obviously. All evidence to the contrary, Spencer normally adhered to a strict ethical code when it came to the crossover between his family and his judging duties. He didn't know how or why or when things had become so murky, but there was no denying that they had.

Or that he didn't care as much about it as he used to.

As he neared the kitchen with both his father and Wheezy in tow, the first thing he noted was that Julio and Xavier had managed to locate his mother and the canister of freshly baked cookies that always sat waiting for them. The second thing he noted was that his mother *did* look exhausted. She was as short as his father was tall, her hair a carefully toned auburn he remembered from his youth. She'd always worn her years well, but something about the dark circles under her eyes and heavy frown lines seemed new.

The reason for this became apparent the moment he crossed the threshold. Her eyes flicked over his shoulder, and when no one appeared behind him, her expression changed from one of expectancy to deep disappointment.

"He didn't come with you?"

All the warm feelings that had flooded Spencer on the porch zipped into a tight ball at the base of his stomach. It felt like lead, but he forced his tone to stay light. "You mean, the three small children and total stranger I brought with me aren't enough?" He leaned in and brushed a kiss on her cheek, careful not to jostle the puppy in his arms. He'd fed enough undersized border collies in his day to have the process perfected. "Caleb sends his love and promises to visit as soon as his schedule opens up."

"That's what you said the last time you visited."

He knew it was. It was the same thing he said *every* time he'd stopped by—not just in the past three months but in the nine-month span preceding it. Caleb wasn't one for paying his parental dues.

"Dad says you guys lucked out and got a litter of nine this time," he said as he indicated the bundle in his arms. "That should bring in a pretty penny."

Since the border collies his parents bred were the only thing his mom loved as much as Caleb, Spencer hoped the distraction would work.

It didn't.

"The last time I called him, he mentioned that you were keeping him busy with some new training client you referred to him. To earn his keep, he said." Her frown deepened, but that didn't stop her from plopping several more cookies in front of the boys. She also reached into a second canister and pulled out a hand-baked dog treat, which she dropped into Wheezy's waiting jaws. It was a good thing Ruby wasn't here to see it, because Spencer knew for a fact that the treats were made with duck fat. "If he's having money trouble, can't you let him stay with you for free? You know how much he depends on you."

"He *is* staying with me for free," Spencer said, but he didn't know why he bothered.

"Then you should have offered to drive him out here with you," his mom said. "Or to wait until he was available so we could all visit at once."

"Justine, we talked about this," his father said, a gentle warning in his voice.

"Yes, and we agreed that Spencer is too hard on his brother. Caleb's going through a rough patch right now. He needs a helping hand, that's all."

It was fortunate for all three of them that Ruby appeared in the kitchen just then, both she and Max wearing clean new clothes. Max looked the same as he always did, his chubby legs protruding from a pair of red shorts that Spencer recalled seeing on both of the other boys at one point in time. Ruby had changed into a yellow sundress that buttoned all the way down her front and reached midcalf. There was nothing the least bit scandalous or revealing about it, but Spencer found himself unable to look away.

She was like the sun walking into the room—and into his life. Every time she appeared, his chest contracted and expanded in equal proportions. He didn't understand it, but he liked it.

He liked it way more than was good for him.

"You didn't tell me that you two started that weird duct-tape separation when you were kids," Ruby said by way of greeting. "Although now that I think about it, I should have known. No rational adult would conceive of such a plan. Let me guess… Your side was the one with all the airplane models lined up in tidy rows?"

She allowed Max to wriggle out of her grasp and dash across the kitchen toward Julio and Xavier. As if they, too, were in on the conspiracy to make Spencer look like a hard-ass of a man who didn't give two damns about his brother, they shared their cookies with Max without being asked.

"For shame." His mother wiped her hands on a dishrag and turned to face him. "Don't tell me they're still doing that? Spencer, how could you? You're thirty years old."

"So is Caleb," he couldn't help pointing out.

"They've got a whole system, actually. With rules and punishments and everything."

His mom tsked disapprovingly at this, but his dad only chuckled. "They've always been a deeply competitive pair," he said. But then he ruined it by adding, "He's doing well, though? Our Caleb? He's…happy?"

Since this question was directed at Ruby, Spencer kept quiet and allowed her to answer it—mostly because he was as curious about the answer as his parents. A month ago, if anyone had asked him about Caleb's well-being, he'd have answered the same way he always had: Caleb was a man who would land on his feet every single time. There were too many people willing to catch him, dozens of safety nets spread out should any of them fail. Even when life was hard for him, he refused to take things any way but easy.

Spencer wasn't so sure about that anymore. On the surface, Caleb was fine: the same happy, carefree man he'd always been. But Spencer knew just how misleading surfaces could be. He'd *always* known it. No two show dogs were created equally. Identical twins could be polar opposites on the inside. A woman's gorgeous exterior might not even hint at the beauty she carried within.

Ruby wrinkled her nose and considered the question for a good thirty seconds before answering. "I haven't known him his whole life the way you have, so it's difficult to say. When he's working—when he's training Wheezy or teaching Caesar new tricks—he seems fine. Productive. Happy, even. It's only when…" Her voice trailed off and she glanced at Spencer, as if unsure whether she was supposed to continue.

He nodded in what he hoped was a reassuring manner.

"He's overcompensating," she said. "That's what it feels like to me, anyway. Like he has to prove not just to the world but to himself that he's okay. I used to see it a lot back when I did beauty pageants. The most confident girls—the ones with the biggest, brightest smiles—were usually the ones who were one ripped seam away from a complete mental breakdown."

The silence that fell over the kitchen caused Ruby to press a hand to her cheek and take a step backward. "Oops. That was more than you wanted to hear, wasn't it? I'm sorry. It's just that I've been spending a lot of time with him lately, and—"

Spencer's mom put a hand on Ruby's shoulder and drove her into one of the stools set up against the breakfast bar. From the look of determination and delight on his mom's face, he knew what was going to happen next.

"I'm going to make you an iced tea," she said. "And then you're going to tell me everything Caleb has been up to."

Chapter 12

BY THE TIME RUBY WAS DONE TELLING MRS. WILSON EVERYTHING she knew about Caleb—in addition to a few innocent lies to pad out the tale—it had begun to grow dark outside. There was no sign of Spencer, the boys, or Wheezy, but this place was huge. They could be anywhere.

She stepped out the back door and immediately felt as though she'd been transported through time. Of all the places she'd have imagined a young, rambunctious Caleb and a young, careful Spencer growing up, a tulip farm and dog ranch an hour's drive north of Seattle wasn't it. They seemed like the type to have had doctors or lawyers for parents—well-to-do and well educated, living in suburban bliss. The wide, expansive sky set against the Cascades was blissful, but for entirely different reasons.

"They'll be out in the kennel, hon," Spencer's mom called from the open window behind her. "There's no getting between a boy and his puppies. Eva's kids are big fans, too."

Ruby couldn't help grinning. Mrs. Wilson—Justine, she'd insisted Ruby call her—hadn't expected something for nothing. For every bit of information Ruby had shared about Caleb, Justine had reciprocated with something about Spencer.

Fact one: He'd been the most easygoing baby in the world—never crying, never making demands, always looking out for his brother. Fact two: He hated Halloween, but it had always been Caleb's favorite holiday, so he always made an attempt to make the biggest and most elaborate costume possible. Best of all was fact three: He used to sleepwalk out to the kennel at night and wake up in a pile of dogs. It got to be such a habit with him that they put a cot out there so he could be comfortable.

The idea of Spencer Wilson—*her* Spencer Wilson—being unable to prevent his inner self from cuddling with puppies in his sleep was too delicious for words.

She thanked Justine for the information and trotted down the steps toward the long, low building located a short distance from the house. She wasn't sure what to expect as she pushed open the door. Instead of the gated sections and sterile smell she associated with most animal shelters, what she found was a cozy-looking rec room with worn couches, half-eaten beanbag chairs, and a big-screen television attached to one wall.

There was also a cot in one corner, which she assumed was Spencer's infamous nocturnal retreat. *Where the cuddling happens.*

"That's funny," she said to Spencer's broad back. He stood looking through a window at the opposite end of the room. "I expected there to be more dogs inside a dog kennel."

At the sound of her voice, Spencer whirled around. He didn't look particularly pleased to see her, his mouth set in a grim line and crinkles of worry etched around his eyes. It was such a departure from the Spencer he'd been when they first arrived—that laughing, almost boyish man enjoying a homecoming—that she inadvertently reached out for him.

He didn't reach back.

"What did you tell her?" he demanded. "What did you say?"

"I'm assuming that the children I've sworn to protect and serve are safely supervised?" she asked by way of reply. "And Wheezy?"

Spencer jerked a thumb at the window. "They're fine. My dad is showing them the puppies. They'll be entertained for at least the next hour." He hesitated. "I should have warned you, Ruby, but I didn't know she was going to pounce like that. My mom, she's… That is… She's not—"

"Relax. I didn't say anything incriminating."

She drew closer so she could peer through the window to the attached room. Sure enough, all of the creatures under her charge were in there. Like her current surroundings, there was something comfortable and lived-in about the space, although with a lot less furniture and a lot more Astroturf. All three of the boys were lying on their stomachs with their heads propped on their hands, watching as a bundle of squirming puppies thronged around an exhausted-looking mother. Wheezy looked equally relaxed. Like the dog who'd recently given life to nine babies, he'd collapsed into an exhausted heap.

"I've never seen them so quiet," she said with a nod toward the boys. "Your dad must be magic."

"He is. Both my parents are."

She could feel Spencer shift to face her and braced herself for more.

"I know I probably sound obsessed, but you don't understand," he said. "My parents worry about Caleb—more than anyone should about a thirty-year-old man, but it's always been that way. He's not good at keeping in touch, so it falls to me to keep them posted. I'm sure you had the best of intentions, but I need to know what you said to my mom so I can run interference—"

When she interrupted him this time, she was careful to put a hand on his forearm and squeeze first. "Spencer, I know. I'm not as stupid as I look. I could tell that she was worried about him and needed reassuring. So that's what I did. I reassured her."

"You did?"

She nodded. "If there's one thing I'm good at, it's handling neurotic mothers. I told her about the barbecues with Eva's family and how much fun he's had training Wheezy and that I'm very sorry, but I won't fall in love with him and whip him into shape as a personal favor to her." She laughed. "Of everything, I think that one hurt her the most. She sounds as though she'd really like to be a grandmother."

Spencer stared, first at her hand and then at her face, studying it as he would a map.

"You're good at a lot of things," he said. "And I never said you look stupid."

She blinked, so startled that she didn't think to filter her response. "You didn't have to say it. I could see it as clearly as you're seeing me right now. You took one look at me and Wheezy standing in that hallway the first day we met and decided you knew everything there was to know."

The tips of his ears turned pink, but he didn't deny the accusation. She appreciated that more than he could possibly realize.

"It's true that I may have jumped to a few conclusions," he said as he placed his hand on top of hers. His fingers were warm and heavy, and they clasped hers with an urgency it was impossible to deny. "And I'm sorry for it—I really am—but when I'm overwhelmed, I retreat. Usually I hide behind Caleb, but he didn't jump in to save me that time."

"To save you?" Her mouth fell open. "From…me?"

"Yes, from you." He shook his head with a self-deprecating grin. "You're stunning, Ruby. You must know that. Every time you walk into a room, I'm *stunned*."

In her short tenure on this planet, Ruby had been called all the synonyms for beautiful that existed in the English language. Men had praised every single one of her body parts, including those of both a visible and private nature. She'd won awards for her ability to look good and pluck at a harp with grace, and she'd enjoyed the social privilege that came with all that.

But right now, with Spencer's hand on hers, his eyes so dark they swallowed her whole, she really, truly believed it—not that she was worth looking at but that she was worth *seeing*.

"Kiss me," she said, unable to look away from his gaze. "Please, Spencer? I've been waiting for you to kiss me for weeks."

Even though she was the one who made the request, the sudden sensation of his mouth against hers was so surprising that she couldn't do anything at first but stand there and allow it to happen. Spencer was always so careful, so methodical in everything he did, that she'd expected him to kiss the same way. However, the man moving his lips over hers was no such thing. As was the case when they'd stood on opposite ends of his living room and bared all, he let himself go in the most glorious of ways. Instead of gently exploring her mouth, nibbling and coaxing the way some men did when kissing a woman for the first time, he went right for the good stuff. There was no hesitation in him, no shyness. The moment she opened her mouth even a fraction, he was claiming her for his own.

With the exception of his lips, no part of his body touched hers. There was something intensely erotic about it—and, she was forced to admit, something intensely *Spencer* about it. She felt the same way whenever he buttoned his cuffs back up or stood just out of reach. His restraint was almost more intoxicating than his touch. It was as though he knew he had the power to break her, but he wouldn't.

Not yet.

He tasted of the cookies his mom had baked for the boys, light and sweet and a little bit chalky. It was such an innocent way for a man to taste—and in the place where he'd grown up—that she couldn't help smiling against his mouth.

"Well, that was very obedient of you," she murmured. "Do you know any other tricks?"

"I know enough," he said, his voice ragged. She wasn't sure if it was the kiss or the dog reference that caused that sharp edge, but she liked it either way. This was the sound of a man who let no challenge go untested, who treated Ruby as his equal in his resolve to get the better of her.

"You told me nothing I did would move you," she pointed out. "'I'm determined not to let you get to me today.' Those were your exact words."

His defense was a simple and powerful one. "You said 'please.'"

Not unsurprisingly, this response set her pulse alight. It was true. She'd asked him to kiss her, and he had—deeply and thoroughly and with so much intensity that her knees started to buckle. How had she not realized it before? Spencer wasn't a man who required a green light or danger word to get started. There was no need to play games and throw porcupines into the ring. Even the thrill of competition was an unnecessary burden.

With this man, all she had to do was ask.

Twining her arms around his neck, she pulled Spencer in for another kiss. This one was *her* doing and hers to control, deep and unrelenting, not just their mouths but their bodies entwined. She couldn't get close enough to him, her legs entangled with his and her hands curling in his hair. If it had been possible to climb him, she'd have done it, curling up in his arms and refusing to leave until all her desires had been sated.

A low hum escaped the back of his throat as he accepted this assault, but he didn't stop kissing her. He shifted his position instead, the entire length of his body drawing closer until she was pressed against the window between the rooms. The sudden shock of that pressure—of his hips holding her in place, of her inability to do anything but let him—sent jolts of pleasure through her, but she wasn't so lost to propriety that she was willing to enact this scene in front of children.

"Um, I know I talk a big game, but I'm not actually a fan of exhibitionism. Especially where minors are concerned." She tilted her head to indicate the window. "Maybe we should take this somewhere else for a few minutes."

He laughed, his breath a whisper against her cheek. "Don't worry. It's a one-way mirror. You didn't think I'd kiss you like that in front of my *father*, did you?"

"I've seen you do a lot more scandalous things than that."

"I could say the same thing about you."

His casual mention of that day in his house only turned Ruby's limbs to liquid all over again, but she forced herself to remain standing. There were couches in here and a cot and a perfectly good wall that she could be pressed up against, but the deep tug of desire would have to wait. Not only were there people in the next room, but she was intrigued enough by the one-way mirror to change course.

"What is this place, anyway?" she asked. "It looks more like a rec room than a dog kennel."

If Spencer was disappointed not to continue their tryst, he didn't let it show. He ran a hand through his hair and followed her gaze over the furnishings.

"That's close to what it is, actually," he said. "As soon as Caleb and I were old enough to be trusted to take care of the puppies, it was our shared job. This was only meant to be the showroom, a place where we could bring a puppy out to meet a potential buyer, but we liked it so much out here that we practically moved in."

She gestured toward the cot. "I heard about the sleepy puppy times."

He coughed heavily. "They got lonely at night. They needed me."

She didn't believe him for a second, but she allowed the comment to pass. There was too much to see here—too much to learn. Even though she'd been spending quite a bit of time inside Spencer's home, he treated that place like it was a battleground. His childhood bedroom had felt much the same, with a line down the middle and carefully delineated spaces for the brothers. Spencer's had been predictably neat and organized, with books and toy models lining the shelves. Caleb's had been much more haphazard and boasted a lot fewer academic posters on the walls.

Out here, however, there was no sign of the fractured relationship between the brothers. It looked like a place where a pair of teenagers could hang out, take care of puppies, and be themselves. Together.

Spencer must have been thinking along the same lines because he cleared his throat and said, "I'm sorry about earlier, when I jumped on you for talking to my mom. It's a tricky subject because Caleb and I aren't exactly getting along right now."

"No kidding?" She laughed and, after a brief check to ensure that the boys were still enthralled with the puppies, lowered herself onto the overstuffed couch along the far wall. It sank under her weight, embracing her like a well-worn hug.

Instead of joining her, Spencer leaned against the wall next to the window and crossed his arms. Ruby would have liked to have him next to her—near her, *on top* of her—but this was good, too. She could see every line of his expression, watch as his eyelashes fluttered and said all the things that he wouldn't.

"Are you ever going to tell me what the feud is about?" she asked. "The *real* feud, not some made-up nonsense about whose turn it is to pick up the dry cleaning."

He hunched one shoulder. "I can't."

"I'm a good listener," she promised. "And there's not much in this world I haven't already seen or heard. Believe me, some of the girls I met growing up had families that made my mom look like a saint. Few things have the power to shock me."

"It's not that. I *want* to tell you, I really do, but Caleb would never forgive me." He hesitated. "Things are already difficult between us. I can't make it worse."

There was something so earnest in his face that her heart gave a lurch. For a man who normally did his best to look impassive, there was an awful lot of emotion in those dark-ringed eyes.

"Whatever it is, I'm sure it can be worked out," she said.

His breath came out in a soft huff. "I'm not. Maybe, if I had a few more months with him, a few more weeks, even…"

Ruby jolted to her feet. Instead of lurching this time, her heart all but stopped. She'd known that something was wrong, but she hadn't realized it went that deep.

"Jesus, Spencer," she said. "Is he *dying*?"

"What? No. No, of course not." He laughed, and even though the sound was shaky, it went a long way in soothing her suddenly jangling nerves. "I'm sorry. I realize how that must have sounded. It's nothing as bad as that."

"Okay, phew." Caleb wasn't her favorite of the Wilson twins, obviously, but she still liked the guy. She hardly wanted to see him in an early grave. "It just seemed like it was possible, that's all. He never goes anywhere except those mysterious dry-cleaning errands, so I thought maybe they were code for the doctor or something. And since he doesn't have any other dog-training clients, I can't imagine what would be keeping him tied to a house where he doesn't have regular access to a bathroom. It's almost like you're running a prison or something."

Spencer's eyelashes fluttered with so much activity that Ruby took a step closer. "Spencer," she said slowly, watching for any clues he might let fall. "Have you imprisoned your brother inside your house?"

"Don't be absurd." He blinked four times in rapid succession. "Why would I do that?"

"I don't know. For the same reason you've imprisoned him on one side of it?"

"I'm not in charge of him. I just share a house with him. Lots of brothers do that."

That was true, but she'd never met any brothers who shared such weirdly sympathetic antagonism.

"Your parents haven't seen him in months." Now that she'd spoken the words about imprisonment aloud, they were starting to make an eerie amount of sense. "Eva said he doesn't go out anymore, not even on dates, and I'm pretty sure he's the sort of man who'd have sex with a lamppost if it flickered seductively at him."

Spencer snorted but didn't say anything, so she kept going.

"He only ever eats Top Ramen or food that he steals from your mini fridge. He desperately needs a haircut. He—"

Spencer interrupted before she could reach the clincher. "He steals my food?"

"Um, yes. All the time. And your clothes and your toothbrush—which is super gross, but he says you have the same DNA in your saliva, so it doesn't matter. And the most compelling argument is that his best friend is a dog. I can't tell you how many times I've walked in on him holding conversations with Caesar—like weird, *long* conversations about the most random things. It reminds me of Tom Hanks and that volleyball from the movie where he's trapped on a desert island for years."

"Wilson," Spencer said.

"What?"

"It's the volleyball's name. Wilson. Caleb and I always used to think it was hilarious that Tom Hanks named it after us, mostly because we couldn't imagine a world that was so lonely you had to invent a friend. That was never our problem. Everywhere we went, the other wasn't far behind." He paused, a frown flickering across his face before being replaced by his more customary grim line. "He really talks to the dog?"

"The last time I came over, he was teaching Caesar to eat Cheetos off his nose."

Spencer released a soft curse. There was nothing angry about it. He seemed mostly defeated. For some reason, that felt a lot worse.

"What is it?" Ruby asked. She risked a hand on Spencer's arm. He felt tense and warm, his latent strength twitching under her fingertips. "What's wrong?"

"You can't tell anyone," he said. "Not our parents, and not Eva or Lawson. It's not that I think you'll run tattling to any of them, but Caleb doesn't want it to get out."

She nodded her agreement. Considering the way Spencer was looking at her, she'd have agreed to a lot more than silence. Something terrible must be going on. Something dark, something secretive, something—

"The truth is, I'm imprisoning him inside my house."

A laugh was the wrong reaction to a situation like this, but one escaped before she could help it. She clapped a hand over her mouth, but it was no use.

She was more relieved than she could say when an answering grin spread across Spencer's face. It was her favorite of all his expressions—this reluctant good humor, this concession that he was human just like all the rest of them—and it quirked his lips in ways that did strange things to her insides.

"I know," he said, shaking his head. "It sounds ridiculous, but it's the truth. The next time you see Caleb, take a good look at his left ankle. There's a reason he doesn't stray too far from home."

Ruby blinked. "He's under house arrest? *That's* what's going on?" Without waiting for Spencer to answer, she added, "Which model does he have? The OM400? That was always Stepfather Un's favorite."

"Stepfather Un?"

Ruby held up three fingers and began ticking them off one by one. "Un. Deux. Trois. My mom and I gave them French numbers so they sounded fancy. What did your brother do? Petty theft? Racketeering? Tax fraud?"

"You seem to know an awful lot about this subject."

She laughed again. Her formal education might be lacking, but she'd graduated from the school of hard knocks early on. "Stepfather Un was always in and out of jail before he bailed on us, but don't look so worried. Stepfather Deux was great—he's the one who taught me how to handle a hammer. I was almost out of the house by the time Stepfather Trois rolled around, so even though he was a bit of a dick, I didn't have much to do with him."

"Jesus, Ruby. How on earth did you turn out to be such a normal, levelheaded person?"

She didn't answer him for the primary reason that she hadn't turned out the least bit normal or levelheaded. Those words didn't apply to a woman who lied about her job, obsessed over a dog that wasn't her own, and strove to win at all costs.

She knew the lie she was living wouldn't last much longer—that she owed it to Spencer to admit the truth about her job and how little she'd accomplished with her education—but it was a lot harder than she'd expected. Mostly because she knew what would happen when she did. He'd stop looking at her with that light in his eyes—that one claiming her as his equal—and that would be the end of it. Of *them*.

As it turned out, she didn't need to answer. Spencer watched through the window at where the three boys were taking turns petting one of the border collie puppies. Something about the scene must have affected him because he sighed and dropped his shoulders a good two inches.

"Gambling is and has always been Caleb's vice. Poker, dice, horse racing, online gaming… It's funny. I don't think he likes any of it all that much, but he's never been able to resist the spirit of competition." He cast a wry glance over his shoulder at her. "Neither of us can, in case you couldn't tell. But while I've learned to channel my energies into the West Coast Canine Classic, he's always been more…adrift."

Ruby understood the sentiment all too well. *Adrift* was the exact word she'd use to describe herself. Finding a cause was easy for a man like Spencer, who was intelligent and driven and knew exactly what he wanted out of life. For people like Caleb—and people like her—there were fewer options.

"He got caught running an illegal gaming website. It was shut down and he was sentenced to six months of house arrest, provided he has supervision—which is me. He also attends a weekly Gamblers Anonymous meeting. That's what the references to dry cleaning are. He can only leave to go to the parole offices or the church basement where the meetings are held."

Ruby nodded. That sounded very similar to what Stepfather Un had undergone back when he and her mom had first gotten married. In fact, she was starting to feel stupid for not seeing it before. She'd been so caught up in the dog training and getting the better of Spencer that she hadn't realized Caleb's behavior was that of a man *unable* to go anywhere instead of one *unwilling* to.

No wonder he flirted so outrageously with her whenever they were together. She was probably the only woman he'd seen in months.

"Poor Caleb," she murmured. "It must be driving him up the walls to be stuck in one place. How much longer does he have?"

"A week."

"Oh, that's good!" She took note of the hard line of Spencer's mouth and quelled her enthusiasm. "Isn't that good?"

"Yes. No. I don't know." He ran a ragged hand through his hair. "I want him to have his freedom back, obviously, but at what cost? He's still the same man he was when he got arrested. He always has been. Fun and charming and *stuck*."

That word struck like a blow to Ruby's heart.

"It's eating my parents up inside, thinking he doesn't want to see them, but what can I do? He made me promise not to tell them." This was uttered with a note of bitterness, but Spencer followed it up with a sigh and a gesture at the boys in the opposite room. "It's hard to believe, but we used to be a lot like that, once upon a time. We used to be friends."

"You're still friends."

He shook his head. "No. Not really. Not anymore."

She didn't believe him. There was no denying that a rivalry existed between them, and the divided house was a strange way to go about living with a person you'd known all your life, but it made a certain kind of sense. Caleb probably didn't have much else going on right now. One dog-training client wasn't much to keep a person busy, and without any other outlet, he had to be mind-numbingly bored. This thing with his brother—this game of good-natured one-upmanship—was all he had to keep him sane.

As someone who didn't have much else going on in her life, she knew. Trying to get the better of Spencer for the past month had done more to start her engines than anything else had for the past ten years. She wasn't sure she'd managed to triumph over him yet or that she ever would, but that didn't seem to matter.

Spencer Wilson was a man worth pursuing, a man whose respect was worth earning. Both she and Caleb knew it, even if Spencer didn't.

"You're too hard on yourself," she said. "He looks up to you."

Spencer snorted. "No, he doesn't. He thinks I'm a stick-in-the-mud who doesn't know how to loosen up or have fun. He's right, too—that's the worst part. I might have a job and a house and a dog show to call my own, but people have always preferred his company to mine."

"Not *all* people," she corrected him.

With those three simple words, Spencer's shoulders came down and all the tension seemed to leave him. He turned toward her with a soft, intimate smile that snagged on every heartstring she possessed.

"Thank you," he said.

She rolled her shoulder in a half shrug, flustered at how easy he made that sound. Like the kiss he'd offered simply because she'd asked for it, his gratitude just *was*.

"And not just for saying that," he added as she struggled to come up with a response. "But for listening. You have no idea how good it feels for someone else to know."

Spencer's dad waved in their general direction, his gesture indicating that it was Ruby's turn to go inside and spend time with the puppies. She'd rather have stayed on this side of the window, but Spencer only nodded his encouragement.

That unsettled just as much as all the rest. She was enjoying her time with Spencer's parents, yes, and it was nice to catch a glimpse of the place—and people—who had created such a worthwhile man, but this was a much more personal look at Spencer's life than she'd been prepared for.

The truth was, Spencer Wilson was no longer just a brooding, annoying stranger who could command her impulses with a flutter of his eyelashes. He was a genuinely nice man who treated her like a human being, too.

And the biggest problem was that although Ruby was smart enough to realize how dangerous that was, she wasn't nearly smart enough to do anything about it.

Chapter 13

IF YOU SLIDE YOUR HAND A LITTLE FURTHER UP MY LEG, YOU'LL FIND that I'm wearing a much more interesting pair of underwear today."

Spencer, whose fingers had been negligently caressing the soft curve of Ruby's calf, didn't raise his head. "I can't. It's too much work. Why don't you take them off and show them to me."

Ruby gave a low chuckle, but that was the extent of her movement. "Are you kidding? If I bend that direction, I'm never getting up again." She paused. "I could describe them to you, if it helps."

Even though every bone in Spencer's body felt as though it had been forcibly extracted, ground up, and then reinserted, he felt a stirring of interest. But only a very *slight* interest. When Eva and Maury got back from their weekend away, they'd better not be pregnant again. The world couldn't handle any more of these children. It would collapse under the groaning weight of all that energy.

"You can go ahead. I'm going to close my eyes for a minute."

He made good on his threat. The pair of them were entangled on the couch in Eva's living room. Once upon a time, it had been overstuffed and blue, but like most of the furniture in this house, it was now a weary, flattened gray. Spencer could relate. Since they'd returned from his parents' house, the boys had used this couch as a trampoline, the foundation for a fort, a wrestling mat, a place to hide the broccoli they refused to eat for dinner, and a mounting block for Wheezy in an attempt to ride him around the living room. The dog had enjoyed that about as much as he and Ruby had, so it was no surprise the golden retriever was also collapsed in one corner, unable to lift so much as an eyebrow.

With his head back against a throw pillow that had also seen better days, Spencer gave himself over to the sensation of being entwined with the softest woman he'd ever touched. It was a good thing their first sexual encounter had taken place on strictly separated sides of a room, because there was no way he'd have lasted as long as he did if she'd been within arm's reach. He didn't know what she did to her skin to make it so silken or how a body that had the same muscles and sinew as his could feel so endlessly supple, but the parts he could reach—ankles and calves and an enticing bit of thigh just above her knee—were like falling into a cloud.

"They're black, for starters. Black lace, but just a tiny scrap that barely covers anything."

The stirring of interest picked up again. Spencer wasn't sure how. After a day of babysitting and dog training and dealing with his parents' disappointment that he wasn't Caleb, he couldn't even think about sex.

Sex, however, was *definitely* thinking about him.

"When you see them from the front, they look like pretty much any other panties. Low on my belly, scalloped edges along my hip bones, the usual. But from behind—oh, Spencer, you have no idea what they do from behind."

Maybe not, but he could imagine it. Of all Ruby's perfectly formed body parts—and there were a lot to choose from—her ass was the one that intrigued him the most. She was a highly active woman, juggling her career and dog training and the Wilson brothers as though they were nothing, and she had the build to prove it. He'd already imagined what it would feel like to grab her by the hips and hold her close; adding the image of black lace was all that was needed to send him over the edge.

"Please don't," he begged. His hand clutched just above her knee, his fingers making soft impressions in the sleek expanse of flesh he encountered there. "I don't have the energy to appreciate them properly. All you're doing right now is torturing me."

Her legs fell open a fraction. It wasn't enough to fully widen her thighs and give him access to the warmest, most enticing parts of her, but it was close enough to count.

"I mean it," he said, sitting up enough so that he could run his hand further up her thigh. She hissed and sank deeper into the couch cushions to give him better access. "Ruby, I'll die if I hear anything more about lace or how it looks on you."

Either she didn't hear him or she didn't care, because she gave a low chuckle and continued taunting him.

"It barely counts as underwear, really. There's just enough fabric to frame my ass but not enough to cover it. If you were to slide your hand up a few inches, you'd see what I mean. Just a wisp, a hint, a delicate vee shape that highlights the curves of my—"

His fingers dug deeper. "Not curves. No curves. I'm begging you."

She scooted her body closer to his. "So many curves, Spencer. Round, taut ones. Soft, supple ones. Ones that jiggle when you smack them."

Spencer groaned. The interest that had been stirring inside him was now fully shaken. Being near this woman always made him acutely aware of what his blood was doing and where it was going, but actually having her in his lap, her legs spreading open for him, his fingers so close to—

His fingers stopped. "Wait a minute. That doesn't feel like lace."

Ruby snapped her legs together in an attempt to prevent him from making a further exploration between her thighs, but it was too late. He'd already reached fabric and the warm, intoxicating heat of her. All she was doing was trapping him in place. He twitched his fingers against the gusset of her panties.

"Uh, I'm no expert, but that feels like cotton."

"It's cheap lace," she protested but with a laugh in her voice. "I never said they were expensive. I like to make them easy to rip off."

There was enough room for him to run a finger along the edge of the fabric. He was well aware that he was stroking a lot more than her underwear at this point, his touch grazing the gentle folds of her body, but he was a man on a mission.

"This feels like *a lot* of cotton," he said as he gave her panties a gentle tug. His forefinger grazed against her clit, which caused a low moan to escape her. As enticing as that sound was and as much as he wanted to follow up on it, he curled his hand to cup her mons instead. His palm lay flat against the front of her, his entire hand reaching between her legs and toward her ass. It was a position he could have held for hours, but he needed to make sure of something first.

It didn't take him long to find what he was looking for. No matter which way he turned his hand or how far up he waggled his fingers, one thing remained the same. "What you're wearing, Ruby Taylor, is no wisp of anything."

Shifting his body so he was no longer pinned underneath her, he used his free hand to lift the skirt of her sundress and peer at whatever was happening underneath. Ruby squealed and tried to hold the fabric down, but Spencer's energy was almost back to its full strength.

Being with Ruby did that, somehow. Her presence restored and revived him, made him feel like a new man. One who laughed and played, who didn't always abide by the rules. One who could be *happy*, if he let himself.

"You're such a liar," he said as he managed to get her skirt lifted to waist-level. The panties she had on were an abomination against sexy underthings. They weren't black or lacy, and they certainly weren't small. White cotton turned gray with multiple washings, they looked like the kind of underwear you'd put on when you planned on chasing small children around for forty-eight hours. "I should have known better than to trust you. What else have you been keeping from me?"

He'd meant it as a joke, a way to segue into the other, more enticing parts of her that lay hidden underneath, but she stopped squirming almost at once. When she pushed her skirt down this time, he didn't try to stop her.

"You can trust me, Spencer," she said as she struggled into a sitting position. The movement slid her bottom half away from him, but it thrust her upper half much closer. So close, in fact, that their lips almost touched. Her breath was warm and beckoned him in, but he didn't think that was why she'd sat up. "I'm not hiding anything that matters. Not really."

Of all the expressions he'd seen cross her face, this was the one that was going to end him. There was such a wistful, pleading note in her melting-chocolate eyes that he couldn't deny her anything.

In that moment, Spencer knew he was in trouble—*real* trouble, the kind that toppled empires and tore families apart. The kind that changed a man forever. There was nothing he wouldn't do for her. With that sincerity and those hideous, adorable granny panties, she had complete power over him.

That was what scared Spencer the most. There was only one other person on the planet who had that power, and look how well he'd handled that. Caleb was about to be released into the world to continue on his self-destructive path, and there was nothing Spencer could do to help him. He could only watch and wait.

"I think I need to take another look underneath your dress," he said. It wasn't at all what he wanted to say, and it didn't begin to capture the emotions that were thrumming like the drums of war in his chest, but it had to be enough. A woman like Ruby—so alive and so physical, so *present* in everything she did—required an alive and physical response. "I can't guarantee that I'll find what I'm looking for under there, but I'm more than willing to try."

"Then it's a good thing I don't have the energy to stop you," she teased.

"I don't know how you managed it, to be honest," he said as he slid his hand toward the hem of her dress. He took the time to enjoy the way she felt through the thin, summery fabric, a liquidity to her limbs that made him think of a cat. "I meant to stick to my resolution *not* to do this. I had a plan of action and everything."

As though reading his mind, she made a low purr of contentment and gave a feline shimmy as she stretched into position. The buttons at the bodice of her dress strained in response. "Oh, really? Why don't you tell it to me, and I'll let you know how it sounds." She laughed. "Well, I already know how it's going to sound, but I want to hear it anyway.

You've got your skintight-black-leather voice on right now. You could tell me anything."

"Trying to provoke me?" he murmured as he gave up on his pursuit of her legs to flip open those straining buttons. He couldn't help himself—there was a glimpse of an equally graying and functional bra underneath. He'd never been so intrigued by a woman's underwear in his life.

"Always," she admitted. "Does it bother you? You're very enticing when you're worked up."

He shook his head, surprised to find that he didn't mind at all. If being worked up meant that this woman would stand across the room from him and dare him to stroke himself, if it meant she'd lay herself out on the couch and invite him to touch any part of her he wanted, then so be it.

He liked who he was around Ruby. He liked this man who joked about black leather, who didn't mind coming undone so long as she was the one in charge of the undoing.

"The biggest part of my plan was to, ah, take care of business before I got here," he said as he got her top button free. As he suspected, a glimpse of whitish cotton peeked back up at him. Considering how that whitish cotton swelled and beckoned toward him, he decided he'd never seen any fabric he liked more. "So that was the first thing I did."

"Wait. What?" She paused in the middle of arching her back, the jut of her breasts causing the second button to undo itself. "You mean you jacked off?"

"Jacked off. Spanked the monkey. Choked the chicken. Wrestled the eel."

She took her underlip between her teeth. "Um… You know a lot of terms for that."

"I was a teenage boy once, all evidence to the contrary. You'll notice the only ones I remember are animal-related. I've always wanted to be a vet."

Her laugh rang out so loudly that she cast a panicked glance toward the boys' rooms, but the one thing Eva and Maury had splurged on in this house was soundproof walls. Lowering her voice a little, she said, "I'm sorry. Please, continue what you were doing. I didn't mean to interrupt."

Since he was in the middle of running a finger lightly along the upper swell of her breast, it took him a moment to remember where he was or what he was supposed to be doing. Exploring the topography of Ruby's form was like traveling to a distant—and wondrous—land.

"Once I, uh, took care of business, I did push-ups." He flipped open the third button of her bodice. This one exposed a lot more than just her bra, offering him a glimpse of the band of skin along her rib cage. It led to the enticing curvature of her waist, which he knew from experience would lead to the equally enticing curvature of her hips. Sucking in a sharp breath, he added, "*Lots* of push-ups."

"One hundred and forty of them?" she teased.

His voice came out as a rasp. "More."

"One hundred and *fifty*?"

He shook his head. The truth was, he'd lost count. Sometime in the past few days, doing push-ups had become synonymous with Ruby standing half-naked with her hand between her legs. He could never go to a gym again.

"Poor baby," she murmured. She placed a hand on top of his before he could reach the fourth button. "You must be exhausted. I'd better get the rest of these for you."

"Don't you dare," he growled. "After all those push-ups, I've earned this."

She arched toward him instead. "Then by all means, don't let me stop you. What else did you include in your plan?"

"Careful breathing. Thoughts of open wounds. A faked phone call from Lawson in case I needed immediate extraction."

With each detail of his plan, Spencer opened a button of her dress. The fourth revealed the neat nip of her waist. The fifth exposed her navel, which formed a perfect circle in the center of her belly. By the time he reached the sixth, he was fully erect and able to count the beat of his pulse by how hard he ached.

"I thought only women did that," she said, gasping a little as he slid a finger underneath the waistband of her panties. "Faked phone calls to get out of unpleasant dates, I mean."

"I wasn't going to fake it to get out of unpleasantness," he protested. "It was to save myself."

Ruby's underwear might have been made of serviceable and breathable cotton, but her skin was pure silk—and the further down her body he went, the smoother it became. He'd just reached the juncture of her thighs when she asked, "Save yourself from what?"

As if he needed to say. The moment his fingers reached what they sought—the warm, slick heat of her—they both knew the answer to that question.

This touch. That pressure. The glory of feeling her squirm underneath him.

"I can't resist anymore, Ruby," he said as he gave her dress a yank and felt the rest of the buttons give way. "I'm sorry."

He wasn't exactly sure what he was apologizing for unless it was the speed with which he pushed her dress aside and removed her panties. As much fun as it had been to make a game of undressing her, the delay was starting to cause a serious strain. He waited only until she'd managed to wriggle her legs free before sliding a hand underneath her hips. She released a sound somewhere between a sigh and a squeal as he planted a kiss on the gentle swell of her lower belly. That sound became much closer to a moan as he kissed her again, further down this time, the damp heat of her clinging to his lips.

Her legs fell open to give him better access. She was all languid limbs and undulating calm, which was why, when he felt a strong grip take hold of his hair, he could only chuckle. As he made a tentative foray between Ruby's legs, kissing her upper thighs and nuzzling at her mons, she grew rapidly more impatient. The movements of her body demanded that he sample her more thoroughly, her fingers weaving through the strands of his hair and refusing to let go.

"I swear on everything you love, Spencer, if you don't stop taunting me like this, I'm going to give you the most agonizing blow job of your life. Don't think I won't. After all my experience standing perfectly still on a stage, I can make *anything* last for hours."

That made him laugh too. "Not that, I'm afraid. If your lips come anywhere near me, I'll last three seconds, tops. There's no way you could stretch that out."

Something about the words being uttered so near to her clit caused a gasp to escape her. Intrigued—and held firmly in place—Spencer gave himself over to the task of seeing what else he could do. That age-old standard, reciting the alphabet, received enthusiastic approval, but not nearly as much as a lightly blown breath alternating with deep, penetrating tastes of her. He adjusted his position slightly, using the leverage of his arm to pull her hips more flush against his face. This caused the grip on his hair to become so intense that he had to wonder what sort of exercises she was doing in her spare time.

All that hair-pulling probably hurt, but he was having a difficult time telling the difference between pleasure and pain as he continued sampling her body with his lips and tongue and even his teeth. The closer he drew to her clit, the more her movements became pleading and frantic—a sensation that was echoed in the tight thrum of his own groin. Unsure whether it was her desire or his that caused him to focus all his energy, he lightly flicked his tongue against her clit until all other thoughts and sensations faded into the background.

He could tell when she came before she did. The tight clenching and unclenching of her body against his lips gave her away.

As the orgasm rocked over her, she bucked and cried out for about two seconds before turning her head into a pillow to mute the sound. Even that inflamed his already scorching desire, especially when she followed it up with a low chuckle.

"I can see why Eva and her husband were so eager for a weekend away," she said. "That was a scream-worthy performance, Spencer. I'm sorry I couldn't go all in."

Scream-worthy? He wasn't sure anyone had said that about him before. Pride puffed his chest and swelled his erection.

"I aim to please," he said. He pulled his arm out from underneath her, but she reached for him before he could fully separate.

"You'll see what I mean in about thirty seconds. It's a lot harder to keep quiet than you think. Pants down, my friend." She licked her lips in anticipation. "I've been wanting to do this for weeks."

She reached for the buckle of his belt, but he pulled away before she could make contact. Her smile dimmed.

"What's wrong?" she asked. "What did I say?"

He shook his head, unable at first to give voice to what he was feeling. A large part of his current thought process was taken up with the desire that refused to abate, a hot, insistent pounding that made it difficult for his thoughts to coalesce into coherency. What was left was busy trying to articulate his feelings.

Because feelings were exactly it. He and Ruby had been playing games for a while now, pushing and pulling in what was rapidly becoming his favorite pastime. It would be all too easy to continue that right now, each of them seeing how fast they could make the other come, torturing each other with teeth and tongues and touch.

That sounded nice—it sounded *wonderful*, actually—but that wasn't fair to either of them. He liked Ruby. He felt things for her that he'd never felt for anyone. He wanted to shake her and kiss her and get the better of her. He wanted to hold her in his arms and make her laugh. He wanted to talk to her about Caleb again and hear her opinion on what he should do next. Her view of the world was wholly unique—cynical yet optimistic, hard-earned wisdom and a true love of humanity rolled into one.

That kind of feeling wasn't a quick blow job in someone else's living room. That kind of feeling deserved more.

"There's a guest room at the end of the hallway," he said, holding out a hand to her. "I stay there sometimes when Eva and I have to work late. Will you come with me?"

She took his hand with narrowed eyes. "Why? What's back there?"

"A bed. Pillows. A door that locks." He squeezed as her fingers threaded through his. Even though this next part was difficult to say, he forced himself to do it. As his earlier attempt at discussing masturbation had proven, he'd never be like the man in one of Ruby's erotica novels, swaggering with confidence and spitting out four-letter words for female anatomy.

He *could* be like the man in one of her romance novels, though.

"If it's all right with you, I'd rather make love the old-fashioned way," he said. "I'd really like to be inside you when I come."

Her hand dropped from his. He was afraid that he'd said something wrong, but she replaced her hand with her whole being.

That was what it felt like, anyway, her arms around his neck and her chest pressed against his. He was painfully aware of her half nudity, of her fluttering dress and naked belly, of the soft swell of her almost-naked breasts against his skin. None of that seemed to matter, however, when she lifted her mouth to his and began relentlessly kissing him. He still tasted of her, but that didn't seem to matter as her mouth sought his. Her hands were once again tangled in his hair, but instead of holding him between her legs, she was holding him in her arms.

This kiss was entirely of Ruby's making, so Spencer allowed himself the luxury of letting her take over. His whole body ached with the need to be inside her, but not nearly as much as his chest ached to have her so willingly and enthusiastically near.

"Just when I think you can't get any better, you go and say something like that." She sucked in a deep and gasping breath as he pulled away. "Yes, Spencer. You can take me to the bedroom and do whatever you want with me. I'm completely yours."

He hadn't been lying when he said he'd stayed in the guest room before. It was tiny, more of a closet than an actual bedroom, with a full-size bed against one wall and piles of outgrown baby toys in the other, but that didn't seem to matter as he and Ruby shoved their way inside. Just having her spread out on a bed in front of him was enough. She'd shed the rest of her clothes somewhere along the way, her naked body a vision from every angle. There was no inhibition in her, no attempt to shield or apologize for anything she had to offer. Spencer suspected it had to do with having been on display in some form or another since she was a kid, but he also attributed it to something innate in Ruby. She possessed something so sublimely accepting, a lack of concern for mundane things like breasts and nipples and legs so long he thought he might get lost in them.

"Fuck me," he said, unable to look away from her.

"I'm trying. If you don't mind a few pointers, I suggest you start by taking off your clothes. We can see where the mood takes us from there."

He chuckled and complied. As he had that day in his house, he felt little hesitation or reserve in disrobing in front of her. He wasn't normally so bold when it came to showing off his body, but something about the way Ruby watched him stripped him of all his reserve. There was that smile playing about the corners of her mouth—the one that didn't think he'd actually go through with it—as well as an appreciation that set fire to his veins once he finally did.

She wanted this. She wanted him.

Him. Spencer Wilson, the lesser twin, the sober veterinarian, the uptight dog-show judge.

"You know you're the most beautiful woman I've ever met, right?" he asked as he made quick work of removing his clothes. He was pretty sure he'd lost a few buttons in the process, and it was going to be difficult to find where he'd thrown his socks, but he couldn't find it in him to care.

Right now, in this moment, he was going to enjoy the hell out of himself.

"You're not so bad yourself," she said with a pointed look at the erection that had finally sprung free.

He shook his head. "I'm not just talking about your body parts. I don't know what it is, Ruby, but when I look at you, I feel…"

It would have been very easy to leave things there, to lower himself to the bed and to the pleasures awaiting him, but he wanted to get this part out first. Sensing it, Ruby lifted herself on one elbow. "What?" she asked, her brows beginning to knit. "What do you feel when you look at me?"

"That beauty is the last thing I care about," he said and immediately took it back. "Wait—no. That isn't it."

He *did* care about beauty. He always had. When he saw a line of perfectly coiffed and trained show dogs, all of them the best examples of their breed, he felt something click inside him. He liked how predictable their points were, how ordered the rules of their existence. Any person from any background could look at them and determine who was the most beautiful of all.

But it wasn't until they started moving that Spencer really fell in love. All those little personality quirks that no amount of good breeding could hide, the stamina and drive to perform for hours on end, the way a dog would sometimes look at him… They knew. The dogs knew he was there to judge them, that he was watching them through cynical eyes.

And the ones he really liked, the ones he always chose as winners, lifted their heads and kept going anyway.

"You don't let anyone tell you how to live your life," he said. It wasn't very sexy talk between two very naked, very eager people, but like those dogs he admired, he kept going anyway. "You don't take no for an answer. You set your sights on a thing and then you go after it with a determination unlike any I've ever seen."

"Um, thank you?"

His laugh came out in a whoosh of relieved air. His fumbled attempts at a compliment hadn't caused her to run screaming from the room yet, so he must be on the right track.

"I admire the hell out of you, Ruby," he said, finally drawing close enough to touch her. He didn't reach for the jutting breasts or the curve of her waist, and he avoided her thighs like they might burn him. Instead, he cupped the side of her face, allowing his thumb to trace the pattern of her softly parted lips. "That's all I'm trying to say."

She took his thumb inside her mouth at the exact same moment she took hold of his erection. *One* of those things would have been enough to drive him out of his mind, which meant the simultaneous sensation rendered him all but useless.

Since he hadn't been kidding about how short a time he had before he lost all sense of self-restraint, he lowered himself to the bed. He would have been happy to stand forever, with Ruby stroking him inside and out, but he really did want to do things properly.

In this instance, *proper* was anything but. The moment his body stretched out along the length of hers, Spencer was reduced to nothing but sensation. Everywhere he touched was soft skin and undulating waves of appreciation. She opened her mouth to kiss him, opened her arms to embrace him, widened her legs to entrap him. She never stopped moving or moaning. Even when she did slow down enough to allow him to trace the outline of her nipple or dip a finger between her legs, her body provided more than enough response for her.

"If you know about this secret sex room, I don't suppose you also know if Eva and Maury keep condoms anywhere, do you?" Ruby asked. Her breath was coming in short, panting bursts by this time, which was a lot better than Spencer was doing, since he was so light-headed that he was pretty sure he hadn't drawn any oxygen into his lungs at all.

It took him a moment to recall his surroundings.

Guest bedroom. Eva's house. Condoms.

"I do, actually." He lingered over a particularly nice kiss, Ruby's breath mingling with his own. As much as he'd have liked to stay there forever, she was right. The sooner he had protection, the better. Every touch of her skin on his erection was sending him closer to the edge.

Pressing his forehead briefly against hers, he added, "But it's better if you don't ask questions."

Nothing could have been more calculated to elicit questions, but Ruby lay and watched as he went to the closet near the back of the room. Opening any closets in Eva and Maury's house was a risk, and this one was no different. The moment he swung open the door, out tumbled a variety of colorful plastic toys.

"I hate to argue with a man on a mission, but are you sure that's the best place to be looking?"

He grinned over his shoulder. "We had a water balloon fight at the beginning of summer. I'm sure they're around here somewhere."

"Uh-oh. Why do I get the feeling there's a story in this?"

"We ran out of balloons after about ten minutes, but the boys wanted to keep playing. Julio said he knew where there were some more hidden inside the house." Spencer found the plastic bin containing all the water toys and held it up in triumph. "Eva and Maury were laughing too hard to correct him. That was the first time I've ever been hit in the face with a water-filled condom. Hopefully, it was also the last. They hurt a lot more than regular water balloons."

Spencer jumped as a pair of very hot, very naked arms encircled him from behind. A kiss that bordered on a bite pricked at his shoulder, and he felt himself shiver in response.

"I've finally figured you out," Ruby cooed. Her breath against his neck only caused the shiver to deepen into a full-body prickle of sensation. "You like kids."

"Of course I do."

"And dogs."

"Obviously."

"And puppies. And kittens. And all things soft and fluffy."

He'd managed to find the box of condoms by this time—the cardboard destroyed by water, but the foil-packaged prophylactics still fully functional—but something about the playful, warning note in Ruby's voice gave him pause.

She slid her hands up his body to his shoulders and whirled him around. If he'd have been ready for it—braced against her touch—he could have easily fought her, but there was a soft, naked woman taunting him while her entire body pressed against his. Fighting was the last thing on his mind.

If he'd thought the press of her breasts against his back was bad, it was nothing compared to the way they felt against his own chest. But then she spoke.

"You're a good man, Spencer Wilson," she said. "Pretty please, will you fuck me now?"

He proved powerless against a request like that one. He'd never be able to say whether it was the claim that he was a good man or the way she said the word *please* that moved him, but moved he was. Without bothering to respond in words, he scooped her deliciously naked body into his arms and tossed her to the bed. She squealed as she landed, her legs falling open and inviting him in, the smile on her face doing much the same.

He *did* like kids, and he did like dogs, and he did like baby animals of all species and varieties, but none of that compared to how he felt about this woman.

Without waiting a moment longer, he opened the condom and slid it along his length. Settling himself between her legs, he breathed deeply as he finally entered her. He kissed and caressed and lost himself in the sensation of Ruby wrapping herself around every part of him.

That was when thought ended and desire took over—where extraordinariness came into play, mostly because it was so simple. Ruby felt good. She tasted good. She made him feel good.

In that moment—feeling her climax beneath him, letting himself go at the same moment he captured her cries with a kiss—he knew his life could never get any better or any easier than this.

"Oh my." Ruby lay panting beneath him, making no move to push him away. If anything, she shifted to better accommodate him, curling her body into a nest that he could settle into for as long as he wanted.

And he wanted. He wanted very much.

"I knew you'd be worth the trouble, but I didn't realize how much," she added as he entwined her legs with his and lay wrapped in her arms. "That was amazing."

"I'm not trouble," he protested. The scent of her hair filled his nostrils, mixing with their lovemaking to create an intoxicating whirl of his senses. "*You* are. I knew you would be from the moment I met you."

Her laughter shook them both, but it dislodged neither. Spencer sank gratefully into her embrace. He knew that Max was likely to wake up at several points during the night and that all three of the kids would be bright-eyed and bushy-tailed long before the sun came up, but for now, he was going to rest.

To relax. To just be himself.

"I still intend to win the dog show, so don't get too comfortable," Ruby warned. She also sighed and nuzzled closer, so he didn't take offense. "I knew the first time I saw you that I wouldn't rest until I had you. And if tonight has proven anything, Spencer, it's that I always get what I want."

Chapter 14

"ARE YOU SURE YOU DON'T WANT TO TAKE ANOTHER PEEK AT THE tiaras?" Ruby's mom once again stood holding the glittering key ring that led to the glories of her past. This time, however, she was standing in front of a filing cabinet in a small back bedroom instead of the storage pod. "Honestly, honey, you're going about this all wrong."

"I think I smell dinner burning." Ruby waited until her mother sniffed the air before snatching the keys. "Ha! You aren't even cooking anything. You're planning on serving me celery sticks and iced wine."

Her mother sniffed. "There's no need to be mean, Ruby. I got you a tub of hummus to go with the celery."

Ruby's stomach rumbled its appreciation. Store-bought hummus might not sound like much to the outside world, but it represented a huge step in the right direction. She might leave this house with actual nutrients in her body.

"Is it the garlicky kind I like?" Ruby asked.

"Of course not. No man is going to want to kiss you if you're running around smelling like an Italian restaurant."

Ruby knew better than to argue. There was no need to point out that things like toothbrushes and mouthwash existed or that people had been consuming garlic for centuries and still managed to further the species. If her mother had once read it in a magazine, it was taken as law.

"Well, I appreciate the hummus all the same." She found the key she was looking for and stabbed it into the lock of the filing cabinet. Like the storage container neatly organized with the vestiges of Ruby's former glory, the filing cabinet was equally organized. A copy of every prize check she'd ever earned, her pageant scores and certificates, newspaper clippings highlighting her successes—if the name Ruby Taylor appeared anywhere in print, her mother had carefully preserved the paper it came on.

"What I *don't* appreciate is your obsession with the past," she said as she fished out an advertisement for a brand of cereal that had long since gone defunct. Her eight-year-old face beamed as she scooped in a mouthful of wheat bran. She'd been hired for the campaign because of her wholesome, all-American appearance, which later turned out to be code for deeply problematic views on eugenics. "Why are you holding onto this ad, Mom? You can hardly put it on a Christmas card and send it out to your friends."

Her mom winced as she plucked the ad from Ruby's hand. "I didn't know how awful the company was at the time. I didn't know much of anything, to be honest. I was twenty six and had just divorced Stepfather Un. Remember? He took everything with him when he left—all the furniture, all the food. He even pulled every last light bulb from its socket. I would have put you in a commercial for *anything* at that point."

Ruby felt a pang as she watched her mother smooth the magazine page and fold it back up, something like reverence in her movements.

"I do remember," Ruby said softly. "You told me we were going to camp inside the apartment for a few weeks—we slept on blankets in the living room and hung a string of Christmas lights from the ceiling so we could pretend they were stars. I thought it was the best thing ever."

"We lived on that racist cereal for three weeks," her mother added thoughtfully. "I lost almost eight pounds. It was the best thing that could have happened, now that I think about it."

"Mom, you don't mean that."

Her mom laughed. "Of course I do. That was when I met Stepfather Deux. I'd never looked so good."

Ruby waited, exasperated, for her mother to expand on the theme. Although there was no denying that Stepfather Deux had changed both their lives for the better, her mother had to see how outrageous it had been—selling her daughter's face to a soulless company, barely surviving in an apartment that had only been paid through the month, a second-hand harp the only item of value they owned.

She didn't.

With a sigh, Ruby turned her attention back to the filing cabinet, her fingers rifling through until she found what she was looking for. Extracting the single sheet, she gave voice to the question that had been taking shape in her mind ever since she'd met Spencer Wilson. "Didn't you ever want more out of life?"

"More?" Her mother blinked. "Of what? Money? Of course I did. What do you think all that work was for?"

Ruby shook her head. She wasn't talking about landing a modeling contract or being discovered by a talent agency. She also wasn't talking about the kind of work she and her mom had always fallen back on—the waitressing and the caregiving, the jobs that never seemed to turn into careers no matter how many years they spent doing them.

"What is that?" Her mom nodded down at the page in her hand. "It doesn't look like much."

"It's not, unfortunately." Ruby grimaced as she glanced at the close-written text. Unlike the rest of the glories in this filing cabinet, this was a sea of mediocrity or, more accurately, C's of mediocrity. "It's my high school transcript. Look. The only class I got an A in was gym, and that was because of all the running and yoga I did. I always beat the other kids in the mile."

Her mom ignored the latter half of her statement. "Your high school transcript? What on earth do you need that for?"

"I don't know yet," Ruby said honestly. She turned her gaze on her mother, aware that this next part was going to be even more painful. "Didn't I win a couple of scholarships at one point? I know those were offered sometimes instead of prize money. A lot of the girls got full rides to college that way."

"*College?* Is that what this is about?"

"Where did they go?" Ruby asked as she began searching through the filing cabinet once again. "You kept literally everything else. Look, you even saved my dental bills."

"I'm sure I don't know what you're talking about." Her mother tossed her head and tried to pull Ruby away from the cabinet. "You can't expect me to remember the exact prize from every pageant you entered."

Ruby leveled her with a hard stare. "Miss Junior Puget Sound, 2006."

Her mother didn't want to answer. The firm set of her lips caused her rose lipstick to smear, and she shook her head until her platinum locks tumbled over her shoulders. Like her daughter, however, Laurel Taylor couldn't resist a challenge once it had been offered.

"Three thousand dollars and a photo shoot with that modeling agency from Portland." Her mom threw up her hands. "There. Are you happy now?"

"Not really. Little Girl Glam, 2004."

Her mom didn't miss a beat. "No prize money for that one. But it did get you entry into Glitz and Rainbows that same year."

"Which…?"

Her mother sighed. "I don't know what good this is doing either of us. You only took second, so it was five hundred dollars. That one hurt. You missed three notes of 'Amazing Grace.'"

Ruby had only vague recollections of those pageants, but she accepted her mother's valuation as truth. When it came to remembering pageant details, Laurel Taylor was as sharp as they came.

"Where did the scholarships go?" Ruby asked again. "And why did we never make a push to use them?"

"Use them for what?" Her mother released a brittle laugh. It was nothing like the spark of sunshine that usually came out of her when she laughed. "Ruby, honey, take a look at that piece of paper in your hand and ask me that question again."

Ruby *did* look at the paper, but she didn't bother to repeat her question. There was no need to remind her mom that there were dozens of community colleges and trade schools in the Seattle area or that some admissions departments looked beyond academics. Her mother could no more envision a life of academia than she could a colony on the moon.

"*You* were the one who wanted to quit the pageants," her mom reminded her. "*You* were the one who insisted on getting a job and making your own way in this world. It's not fair to be mad at me because you don't like the way it turned out."

Ruby closed the drawer, careful to fold and tuck the transcript in her back pocket. As much as she'd have liked to be angry at her mom, she was right. Ruby hadn't made the least push to tally up her scholarship winnings once she'd graduated from high school. She'd wanted to get as far away from pageantry as possible, up to and including the renunciation of everything she'd ever won.

And then…nada. When she'd stopped competing on the stage, she'd stopped trying at everything, allowing herself instead to be carried on a comfortable wave of crappy jobs and even crappier boyfriends.

"This is about that man, isn't it?" Her mom followed her to the kitchen, where Ruby had every intention of eating her feelings in the form of that entire tub of hummus. "The handsome one who's good in bed?"

Ruby wasn't sure if her mom's astuteness or her assumptions startled her more, but she gave a small jump. "I never said he was good in bed."

"Bed, the back seat of your car, a convenient wall—what you do with your gentleman friends is no business of mine." Her mom paused before opening the fridge and pulling out the promised dinner. Much to Ruby's surprise, she didn't just have celery and hummus; there was a whole platter of vegetables and even some pita bread to go along with it.

"They're the low-carb kind, so don't look at me like that." Her mom unwrapped the platter and placed it on the table. "I also picked up a bag of diet dog food in case you brought that animal with you again. Well?"

"Well, what? Why didn't I bring Wheezy? I told you already, he's not my dog. I'm only—"

Her mother waved her off with an impatient hand. "No, not the dog. The man."

Ruby had been afraid of that. She fell to the nearest chair with a thump. "Yes and no," she said before picking up a carrot. Since *she* wasn't required to weigh in for the West Coast Canine Classic, she swirled it generously through the hummus before taking a bite. "It is about him, but it's also not."

When her mom didn't do anything more than twist the top on a bottle of cheap white wine, Ruby forced herself to keep going.

"There's an eensy-weensy chance he thinks I'm a doctor, not a nursing assistant. And an even eensier-weensier one he thinks that because I let him."

Her mother cracked a laugh and began pouring with a generous hand. She plunked several ice cubes in the glass before pushing it across the table at Ruby. "I think you're going to need this. So that's your plan? Go to medical school and become a doctor before he finds out the truth?"

Ruby wasn't going to lie… It wasn't the worst idea in the world. Except for the part where she didn't *want* to be a doctor.

"I don't plan to take it that far," she admitted. "I'm having a personal crisis, that's all. I thought I was doing fine before Spencer and Wheezy and all this dog-training nonsense, but…"

"But?" her mom prompted.

Ruby shook her head, unsure how to answer. The answer—that she wasn't fine and hadn't been for years—would only hurt her mom's feelings, mostly because the things she wanted out of life weren't even close to the things her mother had settled for.

And there it was in plain truth. Ruby wanted more out of her life than to grow old in a job that didn't satisfy her. She didn't want to live in a rented house that left much to the imagination. She didn't want the best parts of her life to exist in a storage pod in the backyard.

"I miss having something to work toward," she admitted, since it was close to the same thing. "Goals and dreams and visions of bright lights. Someone to beat. Something to win."

Her mom nodded as though this made perfect sense. She also ate a pita triangle, which was a thing Ruby had never seen her do before.

"When you set your heart on a thing, you're unstoppable. You always have been."

"Unstoppable?" she echoed. "Me?"

The look her mom leveled on her was the most maternal one she'd ever seen that woman wear. "Ruby, you won more pageants than most of the other girls your age combined. Oh, you whined and moaned and acted as though I was single-handedly ruining your life the whole time, but the moment you set foot on that stage, the entire world fell away. It was like watching a magician pull a dove out of thin air. One moment, there was nothing there and then—BAM!—Ruby Taylor appeared, and nothing else seemed to matter. The other moms *hated* me. The second they saw us drive up, they knew their own little darlings didn't stand a chance."

Ruby could only stare at her. She could count the number of compliments her mother had given her on one hand. Laurel wasn't a woman who fell easily into raptures.

"After you quit, I always assumed you'd find something else to light that fire in you. It's why I kept all your pageant gear. I hoped you might come back to it." She popped another pita triangle in her mouth. "You still can, you know. There are adult pageants and amateur events and—"

"No way. No how. Not for all the money in the world."

Her mom sighed. "I figured that was the case, but I had to try."

Before Ruby could become too alarmed at this sudden shift in her mom's attitude, she added, "Besides, you're so out of practice these days you'd have a better chance of becoming that doctor."

Chapter 15

CALEB, YOU DON'T HAVE TO LEAVE. NOT RIGHT AWAY. YOU CAN LIVE here for a few more months, maybe until you get full-time work or find a new place or—"

Caleb took a deliberate step over the duct-tape line in the living room. He'd been doing it every five minutes since he'd returned to the house without his ankle monitor. Spencer could have pointed out that the rules of the household *technically* still existed, but he didn't bother.

He was too happy for his brother to care about any of that.

He wanted him to be excited about what the future held. He wanted him to feel as though he had something to look forward to. He wanted him to experience even a fraction of the walking-on-air sensation he'd been enjoying since his weekend with Ruby.

"I love you, Spencer, but if I spend another minute inside your house, I'm going to stab my eyes with a fork." Caleb brought his hands down on Spencer's shoulders. "Repeatedly and without remorse."

Spencer was forced into a laugh. An overdramatic and unnecessary reaction was exactly what he'd expect from his brother. "I'm just saying. I know I haven't made things easy on you these past few months, but I can do better. I can *be* better."

Caleb had yet to lift his hands from Spencer's shoulders. Something about the way he held them there—heavy and unrelenting—made Spencer feel as though the worst was yet to come.

He was right.

"I don't know *what* that woman did to you last week, but the next time I see her, I'm not letting her go until I find out."

"I changed my mind," Spencer said, feeling the tips of his ears flame. "You can go now. I'll help you carry your bags to the car."

That only made Caleb laugh. Yet another problem about living with a twin brother was that he knew exactly when Spencer didn't come home for the night.

And Spencer hadn't come home for the night. Or the morning. Or the following two days.

Spencer was careful to avoid his brother's gaze. "Where are you staying, by the way? Mom and Dad would be over the moon to have you." The subject was a dangerous one, but he had to bring it up. "They've been taking your absence to heart, and it would mean a lot to them if—"

A knock at the door interrupted him. Which was probably for the best, because Caleb's grin was starting to dim.

"That's my new landlord right now." Caleb clapped his hands and rushed to answer the door. "So you don't need to worry about me. I've got everything handled."

The sight of three very enthusiastic, very hyperactive Chihuahuas answered the question of who was next in line to take Caleb in. Two of the dogs sported polka-dotted bow ties, while the third wore a matching bow in her hair. Lawson's pack had been over to visit many times before, so they sniffed, ran around in circles, and made a beeline for where Caesar lay in one corner. The bulldog, accustomed to their exuberance, sighed and allowed them to climb all over him. He was probably missing Wheezy, who made a much more restful companion.

"Well, well. You've finally decided you've had enough of living in a tomb, huh?" Lawson extended a hand toward Caleb. In any other man, it might have been taken as an offer of a handshake, but he reached for the overstuffed black garbage bag and hoisted it over his shoulder instead. Lawson had always been a good man to have around when moving. He could lift anything. "Not that your house isn't nice, Spencer, but there's not much…excitement around here, is there?"

Considering the frenzied dog pile in one corner, Caleb's upheaval of belongings, and the way Lawson's cheerful voice boomed, Spencer failed to see how anyone could make such a claim.

"You're doing me a huge favor, Lawson. Thanks." As Caleb turned toward him, Spencer could see that his happy, carefree facade was back. "Lawson's giving me a bedroom *and* a guest bathroom. It's the height of luxury. I'll hardly know what to do with myself."

He hoisted a second black garbage bag and headed out the door to where Lawson's SUV sat parked and waiting.

"I'm sorry I didn't say anything earlier," Lawson said as soon as Caleb was out of earshot. "I wasn't sure if Sanit would be on board, but he's looking forward to having your brother stay with us for a bit. Our own company tends to pall after a while. You don't mind if we steal Caleb from you?"

"Of course not. You're welcome to keep him as long as you like. Just… be careful, okay? And send him back to me if anything gets to be too much."

"You make it sound like he's an escaped convict or something," Lawson joked.

Spencer met his gaze. Lawson and his husband were very nice, very stable human beings, and it would do Caleb a world of good to be around them, but it didn't seem fair for them to take him on without being aware of the extenuating circumstances. Matching his tone to Lawson's, he said, "Would you still take him if he was?"

Lawson shrugged. "Of course. We all need a helping hand sometimes."

He followed this revelation with a hand plunged deep into his pocket. Extracting a folded envelope, he added, "To be honest, Caleb's not the one we're worried about. *You*, however…"

The smallest of Lawson's dogs, a scrapper named Gizmo who could never resist a piece of dangling bait, leaped up and grabbed the envelope before Spencer could make a move for it.

"Dammit, Gizmo!" Lawson cried. "We've talked about this. Spencer, you're going to want to read what's on that. You'd better get it from him."

Caleb reentered the house in time to hear this decree. Since he was closest to the animal, he made a mad dive to get his hands on the envelope. He failed and crashed into the umbrella stand instead. This set up a round of barking protests from the pile of dogs in the corner and only made Gizmo move faster, which upended one of Caleb's black bags of clothes and sent dirty socks flying.

Spencer took one look at the scene of mayhem and announced in his deepest voice: "*Stop*."

It worked exactly the way he expected it to. The Chihuahua, startled into obedience, dropped the envelope. The other three dogs came to attention at the same time. Even Lawson and Caleb seemed to straighten at the sound.

"Don't say it," Spencer warned as he swooped down to grab the crushed envelope. "I already know. All it takes is the sound of my voice to bring everything into order. Dogs listen. Children cry. Cities fall."

But then he grinned. The sound of his voice also made Ruby laugh, and that was worth all the rest.

"Why, Spencer Wilson. Are you *smiling* at me?" Lawson asked.

"Don't bother," Caleb said. "He won't spill any of the sordid details. The only thing I know is that he spent last weekend with Ruby. *All* of last weekend with Ruby."

One of Lawson's eyebrows lifted into an impeccable arch, but he followed it up with a shake of his head. "Then return that envelope. I changed my mind."

Spencer glanced down at the crumpled paper in his hand. "Why? What's in it?"

"A recipe for my great-aunt Ada's pecan pie. I need it back."

Spencer moved the envelope out of reach just as Lawson lunged for it. "You'd better start talking, Lawson."

"I got it mixed up with another envelope. That one's tax receipts for my accountant. It's naked photos of me and Sanit. It's anthrax."

With such promising treats in store, Spencer wasted no time in ripping the envelope open. He had to bob and weave to avoid Lawson's attempts to prevent him, but he was smaller and faster. He was also more determined. If something in this envelope related to Ruby, if she was in danger or needed help or—

"It's a DNA test. A dog DNA test." He glanced sharply up at Lawson. "You had Wheezy tested?"

Lawson gave up on his attempt to get the paper out of Spencer's hand. "You said it was what a real friend would do. Behold me in all my real-friend glory. Interesting revelations in there, don't you think?"

No. There wasn't anything the least bit interesting or revealing in the test results that Spencer held in his hand. They contained everything he'd suspected from the start: Wheezy was no golden retriever. Oh, there was golden blood in him, definitely, and enough of it to make a convincing show, but strains of Lab, Pekingese, and even a small percentage of Saint Bernard diluted the blood.

"I'm sorry," Lawson said. "If I'd have known about you and Ruby, if you'd have told me that you didn't want me to go through with it..."

"What is he?" Caleb plucked the paper from Spencer's hand and gave it a quick perusal. A low whistle escaped his lips. "Well, I'll be damned. She's been playing you this whole time."

"She hasn't been playing me. It's not like that." Spencer snatched the paper back and ripped it in half. Both Lawson and Caleb watched, silent, as the pieces fluttered to the floor.

"Uh, Spencer? Are you okay?" Caleb asked.

"I'm fine, thanks."

Lawson cleared his throat. "You know you can't let that dog enter the show now, right? If word of this got out, we could lose our AKC standing. The rules specifically state that—"

"I know what the rules state."

Caleb and Lawson shared a look that was impossible to misread. They were pretty sure Spencer had just cracked.

"Maybe she didn't know," Lawson suggested, more gently this time. "You said yourself that it's not her dog, that she's acting for a third party. It's possible that this woman she's working for tricked her into it."

"She knows."

The look between the two men intensified until Gizmo grabbed one half of the ripped paper and ran off to enjoy his ill-begotten gains. They all watched the Chihuahua's furtive movements to conceal what he'd done, but only Spencer laughed. It wasn't, as Caleb and Lawson suspected, the laugh of a man who was about to lose the last of his reason.

It was the laugh of a man who'd finally found it.

"It's a small-time dog show, you guys, not the Olympics. Wheezy making an appearance isn't going to break us."

Caleb lifted a hand and placed it against Spencer's forehead. As Spencer expected, his brother's palm felt exactly the same temperature as his skin.

"I'm not sick. I haven't lost my mind. I'm not hopelessly in love." He hesitated. "Well, I'm not so sure about that last one, but you get my point. Is it unethical to knowingly allow a non-purebred dog into a dog show? Sure. Of course. I think we can all agree on that. But it's equally unethical for a judge to allow his twin brother to train some of the entrants, and I've been doing that for years. And let's not even get started on a judge being in a relationship with a handler."

"Are you…in a relationship?" Caleb asked. He didn't voice the rest of the question, which went more along the lines of: *Are you in a relationship, or is it just sex and you're reading way too much into it?*

It was a fair question. There was always a possibility he was reading too much into things because that was what he inevitably did; overthinking was his stock in trade. He looked extensively before he leaped, kicked every tire on a car twice before he bought it.

For once in his life, however, he was letting his emotions take over. He liked Ruby and he liked how Ruby made him feel—and those were the only things that mattered.

"Let's not even get started on a judge *fucking* a handler," Spencer amended. "Does that make you feel better?"

Lawson choked. Caleb grinned.

"*Much* better," Caleb agreed. He cast Spencer a curious glance. "So, that's it, then? You're just going to let Wheezy in the dog show? Against the rules? Knowing he's ineligible and likely to make a fool out of all of us?"

Spencer looked to Lawson for the answer. He already knew what Eva's thoughts on the subject would be. She'd walked into her house late on Sunday evening, seen Spencer and Ruby standing next to one another, and guessed the truth with a squeal and hug for both of them. She'd also been sending Spencer her top wedding-venue choices all week. Any rule-breaking done in the name of romance would get her full approval.

"It's your show, too," Spencer said. "If you're uncomfortable with it, I'll remove Wheezy from the list and talk to Ruby this afternoon."

Lawson lifted both his hands and laughed. "Not on my account, you won't. How much damage could one poorly trained, ill-bred dog do? No, don't answer that. I keep forgetting I've met the poorly trained, ill-bred dog." Gizmo brought Lawson the torn, shredded remains of the letter, and he sobered almost immediately. "Seriously, Spencer. It's no problem. If you want me to forget I ever sent Wheezy's DNA in, it's done. I'll take it to my grave."

Spencer knew he meant it. He was the sort of man you could call to help you bury a dead body, no questions asked. It was a thing Spencer had always known about Lawson, but he'd never had anything approaching a dead body on his hands before.

Allowing a mixed breed in his dog show wasn't as bad as murder, but it was close enough to count. And Spencer regretted nothing.

"Then it's decided. We'll keep this to ourselves, got it? As far as we know, Wheezy is a perfect specimen of a golden retriever. Ruby's worked so hard to get him this far. We might as well give her a chance to see it through."

Both men nodded their agreement. They also both allowed their expressions to fall into enormous grins. Spencer did his best to ignore them, to maintain a dignified upper hand, but there was no use.

"You could *pretend* to be shocked at my lack of morals," he said.

"We could." Caleb slung an arm around his shoulder and squeezed. "But where would the fun be in that?"

Chapter 16

"I DON'T SEE WHY SHE COULDN'T JUST BRING HIM ALONG TO THE ORGY. It was the least she could do after all those orgasms he gave her." From the other side of the living room, Mrs. Orson clucked her tongue. "Ruby, dear, don't you agree?"

Ruby, who had been trying her best to discreetly slip into the book club meeting, gave a sudden start. "Agree with what? I'm sorry I'm so late. I was supposed to get off shift an hour ago, but Harry made me—"

"Multiple orgasms," Mrs. Orson interrupted. Her stern look, leveled at Ruby over a pair of wire-rimmed glasses, made Ruby feel instantly guilty. These poor women had to deal with Harry on a daily basis; the last thing they wanted was for her to introduce him into the book club. This was a place of discourse and literature, of serious discussions about—"Wouldn't you take your gentleman friend along with you to the sex club after that? Or would you leave him home alone to recover and rehydrate?"

Ruby glanced around the room, where half a dozen sweet, elderly women watched her expectantly. Darla Templecombe went so far as to wink.

"Um, I don't take people to sex clubs under any circumstances," Ruby said. "I wouldn't know where to find one."

"Private homes, mostly." Sally York, a stout, pink-haired woman hooked up to an oxygen tank, gave a decisive nod. "The movies always make it look like they operate out of seedy bars, but they're really more like a dinner party than a night out on the town."

The other women agreed as though this made perfect sense—which,

Ruby was willing to acknowledge, it probably did. *She* might not know much about the world of swinging and group sex, but these women had come of age in the 1960s. Their collective knowledge would have made the Marquis de Sade blush.

It would also make Spencer blush. Ruby found herself chuckling inwardly as she imagined telling him about this later. Sharing funny stories from work wasn't something she often did, since few people realized that underneath the laughter lay a deep and unreserved love for the residents, but Spencer would get it.

At least, he *would* get it if she could work up the blasted nerve to tell him the truth.

"What I don't understand is how she could walk after they were done," another woman said. She had a cup of tea at her elbow and a half-eaten slice of banana bread in front of her. "They had sex for forty-four pages. I counted."

"If you factor in a minute per page, it sounds possible."

"I think it's closer to five minutes per page. Look at the beginning of the sixth chapter. It'd take twice that long just to get in position. That poor girl must have a third leg to make it work." The speaker, Lorraine Dewan, was the owner of the Maltese that Harry had once thrown in the pool. "We'll start reading aloud, dear, and you can act out the parts. You look flexible. Who has a timer?"

Ruby held up her hands and started backing away toward the kitchen as the women fished out their cell phones and fought over who would be the timekeeper. She was happy to participate in their conversations and eat their baked goods, but she drew the line at re-creating sex acts in a living room covered with hand-crocheted doilies. She'd once attended a wake here, for crying out loud.

"Don't be such a prude, Ruby. We promise not to record it."

"It'll be good for you, dear. You might learn a thing or two."

"Now look what you've done. You scared her off." In a louder voice, Mrs. Orson added, "Eat some of the bread, Ruby, and come back in thirty minutes. There's banana or pumpkin. We'll see how you feel about it then."

It had been Ruby's intention to generously butter and eat the largest slice of banana bread that sat on the veiny granite countertop, but at Mrs. Orson's words, she crumbled off one corner and smelled it. The skunky scent that assailed her nostrils had her chuckling—and also straying far from the plate. It wasn't that she was morally opposed to edibles, since they lived in Washington state and it was perfectly legal, but she *was* morally opposed to getting high while she was in her scrubs—and while Harry was still somewhere on the premises. It would be just like him to change her time card to make it look like she was still on the clock.

Since she wasn't brave enough to venture into the living room until the pot had mellowed the women out, she began tackling the pile of dishes in the kitchen instead. Mrs. Orson came in about halfway through, her hip against the kitchen island as she watched Ruby work.

"Oh, good. I was hoping someone would get to those. Aren't you a love?"

"No. I'm avoiding the living room until you guys are done reenacting sex scenes."

"If that's the case, then you might as well organize the pantry. Unless Lorraine throws her hip out again, it's going to be a while."

A burst of laughter from the other room confirmed Mrs. Orson's prediction. That didn't sound at all like women who were dislodging joints; it sounded like women who were smoking them.

Ruby paused in the act of rinsing out a large mixing bowl. "How much THC did you guys put in that banana bread, anyway?"

"Enough. Darla got her prescription filled this morning. It's the only thing that makes her cooking palatable."

Ruby doubted any amount of marijuana could do that, but there was no denying that the women were enjoying themselves. As well they should. They'd lived long lives, full lives, *active* lives. They were rich with experiences and memories—and all the ups and downs that accompanied them. Even being in the next room washing their dishes was giving her strength.

In fact, she was halfway tempted to pull out the college application she'd printed out in Harry's office when he was taking one of his many smoke breaks earlier today. North Seattle College wasn't the most prestigious educational institution, and their two-year nursing program was only a stepping-stone toward a more formal degree, but Ruby needed to talk to *someone* about it. Her mom wasn't ready to understand what a big deal this was for her, and Eva was out for obvious reasons.

And the one person she wanted to tell most—Spencer—was a definite no-go.

"Where is Wheezy, by the way?" Ruby asked, mostly by way of changing the subject. She made a show of looking around the kitchen. "Did he go into hiding when I came in? Typical. He's starting to loathe the very sight of me."

"He's taking a nap," Mrs. Orson replied. "Starvation makes him sleepy."

It was on the tip of Ruby's tongue to point out that beauty was pain and that no one accomplished anything in life without some good, old-fashioned suffering, but her mother's aphorisms felt bitter on her tongue. Okay, so Wheezy wasn't what everyone else would consider an ideal example of a golden retriever, but why did that matter? He was easygoing and good with kids. He brought Mrs. Orson happiness. He went along with whatever adventure Ruby dragged him into and never once showed signs of aggression about it.

In other words, being a show dog wasn't everything. If anyone was qualified to make that judgment, it was Ruby.

She was prevented from saying any of this by a voice calling from the next room. "Rosemary, bring in the pumpkin bread! We're ready for another round."

"Oh, no you don't," Ruby warned Mrs. Orson. "I think you should let the first round settle in first."

She searched for the bread in question so she could hide it, but other than a bowl of oranges and two half-empty bottles of wine, there was nothing on the kitchen counter.

"Uh-oh. Did you guys already eat it and forget? You did that last time, and we couldn't find Sally for three hours. Remember? She walked all the way down to the taco stand on the corner and back—and with her knee."

"I could have sworn it was just here." Mrs. Orson searched in the silverware drawer and on top of the fridge. "You don't suppose Harry snuck in here and stole it, do you?"

"I wouldn't put it past him to try," Ruby said. As she was of a more practical and less high frame of mind, she also looked inside the refrigerator and the bread box. There was no sign of the missing dessert in either.

A sudden fear seized her, taking hold like a hand over her throat. "Mrs. Orson, has Wheezy been in this kitchen?"

"Of course he's been in the kitchen. He practically haunts the place. Every crumb is the potential for salvation."

"Was he in here unattended?" Ruby persisted. This was one of the wheelchair-accessible units, so the counters were a few inches lower than the modern standard. It would have been very easy for a dog to get up on his hind legs and enjoy an all-you-can-eat buffet. Especially if he'd been on a diet for the better part of the past two months. "Mrs. Orson, we need to find him. *Now.*"

Her worried tone had its intended effect. Mrs. Orson blinked and uttered a faint "He's in the bedroom, most likely. Or out back. He can't have gone far."

Ruby sincerely hoped so. She was no expert on dogs or marijuana, but she knew that an entire loaf of *anything* couldn't have been good for him. Dashing down the hallway, she pushed open every door she passed. The bathroom and linen closet were empty, but when she reached the bedroom at the back, it was to find a heavy, unmoving lump behind the door.

"He's in here," she called. "Wheezy, love. You have to move. Or roll. Or slump a few inches. I can't get in."

Since she'd never used the terms *Wheezy* and *love* in the same sentence before, she could only assume he hadn't understood.

"Wheezy, you beast. You devil. You greedy, addlepated nuisance of a—"

"Why are you yelling at him?" Mrs. Orson drew close and pressed her face against the narrow opening. "Wheezy, my pet. Ruby doesn't mean it. Listen to what she says. Help us open the door."

He didn't respond to either approach. Although Ruby was tempted to chalk this up to his unwillingness to conform to accepted standards of behavior, she knew better. They'd come too far, she and Wheezy. He was the reason she got up every morning with a smile on her face. He was why she was suddenly exploring career options and feeling excited about her future. He was responsible for introducing her to a whole new group of people who saw her not just as a pretty face but as someone worth getting to know.

With a flash, Ruby realized what she had to do. She needed help, and she needed it fast—and there was only one person in the world who could be relied upon to provide it, no questions asked.

She tossed Mrs. Orson her cell phone. "Call Spencer Wilson. Tell him we need him right away. I'm going to have to go in through the window."

"Spencer Wilson?" Mrs. Orson echoed. Her fingers flew as she scrolled through Ruby's contact list. "Are you sure he's in here? I don't see his name."

Ruby paused just long enough to call back, "He's listed under Porcupine," before darting out to the back door.

Although the house's countertops and bathrooms were wheelchair-accessible, no one had thought to lower the bedroom window to make a convenient escape—or entrance—route to the house. The window she wanted was located above a colorful row of chrysanthemums, which made a picturesque setting but also rendered Ruby's task a lot more difficult.

It just so happened that she was allergic to chrysanthemums. *Severely* so. Her mother had made the discovery when eight-year-old Ruby had been presented with a bouquet after a pageant win. The rash that covered her arms, neck, and face had taken weeks to clear up—weeks in which she'd been forced to remain indoors and out of sight so no one would see the splotchy mess of her skin.

"Wheezy, you'd better really be sick and not just high as all get-out," she muttered as she located a cement birdbath and started dragging it toward the window. She did her best to avoid touching the flowers, but there was no way to get the birdbath in place without brushing a few of them away. If history planned on repeating itself, the itching would start any minute now. "If all you get out of this are some profound insights on the existentialism of man and a case of the munchies, I'll never forgive you."

She was aware of the women in the book club filing out to watch as she pushed out the window screen and began jimmying her body through. A few of them shouted words of encouragement. Darla gave her rear end a push. And Sally, after Ruby had to twist and turn to get her body through without dislocating any of her major joints, said, "I told you she'd be flexible."

She didn't have time to reply. The moment she landed on the beige carpet with a soft thud, she realized that Wheezy wasn't enjoying his high. He was awake but barely, his body slumped against the door as though he'd never be able to move it again. His brown eyes were glazed in a way that barely registered her presence, and drool fell out of the side of his mouth in huge, globby rivulets.

"Oh, you poor honey," she cried, falling to her knees in front of him. She had no idea what she was supposed to do in this situation—if she was supposed to make him throw up or give him water or hold his paw until the worst of it was over, so she did the only thing she could think of.

She shifted her body as close as she could get and held him. His head lay passively in her lap, which was all the sign she needed to know that he wasn't okay. Wheezy would never willingly lower himself to cuddle with her.

With a quick prayer that Spencer would get here soon, she began murmuring soothing, nonsensical words, keeping the dialogue going even when the itching began.

House calls had always been Spencer's favorite part about being a veterinarian. After graduation, he'd toyed with the idea of setting up a rural practice that would require him to spend the majority of his time on the road and in the homes of those he served, but Eva had convinced him to set up shop in the city instead.

He was glad she'd done it, but he still enjoyed the simple pleasures of meeting an animal on his own turf, to provide care in an environment that was comfortable and familiar. Every pet, from a tarantula to a pot-bellied pig, showed to best advantage at home.

Except, of course, Wheezy.

"How much marijuana did he consume, and how long ago would you say it entered his system?" he asked as walked into the bedroom where the group of formidable old women had directed him. He wasn't the least bit surprised to find the golden retriever in a state of psychoactive lethargy, his breathing and heart rate slowed as the drug took effect, but he *was* surprised by the state of the woman holding him in her lap.

Ruby looked—and smelled—as if she'd been through war. She'd obviously been at work for most of the day, her scrubs wrinkled and her hair once again pulled back in a tousled ponytail, but that wasn't what struck him most. For reasons he had yet to understand, her hands and arms were covered in a series of splotchy red welts that seemed to be working their way up her neck and toward her face. For reasons he *did* understand, the scent of dog urine floated around her like a cloud. Wheezy had obviously lost control of his bladder at some point.

"No one seems to know the exact amount, but from the way the other loaf of bread smelled, I'm guessing quite a bit—and it was medical-grade, so it's the strong stuff. He ate it before I got here, which was a few minutes after five." This information was rattled off efficiently and in a manner that did Ruby's scrubs justice. When she glanced up, however, it was with the expression of a woman who was prepared to hear the worst. "He's really out of it, Spencer. I don't think he's aware that I'm here."

"He knows." Spencer had no doubts on that score. The dog was curled up in her lap, soft yaps escaping every time she lifted her hand from his head. Her presence was the only thing keeping him from falling into a drug-fueled panic. "No—don't get up. I'll examine him where he is."

The examination didn't take long. Ever since the legalization of cannabis and cannabis-related products—especially edibles—the number of accidental canine overdoses had been growing. Dogs never could resist fresh-baked goods, regardless of what was in them. While dangerous, eating them was rarely life-threatening, which seemed to be the case here.

"There wasn't anything chocolate in the bread, was there?" he asked, glancing up at the woman who'd come in to watch the exam take place. From the look of concern on her well-lined face, he was guessing this was the infamous Mrs. Orson.

"No...oh, no," she murmured. "Ruby made us throw out all the chocolate in the house weeks ago. The chips and cookies, too."

Spencer hid a smile at the outrage in the woman's voice. Ruby hadn't been pleased with his initial dietary advice, but it was obvious she'd been determined to see it through, even against a sweet old lady's wishes. Which was just like Ruby. Although she might not like a thing, she gritted her teeth and pushed through.

Even the way she was sitting on the bedroom floor, her whole body vibrating with the need to scratch at her red-welted skin, made him want to pull her in his arms and kiss her. She was uncomfortable and unhappy, and her day was about to get a lot worse, but not by so much as a flutter of her eyelashes did she let it show.

"Well, the good news is, Wheezy isn't going to die," he announced.

In true Ruby fashion, she was quick to pick up his real meaning. "What's the bad news?"

"He isn't going to like my recommended treatment."

"If things are that bad, why are you smiling at me?"

He smiled wider. "Because you're not going to like my recommended treatment, either." He reached for his veterinary bag. "How are you at giving enemas?"

Chapter 17

RUBY ITCHED ALL OVER. HER FACE WAS A SPLOTCHY MESS, SHE WAS urine-soaked and sitting on a bathroom floor, and she was holding a syringe that Spencer had just pulled out of Wheezy's butt. There seemed no possible way for this day to get worse.

"I came as soon as I heard what happened," a male voice said—a whining, nasally, *walrus*-y male voice. "How could you let this happen, Ruby? What were you thinking?"

Ruby closed her eyes and prayed for the floor to open up and swallow her whole.

It didn't.

Aware that Spencer was watching her with the intensity of a man who was trained to diagnose problems on sight, she stretched her lips into a smile and turned to face Harry. She had no idea how he knew about Wheezy's mishap or why Mrs. Orson had allowed him inside the house, but he'd obviously come running the second he heard.

He would. The man was drawn to drama like a serial killer to the scene of his own crime.

"Hello, Harry," she said, using the same sweet voice she always used to placate him. It was harder to do now that her hands and arms felt like they were on fire, but this was what she'd been training her whole life for. There would be no fidgeting, no sign of distress; she was nothing but a perfect smile and inherent grace. "I'm so sorry you had to come all this way. If you'd called first, I could have saved you the trouble."

"Fuck me!" A grimace twitched the bushy ends of his mustache. "What happened to your face?"

She ignored him. She'd had plenty of time while trying *not* to watch Spencer flush out Wheezy's digestive track to examine herself in the bathroom mirror. The sight wasn't a pretty one. Either her allergy to chrysanthemums had gotten worse with age, or there was something particularly potent about Mrs. Orson's crop, because it looked as though she belonged in the infectious ward.

Unlike Harry, however, Spencer had yet to say one word about it. He was much too busy for that. In addition to the enema—which would, he said, need to be repeated in about eight hours—he'd administered active charcoal to settle the dog's stomach and absorb the worst of the toxins.

"I know I'm off the clock, but I felt it was my duty to stay and offer a hand," she said. At a nod from Spencer, she handed the syringe back to him. "This is Dr. Wilson, Wheezy's vet."

She'd hoped that the introduction would stop Harry from asking questions and pushing himself in where he didn't belong, but like the bathroom floor remaining intact, it didn't work.

"I'm going to need you to take a drug test before you head home," Harry said. "In case you've forgotten, it's against policy to indulge in narcotics with the residents."

It was on the tip of her tongue to ask what the policy was regarding *stealing* narcotics from the residents, but Spencer had tilted his head and was staring at her. He was far too intelligent a man not to pick up on the pedantic way Harry was treating her.

So this is it, then. The dark confession, the ugly truth, the way it all would come to an end. Ruby was finally going to be outed as a liar and a fraud, and Harry motherfucking Gunderson was going to be the one to do it.

It was that thought more than anything that pushed her into action. Her stomach felt like she'd eaten twelve lead weights, and her heart skittered worse than the first time she'd set foot on a stage, but she could not, *would* not allow Harry to push her around anymore. It had been wrong of her to mislead Spencer, and there was a good chance a man like him would never forgive her for it, but she was no longer content to sit back and let life happen to her.

Ruby Taylor was officially back.

"It's weed, Harry, not meth, and what I do on my own time is none of your business." She snapped her latex gloves off with the ease of long practice—of thousands of catheters cleaned and baths given, of temperatures taken and wounds dressed. Nothing she'd done in the past decade had been particularly glamorous, but it *had* mattered. The only shame was that it had taken her so long to realize it. "I'm not going to explain myself to you or apologize for my actions. And I'm definitely not letting you administer a drug test unless you can show me where in the employment contract it says you can."

"It's common sense, Ruby. Anyone with half a brain would know that you can't just sit around rolling joints with the residents. You work here, remember? You work for *me*."

"Not anymore, I don't," she said. She tossed the gloves into the trash bin with a satisfying swish. "I quit."

It should have been a moment for triumph—and in many ways, it was—but Harry looked down at the welted red skin of her hands with something like horror. She didn't know why that upset her more than all the rest, but it did. She'd just put this man in his place and quit her job. She'd taken a stand. And *still* he only focused on her exterior. She could spend three decades working here, and Harry would never see her as more than her outward parts.

"If you dare to comment on my appearance again, so help me, I'll report you for sexual harassment before I go," she said with a hard set of her jaw. "And abuse of power and emotional badgering and—"

"General unpleasantness," Spencer supplied.

Before she realized what was happening, Spencer rose to his feet and placed himself at her back. Even though no part of him touched her, she could feel every muscle in his body—the latent strength and warm, solid mass of him. She wasn't sure if it was the physical proximity that was making her heart pick up like that or if it was the fact that he was standing up for her—literally—but there was no denying the uptick in her blood flow.

He knew the truth. He knew the truth and he was still here.

"I don't know who you are or why you've come, but you should know that Ruby saved this animal's life today," Spencer said and in a voice that skipped the leather to go straight for steel. "I've never seen anyone deal with an asshole the way she has."

Ruby choked back a laugh as the full weight of Spencer's double entendre hit home. From the look on Harry's face, equal parts outraged and insulted, it was clear he understood what Spencer was getting at.

"You could say that I've been dealing with assholes my whole life," Ruby said sweetly.

"You can't lodge a complaint about general unpleasantness," Harry muttered, though he was already stepping backward toward the door. "And I never sexually harassed you, Ruby, not once. I'll swear to that under oath. You're not my type."

He meant the words as an insult, but Ruby couldn't think of a better compliment to give a woman.

"I *could* lodge a complaint about all the prescription drugs that have gone missing around here, so don't even start," she countered. "And sexual harassment isn't just hitting on a woman, you nitwit. You've been making snide comments about my appearance since the moment I started working here. You and management both."

Harry's face grew red, then purple, then white. "You can't prove anything."

He was right. She had no proof that he'd been stealing from the clients, and any claims she made about him making the workplace an uncomfortable environment would be a case of he-said, she-said—and management had already shown whose side they'd be more likely to take.

Not that there was any way in hell she was letting him know that.

"You'd better hope so," she said, still in that sweet voice. "Now, if you'll excuse me, I need to finish up here before I gather the things from my locker. You'll pass my resignation along to the proper channels?"

She didn't wait for an answer, turning instead to address Spencer, who was still standing like a suit of armor at her back—not protective but prepared should the situation require. His intensity was so unsettling that she forgot herself and scratched at her wrist, an action that only made the rest of her body flare up and make similar demands.

It was a lot like returning to the stage—*to life*—after ten years of stasis. For a full decade, Ruby had managed to quell every natural impulse and desire she had, to keep her head down and her sights low, to accept the bare minimum and be grateful for it. Doing so had helped her to leave the past behind, but at the cost of her future.

Not anymore. She might be uncomfortable and uncertain and unemployed, but at least she was those things on her own terms.

"Shut the door behind you when you go, please," she called as a parting shot. "Wheezy needs to rest, and it's best if he has some peace and quiet while he does it."

The bathroom door slammed shut. The vibrations shook the room, but the dog slumbering in the bathtub didn't even blink. Poor Wheezy was done in. Ruby was tempted to climb in and join him for a weary and well-earned nap, but Spencer cleared his throat before she could give in to the impulse.

She braced herself for what came next.

"I don't think I like that man very much," he said.

Ruby was startled into a shaky laugh. That wasn't how she'd expected Spencer to start the conversation, but it was just like him to cut straight to the heart of the matter.

"I *know* I don't like that man very much," she countered. "I never have."

"Does he really steal drugs?"

She nodded. "I've never caught him at it, but yes. It's not that uncommon, unfortunately. A lot of people work in places like this so they can take advantage of the residents."

"You don't." He didn't phrase it as a question.

"My mother has high hopes that I'll rope some sweet old man with an amazing life insurance policy into marriage, but no, I don't." Unlike Harry, Ruby didn't waver under the power of Spencer's stare. It was his intense stare, the one that fired her blood in every possible way. "I'm also not a doctor, in case that wasn't obvious. I'm a nursing assistant—or, rather, I was until about five minutes ago."

"A nursing assistant," he echoed.

"Who makes fourteen dollars an hour and barely qualified for her CNA exam and has been passed over for every single promotion she's applied for." She paused, allowing him a moment to react, but he didn't move—not even to blink. The moment of truth had come at last. "This is where I should also admit that my bank account has exactly forty-three dollars in it. I also graduated from high school by the skin of my teeth and have no real skills except the ability to walk elegantly across a stage. When it comes to my life, it's a case of what you see is what you get. Literally. A pretty package, and that's about it."

She waited again, her breath caught in her lungs. She didn't want to exhale for fear that it would disturb the balance of the room. Its quiet expectancy carried a feeling that she stood on a precipice. The slightest brush, the softest whisper, and she'd be pushed over the edge.

Which is exactly what happened. As she stood there staring up at Spencer, both willing and not willing him to speak, she braced herself for the worst. He'd hate her. He'd revile her. Or, worst of all, he'd look down on her.

He did none of those things. Instead, he crossed the room in one powerful stride. He came so close that his hips touched hers, holding but not pinning her against the vanity. She could feel the powerful press of his thighs, the heat of a body that seemed to thrum with some unspoken need. More curious than alarmed, she waited to see what he would do.

His hands came up, a low growl escaping his throat before any words could form. Even that didn't scare her, especially when his hands stopped on either side of her face, his palms hovering above her cheeks.

"Goddammit, Ruby," he said, his low growl still evident in the rumbling way the words came out. "I really want to kiss you right now."

"You do?" Something in her throat caught and clenched. He wasn't going to storm out the door. He was still here and with *such* a look in his eyes. It was his challenging look, his I-cannot-fight-this-attraction look. "What's stopping you?"

He released a shaky laugh, his hands still suspended above her skin, the heat of him causing a rush of sensation to overtake her. "Several things," he said, "but none of them as pressing as the fact that I just had my hands up a dog's ass."

She laughed so hard that he was forced to take a step back. She probably sounded unhinged—she *felt* unhinged—but her relief was so strong that it came out in a burst of sudden, overwhelming glee.

"That might be the most romantic thing anyone has ever said to me," she confessed—and it was the truth. Sweet nothings and flowery compliments had nothing on a man who had just saved a dog's life, taken down Harry Gunderson, and *not* fled the moment the real Ruby Taylor reared her not-so-pretty head.

"Ten minutes," he said as he stepped back. "Give me ten minutes to get cleaned up, and then we'll talk."

"We'll talk?" she echoed, somewhat disappointed. A conversation between them was inevitable, it was true, but she'd much rather do the kissing first. It was so much more enjoyable, so much easier than all the rest.

Which was why she nodded and accepted his offer. It might be easier to use sex and attraction to smooth things out between them, but Ruby didn't want the easy way. Not when it came to Spencer. Not when it came to the things worth fighting for.

"I should probably go clear out my locker anyway," she admitted. "There's not much in there, but it'd be just like Harry to change the locks before I can get to it."

"Caleb tried that with the front door the day he moved in," Spencer admitted with a shake of his head. "But then he couldn't pay the locksmith, so I got all his copies of the keys."

"Someday, you're going to have tell me the entire story of how you two started that game," she said.

Mentioning someday—a future between them—caused something to spark in Spencer's dark eyes. "Someday," he promised, "I will."

Chapter 18

SPENCER WAS NEVER ONE TO RUSH THE JOB. HE WAS ALWAYS meticulous when it came to washing up both before and after seeing an animal. His surgeries ran a little long because he liked to double-check the sutures. Eva and Lawson even joked that he'd gladly spend two hours judging each individual animal during the West Coast Canine Classic, despite the fact that the entire show was meant to be completed in an afternoon.

He finished cleaning up after Wheezy and putting away his supplies in under six minutes flat.

Ruby must have been equally determined because she was sitting on the front steps of Mrs. Orson's house when he emerged, a cardboard box sitting next to her. When he glanced inside it, he winced. A reusable lunch box, deflated and travel-stained, sat in one corner. A set of purple scrubs and a worn pair of sneakers sat in the other. On top of it all was a black-covered novel with what looked suspiciously like a nipple peeking through.

An entire career, summed up in one small parcel. A career that was, to all intents and purposes, over.

"Is that the infamous porcupine book?" he asked as he approached. He forced himself to speak lightly, as though it was perfectly ordinary to hold a conversation like this on an old woman's front porch while several walker-laden men shuffled down the sidewalk in front of them.

Ruby twisted to look up at him, her eyes squinted against the setting sun. She was, without question, the most beautiful woman he'd ever seen. The red, angry mottling of her rash looked even redder and angrier in the outdoor light. Exhaustion darkened the hollows under her eyes, and her usual curls hung limp around her shoulders. She looked like a woman who'd been through battle and emerged—not victorious, exactly, but with her head held high.

God, he loved that about her.

His chest clenched as he realized that he loved a lot more than that. He shot a hand out to brace himself on the porch railing, his whole body reeling with the implication of what he was looking at—of *who* he was looking at.

Ruby Taylor. The woman he loved.

As her lips lifted in a half smile, mischief lighting her eyes, he almost staggered where he stood. "You'd better be careful throwing that word around. I know of at least three seedy motels within walking distance." She tilted her head toward the house. "Is everything okay in there?"

The calm way she asked this question, as though the fact that she was jobless and in desperate need of medical attention meant nothing, did little to help the sudden reeling inside Spencer's head.

"It's fine," he said. "He's fine. Everything is fine."

His incoherence caused her smile to deepen. Lifting the box out of the way, she patted the step next to her. "That's good. I gave the ladies a stern lecture about leaving narcotics out and sent them to their rooms to think about what they've done." Her smile dropped as suddenly as it had appeared. "Man, I'm going to miss this place. Is that pathetic?"

Spencer lowered himself to sit, careful not to touch any part of her. Not because he didn't want to but because he desperately, feverishly *did*. The air between them pulsated with heat and the crackling of untapped energy, but he refused to stick so much as a toe in it. He'd promised a conversation, so a conversation was exactly what he intended to have.

"How long did you work here?" he asked instead.

"A long time. Almost a decade." As though unaware of the embargo he'd placed on the space between their bodies, she put a hand on his arm. "I never meant to lie about my job, Spencer. It was wrong of me to let it go on as long as I did, and I meant to tell you, I really did. But when you first assumed I was a doctor..." She lifted her hand away and pressed it to her cheek instead. "In that moment, I'd have said anything to get the better of you. You looked *so* incredulous, like it would have been more believable if I'd said I hatched from a dinosaur egg."

It was true. Incredulity was exactly what he'd felt in that moment, but there was more to it than that. He'd also felt admiration for how dedicated she was to her job, seen how much it meant to her—the same amount as his own job meant to him. As far as he could tell, that was still true. She obviously loved this place, and from the way those women had turned to her when things got rough, it was obvious this place loved her back.

"I don't care what your job is, Ruby. You could scrub toilets, and it wouldn't make any difference to me."

"I *do* scrub toilets," she responded. "That's literally in the job description."

Spencer rolled his shoulder in a half shrug. He wasn't sure how to make her realize that he was in earnest, that the *what* of her profession wasn't what impressed him. It was the *how* of it that sent him reeling. How she showed up every day, how she gave it her all, how her presence positively impacted all those around her. By her own admission, she earned minimum wage, an income that justified punching a clock, fulfilling her duties, and little more.

But she was a part of a book club here. She trained Wheezy for hours every day. She knew all the residents by name and was on familiar and comfortable footing with them.

In this, as in all things, she gave of herself *fully*.

"Whether you're a nursing assistant or a doctor, I admire what you do," he said, knowing it was only half of what he wanted to say but unsure how to articulate the rest. What he really admired, and what he really loved, was *her*. "That's the only thing that matters. I can forgive the rest."

Next to him, she stiffened. The air between them—the air that had been crackling with so much promise seconds earlier—went flat.

"Forgive the rest?" she echoed.

It hadn't been his intention to bring up Wheezy's blood test, but the tone in her voice sent him into a sudden panic. She sounded cold and hard and a lot like he did when he was doing his best not to show Caleb how disappointed he was.

Jesus. No wonder Caleb hated it.

He tried for a smile. "You didn't think I wouldn't find out about Wheezy's pedigree, did you?" He tilted his head back toward the house, where the not-quite-a-golden-retriever slumbered. "Don't worry. I won't tell anyone. As far as the West Coast Canine Classic is concerned, he has all the right papers, and you two are more than welcome to stick around and participate. Although I *am* curious. Where did they come from? For forgeries, they were well done."

This confession didn't, as he'd hoped, loosen Ruby back up. She shot to her feet like a bolt. Something about the way she loomed made her seem twelve feet tall.

He fumbled against the cardboard box of her belongings as he rose to join her. "What?" he asked, searching her face for clues as to what had gone wrong. "What did I say?"

"You know about Wheezy? How? When?"

"I mean, I knew from the first moment I saw him. He's a good-looking animal, yes, and you could probably pull him off as a purebred golden retriever to anyone else, but judging every little detail is my thing. It's what I do. Or what I always used to do, anyway." He paused, doing his best to get the next part right. There was no denying that he was sometimes *too* good at that aspect of his life, especially when it came to his brother, but that was the point. He was getting better. He was learning. Ruby had taught him that. "But it doesn't matter to me anymore. That's what I'm trying to say. Lawson got a DNA sample and had it tested, but we tossed it out. No one has to know if you don't tell them."

A strange flicker crossed her face. It was similar to her look of steely determination, of her resolve to win no matter what the costs, and was a sight to behold. It was also scary as all get-out. They weren't trying to one-up each other now. They were on the same side.

Right?

"So…you forgive me for lying to you about my job?" she asked, speaking as though from the end of a long, dark tunnel.

"Yes."

"And you also forgive me for lying about Wheezy's eligibility?"

"Can't you see?" he asked, almost desperate at how distant she sounded, how far out of reach. "Of course I don't care what you do for a living. Or what you said to get Wheezy into the show. It doesn't mean anything—none of it means anything. Not after the things we shared, the things we *did*."

She narrowed her eyes and studied him, distractedly scratching at her jawline with long, jerky movements. He wanted to tell her not to do that, to suggest that she take a Benadryl before those welts got even more inflamed than they already were—but he didn't dare.

"And what if I asked you to let us win, me and Wheezy?" she asked. "Could you slip us a few extra points?"

"Probably. There are certain categories where we get extra leeway—"

"Or get us in good with Lawson and Eva?" she persisted. "Make sure they're willing to throw the contest our way?"

"If it's that important to you, I could talk to them, but…" Spencer glanced around, bewildered to find himself still standing on Mrs. Orson's porch, still in the same world he'd been part of when he arrived. "What are you asking? You want me to cheat and let Wheezy win?"

"Yes. That's exactly it." She stopped scratching and dropped her hand like a deadweight. "And you'll give it to me, won't you? Just like that, no questions asked. Because we're fucking? Because we fucked?"

There was nothing soft about the way she used that word—fucking, fucked, *fuck*.

"I'd give you anything." He lifted a hand and reached for her. She allowed him to make contact, but it felt like grabbing a marble statue.

"You just lost your job of ten years, Ruby. And you're obviously in a lot of discomfort right now. Why don't you come back to my house? I have some medical supplies, and without Caleb there, you're free to crash if you need to. We can—"

"She doesn't need to crash at your house." A now-familiar woman's voice sounded behind him. Spencer turned to find Mrs. Orson standing in the doorway to her house, her slight frame swathed in a colorful quilt, a pair of pink-rimmed reading glasses perched on the end of her nose. There shouldn't have been anything intimidating about an eighty-year-old woman who weighed as much as a sack of potatoes, but Spencer felt a quaver unlike any other.

That woman would end him, if given half a chance. Both of these women would.

"I have enough medication around this place to perform heart surgery, should Ruby require it, and she has a place on my couch for as long as I continue to live and breathe on this planet. There's no need for you to stick around." Mrs. Orson held out a hand. The quilt fell from around her, opening like a queen's robe. "Come, Ruby. There's something I want to talk to you about."

Spencer glanced back and forth between the two women, so far out of his depth now that he might as well have been buried at the bottom of the Bermuda Triangle. The look of understanding that passed from Mrs. Orson to Ruby and back again made him realize that they were both upset. With him.

He wanted to defend himself, to point out that he was only trying to help, but if there was one thing Spencer was good at, it was knowing when he wasn't wanted.

From the rough way Ruby picked up the box containing ten years' worth of both nothing and everything, Spencer could tell he *definitely* wasn't wanted.

She hoisted the box against her hip and held it there for a moment—no more than a few seconds, but it felt like an eternity.

"Thank you for helping Wheezy today." There was a chill in her voice that he'd never heard there before. "And for all your assistance in training him. But I'd rather you didn't fix your dog show in my favor, if it's all the same to you."

"That's not what I—" he began, but there was no use. Everything about her posture indicated that she was done with this conversation and, by extension, him.

Chapter 19

THERE'S NO NEED FOR YOU TO GO TO ALL THIS TROUBLE, MRS. Orson." Ruby set her box on the kitchen counter and watched as the older woman bustled around the kitchen, putting hot water on to boil and pulling out a Tupperware container of various tea bags that Ruby knew for a fact had been left by the previous resident. "It's, like, eighty degrees outside. I don't think hot tea is going to help with my rash."

"Hot tea always helps," she said firmly. "Especially if you grab the whiskey from inside the flour canister to give it an edge."

"The flour canister? Really?"

Mrs. Orson glanced over her shoulder. "My ex-husband never liked to see a woman drink, so I got in the habit of keeping it hidden. To this day, I have no idea what he thinks I was doing alone in the kitchen every night."

Ruby was shaken and reeling from her interaction with Spencer, but she followed Mrs. Orson's orders. Although she wanted to get home to lick her wounds—both metaphorical and literal—in peace, she had to admit there were worse things in the world than being coddled by a sweet, elderly woman with a penchant for—

"Wait a minute." She paused in the middle of popping the top off the flour canister. "Did you say your *ex*-husband?"

Mrs. Orson shuddered. She'd given up on the quilt she'd been wrapped up in—for effect, no doubt—and was swathed in a chic paisley scarf instead. The ends of it quivered with her body's movements. "Yes, thank goodness. Didn't I tell you? The divorce came through earlier this week. That's why the girls and I were hitting the banana bread so hard. We were celebrating." She turned to find Ruby's hand still suspended on the canister and took it from her. Assuming Ruby was having a hard time with the lid, she gave it a strong-gripped twist and pop. "There you go, love. Pour with a heavy hand. You look like you could use it."

Mrs. Orson finished pouring the cups of stale tea and held them out for Ruby to add hard—and expensive—liquor.

This time, Ruby didn't do as she asked.

"Mrs. Orson, what do you mean, you got divorced from your husband? He's alive? You're not a widow?"

Mrs. Orson shook her head, a mischievous, dangerous smile playing on the edges of her lips. "I thought about it all the time, if that helps. Arsenic in his pot roast. A snip to his brake line. A long walk on a cliff's edge when the wind was rising." She took the bottle from Ruby and poured. "Despite my dreaming, I could never make myself go through with it. Pity. I would have looked so good in black."

Ruby could only stare as Mrs. Orson took both cups and saucers in her firm, unshaking grip and moved toward the living room.

"Peek in the bathroom to check on Wheezy before we settle for our chat, would you? You'll find antihistamines in the second drawer down if you want to do something about that face—or, if you need something stronger, I think there's morphine inside the douche box. It might be expired, though."

Ruby couldn't find it in her to be shocked or outraged by any of the words coming out of Mrs. Orson's mouth. The fact that she stored out-of-date morphine inside feminine hygiene product boxes was no more surprising than the fact that her dear, departed husband was neither dear nor departed after all.

And *both* of those things had no power over her while Spencer's words were still rolling like pinballs inside her head. He'd offered to throw his dog show for her. He'd offered to throw his dog show for her for no reason other than the fact that they were sleeping together.

And worse than that, he'd offered her *forgiveness* for it.

She bit back a sob as she searched through the bathroom drawers for the promised antihistamines. It was more of an angry sob than a sad one, even if her eyes were having a hard time getting the message. She dashed a hand at the back of her cheek with one hand while searching through a trove of medications with the other. There was a good chance that what she ended up taking was yet another baby aspirin with the letter scraped off, but it wasn't like it mattered. She was going to be a bloaty, itchy mess no matter what she ingested.

As if in solidarity, Wheezy let out a high-pitched whine, his legs twitching with dreamy sleep. Ruby put a hand on his heaving side to calm him. She was surprised to find that the warm bulk of him—that hefty, stubborn mass—did more to calm herself instead.

"I know, Wheezy," she murmured, careful not to wake him. "It's been a rough day, but we'll get through it. Fighters like you and me always do."

With a deep, resolute breath and a quick adjustment of Wheezy's blanket so he was better tucked in, she headed out of the bathroom to face Mrs. Orson. She had no idea what that woman was going to throw at her next, but she was strangely eager to find out.

"I'm not going to tell you where I got Wheezy's papers" was the first thing Mrs. Orson said as soon as Ruby walked into the living room. "If you don't know, then you can't be held liable for any inaccuracies that may have accidentally slipped in. Let's get that clear right away."

Ruby halted, her hand on the doorjamb to settle herself. Maybe she wasn't so eager to talk to this woman after all. Mrs. Orson was supposed to tell her about Norbert, not Spencer.

Spencer, she knew. Spencer, she understood.

"It doesn't matter." Ruby set her jaw. "We're not going anywhere near that dog show."

"Oh, you're going to be in it. And you're going to win. You promised me, remember?"

Ruby couldn't recall *promising* to do anything, but she was willing to play along for the sake of this conversation. Taking a few tentative steps into the room, she moved behind the nearest couch. She used the back of it to brace herself.

She wanted to stay standing for this. She *would* stay standing for this.

That was the thing Spencer hadn't understood—the thing he'd crushed with his sweet, stupid smile and his even sweeter, stupider offer to throw away the West Coast Canine Classic. After everything Ruby had done to get to this point, the lies she'd told and the work she'd put in, the way she'd clawed her way out of the grave she'd buried herself in for the past ten years, she was supposed to win the dog show on her own two feet—or at least to *lose* the dog show on her own two feet.

That was the whole point of Spencer. Unlike everyone else in her life, Spencer had never once hinted that she could use her looks as an all-access pass to the future of her dreams. In fact, he did the exact opposite. He liked her *in spite* of her face. He kissed her only after she dared him into it. He refused to be charmed by Wheezy's soft brown eyes—or by her own.

Until today. Today, she'd been at her lowest point: covered in a rash and worried about Wheezy, caught in a lie and fired from her job. And instead of taking her by the shoulders and telling her that she was a strong, capable human being who had yet to balk at anything life had thrown at her, he'd offered her the easy way out.

He'd meant it, too—that was the worst part. He'd have whisked her into his car and driven her home, where he'd have done all those things her mother dreamed of: given her money and gifts and a dog-show trophy, provided a future where she didn't have to do anything but be a pleasing addition to his life. In other words, he'd forgive her for her little foibles, and all she had to do in return was smile gratefully for it.

The thought was enough to make Ruby scream. And cry. In no particular order.

"You only have his word for it that Wheezy isn't a purebred golden retriever," Mrs. Orson said. Her voice was soothing in ways that mocked the roiling of Ruby's blood. "How do we know his test was valid? Was it done in a lab? Was he careful not to cross-contaminate the sample with all the other animals under his care?"

"Mrs. Orson, you don't understand. It's not about Wheezy's bloodlines anymore. I'm starting to think it never was."

"Of course it wasn't." Mrs. Orson patted the couch cushion next to her. When Ruby didn't sit, she patted harder. "I can feel the bones in my frail, osteoporotic hands starting to crack, dear. Please sit before they break."

Mrs. Orson's hands were fine, as Ruby was well aware, but she gave in and sat anyway. There was no telling how far Mrs. Orson would take the farce, and the last thing she wanted was to have to call another medical professional into this house. Look what had happened with the last one.

"There are only two things in this world that my ex-husband loves," Mrs. Orson said the moment Ruby's butt hit the cushion. She spoke as one making a formal announcement. "One of them is himself."

Ruby could guess her line. "And the other is Wheezy?"

Mrs. Orson nodded, a pleased smile folding the lines of her face. That gentle serenity was at odds with what came out of her mouth next. "And since I was too chickenhearted to take the first one, I decided to take the second."

Ruby turned to stare at her. "You *stole* Wheezy?"

Mrs. Orson waved an airy hand. "It's a community-property state. Wheezy is technically half mine. Everything of Norbert's is half mine, including the money he made running one of the biggest and scammiest insurance companies in greater Seattle. Why do you think I'm so comfortably situated now?"

Ruby could only shake her head. She should have introduced this woman to her mother months ago. If everything Mrs. Orson was saying was true, they had quite a bit in common.

"Norbert had been training Wheezy to appear in dog shows since the day he brought him home." Her tone took on a narrative lull that encouraged Ruby to relax against the cushions. "Nothing was too good for him. Training, grooming, professional dog walkers, a chef."

"Wait—a *dog* chef? That's a thing?"

"Don't interrupt me." Mrs. Orson tapped her pursed lips with her forefinger. "The point is, he lavished more love and attention on that animal in five months than I got in fifty years. Think about that. Fifty *years*, Ruby. My whole life. My youth. My beauty… Oh yes. You aren't the only one with a nice pair of legs, so don't look so surprised. I was quite a dish, back in my day. And I wasted it on that scoundrel."

There were a lot of reasons why a man could be labeled a scoundrel, but something about Mrs. Orson's tiny, resolute frame made Ruby's heart squeeze. Any man who'd been given the gift of this woman in his life and wasted it, *hurt* her in any way…

"My family didn't believe in divorce, so I took what had been offered and tried to make the best of it. I'd have kept doing it, too, if it wasn't for that dog." The serene, playful smile was back on her face. "Try as Norbert might, he could never make anything of Wheezy. Oh, he knows all the commands, don't you worry. And he'll do them when he feels like it, but he never feels like it when Norbert is in the room."

Although Ruby had been told not to interrupt, she couldn't help inserting a question. "But you asked me that day if Spencer had a commanding voice. You said Wheezy responds best to authority."

"And so he does, when he likes a person. The problem is, he doesn't like very many people." She paused. "He likes your Spencer."

"He's not my Spencer," Ruby corrected her.

"After that display out on my front porch, I think we both know that's a lie."

Ruby's cheeks flushed even more than they already were. It might have been the effect of the antihistamine taking hold, but she doubted it. This was shame and embarrassment and unadulterated pleasure all at once.

"You heard what he said," she protested, pushing that pleasure down as far as it could go. "About allowing Wheezy into the competition, about letting him win. As if there's no way either of us could *imagine* success otherwise. As though we're nothing without him."

Mrs. Orson nodded and took Ruby's hand in her own. Ruby loved the way her skin felt, like a well-worn blanket.

Like so many things about this woman, however, looks were deceiving.

"Which is why you and Wheezy are going to be in that show next week."

"Mrs. Orson, I don't think you understand—" She tried to take her hand back, but Mrs. Orson held her firm. The soft skin and gentle fingers transformed at once to a predator's talons.

"As soon as Norbert realized that he couldn't push Wheezy around, he looked into the breeder. He needed someone to blame… He's always been a blamer. When he found out they may have lied about Wheezy's origins, he demanded his money back with reparations. For all I know, he got them. I don't care. Wheezy and I didn't stay long enough to find out."

"You left him."

"Wheezy gave me the strength to do it. Norbert pushed me around for fifty years, and I took it. But when he turned on that dog…" She shook her head, her fingers pressing so hard into Ruby's hand that the pain was starting to overtake the itching. She didn't pull away, though. There was something profoundly comforting in that strength. "Don't take this the wrong way, but you remind me of Wheezy."

Ruby knew it to be the truth—and not just because of those golden curls and brown eyes. Wheezy was a well-trained animal who refused to become a star on someone else's terms. He refused to do *anything* on someone else's terms…unless, of course, that someone was Spencer Wilson.

Which was exactly the problem. Trying to get the better of Spencer had brought her back to life, yes, but he couldn't be her reason for staying that way. It was just another form of pageantry, something else to hitch her wagon to.

She liked Spencer. She probably even loved him. But for the first time in her life, she loved herself more.

"I can't take Wheezy to the West Coast Canine Classic," Ruby said. She finally managed to wrest her hand free of Mrs. Orson's. "Don't you see? I'd be playing into Spencer's game, trying to mold myself to fit someone else's rules."

Mrs. Orson laughed—that deep, body-shaking, beautiful laugh. Ruby couldn't help but feel sorry for Norbert, wherever he was. He'd missed out on something wonderful when he tried to quash this woman's spirit.

"Then don't follow his rules, dear," she said. "Follow your own."

Ruby stared at Mrs. Orson, that soft, beautiful face going in and out of focus. This thing she was saying—this idea she was proposing—was both the easiest and the most difficult thing in the world. For Ruby's entire life, she'd been told to change herself to fit predetermined criteria. To win a pageant, to get a man, to hold down a job.

What Mrs. Orson was suggesting was the exact opposite.

"You brilliant, beautiful woman!" Ruby sprang to her feet. The antihistamine had started to make her woozy, but she didn't care. She welcomed that feeling of being off-balance, of not knowing herself to be on solid ground. Leaning down, she pressed a loud and smacking kiss on Mrs. Orson's cheek. "You really think I can do it?"

"You can do anything you put your mind to. Take it from a woman who spent far too many years doing what she was told. Life is so much better when you live it on your own terms."

Chapter 20

"CAESAR, BUDDY, YOU HAVE TO STOP THIS."

Spencer paused in the middle of scrubbing his kitchen sink, surgical gloves up to his elbows and a container of bleach by his side. Growing up, his mom had always been a cathartic cleaner—the more upset she'd been, the harder she'd scrubbed. He could still remember the morning after Caleb had been first expelled from school for one of his many teenage escapades. Spencer had woken up at four o'clock to find his mom on hands and knees, taking a toothbrush to every inch of grout in the guest bathroom.

He hadn't been scrubbing *quite* that long yet, but there was still time.

"I mean it, Caesar. Come over here."

The bulldog, who was lying by the front door with his head on his paws and heaving a forlorn sigh every ten seconds, responded with—what else?—another forlorn sigh.

"It hurts my feelings. You do realize that, right?" Spencer gave up on the sink, peeling off his gloves with a snap. All traces of Caleb were now removed from the kitchen—the stacks of old takeout in the refrigerator, the garbage that hadn't been emptied in over a week, the cheap bottles of whiskey that had replaced normal things like ketchup and sriracha. From the way the kitchen sparkled and gleamed, Spencer's house was finally starting to look the way it used to.

Cold. Sterile. *Empty.*

"It's not like he's dead," Spencer said. "I could text him right now, and he'd be here in ten minutes. Probably less."

The look Caesar gave him, his eyes wet and accusatory, dared him to make good on that threat. It was a feeling Spencer understood well. Since the moment he'd driven away from Mrs. Orson's house—and away from Ruby—all he'd wanted to do was to call his brother. Caleb was the last man anyone should turn to for relationship advice, and he'd probably spend half the time laughing at how badly Spencer had messed things up, but he didn't care.

He wanted his brother. And Caesar, unable to eat or sleep or do anything without his favorite Wilson twin near, felt the same.

"You could at least pretend to love me," Spencer accused as he slid down the wall and came to rest beside the dog. Caesar didn't go so far as to shower him with affection, but he did roll his head onto Spencer's lap, which counted for something. "I'm the one you're stuck with, so you might as well make the best of it."

Caesar's warm, heavy bulk went a long way in soothing Spencer's lacerated feelings. Even though he was the animal's second choice, he was grateful to have him near. There were some things a man wasn't meant to bear alone.

A broken heart was one of them—especially since he didn't know *why* it had happened. Ruby was the person who was supposed to see behind the stiff facade to the man he was underneath, the person who stepped up and met him challenge for challenge.

She was smart and strong and everything he desired…and she wanted nothing to do with him.

A loud thumping caused both Spencer and Caesar to jump. Spencer was so deep in his morose reflections that it took him a moment to identify the cause, but Caesar was on his feet and whirling in circles right away. His stub of a tail waggled back and forth, both his age and his stupor forgotten in a sudden burst of joy.

The thump sounded again, followed immediately by a jingle of the front doorknob.

"I know you're in there, Spencer!" Caleb's voice—mocking and loud and more welcome than Caleb would ever know—blared through the door. "And I can see that you had the locks changed again. Very funny. Let me in."

Spencer scrambled to his feet and unlocked the door. It swung open, missing his face by inches, but he couldn't find it in him to care. The sight of his brother—in ratty jeans and a well-worn band T-shirt, his hair still too long and his shoes coming apart at the soles—was so welcome that Spencer wrapped him in a hug as he pulled him through the door.

And Spencer—who rarely initiated a hug with anyone, who hadn't done more than shake hands with his brother in years—wasn't the first to let go.

"Well, shit." Caleb's soft laugh sounded as he extricated himself from Spencer's grasp. He stepped back and took a good look at Spencer's face. Those dark eyes, so much like his own, didn't stop searching until they found what they were looking for—and what he found wasn't good. "Eva wasn't kidding, was she? You're in rough shape."

Spencer didn't bother to deny it. "Eva called you?"

"Eva called me. Eva texted me. Eva stopped by Lawson's house and demanded that I do something." Caleb laughed again, but the sound carried more concern than delight this time. "I thought she was exaggerating when she said you've done nothing but mope for the past few days, but she was right. You look like hell."

"I feel like hell," Spencer admitted. "But you'd better do something about this dog of yours because he's not going to stop until you pet him."

"He's not my dog," Caleb said, but they both knew it wasn't true. As his brother crouched down to say hello to the bulldog, it was evident that Caesar had long since made his choice. He whimpered and burrowed as though he wouldn't be satisfied until he shared Caleb's skin. "Don't take it to heart, Brother dear. I'm the one who really carries roast beef in my pocket."

"As soon as you have somewhere permanent to live, you can have him." Spencer gestured for Caleb to come the rest of the way in the house, where the duct-tape line was starting to peel in several places. "I'll miss the old rascal, but it's obvious he prefers you to me. I don't have the heart to stand in the way of true love."

Caleb released a low whistle. "It's as bad as that, huh?"

Spencer didn't have to answer. Caleb already knew.

"Then you'd better tell me what happened," Caleb said. He came into the house, glanced around at the newly cleaned interior, and shook his head. "And don't leave anything out. I haven't seen the place look like this since the day I moved in."

Spencer watched as his brother settled himself on the couch and patted for Caesar to join him. The ancient bulldog had trouble pulling himself up to that height, and Spencer had long since given up on asking him to make the attempt, but he managed to do it.

He did it because Caleb was the one asking. He did it because he wanted nothing more than to be near the person he loved most.

"How do you do it?" Spencer asked with a nod down at the pair of them.

Caleb lifted an enquiring eyebrow. "How do I make Caesar love me?"

"Caesar. Mom and Dad. Eva. Everyone." Spencer tried not to sound bitter, but he didn't have much success. He sounded bitter because he *was* bitter. "How is it that you can disappear for months at a time—years, even—and show up only to have everyone fall at your feet? What is it about you that's so lovable? *What do you have that I don't?*"

That last question came out dangerous, and Spencer could only hope his brother understood that his anger had nothing to do with Caleb and everything to do with himself. His whole life, he'd done all the things he was supposed to: got good grades, was kind to animals, paid his bills on time, and bailed his brother out when he needed it. When none of that made him happy, he'd changed course. He'd fallen for Ruby, broken all his self-imposed rules, and offered her everything he had.

And she'd rejected him.

"Is this a trick question?" Caleb stopped in the middle of petting Caesar, his hands poised motionless above his fur.

"Of course it's not." Spencer sank to the recliner nearest the couch, suddenly so weary that he could no longer remain standing. "Our whole lives, everyone has liked you better than me. Hell, *I* like you better than me. It doesn't matter what you do or how bad you mess up. The doors always stay open."

"Spencer. Are you being an idiot on purpose?"

"What? It's true. Do you know the first thing Mom asks anytime I visit her? 'How's Caleb?' 'What's Caleb up to?' 'Why didn't you bring Caleb along?'" He shook his head. "She couldn't care less whether or not I'm there. I'm only valuable as a conduit to you."

"That's the stupidest thing I've ever heard."

"People light up when you walk into a room," Spencer continued. "It never used to bother me—not really, not in any way that mattered. I mean, it was *annoying*, obviously, but that was fine. You could be the shiny twin, the happy twin, the better-looking twin. I didn't need any of that. I had my work and my dog show. I had Eva and Maury and Lawson."

"You still have all those things," Caleb pointed out.

He wasn't wrong. Spencer did have all those things, and there was a good chance he always would. His friends had always been there for him, and the world would always need veterinarians. His place in life—at least on the surface—was secure. And had he never met Ruby, it might have been enough. He could have continued along in his narrow little world, content with how small it was, how rigid, never knowing what lay outside the duct-taped line he'd put around his heart.

But he *had* met her, and he'd fallen in love with her, and the duct-taped line around his heart was as useless as the one on his living room floor.

"She doesn't want anything to do with me," Spencer said, his voice cracking. He didn't say who the *she* in question was, but there was no need. "I told her I didn't care about her stupid job or Wheezy's stupid papers, that I'd throw the whole damn dog show out the window if it would make her happy. I offered her everything I have, and she just… quit."

"She quit."

"Yes."

"Ruby quit."

"Caleb, now's not the time to mess with me. Can't you tell I'm barely holding on here?"

Apparently, he couldn't. "*Ruby* quit," Caleb said again, this time emphasizing her name. "The same Ruby who's haunted this place for two months? The same Ruby who drags an unwilling dog on a three-mile walk every day? The same Ruby who built a stage in the backyard and watched every single Westminster Dog Show recording in existence?"

That last one caught Spencer's interest. "She watched all of them?"

"Of course she did. I once mentioned—in passing, mind you—that she could catch up on a few championship rounds to see what real winners looked like. Three days later, she could name every single Best in Show dating back to the '70s. Their breeds, their names, *and* their handlers. I was curious about that last one, but she admitted to emailing a few of them for advice."

Spencer gave a reluctant chuckle. That sounded like the Ruby he knew—the one who'd stop at nothing to get her way, who refused to let anything stand between her and what she wanted most.

Only she doesn't want me. I'm the one thing she didn't bother fighting for.

Caleb must have noticed the sudden shift in Spencer's mood because he heaved a sigh and held out an imperative hand. "Give me ten dollars."

"What? Why? Use your own money."

"I don't have any money. You know that better than anyone. Just hand it over."

Spencer was curious enough to reach for his wallet and extract a bill. "All I have is a fifty," he said as he handed it over.

"Of course you do." Caleb held the bill up between two fingers. "I'll bet you this fifty bucks that I can hop on one leg longer than you."

Spencer could only stare at his brother. Never mind that there were far more important matters weighing him down right now; the idea of Caleb placing a bet against him with his own money was ridiculous. Not to mention entirely against the rehabilitation that was supposed to have made him a functioning member of society.

"Right or left, I don't care. You pick." Caleb nudged Caesar aside and got to his feet. He looked so casually confident, so sure of himself, that Spencer felt his every competitive instinct sit up and take notice.

He steeled both his jaw and his resolve against those instincts. "I'm not playing this game with you," he said.

"Why? Afraid I'll win?"

"Of course not. It has nothing to do with winning or losing. You shouldn't be gambling, that's all."

"You shouldn't have slept with an entrant in your dog show, yet here we are."

Spencer's jaw tightened even more. He could list all the things he shouldn't have done where Ruby was concerned, but none of that mattered. It was the thing he *couldn't* list—that mysterious thing he'd done wrong—that was going to end him.

"It's different," he protested. "You only just got the ankle monitor off. If you're already slipping back into your old habits, you need more meetings, more classes. If money is an issue, I'll pay for them. I'll find you a good therapist, someone you can talk to when the urge gets to be too much—"

Caleb cut him short by starting to hop on his right leg. He did it with so much deliberation, so much intent, that Spencer knew he was being provoked.

"You're going to have a lot of catching up to do," Caleb taunted. He waved the fifty-dollar bill in the air as though fanning himself. "You'd better get in on this while the getting's good."

Spencer shook his head. "If you want the fifty that bad, you can have it. Hell, you can have fifty *thousand* if you really need it. You just have to promise not to gamble with it."

Caleb stopped hopping as suddenly as he'd begun. The bill fluttered to the floor, where it lay like a piece of discarded confetti. Neither of them made a move to pick it up.

"You'd do it, wouldn't you?" Caleb asked, and with a hard note in his voice that Spencer couldn't remember hearing there before. "If I promised to be a good boy and keep my head down, put it to good use by investing it in my future."

"Of course I would," Spencer said, though not without wariness. He didn't like the way Caleb's face was so unmoving and still. It reminded him of how Ruby had looked on the porch. "All you've ever had to do is ask."

"Fuck you, Spencer."

Spencer blinked. There was no vehemence in Caleb's voice, no anger. Just that chill, that same Ruby chill. "What do you mean?" he asked.

"I mean, fuck you. Fuck your offer and fuck your fifty dollars and fuck gambling therapy."

"You're the one who wanted to hop," he protested. "Not me."

"I don't want to hop, you idiot. I don't even want to gamble all that much, to be honest. It's never been my favorite thing."

That feeling was back—of being lost at sea, of drifting away into a world Spencer had only ever seen through a warped glass. "But you were arrested for running an illegal gambling website."

"Yeah—one that I coded and built all by myself. One that employed three independent contractors before it was brought down." Caleb brought his hands down on Spencer's shoulders and squeezed. Hard. "You're one of the smartest people I know. How you can be so stupid is beyond me."

Stupid wasn't a word that got slung at Spencer very often, but he was in no position to deny it. Considering how far out of his depth he was right now, he felt like the least intelligent person on the face of the planet.

"It's not about the gambling," Caleb said. "It's never been about the gambling. I could have just as easily fallen into forgery or petty theft. The *what* of it doesn't matter, just so long as there's an element of danger. I don't know if you've noticed, but it just so happens that my skill set leans toward a high tolerance for risk."

"Do you even know how to forge things?" was all Spencer could think to reply.

Caleb squeezed his shoulders one last time before letting go. "I can't win, Spencer. I can never win."

In that instant, Spencer knew they weren't talking about winning or losing at a game of chance. They were talking about something a lot more important than that.

"Our whole lives, you've been better than me at everything," Caleb said, confirming Spencer's suspicions. "You got better grades. You did your chores on time. You remembered to feed the dogs in the kennel every morning and to always say 'please' and 'thank you.'"

"Thank you?" Spencer tried now.

Caleb chuckled. "That's not what I mean, and you know it. You were so damn good at everything, Spencer. You still are. No one ever doubted that you'd go to college and make something of yourself or that if you one day decided to run a dog show, you'd do it so well that people would travel hundreds of miles to make their pets preen in front of you. From the day we were born, your success was pretty much guaranteed."

"That's not true—" Spencer began, but Caleb wasn't done yet.

"I've tried to do the same. Hit the books, study hard, mold myself into someone like you. It didn't work, obviously, but no one could accuse me of not trying. Hell, I became a dog trainer for the sole reason that it was as close to a veterinarian as I could get without a degree. And I'm not even all that skilled at it."

"You are skilled at it."

Caleb snorted. "If Wheezy is any indication, I think we both know that's a lie—but even that is just like you, isn't it? Pretending I have half your drive and intelligence, that I could make something of myself if I dug in and applied myself."

It was on the tip of Spencer's tongue to point out that everything he'd just said was true and that the sky was the limit when it came to the things Caleb could do in this world, but he didn't. Something approaching understanding was starting to seep its way into his brain, hazy now but gaining clarity the longer Caleb stood there talking.

"You're just so damn *good* at everything all the time." Caleb spoke without bitterness. "I'd hate you for it if I didn't love you so much, but I do. Love you, I mean."

Spencer swallowed a lump.

"It's why I keep falling into the same messes. I play poker and build illegal websites and do so many push-ups that I'm pretty sure I've pulled, like, twelve muscles." Caleb's voice grew quiet. "If I'm right—and I think I am—it's also why Ruby has spent every waking hour of the past eight weeks training that completely worthless dog."

Spencer didn't ask. He couldn't.

"She doesn't want you to give her the dog-show trophy, Spencer. She wants to earn it." Caleb gave a rueful shake of his head. "Even if she fails, even if she falls flat on her face and ends up with an ankle monitor and six months of house arrest, she'll get back up and keep fighting. Don't you get it? We don't want to be your shadow. We want to be your *equal*."

"My equal?" Spencer echoed.

"Or as close to it as we can get anyway." Caleb shrugged. "And even though we know it's not really possible—that you're always going to be one step ahead, with a wallet full of cash and a head full of information—we're not going to give up the pursuit. That's the whole point. You force us to try. You make us want to be better. Hell, Spencer. You *do* make us better."

There was a lot to unpack in everything Caleb had just said, but one question loomed at the forefront. Spencer gave in and asked.

"You think Ruby loves me?"

Caleb's laughter did much to dispel the tension that had fallen over the room. "*That*'s your takeaway from all this?"

Spencer felt the tips of his ears grow warm. "It's just that you said you'd hate me if you didn't love me so much. I know I don't deserve any of it, but if you think Ruby is the same, that she feels the way you do—"

"She does."

Spencer wished he could be so sure. Caleb hadn't been there when Ruby had turned him away, so upset she was practically vibrating, everything about her signaling that she wanted nothing to do with him.

He *had* been there for all the rest, though. For every single high point in Spencer's life, for just as many of the lows. Even when relations between them were so strained that they had to put a literal line between them, Caleb showed up. That was more important than all the money in the world, worth more than a stable job and a predicable daily routine.

"I messed up, didn't I?" Spencer said.

It was a rhetorical question, but Caleb answered it anyway.

"Oh, absolutely. I don't know what you were thinking, offering that woman an easy way out." He laughed. "Even I would have known better than that, and I'm not the one with a college degree and a clean criminal record."

Spencer felt a strange combination of relief and dread, a sensation that everything was right with the world and also terribly, horribly wrong. "You really don't care that much about gambling?"

Caleb shrugged. "Not unless I'm staking myself against you. It was a means to an end, that's all."

"You don't plan on breaking any more laws?"

"I can't promise I won't run the occasional red light, but no. I've learned my lesson. I appreciate you bailing me out and taking me in, and I doubt I'll ever be able to repay you for it, but I don't think I can stand the sight of this house much longer. Or, to be honest, your grumpy, unshaven face in the morning."

Spencer released a shaky laugh. That sounded so much like the Caleb he used to know—the brother who was as much his friend as his foe—that life was suddenly taking on a much sunnier aspect.

"And you'll go see Mom and Dad?" he persisted. "Now that you're free?"

Caleb pulled a grimace. "If it's that important to you, yes."

"It is."

His brother nodded once. Even though Caleb didn't like it, and he wouldn't enjoy their mom's loving recriminations, Spencer knew he'd make good on his promise. He always had. That was something he'd forgotten in all the anxiety and annoyance of the past few months. Caleb didn't always make the same choices Spencer would, but when he said he'd do a thing, he'd do it even if it cost him everything he had.

Just like someone else he knew.

"For the record, you're not my equal," Spencer said, drawing a deep breath. This next part was going to be difficult, but it had to be said. "Not in the things that matter."

A hurt expression crossed Caleb's face. "Even after everything I just said, everything we just—"

"When it comes to people, you're unquestionably my master." Spencer ran a hand through his hair and released a shaky laugh. "And I want you—no, I *need* you—to teach me. People like you. People freaking love you. Tell me, Caleb. What can I do to get Ruby back?"

Caleb's wince turned to a wide, beaming smile. "Oh, Spencer. And here I thought you'd never ask."

Chapter 21

WELL, IT'S NOT HOW I ALWAYS IMAGINED YOU RETURNING TO THE stage, but I suppose it's better than nothing." Ruby's mother held up a bottle of hair spray and started to apply it. Everywhere. Hair and face and, most important, all those spots where dress met skin. Although the modern style was to rely on tape and clever stitchery to hold a pageant gown in place, Laurel held true to the traditions.

Hair spray fixed everything.

"I've got to say, Ruby, I didn't think the dress would look as good as it did when you were seventeen, but I was wrong. Now that your breasts have dropped a few inches, the neckline looks quite nice."

Ruby choked. At her feet, Wheezy made a similar sound, but that was because he'd inhaled far more of the hair spray than was good for him.

"If you think your boobs have started losing the fight against gravity now, wait until you get to be my age." Mrs. Orson, who sat well out of hair-spray range on a velvet settee on the opposite end of the dressing room, heaved a despairing sigh. "These days, they look like a pair of deflated balloons filled with cottage cheese."

Ruby choked again, the sound bordering on a laugh. It was a daring move in more ways than one. Not only was laughter forbidden in the sacred dressing room—a small bedroom that her mother had converted to her own personal closet—but her mother hadn't yet Vaselined her teeth. Her smile needed to be picture perfect before she was allowed to roll it out.

But her mom, giddy with all the sequins and sparkles that surrounded them, gave up and joined in.

"Oh dear. They really do, don't they?" Laurel placed her hands underneath her breasts and hoisted them to unearthly heights. "I've been thinking about having mine done while there's still enough elasticity in my skin to hold them up."

"I think you should do it," Mrs. Orson agreed. "My friend Darla had hers done about a decade ago. The rest of her is like wet crepe paper, but her décolletage looks fantastic."

If Ruby wasn't standing in the middle of her mother's dressing room, a pair of towering silver heels on her feet and her hair so tall it practically brushed the ceiling, she'd have supposed she was dreaming. Never, in her wildest imaginings, could she have pictured her mother and Mrs. Orson casually discussing aging female bodies. Especially not while she was wearing a long, sweeping, off-the-shoulder ballgown that weighed almost as much as Wheezy did.

It was one of the last gowns she'd ever worn, a spangled teal monstrosity that cost more than her car. The sweeping hem had to be carried by hand—or by an attendant—but her mother was right about the neckline. The dress fit her woman's body much better than it ever had her teenage one.

A lot of things about this moment felt that way. As a teenager, she hadn't been able to appreciate how nice it was to spend this time with her mother. So many other parents were dedicated to their jobs and their hobbies and their travels—but not Laurel. Every ounce of energy she'd possessed had been channeled into her offspring.

It had been infuriating and exhausting, yes, but she'd been there. Just like she was now.

Ruby stepped down from the literal pedestal she'd been placed upon and pulled her mother into a hug. She could hear the muffled sounds of Laurel's protests and admonitions, but she didn't care. Her dress might wrinkle and sag, and her makeup might smear, but she wasn't planning on winning a beauty pageant today.

She wasn't planning on winning a dog show either, but anyone standing in the room with them right now would be able to tell that. Sometime in the past week, Wheezy had enjoyed an altercation with a raccoon. A large chunk of fur was missing from underneath his ear, and Mrs. Orson's attempts to cut the rest of his hair to match hadn't gone well. He'd never looked worse.

Since he hadn't seen Spencer in over a week, he'd also never acted worse. Even the recording of Spencer's voice seemed to be losing its hold over him.

He missed having the real man around. So did Ruby.

"Well, this is it, then. Showtime." Mrs. Orson struggled to get to her feet. Ruby made a motion to help her, but her mom was on alert and beat her to it.

Although she'd been hesitant to introduce the two women to each other, there'd been no need. They got along in ways that both delighted and terrified her. Half of her was pretty sure her mom was going to try the old woo-the-elderly-to-get-put-in-the-will routine, but the other half thought they might actually become friends. They'd both been burned by love and enjoyed nothing more than telling Ruby what to do. Relationships had been founded on less.

"I think you look very nice, dear. A bit tarty, but that's how I like it." Mrs. Orson glanced at Ruby's mom. "You've worked a miracle on her skin, by the way. I had no idea glitter was so concealing. I barely notice the rash anymore."

"I wanted to send her through a fake tan spray, but she wouldn't go." Laurel clucked her tongue. "She won't win any awards looking like that, but I've done the best I could. The rest is up to her."

"Technically, the rest is up to Wheezy." Ruby nudged the golden retriever with the tip of one delicately shod foot. When that didn't do more than cause him to grumble, she nudged harder. "Come on, slugabed. It's now or never. All the other dogs have been getting ready since sunrise."

Wheezy rolled his eyes at her, looking exactly like Ruby had felt for the majority of her teenage life. Nothing was worse than slapping on a pair of heels and trotting around for a bunch of judges when all you wanted was to curl in a ball and cry, but that was the point. When you wanted something—*truly* wanted it—you had to suck it up and do it anyway.

That was the one thing Ruby had forgotten, the one thing she should have held on to as she ventured out into the real world for the first time. *Naive* wasn't a word she'd have used to describe the hard-edged eighteen-year-old she'd once been, but that was the word that fit. Gowns were just sequin-covered fabric and trophies were only plated gold, but the drive it took to succeed in the world of pageantry—the determination, grit, and fierce, unyielding passion—was something special.

And she'd turned her back on it. She'd let it go.

"Not anymore," she said aloud. The words were more for herself than for Wheezy, but he recognized the tone and heaved a sigh. He also heaved himself to his feet. He looked worse standing up than he had lying down, but that was okay.

Wheezy wasn't going to win the West Coast Canine Classic. He wasn't even going to come close. But he'd put in the effort and she'd promised Mrs. Orson to give him this opportunity, so they were going anyway.

And if Spencer so much as hinted that he'd slip Wheezy a few extra points when Eva's and Lawson's backs were turned, she was going to tell him exactly what he could do with them. His pity could go in the garbage and his charity up his ass.

She had her pageant face on and her dress zipped tight. She was ready.

"The doors don't open to the public until three o'clock, so you two will have to find something to amuse yourselves until then." She cast a stern look at the two women, who were already making plans for a liquid lunch at a nearby bar. "Please don't embarrass me. Or Wheezy. We've both worked really hard for this."

She expected at least one of them to reply with something sarcastic and scathing, but the two women shared a look before pulling her into their arms.

"I'm so proud of you, Ruby," one of them said. Ruby thought it might have been her mom, but she couldn't be sure. And to be perfectly honest, she didn't care. Both of these women meant so much to her—the one because she'd raised her to be a warrior, and the other because she'd reminded her what it meant to fight.

"I'm proud of me, too," she said somewhat mistily. "But for the love of everything, please don't show up drunk."

The day of the West Coast Canine Classic was always chaotic.

Most of the stage was set up in the two days preceding the event. They timed the show to occur in summer so they had free access to the high school gymnasium, where vendors and rental companies transformed the bleak white walls into a glittering blue-and-gold canopy. Fortunately for Spencer, Lawson always handled most of the details out front. Spencer was fine setting the locker rooms up as temporary dog dressing rooms, and he was happy helping the Rotary Club set up concessions, but dangling tassels from the ceiling and aiming spotlights had never been his strong suit.

"She's not here yet, so don't ask." Caleb sauntered up with his hands driven deep in his pockets, looking as though he didn't have a care in the world—which he probably didn't. Spencer's brother had been nothing but supportive over the last few days, but that was easy when everything he cared about wasn't on the line. "And, yes, I double-checked to make sure she and Wheezy are still on the list. As far as everyone here is concerned, she's nothing more than an ordinary entrant with a well-trained and well-bred dog to show—though I'm sure they'll revise that opinion after three-point-four seconds."

Spencer knew his brother was just trying to calm his nerves, but that only served to make them jitter harder.

"What if she doesn't come?" he demanded. "What if I never see her again?"

Caleb cast an obvious look around the main gym, where Lawson was overseeing the final touches being put into place. About half the dogs were already here, many of them in curlers with scarves wrapped around their carefully coiffed hair as they underwent their final preparations. An air of expectancy and excitement filled the air, months of hard work finally coming together. A few dogs were sniffing out the obstacle course; a few more were sniffing each other. It was all so familiar to Spencer, his favorite day of the year. Christmas was fine and birthdays were okay, but this—*this* was something worth celebrating.

Dogs. Dogs everywhere. Dogs who'd worked hard and played hard and lived hard. Dogs who *loved* hard.

"You see that bichon frise in the corner near the drinking fountains?" Caleb asked.

"Yes. That's Mortimer. He won his breed last year, though he couldn't eke it out over the Afghan for Best in Show."

"Oh my God, Spencer. You're pathetic."

"What? You asked."

Caleb nodded in the other direction, to where a Labrador was sitting stately and serene while his owner chatted at length with a breeder who was a friend of their parents. "And what about that Lab sitting with the Jacksons?"

Was this supposed to be some kind of test? To see how much time and mental energy Spencer dedicated to the West Coast Canine Classic? There was no need to play games—Spencer could tell him the answer.

A lot. It was a lot.

"You mean Nightmare? She's didn't place last year, but I feel like that might change. She's really improved her performance in the show ring. They have their sights set on Westminster."

Caleb nodded. "See? You have nothing to worry about. Ruby will be here."

As much as Spencer wanted—*needed*—to hear that, he didn't follow. "What does Nightmare have to do with it?"

"These dogs are the cream of the crop when it comes to Seattle. The most prestigious, the elites of the elite." Caleb laughed—actually laughed, as though Spencer's entire life's happiness didn't depend on the appearance of one woman. "Ruby will be here. That woman wouldn't pass up a chance to compete with the best. I don't think she can."

Spencer's whole heart yearned for that to be true—and, acknowledging his brother's certainty, he allowed himself to hope. For the past five days, all he'd wanted was to call Ruby up, send her an official invitation to the dog show, park himself in front of her apartment door and beg her to give him another chance. But he'd put himself in Caleb's hands for a reason.

"Okay." Spencer fingered the neckline of his shirt, which wasn't, for the first time in his life, buttoned up all the way to the top. It felt foreign, that open splay, the brush of air at his throat, but he liked it. "I believe you. She'll be here."

No sooner were the words out of his mouth than a commotion near the front drew his attention. He knew, without turning his eyes in that direction, that it was her. It had to be. No one else could enter a room in such a way that there were literal gasps from the crowd—of awe and wonder, of unadulterated delight.

"Fuck me." His brother released a low whistle. "I think maybe you should run and hide while you still have a chance. You're in a hell of a lot of trouble, Spencer. More than I could handle, that's for sure."

Although Spencer had promised to start taking more of his brother's advice, there was no way he was going to run away now. Not when every cell in his body was suddenly soaring. She was here. She'd come. She wasn't giving up on—

"Fuck me." Spencer echoed Caleb's words almost perfectly, though his mouth had grown so dry there was no way he could even pretend to whistle. There, at the threshold to a high school gymnasium filled with dogs, stood the most beautiful woman in the world.

She was also the most out of place. Although plenty of people dressed up for the event—some even coordinated their outfits to match their dog's—no one could boast a long, blue-green gown that dazzled in the light and skin that glowed with ethereal incandescence. Or, you know, a literal crown upon their head.

Despite how much she stood out, Ruby didn't bat a single false eyelash. She swept into the gym as though she owned it, unaware or uncaring of anything but the movement of her own feet.

At the sight of it—of *her*—Spencer's breath caught in his throat and almost choked him. Not because of how she looked but because of what that confident, unerring stride signified. That was the Ruby Taylor who competed to win. That was the Ruby Taylor who could conquer the world.

That was the Ruby Taylor he loved.

Spencer had no idea how long he might have stood there gawking, but the murmuring of the crowd was broken by a loud bark and the sudden scuffle of claws on hardwood. He barely had time to register the sight of a gawky, poorly groomed golden retriever headed his way before he was knocked flat on his back.

Wheezy was on top of him before he hit the floor, the dog's paws pushing at his face and his tongue working its way into places Spencer would have preferred to keep dry. Instead of feeling embarrassed at being caught in this state—making a fool out of himself in front of not just Ruby but a hundred people he considered his peers—he gave in and let the dog say hello.

"I've missed you, too, buddy," he said, running his hands over those golden curls, shorn too short but still like silk between his fingers. "I'm glad to see you've recovered from your overdose, but I don't know that I approve of the new look. Yes, yes, I know. It'll grow back. There's no need to bite me."

"Oh, for the love of everything. Must you two be so dramatic all the time?" Ruby appeared above them both, shining with a glittering light that had to be manufactured. As she came into focus, Spencer could see that it *was* manufactured. In addition to more crystal beads than he'd ever seen collected in one place before, she seemed to have been decked out from head to toe in some kind of glitter. "You're making a scene."

Spencer could have easily pointed out that a man being licked on a gymnasium floor was nothing compared to a fully gowned beauty pageant queen gliding around as though walking on air, but he didn't. He was too happy to see her—scowling, the light of battle in her eyes.

She was back.

"Hello, Ruby," he said in as level a voice as he could muster. He had to physically set Wheezy aside in order to struggle up to a seated position, but the dog was in a compliant mood for once. "I was hoping to see you today."

Her eyes narrowed at this, a suspicious twitch at the side of her mouth. "Why? What have you done?"

"You look beautiful. The glitter suits you."

The compliment did little to reduce her suspicions, even though Spencer was speaking the truth. She might have a complicated relationship with pageantry, but it was obvious she'd been born to wear a crown.

"He's right, you know." Caleb stepped forward and grabbed both of Ruby's hands. Without any hesitancy, he yanked. She was propelled into his arms, where he laughed and pressed a quick kiss on either of her cheeks. "You are, without a doubt, the most gorgeous bitch in this place, and I mean that literally."

Ruby rolled her eyes. "Why do I get the feeling that's not a compliment?"

"Because you didn't grow up around show dogs the way we did. Believe me when I tell you that we are surrounded by some of the best specimens of bitchery the world has to offer." Caleb reached down and patted Wheezy's head. "Present company excluded, of course."

Wheezy took no offense at this. He sat at Spencer's feet, looking unkempt and more like a dog than Spencer had ever seen him, with his tongue lolling and an occasional thump of his tail.

"Shouldn't you be passing around your business card and trying to drum up business or something?" Spencer asked with a pointed look toward the rest of the gym—*anywhere* in the rest of the gym. "I thought you came here to schmooze."

"I *am* schmoozing," Caleb protested with a wink at Ruby. "But I can take a hint when it's being thrown at my face. Ruby, if this were a competition for humans, you'd be far and away the winner. Since it's one for dogs, I can only wish you luck." He glanced down at Wheezy, who was scratching at his ear with uncouth enthusiasm, and laughed. "Lots of it."

With a whistle on his lips and a twinkle in his eye, Caleb took himself off.

"Eva is around here somewhere, and I know she wanted to say hello, but I wouldn't seek out Lawson unless you want to be put to work hanging bunting." Spencer spoke as though the entire last week hadn't happened. It *had* happened, as the dark scruff along his jaw and the rings under his eyes could attest, but he was trying not to dwell too much on that. For once in his life, he wasn't the well-put-together, well-rested man who had everything figured out. He was sad and exhausted, but he was also hopeful.

She was here. She'd come. She meant to see this thing through to the end.

"My parents will also probably accost you at some point, but they won't bother you for long. They're friends with a lot of the other breeders, so this is their social event of the year."

Ruby gave a startled jump. Her skin shimmered as the glitter caught the light, but Spencer was pretty sure he caught a glimpse of red rising up from the neckline of her gown and creeping up the right side of her neck. He'd been trying not to focus too much on how bare and enticing the skin of her shoulders was, but that sudden flash held him transfixed. He lifted a hand to touch her before remembering where—and who—he was and dropping his hand.

"Your rash isn't healed yet?" he asked just as she stammered a nervous "Your parents are here?"

She was the first to corral her thoughts. "I'm feeling much better now, thanks." And, more stiffly, "Of course I'll say hello to your parents, but I'm not really here for a friendly visit. I came to compete. Wheezy and I both did."

"I know. I look forward to your performance."

The suspicion that had carried her over here magnified tenfold. "Why? What did you do?"

"Nothing."

"Spencer, if you said anything to anyone—if you changed the scoring categories in any way…"

"I didn't touch a thing."

"Then why do you look so smug?"

He had no idea that he looked anything but hopelessly in love. "I'm not smug. I'm happy to see you, that's all." It was a moment for intimacy and a low, quiet voice, but he had to raise his to be heard over the general din. "I've missed you."

This confession did little to reassure her. Although she already stood like a beacon, she straightened and seemed to gain two inches in the process. "I swear on everything you love, Spencer, if you did anything to grease Wheezy's wheels, I'll never forgive you. I know you meant to be nice and that you thought you were doing me a favor by handing me a dog-show trophy, but if that's the person you think I am, then—"

"You," he said, unable and unwilling to let her finish that sentence. He knew how it ended: *then we're through, then I never want to see you again, then you aren't the man I need you to be*. Each one of those options made his blood run cold.

She blinked, clearly taken aback. "Me what?"

"You swore on everything I love," he said. This was dangerous territory, but he had to say it. She had to know. "That's you. You're everything I love."

Instead of being touched by this confession, Ruby put her hands on her hips. "Spencer, don't."

"Sorry. I know there's a good chance you don't feel the same, but I had to say it."

"Well, don't say it again. I'm here to win a dog show, not entrap one of the judges into doing my bidding." She cast a quick furtive glance around the gym. Several people were watching them, some sidling close enough to overhear, so she leaned close and lowered her voice. "I don't need your charity. I know my life isn't the glamorous picture I made it out to be, but it's mine. I'm sorry for lying about what I did for a living, but I'm not sorry for who I am. If you aren't willing to hold Wheezy—and me—to the same high standards you hold for everyone else, then we have no place here."

"Then it's a good thing I'm not one of the judges," he said.

There was no way Wheezy could understand the conversation they were having, but the length of it was starting to make him feel neglected. He fell to the floor with a dramatic slump. Since Ruby was holding the other end of his leash, she slumped with him.

"Wait—what? Spencer. *What?*"

He smiled. He hadn't been sure that such a thing was possible when so much between them was up in the air, but the look of incredulity she shot him demanded nothing less. His parents and Lawson had experienced similar reactions to the news, though Lawson must have sensed something was up because he got over it pretty quickly. And as for Eva, well, Spencer's ears were still ringing with her response.

She'd been disbelieving and then outraged and then had burst into a flood of tears. Spencer had found that last reaction bewildering until Maury showed up with a box of tissues and a comforting arm. Early pregnancy always hit Eva that way. They had to issue a blanket statement at work that the veterinarian sobbing over every kitten's perfect toe beans wasn't a sign that the animal had to be put down.

Through those tears, Eva had called him every bad name she knew. Considering she was bilingual and had grown up with a father who hadn't shied away from teaching his kids all the best Spanish swear words, they had numbered quite a few.

"If it makes you feel any better, I've already been raked over the coals by Eva," he said. "Several times, in fact."

"Eva?" Ruby echoed with another glance around the gym. She didn't find what she was looking for. Eva was busy backstage making sure that everything unrolled exactly as it should. Early pregnancy made her weepy, but it didn't quell her energy levels in the least.

"She'll probably come find you later, so you don't have to worry. You'll have plenty of time to abuse me behind my back. I can't decide whether she's angrier at me for giving up my judging post or being so stupid as to offer to throw the show for you, but I'm leaning toward the second one." His smile faltered. "I didn't realize what I was doing, Ruby. I mean, I *did*, obviously, but not what it meant—not what an insult it would be to someone as strong and capable as you. I wanted to whisk you into my arms and kiss away every problem you have. Hell, I still do—and if I thought for one second it was what you needed from me, I'd do it. But I know now what a terrible idea that is. Caleb set me straight."

This apology didn't appear to comfort her. Her mouth flattened to a thin line.

"Take it back," she demanded.

"What? The fact that I love you? I can't."

"It's not true," she countered with an angry wave of her hand. "The thing you really love is this dog show. You know it as well as I do. The rules and the neat little rows of animals, the way all of them do exactly what they're told."

"I can still love it without being a judge."

She seemed perilously close to stomping her foot at him, but Spencer knew she wouldn't. Ruby was no stranger to maintaining her composure under pressure. "Spencer, it's not any better. Don't you get it? Whether you're offering to hand me a trophy or resigning from the judging panel, it all boils down to the same thing. I don't want you to change your principles for me. I don't want you to change anything."

His heart gave a lopsided thump. "You wouldn't change anything? Anything at all?"

A small grunt of irritation escaped her lips. "You're a stubborn, judgmental, competitive neat freak, but that's what I love about you. Lov*ed*," she corrected herself hastily, but it was too late. The word had escaped. It was in the air now, pulsating between them, stripping every other human and animal in the room away.

"You're such a bastard, you know that? You were supposed to be the one man who didn't give me a free pass because of how I look, who didn't smooth my path because you wanted to sleep with me. For the past two months, I've woken up every single day determined to make the most of every minute—to beat you at your own game, to force myself to match you stride for stride. Do you know how long it's been since I've felt that way? Since I've been anything but resigned and bored with my life?"

He shook his head. "No. Tell me."

That pushed her even closer to the brink. Tucking a wayward strand of hair behind her ear, she took a step toward him. It was a step of intent and challenge, and it made every nerve ending he had vibrate at once. "Ten years. Ten long, flat, wasted years."

"They weren't wasted," he said and meant it. "I think you're pretty amazing just the way you are."

"No." She flung a hand up and stepped back once again, but the distance didn't matter. His nerve endings hadn't stopped reacting to her presence. She didn't want to change him. She liked—no, *loved*—him the way he was.

Spencer Wilson, veterinarian and former dog-show judge, a little stiff upon first meeting but not a bad guy once you got to know him.

"You don't get to say that and then refuse to judge me and Wheezy," she said. "You don't get to say that and then resign. I can take whatever you have to throw at me. I *will* take it. And then I'll come back next year and try again—and the year after that and the year after that. It might take me another decade, but you'll see what I'm capable of."

His heart swelled at the fierce determination that tightened her jaw and pursed her lips, caused the skin underneath all that glitter to glow.

"I already know what you're capable of," he said. "And I became ineligible as a judge the moment you stood in my living room and dared me to admit how I felt about you. You know that as well as I do."

She faltered, the firm set of her lips quavering at the edges. Tears sparked in her eyes, but he already knew she wouldn't let them fall.

"You are, without a doubt, the most determined, kindhearted, resilient person I know," he said. He gave in to the urge to grab her hand.

Like the rest of her, it was shining and perfect from a distance. Up close, however, it still bore several large welts and angry red patches.

He lifted that perfectly imperfect hand to his lips and kissed it.

"I don't need a pageant or a dog show to tell me any of that. Trust me—anyone who's spent more than five minutes in your company knows it." Ruby made a motion to draw her hand away, but he held fast. "Which is why I found a replacement judge who will not only rip you and Wheezy to pieces but who will most likely leave both of you in tears before this day is through."

Her hand stilled in his. "You did what?"

He chuckled softly. "Did you think I was going to leave this whole thing to Eva and Lawson? I love them both to death, but they're not nearly harsh enough to provide the criticism these animals need. And yes, Wheezy, I'm talking to you. You are, without a doubt, the poorest specimen of a show dog I've ever seen in my life. Even with those falsified papers—"

Ruby stiffened and placed herself in a protective stance in front of the dog. "You can't prove that DNA test was his. I never agreed to it. Mrs. Orson didn't give her consent."

"Even with those falsified papers," he echoed, fighting the laugh that rose to his lips, "I predict that you two will go down as the worst candidates the West Coast Canine Classic has ever had the misfortune to see. And I'm including a few years ago when a bull terrier and an Irish wolfhound got into the school kitchen and ate three bags of frozen fish sticks."

"Is that a challenge?" she asked, her shoulders squared to meet him. Spencer had never been so happy to see anything in his life. There was still a lot that had to be said between them, and he wasn't sure if Ruby would ever be able to forgive him, but she was back to fighting form, and that was all that mattered.

"Yes, Ruby," he said, meeting her gaze and holding it. "It is."

"Then you'd better point me in the direction of the dressing room." She wrapped the end of Wheezy's leash firmly around her hand and gave it a tug. "Wheezy and I have a lot of work to do."

Chapter 22

THAT DOG, I'M SORRY TO SAY, IS THE LEAST QUALIFIED GOLDEN retriever I've ever witnessed in action."

Ruby stood in the center of the show ring, where Wheezy lay in an unmoving heap. Several hundred people were seated on the bleachers on either side of her—both unfamiliar faces and familiar ones, including Mrs. Orson, her mother, and Eva's entire family. An announcer in a gold jacket stood poised with a microphone placed to his lips, but for the first time in the hour he'd been at work, he had nothing to say.

The judge was saying it all for him.

"I don't know who sold you this animal or what convinced you to enter him in a dog show, but he's an abomination against everything the AKC upholds." The judge, a woman of about Ruby's age in a well-cut suit and black head wrap, lifted a finger and pointed it at Wheezy. "He's sluggish. He has poor stature. His head is well formed and he has intelligent eyes, but he needs some serious grooming before he comes anywhere near this competition again. And don't even get me started on his training."

Ruby nodded her understanding and continued to let the wave of criticism wash over her. It felt good, like a baptismal cleansing followed by a painfully deep massage. She knew it. She'd known it all along. Wheezy was the last dog on earth who should be given a trophy, either because she was in a sort-of relationship with one of the dog-show organizers or because he was anything approaching show-quality.

He was, quite literally, the worst.

Ruby braced herself for more feedback along the same lines. It was no more than she deserved. For the past ten minutes, she'd been unable to haul Wheezy away from the show ring. Exhausted with the labors of being brushed and fed and lavished with an inordinate amount of care, he'd had enough.

But when the judge spoke again, it wasn't to her.

"Then again, I don't know what I expected from an animal trained by Caleb Wilson. Let me guess... You thought you could charm him into doing your bidding, is that it? A smile and a laugh, and you'd have him eating out of the palm of your hand?"

Caleb nudged Ruby out of the way to take her place in the hot seat. Like her, he'd been unable to get Wheezy to do much of anything once the dog decided that the most ideal place to nap was directly in front of the judging table. Unlike her, he'd been laughing almost the whole time.

"I can't charm anyone into doing something they weren't already planning to do," he countered. "You should know that better than anyone, Jada. I only provide an outlet for the urges that are already there."

Ruby had never been more grateful for her years of stage training. She called on every ounce of willpower she had to stop herself from laughing out loud. She'd been so caught up in getting Wheezy to jump through at least *one* hoop before he exited the show ring that she'd failed to notice the way that judge was eyeing Caleb.

It was a sensation she'd felt toward the other Wilson twin far too many times to be ignorant of its power. There was deep, unyielding annoyance in that gaze...and way more lust than was good for anyone.

On the other side of the judges' table, Eva covered her own amusement with a cough. "As much as I'm sure we'd all love to debate Mr. Wilson's capabilities as a dog trainer, I think we should get things moving. Lawson, do you think you could, ah, urge our contestant to leave the ring?"

Lawson rose to his feet and cracked his knuckles. With an apologetic shrug for Ruby, he started to make his way toward them. The sound of a familiar male voice stopped him before he made it halfway.

"I probably should have mentioned that the replacement judge I chose and my brother have a somewhat…torrid history," that voice said near her ear. Spencer was so close that Ruby could feel the vibrations of his breath tingling up and down her spine. "I don't know all the details, but from what I understand, Jada once threw his television out a window. I can't say I blame her. I'm often tempted to do the same."

Ruby felt her lips start to twitch.

"I wanted to make sure you didn't feel like I was favoring you in any way, so one of Caleb's angry ex-girlfriends seemed like the best way to go. There were several to choose from, but Jada has always been my favorite."

The twitch of her lips became a bona fide smile.

"Sorry about this, your honors." He gave the judges a small wave before stepping forward with a cheeseburger in his hand. "I'll have him cleared away and out of your hair in a second."

Eva and Lawson could tell what was coming next, but Jada only stood and stared as Spencer dangled the cheeseburger at Wheezy with a complete lack of irony.

"What are you giving that dog, Spencer?" Jada demanded. "He's already fifteen pounds over show weight."

Despite all her mother's admonitions echoing inside her head, the laughter finally escaped. In the past hour, Ruby had withstood a useless show dog, a restlessly agitated crowd, and a torrent of abuse from the harshest judge she'd ever met—and without so much as a blink of her false eyelashes. The sight of Spencer luring Wheezy out of the gym with a cheeseburger, however, was the thing that was going to break her.

"Don't worry," Spencer said cheerfully. "I'm not going to give it to him. The carrot in my pocket is the only treat he's getting today."

Spencer proceeded to make light work of removing Wheezy from the center circle. Ruby could have sworn the two of them must have planned it ahead of time, because Wheezy sprang to his feet and trotted out of the room with barely a second glance at the food in Spencer's hand.

Since her work here was unarguably done, Ruby lifted her hand in her most pageanty wave and followed them to the utility hallway, the crowd roaring with laughter behind them.

"I hope you're happy with that little performance," Spencer said as she shut the gym door. He tossed the cheeseburger to the dog, who promptly wolfed it down. "I don't think I've ever seen anything less dignified in my whole life."

She paused a moment to give her eyes a chance to adjust—and for her heart to adapt to the sudden tightening that enfolded it. That sounded exactly like the Spencer she knew, the Spencer she'd fallen in love with. A little bit stern and a whole lot sexy, refusing to settle for anything other than the best.

"I hope you're talking to the dog right now, because my execution out there was flawless," she said.

He turned, his eyes widened in surprise. "Ruby! I didn't know you followed me." He lifted a hand to reach for her before dropping it again. "Of course I was talking to Wheezy. I would never say that about you, *could* never—"

"I repeat," she said carefully, "my execution was flawless. Obedient and beautiful and everything you look for in a contestant."

Wheezy must have noticed the tense note in her voice because he finished his snack and cocked a quizzical head at her. The golden retriever understood what Spencer hadn't yet—that what she needed from him weren't flowery compliments on how she looked and sweet nothings about her performance. Those things were fine in a man she dated casually or saw only on weekends, but when it came to her partner—her equal—she demanded a lot more.

She didn't move, not even to blink, her breath suspended as she waited for him to respond.

It was worth the wait. *He* was worth it.

"If you believe that, then you don't know anything about me." He took a step closer, drawing so near that the air around her was displaced. There was no touching, but she could feel the warmth of him, the familiar comforts of his strength and solidity. "Anyone—any animal, I mean—can learn how to follow the rules. When it comes to a *real* winner, what I like is a combination of personality, strength, and resilience."

"Oh?" Her heart thumped heavily, her stomach settling somewhere between knots and butterflies. He was doing it. He was playing the game. He was meeting her exactly where she needed him to be.

"It's not an easy combination to find, especially in the more decorative breeds."

"Who are you calling decorative?" she demanded.

"Not Wheezy, that's for sure." He leaned close, his lips not quite touching hers. She could taste the outline of them, sense the quiver as they drew near. "I had a different creature in mind."

"Tell me more," she said. "What else do you like?"

"Well, the shape of the head is very important."

Considering that their mouths were almost brushing, their bodies drawn like magnets toward each other, this was a moment for eloquence and sexual promise—for the eternal language of love. Instead, something perilously like a giggle rose to her lips.

"I like a good set of haunches, too," he said. She felt the curve of his smile. "Strong and firm—something you can feel pulsing under your hand."

"This is starting to sound like an awfully tall order."

"It is," he said, and this time, all the humor went out of his voice. "About five foot nine, is my guess."

She stiffened.

"I know you don't want to hear it, Ruby," he said. "You want me to be the man who challenges you and pushes you, who looks at you and sees not just a beautiful woman but a force to be reckoned with—and I do. I promise I do."

"But?"

His hand came up and cupped the side of her face. She didn't want to lean into it—didn't want to need him—but she did. She so completely did.

"But I also love you. More than I thought possible—more than all the dog shows and beauty pageants in the world. More than my job and my house and everything else that I've come to realize doesn't matter if I don't have you to share them with."

"You gave up your dog show for me," she said. "I told you not to do that."

"I didn't give it up. I recused myself. It's different."

"How do you figure?"

He paused. In the long moment that ensued, Ruby's heart leapt to her throat and stayed there. Spencer's next words mattered so much more than he knew.

"The truth is, I've lost my taste for judging," he said. He shrugged his shoulder in a way that reinforced his words, but she couldn't bring herself to believe it. "I know it sounds stupid, but it's true. I'm tired of looking at the world like I'm running through a checklist, seeing things only in accordance with a predetermined set of rules. Sometimes, I just want to like a dog for being a very good dog. And I want to love a woman for the exact same reason."

"Spencer, you don't mean it," she begged, but her heart wasn't in it. She wanted him to mean it. She *needed* him to.

"Would it help if I also told you that it was a really bad move to put glitter on top of your rash?" he asked. "And that you're starting to look like a plague victim again?"

Her chest expanded until it seemed that the whole of the universe wouldn't be enough to contain it. That had to be the strangest declaration of love she'd ever heard, but it was also the best. Because it came from Spencer. Because it didn't allow either of them to be complacent. With this man by her side, she'd always be on her toes.

"I don't need you to give me medical advice," she said, but there was no sting to her words. Only her face. "For your information, you're speaking to a woman who was recently accepted into the nursing program at North Seattle College. I'm practically an expert."

Spencer broke out into one of the widest and most genuine smiles she'd seen from him. There was no sign of the dark-lashed, brooding menace of their earlier meetings. There was only a man who was prepared to share her every sorrow, her every joy. Her life.

"Ruby, that's fantastic. You'll be an amazing nurse."

"I know I will. I've already given a dog an enema. I'm pretty sure it's all downhill from there."

Mentioning the enema caused a whimper to sound from the direction of their feet. Wheezy sat up at full attention, full of the energy he'd been lacking during the dog show.

"Wheezy, is that another word you like?" Ruby asked. She tried again. "Enema. E-ne-ma."

With a start, Wheezy took off running down the hallway, his leash dragging behind him. She'd never seen him move so fast and would have taken off after him, but Spencer put his arms around her waist and refused to let go.

"There's nothing down there but locked doors and an empty stairwell. He'll be fine."

"I'm not worried about his health and safety," she countered. "I'm just curious what else that word will get him to do. Maybe that's the secret to his success. You can train him with mayonnaise. I can train him with enemas."

Spencer's whole body shook with laughter as he tightened his grip and pulled her in. "You are not running around on a stage shouting 'enema' at a dog. This is a family show."

"I'll shout anything I want," she said, but considering that Spencer had started kissing her, she wasn't sure he heard her.

Just to check—and to ensure that the kissing didn't stop anytime soon—she added, "Something like...porcupine."

He pulled back, with laughter lifting his lips and a dark, meaningful glint in his eyes. "Don't even think about it. I finally found a copy of that book, and I've never been so scandalized in my life. You can't possibly expect me to do all those things. Some of them didn't seem physically possible."

Ruby's heart, already so full, practically overflowed. "You read it?"

"Of course I did," he said. He dropped a kiss up her jawline and down her neck, not stopping until he was buried deep in her hair. "I'm not saying I want to join your book club, but I'm starting to see the appeal."

"Oh, really?" She arched her neck to give him better access, reveling in the soft, sensual way he trailed kisses everywhere he landed. He might not be up to porcupine levels of daring—yet—but Ruby wasn't a woman to give in easily. "And what's that?"

"They always end happily," he said and swept her into his arms. "Just like you and me."

Epilogue

THE THING IS, RUBY, YOU'D REALLY BE DOING US A FAVOR. WE DON'T have anyone else."

Ruby sat cross-legged in the middle of Spencer's bed, her phone on speaker. Not only had Spencer come in to hear what Parkwood Manor had to say that was so urgent it interrupted dinner, but Caleb, Mrs. Orson, Eva, and at least two of her children also seemed to be pushing their way in.

The room was packed. It was a good thing Spencer was so tidy.

"I appreciate the offer, I really do, but I'm no longer interested in being a nursing assistant. I don't know if you heard, but I recently started college classes and—"

"We'll give you a raise. You can set your own hours. We're really struggling here. Harry left us in a huge mess."

A muffled cackle arose from the assembled crowd. Ruby mistrusted that sound almost as much as she mistrusted this unprecedented show of begging and generosity from her former employers.

"What kind of mess?" she asked.

"You haven't heard?" A groan sounded on the other end of the line. "There was a sting operation. An exposé. Someone uncovered a drug ring that Harry was running behind everyone's backs."

All those things sounded less like Harry Gunderson and more like Rosemary Orson. Ruby turned to the older woman with a glare. Sure enough, Mrs. Orson was laughing to herself and stroking her chin like a cartoon villain.

"I'm sorry to hear that," Ruby said, trying to keep her voice from wavering. "But if you'll recall, I warned you about him."

"Yes, and that's why we're prepared to offer you—"

"You told me to stop being so dramatic."

Her former boss cleared his throat nervously. "I apologize for that, but at the time—"

"You said I wasn't qualified to make those kinds of judgment calls."

"Did I? I don't recall—"

Ruby decided she was done with the groveling. She was only a few weeks into her new classes at the community college, and getting into the groove of higher education after her disastrous high school career was a lot more challenging than she'd thought it would be, but that was half the fun. There was no way she was going back now—not for anything Parkwood Manor had to offer.

"What kind of sting operation was it?" she asked.

"That's confidential information, I'm afraid." Now that her ex-boss had been rejected, he was back to sounding stiff and pompous. "I can only tell you if you come back as an employee."

Considering how hard Mrs. Orson was struggling to keep her composure, Ruby was pretty sure she had access to all the confidential information she needed.

"As tempting as the offer is, I'm a solid no," she said sweetly. "But I'm sure I'll see you around. Now that I'm just a visitor and all. Buh-bye!"

She hung up the phone before the voices around her broke into a babble. Amid the exclamations, Ruby zeroed in on the one person who had all the answers.

"Mrs. Orson, what did you do?"

"I don't know what you mean, dear. Have you started the new novel for book club yet? Darla and I aren't sure about it yet. The hero is a touch milquetoast for our tastes. We like a man who takes control in the bedroom. Don't you agree, Spencer?"

Spencer took a step back, his hands up. "I'm not touching this one."

"And I'm not letting you change the subject," Ruby said. Xavier crawled up onto the bed and placed himself in Ruby's lap. Ever since the news of his mother's fourth pregnancy, he'd been feeling a little overwhelmed, so he popped a thumb in his mouth and settled in. Ruby put an arm around him but refused to be distracted. "What kind of sting operation did you run, and why wasn't I invited to be a part of it?"

"I told you we had it handled."

"Did you plant drugs on him? Put dye in the fake pills so his mouth turned blue? Poison him?"

Mrs. Orson laughed. "Poison didn't occur to us. That would have been fun, too."

"Please don't give her any ideas." Spencer groaned and joined Ruby on the bed.

No sooner had he settled himself in than a small creature climbed up into his lap as well. His wasn't human. The three-month-old border collie had cost them a small fortune—Spencer's parents didn't believe in family discounts—but he'd been worth every penny. Ruby didn't know much about dog breeding, but even she could see that the perfect black-and-white patchwork of his fur was something to behold.

Not that it mattered. Spencer refused to train him to do anything but cuddle. Since they only had partial custody of Caesar these days, and Wheezy only paid them an occasional visit, it had seemed wise to add to their collection. There was more than enough love in this house to go around.

"If you didn't plant drugs, what did you do?" Ruby asked. "Or—wait. Is it possible to be an accessory after the fact? Maybe I don't want to know."

Mrs. Orson laughed. "We didn't break any laws, so don't look so worried. It was your mother's idea, actually. We videotaped him in the act."

Ruby and Spencer shared a look of understanding. Of all the things Ruby had never expected out of a relationship like this one, the sharing of family burdens was at the top of the list. The day she and Spencer had decided to make things official, she'd acquired a charmingly unreliable twin brother and he'd been granted a dramatically overbearing mother.

It was wonderful.

"I helped them set it up," Caleb said. "I had no idea your mom was such an audiovisual enthusiast. Some of that equipment she has is really valuable."

"Equipment?" Ruby echoed. "What kind of equipment could she possibly have?"

"She said something about it belonging to Stepfather Trois," Mrs. Orson said. "Apparently, he was a big fan of recording them during—"

Spencer had spent enough time learning about Ruby's trio of stepfathers that he jumped to his feet and brought the entire conversation to an end. He also somehow managed to get everyone out the door, including Xavier, and all while the puppy remained cradled in his arms.

"That was a close one," he said as he pushed the bedroom door shut and leaned against it to prevent anyone from sneaking back inside. "What happened to Stepfather Trois, if you don't mind me asking? I know the first one snuck out in the dead of night and the second one left in a fury, but where did the third one go?"

Ruby shrugged and unfolded herself from the bed. They'd eventually have to get back out to the barbecue, but it was nice to have this moment first. She drew close and ran a finger under the puppy's chin. The tiny puppy allowed it but didn't bask in it—which made sense. He liked Spencer best.

So did Ruby.

"For all I know, she murdered him and buried him out somewhere underneath all my old pageant stuff," she admitted. "Maybe that's why she won't get rid of it. It's hiding the bones of all the men who broke her heart. We Taylor women aren't easily scorned."

"Is that a threat?" Spencer asked. He didn't sound alarmed so much as intrigued.

"You know me, Spencer," she said and grinned. "Nothing I say is a threat. Only a challenge."

This sparkling, escapist, feel-good rom-com brings together a grumpy hero, a sunshiney heroine, delicious forced proximity, and enough puppies to make anyone smile.

When Sophie Vasquez and her sisters dreamed up Puppy Promise—their service puppy training school—it was supposed to be her chance to bring some good into the world. But how can she expect to do anything when no one will take her seriously?

Enter Harrison Parks: a rough, gruff, take-no-bull wildlife firefighter in need of a diabetic service dog. He couldn't be a more unlikely fit for Sophie or Bubbles—the sweet puppy she knows will be his perfect partner—but when Sophie insists he give them both a shot, something unexpected happens: he listens. Even better, he keeps on listening, even as Sophie and Bubbles turn his lonely, uber-masculine world upside-down.

As it turns out, they all have something to prove...and more than enough room in their hearts for a little puppy love.

Chapter 1

NOW *THAT* WAS A DOG.

Harrison Parks stood in front of the Great Dane puppy, watching as he stumbled over his feet and struggled with the weight of his oversize head. Already, the animal's sleek gray fur was something to behold, those beautiful eyes like the sky after a rainstorm. It was easy to see what he would someday become—majestic and muscled and massive, more like a trusty steed than a canine.

"He's perfect. Where do I sign?"

A cough sounded at his back. "Um, that's a Great Dane."

Harrison turned to find the slight, well-dressed woman who'd greeted him at the door. She looked apologetic and hesitant and, well, the same way most people looked when they met him for the first time.

In other words, like this was the last place in the world she wanted to be—and he the last man she wanted there with her.

"I thought he might be." He attempted a smile. "What's his name?"

"Rock."

Yes. Rock—durable and solid, the kind of dog a man could count on. Harrison crouched and put a hand out to the animal, his fingers closed in a fist the way the woman, Sophie Vasquez, had shown him. It seemed like overkill, this careful approach to an animal who hadn't yet reached six months of age, but what did he know? The closest he'd come to having a pet was the raccoon that lived under his back porch.

"I think he likes me."

Sophie coughed again, louder this time. "Rock is great, but he's a stability dog, I'm afraid."

Harrison turned to look up at her, struck again by how out of place she seemed among this room of scurrying puppies. It wasn't just her air of fragility, which made it seem as though a strong wind would topple her over. It wasn't her age either, although her short crop of dark brown hair and her round, sweet face made him suspect she was still in the youthful flush of her twenties.

No, it was the ruffled dress she wore, which seemed better suited for a tea party than a dog kennel.

He did his best to smile again. He was trying *not* to scare her away within the first ten minutes. It wouldn't be the first time he'd done that to a woman. Or a man. Or, if he was being honest, any living creature with a heart in its chest and eyes in its head. He wasn't saying he was a *bad*-looking man—a bit rough around the edges, maybe—but he did have a tendency to come across more forcefully than he intended. His friends blamed it on what they called his "resting brick face." *Like you're going to throw the next man who crosses you into a brick wall*, they laughed.

Which was all well and good after a long day of work, but it wasn't the least bit helpful here.

Just smile and relax, they said. *Be yourself. And for God's sake, lower your guard an inch or two to let in some air.*

Well, he'd tried. The smile—both of them—had already fallen flat, and the idea of relaxing under that woman's wide-eyed stare was impossible. No one had warned him that the puppy trainer was going to be a delicate, fragile wisp of feminine perfection. One of those things he *might* have been able to handle, but all of them?

Yeah, his guard was going to stay right where it was. It gave him someplace to hide.

"What's a stability dog?" he managed to ask.

"Well," she began, "some of our clients need dogs that can provide physical support."

When he didn't do more than nod encouragingly, she added, "As he grows up, Rock will be great at leading someone with vision issues or providing a safe landing for someone prone to seizures. You know—for stability."

"Oh." Harrison blinked. "I don't need that."

"Not really, no."

"Well, what about that one, then? He looks like he knows his way around a back alley or two."

He nodded toward the bulldog in the next slot over. Like Rock the Great Dane, this one was prancing about in one of a dozen half-walled pens built in an extension off the back of Sophie's house. Unlike other dog kennels, Puppy Promise kept none of their animals fully caged in. They had room to climb and jump and pop their heads up to say a friendly hello to their neighbors. And they did too, wet noses being pressed and kissed from one animal to another. When added to the bright-blue walls and not-unpleasant smell of organic cleaning solutions and puppy breath, the result was strangely inviting.

"Rusty?" Sophie asked as the wriggling, wrinkly puppy came bounding forward. His expression held a belligerence that appealed to Harrison on a visceral level. This dog might not be as physically intimidating as a Great Dane, but he sensed a kindred spirit. *Grump and grumpier.* "No, you don't want him. He'll be a nice emotional support dog someday, but he can't smell worth anything."

Harrison bit back his disappointment and allowed his gaze to skim over the other options. He immediately bypassed a tall white poodle that looked as if it had been recently permed and a tiny, yappy thing with eyes like raisins. A soft golden retriever with a mournful expression peeped up at him from the corner. "How about—"

Sophie coughed once more, cutting him short. When he turned to see what the problem was this time, he found her standing a few paces back, holding her hands out in front of her as if warding him off. His gaze was immediately drawn to those hands—so smooth and soft, her nails carefully polished to match her outfit. His own hands were like burned leather, cracked and callused all over. That was what happened when you spent half of your life battling wildfires. What the elements didn't scorch, the flames did.

"What is it?" he asked, his heart sinking at the sight of those hands. They were *nice* hands, obviously, but he knew what that gesture meant. *Harrison Parks has done it again.* Ten minutes in this woman's company and she'd already seen through his sorry exterior to the even sorrier contents of his soul.

"The truth is, Mr. Parks, we only have one dog right now that matches your specific needs."

"Okay." He swallowed. "Which one is he?"

"He's a female, actually. And she's really sweet."

"Female? Sweet?" Harrison could work with that. In fact, he quite liked both of those things, despite all evidence to the contrary.

"Oh yes. You wouldn't believe the nose she's got on her. I don't think I've ever worked with a more promising puppy. We were lucky to get our hands on her. Most of our animals come from breeders, but this one was rescued from a puppy mill. She's fantastic, even if she is still a little skittish."

Skittish could have applied to several people in his life right now, including the woman standing opposite him. Ever since *the episode* last week, everyone—from his boss at the Department of Natural Resources to his doctors to his very own father—was acting as though he, like Sophie Vasquez, was one strong wind away from toppling over.

But he was *fine.* It was one small coma. He'd get a dog, and it wouldn't happen again.

"She may need some extra work because of it, but I promise she'll be worth it in the end." Sophie broke into a smile—her first since he'd walked in. It struck him forcibly that it was a good thing she'd been too wary to pull it out before now. A smile like that, so warm and real, was a transformative thing. It made him almost happy to be here.

Almost.

"The best things in life usually are, don't you think?" Without waiting for an answer, she added, "Come on. I'll introduce you. She's been eyeing you since we walked in. I think she knows you're going to become good friends."

Harrison didn't have time to fully absorb that remark before a tiny bark assailed his ears. A *very* tiny bark. One might even call it a yap.

"The great thing about this dog is that she's highly portable. You can carry her everywhere."

Portable? Carry her?

He stopped and tried to dig his feet into the concrete, suddenly seeing the oncoming disaster with perfect clarity. Unfortunately, there were some things he couldn't resist, no matter how hard he tried.

One was the power of a beautiful woman's smile.

Another was the force of a 100,000-acre forest fire devouring everything in its path.

And a third, apparently, was a pair of raisin eyes lifted to his in trusting supplication.

"You've got to be kidding me," he said as the miniature ball of fluff twirled and stuck a small pink tongue out the side of her mouth.

This couldn't be right. He was a man who spent literal *weeks* in the wilderness, fighting fatigue and flames. He walked for days with an ax over one shoulder and a team of men at his back. He needed a trusted companion, a sturdy beast he could count on to keep him alive.

Not...

"This is a joke, right? Someone put you up to it?"

"No joke, Mr. Parks," Sophie said. "Please allow me to introduce you to your new diabetic service dog, Bubbles."

It was a truth universally acknowledged that a large, gruff man in search of a puppy would always choose the largest, gruffest one he could find.

Sophie didn't know how or why it happened, but every time a man entered the kennel, he was drawn inexorably toward the animal most like him in appearance. It was as though they walked up to each pen and, instead of seeing the puppy for its strengths and talents, they saw a mirror instead. Like getting dressed in the morning or buying a car, they wanted a puppy that exactly reflected the image they presented to the world.

Which was why she'd known, the second Harrison Parks walked in the door, that she was doomed.

"Now, I know what you're thinking," she said, watching the expression that crossed his face as his gaze shifted from Bubbles to the Great Dane and back again. *Disappointment* was a disappointingly inadequate word for it.

"No, you don't."

"And I know she's probably not what you had in mind when you signed up for this, but she's very suitable for your needs."

"No, she's not."

"Small dogs require a lot of care, which means you'll be forced to slow down a little when you're working. That's a good thing, right? To be reminded to take more breaks, to put your needs first?"

"No, that's a terrible thing."

"Plus, Pomeranians are much better suited for this type of job than you'd think. They have exceptional noses."

"No."

That was all he offered this time—just that one syllable, that one deeply rumbling sound, a death knell meant to end any and all discussion on a project that she'd thrown her whole self into prepping for. She wasn't sure which part of it caused her to crack, but she suspected it was that last one.

Well, either that or the fact that he looked so unfairly good while he did it. From the top of his disheveled brown locks to the tips of his heavy work boots, Harrison Parks was exactly what she'd imagined when she'd heard about his case. The man was a wildland firefighter, a hero. Every year, when flames swept across the dry lands of the Pacific Northwest's interior, he headed out with his hose and his determination until every last spark was gone. He was tall and muscular, his expression weary with the devastation he'd seen.

A bit on the crusty side, Oscar had described him, *but totally harmless.*

What he hadn't said was that Harrison was also a half-buttoned flannel shirt away from being the quintessential lumbersexual—rugged and outdoorsy and built like a tank.

In other words, he was a Great Dane. A bulldog.

And he wasn't giving either Bubbles or her a fair shot.

"Listen, Mr. Parks." The sharp rap of her voice startled even herself. "I appreciate that Bubbles isn't what you had in mind, but you need to at least consider what she has to offer."

His gaze—that hard, disappointed one—snapped in her direction, and Sophie instinctively froze. Now that she'd uttered her reproach, she wasn't sure what came next. Her sister Lila would probably segue into an articulate and professional speech about the Pomeranian's finer points. Her other sister, Dawn, would try a coy smile and a low purr to get her way.

Sophie didn't have any such methods for handling recalcitrant clients. No one had let her *have* a recalcitrant client before.

"She's not nearly as bad as you think," she said, soldiering on. "In fact, I think you'll like her. You just have to take a deep breath and give her a try."

He held her stare, his eyes a stony gray that made her think of battlements and cavernous quarries, but at least he complied. Even breathing, he seemed to be exercising every muscle in his body, the swell of his massive chest like an ocean rising.

It worked though. Already, he looked much less like he wanted to storm out the door and report her to the authorities—or, worse, to her sisters.

"Okay," he said. "I'm breathing. What's next?"

Sophie blinked. Breathing had seemed like the most logical first step, but she had no idea what came after that.

Yes, she did. *Cuddles.* No one could resist puppy cuddles—it was almost as universally acknowledged as the fact that Harrison had chosen the Great Dane as his first pick. Maybe she wouldn't be so bad at this after all.

"That all depends on you," she said. "Would you rather climb into the kennel with Bubbles for your introductory session or take her outside?"

For the second time in as many minutes, his gaze sharpened as though he couldn't believe what he was hearing. He didn't blink or move, just stood there staring at her as though he were looking through a ghost. People did that quite a lot actually—looked through her as though she were nothing—but not like this.

He didn't seem dismissive of her or more interested in the greener pastures that lay beyond. He seemed, well, scared.

"You want *me*"—he pointed at himself—"to climb in *there*? Do you have any idea how far the human body can feasibly bend?"

Sophie had to tamp down a laugh. Now that he'd pointed it out, the idea of that six-foot bear of a man climbing into a pen and snuggling with a baby Pomeranian did seem a little preposterous.

"Outside it is, then," she said. "Just scoop her on up. Don't worry—she won't be afraid of you. She likes to be carried."

He didn't, as she'd hoped, follow her orders. Instead, he glanced down at the little puppy, his brow growing heavier the longer he stood there. It was the same glower that had made him seem so fierce when he'd first walked in.

It didn't seem nearly as intimidating when he shook his head and said, "No, thank you."

She laughed again, unable to stop it from fully releasing this time. All of her tension seemed to be seeping out the more she realized this man was nowhere near as hard as his gruff expression indicated. *All bark and no bite.* "Well, at least you're being more polite about it. I promise she won't bite, and she won't pee all over you. She's a very good girl. Aren't you, Bubbles? Aren't you the most precious little ball o' fluff?"

Harrison took a wide step back from the pen and clasped his hands behind his back. If Sophie didn't know better, she'd think he was afraid of touching the puppy for fear she would infect him with her adorableness.

"No way. I'm not calling her that."

"What? Bubbles?" Laughter welled up in her throat. He was *totally* afraid of her adorableness. "Or precious little ball o' fluff?"

His only answer was a snort. Well, that and another one of those wary looks at the puppy.

"What's wrong?" Sophie asked. "She's just a honey-bunny banana muffin."

"*What?*"

"The fluffiest lady in fluffy town."

"Now see here," he commanded. "You might be able to force this animal on me, but you can't make me say any of that."

No, she couldn't. Sophie couldn't make anybody do anything. She couldn't even get rid of those pushy satellite TV salesmen who still tried door-to-door tactics. The last time someone had asked her to switch cable companies, she'd ended up serving him lemonade and buying 230 sports channels that she and her sisters never watched.

None of that seemed to matter to this man. He was a good head taller than her, outweighed her by the size of the Great Dane puppy, and wore a scowl that could have stripped paint from the walls. But as she took a step closer, he only shook his head in a frantic effort to keep her at bay. It made her feel unexpectedly powerful. Unexpectedly *good.*

"Don't say any more," he warned. "I can't be held responsible for my actions if you do."

"It's all right," she said, feeding off that sense of power, feeling herself coming alive under it. "I can take it."

And then he smiled—for real this time.

Her heart suddenly felt three sizes too big for her chest. She'd known smiles to change a man's appearance before, but not like this. This wasn't a charming smile or a kind smile or even a dashing smile. It was *devastating*, plain and simple. All those lines and creases, the well-worn care that was etched so deeply into his skin—they disappeared only to be replaced by an expression so startlingly warm and inviting that Sophie had no choice but to fall right in.

"Sweet, soft snookums," she said somewhat breathlessly. She could have stopped there, but the urge to babble overcame her. In all honesty, it was a wonder that she was able to speak at all. "Plush princess paddy-winkle. Beautiful bitty baby Bubbles."

That last one broke him. The smile vanished, but only because it lifted into a laugh.

"Oh, hell no," he said. His voice was no less gravelly than it had been before, that deep sound rumbling throughout the kennel, but Sophie detected something new—something *alive*—underscoring it. "If you think I'm going to stand here and let you make a fool out of me, you're sorely mistaken. I'm taking that goddamn Great Dane home with me, and nothing you do or say will stop me." It was said like a dare—almost as if he wanted her to try. Were they…flirting?

Unfortunately, there was no time to find out. Just as she was about to gamely rise to his bait, a voice spoke up from behind them.

"I beg your pardon?" Her sister Lila's voice, normally so polished, acted like a shock of cold water over the proceedings. Sophie turned to find her standing at the top of the steps leading from the kennel to the house they shared. "Is there a problem out here?"

Sophie did her best to put on her usual bright smile, but Lila wasn't looking at her. Her oldest sister—a tall, statuesque beauty who could command the attention of an entire room simply by walking into it—was staring at Harrison with a look that would have done their mother proud. It told Harrison that if he said one more word, goddamned or otherwise, he'd risk the full weight of her wrath.

Of course, when she spoke, her words were nothing but professional.

"I'm terribly sorry if there's been a misunderstanding," she said, and moved elegantly down the steps. Each click of her heels on the cement carried its own warning. "Perhaps I can be of assistance."

"Assistance?" Harrison echoed. All signs of laughter and friendliness had been wiped from his face, replaced once again by the hard wall that he had carried in here.

Lila inclined her head in slight acknowledgment. "Yes. Did I hear you correctly when you stated your preference for the Great Dane over Sophie's selection?"

"You mean Rock?"

Lila nodded.

"Rock. Yes. Rock." Harrison swallowed heavily, glancing back and forth between the sisters. "That's the one I want. The one that's too big to squish."

Lila smiled, but it didn't touch her eyes. She tsked softly. "You have good taste, but I'm afraid he's not available. He's already been assigned to another case. I'm sure Sophie explained that to you already."

"Actually, I—" Sophie caught Lila's eye and clamped her mouth shut. *Of course.* It hadn't even occurred to her to try a discreet lie. When a client wanted what they couldn't have, you were supposed to redirect them, not antagonize them. *Why didn't I think of that?* "Um, no. I hadn't gotten around to it yet."

"So it would seem. Mr. Parks, why don't you come inside with me and we'll work it out? There's no need to upset the puppies with all this arguing."

"He wasn't arguing." Sophie tried to explain but was once again quelled by a look from Lila. What else could she do? Technically, he *had* been arguing—and she'd been egging him on. She'd been *loving it.*

What is wrong with me?

"This is all my boss's fault," Harrison said. His words were abrupt, his movements even more so. "I didn't even want a dog in the first place."

"It's a tricky business, matching people and puppies," Lila said, trying to soothe. "Every temperament is different—even we don't always get it right on the first try. Do we, Soph?"

Sophie knew that her sister was only trying to make up for this intrusion, including her in the conversation so she wouldn't lose *all* her professional footing in front of the client, but she couldn't help but feel miserable. What Lila really meant—and what Lila would never say—was that *Sophie* didn't always get it right on the first try.

She managed a weak smile. "No, it's not always easy."

"There. You see?" Lila extended her hand toward Harrison. "Come inside. We'll be more comfortable having this conversation in the kitchen."

"*No*." He jerked back as though Lila had shot a lightning bolt from her fingertips. "I mean, no thank you. I'm leaving. That puppy can't… There's no way I…"

He paused and took one of Sophie's deep breaths, a thing she might have appreciated if not for the look of painful reproach he shot her as he did it.

"This was a mistake," he said curtly.

And that was all. Turning on his heel, he made for the back door to the kennel.

Sophie wanted to say something to stop him—apologize maybe, or beg him to give her another chance—but he was already swinging through the door by the time she found her tongue.

"Well." Lila was the first to break the silence that followed Harrison's sudden departure. "Oscar wasn't exaggerating about him, was he?"

When Sophie didn't respond, her eyes still fixed on the gentle sway of the door as if waiting for Harrison to reappear, Lila softened her voice. "That was a pretty nasty scene I walked into. You okay, Soph?"

It was exactly like her sister to ask that question. Given the way things had turned out, Lila could have dumped any number of reproaches on Sophie's head, including the fact that she hadn't wanted Sophie to take on this case in the first place, but of course, she didn't. She never would.

Money meant nothing when compared to Sophie's happiness. Work was secondary to making sure Sophie was taken care of.

Which was why Sophie shook her head. She wasn't okay, not by a long shot. She felt humiliated and ashamed and, well, *small*—but more than that, she felt a strong compulsion to meet Harrison Parks on neutral territory once again. At first, he'd looked at her the way everyone always did, but then, when she'd pushed back, there'd been a spark in his eyes she desperately wanted to see again.

"I'm a little rattled, to be honest," Sophie said. "He's not like anyone I've ever met before."

"No," Lila agreed. "Some men are just like that, I'm afraid."

It was on the tip of Sophie's tongue to ask what Lila meant, but she stopped herself just in time. She already knew what Lila was thinking, because it was the same thing she'd thought when Harrison Parks had first knocked on the door.

This is a man who doesn't like to be told what to do. This is a man to be wary of.

But Lila hadn't seen that smile. Lila hadn't been there when he'd quaked at the mere thought of touching such a precious, golden-haired lump as Bubbles. Lila hadn't felt the surge of exhilaration that had come from confronting him…and *winning*.

"And he wasn't necessarily wrong," Lila added. Her hand touched Sophie's shoulder. "I did warn you that Bubbles might not make a good service dog, sweetie. Not every puppy is cut out for this kind of work."

Sophie glanced down at the animal under consideration, a pang of mingled frustration and disappointment filling her gut. Okay, so Bubbles wasn't the most impressive puppy to come under their care—she was small and soft and had lingering issues from the trauma of the puppy mill—but that didn't make her *useless*.

"Don't worry about it," Lila continued softly. "There will be other cases. One unhappy customer won't make or break us. I'll call Oscar and get everything straightened out."

"No, don't." Sophie spoke sharply, using the same tone that had snapped out when Harrison had initially refused Bubbles. At her sister's raised brow, she hastily amended it with, "I'll talk to him. It's my responsibility. I'm the one who mishandled the situation."

Lila's brow didn't come down, but she accepted Sophie's decree with a nod. "Sure thing, Soph. Take the rest of the day off. Go see Oscar. He always makes you feel better."

Sophie offered her a tight smile but didn't say anything. Oscar *did* always make her feel better, but that wasn't what she meant. She didn't want a day off. She didn't want someone to hug her and placate her and tell her everything would be all right.

What she wanted—no, what she *needed*—was to get her client back.

Glancing down at the Pomeranian, who was staring at the back door as if she too expected Harrison to come waltzing back through it at any moment, Sophie decided that was exactly what she'd do too.

Even if it was only so she could feel that sudden spark of battle coming alive inside her again.

chapter 2

YOU SAID HE WAS GOING TO BE TRICKY."

Sophie walked through Oscar's door at the Deer Park Department of Natural Resources without knocking. His office was a small, one-room affair used mostly for administrative purposes, but he could be found there almost around the clock during the wildfire off-season. The May weather was still damp enough to stave off most forest fires, so she knew he'd be in.

"Did I?" Oscar didn't bother to look up from the stack of papers he was sorting on his desk. "I must have been in a good mood."

"You said he had a tendency toward stubbornness."

"From your tone, I'm guessing you disagree."

"You said I should tread warily."

"Actually, I believe my exact words were, *you should wear a hazmat suit underneath a flak jacket*, but you've always had more tact than I do."

She clamped her lips and crossed her arms, stopping short of tapping her foot on the floor. It took a full twenty seconds for Oscar to give in and glance at her, but Sophie was nothing if not patient. It was the one virtue all good dog trainers needed.

When he did finally look up, it was with a wry twist to his smile. The heavy lines of the older man's face were both familiar and friendly, but she knew better than to take the wire-rimmed glasses perched on the end of his nose and the bushy gray mustache as signs of a jolly, grandfatherly type. Oscar was as tough as they came.

He sighed and pulled the glasses off. "Oh dear. What did he do?"

Sophie lowered herself into the lone chair that was squeezed in the room with him. The DNR, as it was more affectionately known, was at least accommodating enough to give him one extra seat.

She could be accommodating where this man was concerned too. After all, she owed him her life.

"Let's just say he decided to dispense with our services," she said.

Oscar sighed again, this time with world-weary resignation, and pinched the bridge of his nose. "He stormed out the second he saw the dog, didn't he?"

"Um."

"Sophie?"

"Not exactly?" She frowned and picked at a hangnail. "I mean, he wasn't *happy* about Bubbles, but that wasn't what ruined things. I, um, may have spoken to him in baby talk for a large portion of the time."

Oscar's entire body stilled. "I'm sorry?"

"It made sense at the time, I swear. He liked it."

"He liked it? Harrison Parks—*my* Harrison Parks—let you whisper sweet nothings to him?"

"They *weren't* sweet nothings," she protested, hoping she didn't sound nearly as foolish as she felt. "I was only trying to get him to relax a little. And I did too—he was smiling and everything. But then Lila came in and misunderstood, and, well…" She let her voice trail off.

Oscar was familiar enough with her sister to fill in the blanks. Sophie was afraid that he'd do that thing where he pinched his nose in dismay again, but all he did was fall into a crack of laughter. Well, that and reach into his desk drawer to extract a bottle of Wild Turkey and two mismatched glasses. He poured out a finger for each of them and pushed one across the crowded desktop.

She stared at it. "I don't understand. What's this for?"

"Because, my dear, you've earned it."

She lifted the glass but didn't sip. "I have? But I told you—he left. *Without* a puppy."

"You also told me that he smiled. That's half the battle right there. Drink up."

Sophie wasn't much of a day drinker, but the memory of Harrison's smile seemed deserving of a good toast. Following Oscar's lead, she clinked her glass against his and took a generous sip. It burned and not in a good way, but she managed to swallow.

"Now." Oscar leaned back in his chair, which creaked as his full weight sank in. "Why don't you tell me exactly what happened? I should have been clearer about how difficult Harrison can be to work with. He's a hell of a firefighter, but he's not what you'd call a people person."

"Oh, don't worry—you were plenty up-front about that. What I don't understand is why you didn't tell me how nervous he is."

Oscar sat up. "Nervous?"

She nodded and took another sip of the bourbon. It burned just as much as the first time, but it gave her the courage she needed to keep going. "I think he was afraid that he'd, um, *squish* Bubbles. That was the impression I got anyway. He wanted the biggest, baddest dog we had, and when I told him that wasn't an option, he sort of got this panicked look in his eye."

"You saw all that?"

Sophie shrugged. It sounded ridiculous, she knew, but how else could she explain it? "From the way he reacted, it was like I'd asked him to carry around a cracked egg for the rest of his life."

"No, he wouldn't like that." Oscar chuckled. "He wouldn't like that at all."

"That was where the baby talk came in. Just some cute names I have for Bubbles, you know? I was trying to get him to say a few of them, which was when he started yelling. It wasn't *real* yelling, but Lila walked in right in the middle of it and couldn't tell the difference. Do you know no one has ever yelled at me before?"

Oscar tugged one end of his mustache. "Is that so?"

"Not once. Not even a little." She sighed, remembering. "It was nice."

"*Nice?*"

"I think you should yell at me for screwing everything up. It might help. Go ahead. I don't mind."

Oscar only shook his head, which just went to show how right she was. In the entirety of her childhood and adult memories, she couldn't even remember anyone sitting her down and giving her a stern talking-to.

"Anyway, that's why I'd like to try again," she said. "If you can convince him to work with me, that is. I'm, um, not sure he'll want to."

For the first time since she'd walked into this office, Oscar allowed a frown to appear. "Oh, he'll work with you, all right. I don't care what tactics you have to resort to—baby talk, speaking in tongues, making him carry a dozen cracked eggs. After what happened last week..."

Sophie didn't say anything, content to let Oscar lapse into thought for as long as he needed. From the report she'd read, it sounded as though Harrison Parks was lucky to be alive. He'd slipped into a diabetic coma after his continuous glucose monitor malfunctioned during a routine wildfire training exercise. Had he been out on a call somewhere remote or inaccessible by road—both common during the height of the wildfire season—they may not have been able to get him to a hospital in time.

As if following the exact thread of her thoughts, Oscar's mouth firmed in a hard line. "If he wants to see any action on the ground this summer, he'll do it. And he'll *like* it, by God. I'm not putting him through that again without some kind of protection in place."

"No, of course not," Sophie said meekly.

"A puppy's the only recourse I have left, short of putting him behind a desk."

"He doesn't seem like the sort to appreciate that," Sophie agreed.

Oscar sighed and scrubbed a hand over his mouth. His glance, when it met hers, was pointed. "He won't make this easy on you, Sophie, not for one minute. I've never known anyone so wrapped up in barbed wire. Are you sure you're up for it?"

"Absolutely," she said the word automatically.

It wasn't automatic enough.

"You're saving my skin to take his case at the last minute like this, but I won't hold it against you if you pass. Especially now that you've met him. And Lila wasn't sure if this dog of yours would be up to the task, so..."

At the mention of her sister's name, Sophie's chin lifted a good inch. "I know what you're thinking, but it's not like that. Bubbles had a rocky start in life, yes, but she can do the job. I know she can." She hesitated before bringing her chin up even more. "And so can I."

His expression softened. "Of course you can, kiddo. Lila's just looking out for you, that's all. We both are."

Any desire she might have had to abandon this project died at once. It was the *kiddo* that did it, the reminder that the history she and Oscar shared was forged in blood a long time ago.

Literally. Once upon a time, this man had leeched the marrow from his bones for her. Once upon a time, he'd undergone extreme pain and hospitalization so she could have another chance at life. It had been eleven years since the bone marrow transplant took successfully and her leukemia went into remission, but that didn't mean Sophie had forgotten.

She'd *never* forget. She couldn't. No one in her life—family, friend, or foe—would let her.

"Bubbles is a lot tougher than she looks," she said as she raised her eyes to Oscar's. "Please let me do this for you, Oscar. For you and for Harrison."

And, she didn't need to add, *for me*.

"I don't know..." Oscar began.

"I'll find a way to make it work," she said. "That's a promise. Even if I have to beg him to come back on my knees. Even if I have to make him yell at me every day for six weeks to do it."

Oscar rolled his shoulders in a gesture of capitulation. With that one small move, Sophie knew she was getting another chance.

Her life was filled with second chances. She sometimes wondered what she'd done to deserve so much.

"He's rough, but he's not that rough. I doubt he'll yell at you for the whole six weeks." Oscar grinned and added, "Four at the very most."

chapter 3

OSCAR MUST HAVE WORKED FAST.

Sophie arrived home from Deer Park to find a house full of people. In addition to her two sisters, who were holding court over a pot of tea in the kitchen, Harrison sat hulking in one corner, looking like a man undergoing extreme torture.

"You know it's going to be a good date when the guy leads with something like that." Dawn winked at Sophie as she stepped into the room. "We broke at least three laws that night. Four if you count some of the really prudish ones in Kentucky. Speaking of, look who's finally returned to the fold. Hello, Soph. You have a visitor."

At the mention of her name, Harrison sprang to his feet, almost knocking over the wooden chair in the process. He was surprisingly swift for a man of his size, but that might have been because she'd never seen anyone look so delighted to see her.

"Oh, thank God," he said. "I've been here for forty-five minutes already."

Right. That wasn't delight so much as it was a deep, profound relief. And who could blame him? Dawn and Lila together in one room were a lot for any man to handle, let alone one who clearly didn't enjoy the social niceties.

"Forty-five minutes?" Sophie asked with a quick check at the clock. "Oscar couldn't have possibly had time to call you. I was still with him at that point."

"What the hell does this have to do with Oscar?" Harrison demanded. Then, as if aware that he was addressing a room of three women rather than a firing squad, he took a deep breath and added, "I, uh, came to apologize. For earlier. About the puppy."

Sophie hadn't had a chance to apprise Dawn of the day's events, but one look at her sister's face and it was obvious she was up to speed. With that kind of giddy glee lighting her from within, Dawn obviously thought this whole thing was hilarious. Lila mostly looked worried.

Neither of those reactions was surprising. Lila had always carried herself with a serene grace that matched her status as the eldest in the family. It also matched her tailored clothes and the topknot she wound her almost waist-length hair into. Dawn wore her own dark locks—a gift, along with the sisters' deep-brown eyes and light-brown skin, from the Vasquez side of their family—in a tousled bob that made the most of her natural waves. Her wide, sunny face was sprinkled with freckles and a smile to match. Lila's demeanor was one men could admire; Dawn's one they couldn't help but be charmed by.

It was only Sophie who lagged behind. She'd done the best she could to distinguish herself from her sisters, her short, boyish figure offset by a pixie cut that made the most of her delicate features, but it was no use. When the three of them stood side by side, she inevitably faded into the background.

Or, rather, she *used* to fade into the background. From the way Harrison was looking at her, like she was his walking savior, she couldn't help but feel a warm glow start to take over.

"There's nothing to apologize for," she said with what she hoped was breezy unconcern. "It was a slight misunderstanding, that's all. I should have warned you ahead of time that your animal had already been selected for you."

"About that..." Lila began, but Sophie turned to her with an imploring look. Lila might technically be the one in charge of Puppy Promise, the service-dog training organization that provided the Vasquez sisters with their life's purpose, but Sophie needed this. *Bubbles* needed this.

Lila had been uncomfortable with the idea of using a puppy mill dog from the start, since the poor thing had obviously been subjected to more than one cruelty in her short life, but Sophie had no doubts on that score. Five minutes in that animal's company had been more than enough to convince her that she was worth taking on.

With some animals—some people—you just *knew*.

"I realize Bubbles isn't much to look at, but she's smart and eager to learn. All she needs is a chance to prove herself."

Harrison didn't say anything. He kept watching her in that intense, panicked way, as if he couldn't make up his mind whether to sit down again or run screaming from the room.

Please don't run screaming from the room, she wanted to beg him. *Please don't run screaming from* me.

"What do you say we make ourselves scarce, Lil?" Dawn asked, a deep dimple appearing in her right cheek. "Scott has that new litter of blue heelers he wanted us to come take a look at."

"But we don't need any—"

"They're very promising. I bet they'll get snatched up quickly. We'll need to act fast if we want to make an offer."

"But—"

Dawn took one glance at Sophie's face and put on her sternest expression. "*Now*, Lila."

It took Lila a good ten seconds to pick up on the subtext and agree to give Sophie and Harrison some space. Harrison was much quicker on the uptake.

"A blue heeler?" he asked. "Are they good at—what did you call it—scent detection?"

"Yes, they are," Sophie said. In fact, given Harrison's obvious preference for dogs with size to recommend them, a blue heeler would be a perfect fit. Their noses were more than adequate to pick up on the subtle changes in human saliva that occurred when blood sugars rose or fell, and the larger dog would be able to keep up with him as he plunged through forest undergrowth.

In any other situation, she'd have allowed the client's preferences to outweigh her own. In this situation, however, she was taking a stand.

Bubbles could *do* this. Sophie had done her research, looked into other fire workers with needs similar to Harrison's, and hand selected an animal based on a careful study of his medical and professional records. This wasn't some idea she'd come up with on the fly.

"I've already talked to Oscar about this, and he agrees with me." She crossed her arms and did her best imitation of a woman who inspired awe and confidence in others. "It's Bubbles, or you don't go back to the field."

As it turned out, admitting to a man that she'd run tattling to his boss wasn't an ideal way to win him over. Instead of submitting to her autocratic decree, Harrison's stance became even more rigid.

Sophie's natural inclination was to turn to her sisters for help, but she pushed the urge down as far as it would go. To admit defeat now would only foster Lila's belief that they should have passed on this case. Sophie'd be back on basic training, once again spending her days teaching puppies how to sit and where to pee.

All things that needed to be done, of course, but those were the easy tasks, the *safe* ones. The kinds of things a fluffy, skittish ball of fur might be expected to tackle.

"If you're willing to try again, I'll bring Bubbles out to the side yard so you two can get to know one another. But you have to promise not to reject her this time. She didn't like it." Almost as an afterthought, she added, "And neither did I."

"Well done, Soph!" Dawn cheered from the doorway. Before Lila could say anything to undermine Sophie's swell of confidence, Dawn bustled them both out of the kitchen.

It was a strange location for an impasse. The house Sophie shared with her sisters was as dainty and feminine as Harrison was rough and masculine. Everywhere the eye landed were massive doilies and vintage finds, with dried flowers next to the sink and artfully arranged silver teaspoons hanging on the wall. Only the kennel through the back door gave any indication that this was as much a place of business as it was a home. Harrison wasn't so tall that his head brushed the ceiling or anything, but he did have a way of filling the space in a way that felt both unfamiliar and unsettling.

It's not just his size, Sophie thought. *It's him.* Whatever else might be said about this man, he was certainly a presence. Being in the same room with him seemed to kindle an awareness in every part of her—a *tingling* awareness that started in her toes and worked upward from there. It was almost as though her limbs were awakening from a long, numbing sleep, and she wasn't sure they were ready to support her weight just yet.

"So you really *do* know Oscar," Harrison said by way of breaking their strange stalemate.

"Oh. Um." Sophie blinked. She'd assumed, when Oscar had asked them to take on this case, that he would have told Harrison all about their personal history. That he hadn't—and most likely wouldn't unless Sophie gave him permission to—said a lot about him. "Yes, actually. He and I go a long way back. He asked me to take your case as a kind of favor."

A look of strange relief swept over Harrison's face. His shoulders actually sagged a little. "Then *that* explains why you put up with me for as long as you did. What did he say about me?"

"Um."

"You don't have to hold back on my account. He won't have said anything I haven't heard a hundred times already, believe me."

As if the sudden turn of conversation wasn't strange enough, Harrison paused and pulled out a chair for her. It was *her* chair, obviously, and he was offering it in *her* house, but the gallantry of the gesture was still forefront in her mind.

She didn't sit though. She was already so dwarfed by this man.

"Please," he said, his voice rough. "One of the things Oscar should have told you first is that my bark is a lot worse than my bite."

With that, Sophie relented. She didn't know if it was the reference to canines that did it, or the fact that he sounded so forlorn, but she took the proffered seat and watched as he lowered himself into the opposite chair. Even in a seated position, he still dwarfed her. Those powerful thighs, the broad shoulders hunched as if ready to pounce—there was no other way she *could* feel in his presence.

Before she could think of a tactful way to disclose her earlier conversation with Oscar, Harrison lifted one massive hand and started ticking off fingers instead.

"I don't take orders well. I don't know how to interact with others in a way that doesn't make them uncomfortable. I'd rather cut off my own foot than admit to a weakness." He paused and considered the matter before turning a look of inquiry her way. "Let's see…which one am I missing?"

Heat rose to the surface of her skin. Sophie didn't believe any of those things, not when he'd made such a generous and obviously painful effort to return here and apologize of his own volition, but she could see how someone meeting him for the first time might get that impression. Those deep lines, that unsmiling expression… He just looked so *hard.*

Harrison took one look at her flaming face and swore. "Dammit. He didn't sugarcoat it, did he? Did he tell you how half the volunteer firefighters I train end up quitting after less than a week or that some of them take one look at me and don't even last the day?"

Sophie had no idea how to answer that question, so she didn't try. Dawn would have been able to turn it to a joke, but her sister wasn't here. She'd scurried off so Sophie could have at least one opportunity to prove herself.

"The week," Harrison repeated carefully, "or the day?"

She began tracing the outline of a red wine ring on the table. "Do people really quit after one day?"

"Your sister took my measure this morning after knowing me for thirty seconds," he said. "What do you think?"

Yes, people probably did quit that fast. But people also took one look at her and assumed she had no more courage than a mouse, so what did they know?

"I'm not going to quit, Mr. Parks," she said. "Oscar asked me to help you, and that's exactly what I intend to do. You're not the only one with flaws, you know."

When he didn't say anything, she held up her hand and started ticking off her own fingers.

"I'm the baby of the family, and it shows. I'm dependent on my sisters for almost everything. I've never gone anywhere or done anything on my own." She paused. This next one was going to be the toughest to get out.

As if sensing that, Harrison cleared his throat. "Anything else?"

She shifted in her seat. "I'm a little intimidated by you, to be honest." She met his gaze and was surprised to find that he was regarding her with alarm. "But it won't get in the way of the job, I promise. Bubbles is an amazing puppy, and I've got a whole training plan worked out for the next six weeks. I realize that neither one of us is what you were expecting when you signed on for a service dog, but I want to do this."

I can *do this.*

"Please, Mr. Parks?" she asked, her voice wavering. Whatever bravery his confession had conjured in her was quickly waning under his continued scrutiny. "You might not think much of me yet, but I have a tendency to grow on people, I swear. I'm like a friendly goiter."

"Harrison," he said.

"What?"

He sat up, no longer hunched as if ready to pounce. "If we're going to be working together, I insist you call me Harrison."

Her first feeling was one of relief—she'd actually done it. She'd gotten through to him. He was going through with the plan and without Oscar being the one pulling the strings.

Her second feeling was more difficult to pin down. This small victory was just the start of the process. If even one-tenth of the things Oscar had said about Harrison were true, there were countless skirmishes ahead.

Strangely enough, she wasn't scared by the prospect. She'd already engaged him in one battle and come out victorious. The idea of waging another campaign—a *lengthy* one this time—made her chest swell.

She'd waited twenty-six years for an opportunity like this.

She stuck her hand out, determined to make their partnership official. It was a good ten seconds before Harrison put her out of her misery, but the end result was worth it. His palm was callused and hard, his skin surprisingly cool for a man of his size. His grip was also much gentler than she expected. She assumed he'd have one of those hypermasculine handshakes, the kind that wrenched her arm out of its socket and nearly crushed the bones of her fingers, but as his palm lingered against hers, it felt more like he was holding her hand than striking a deal.

But his next words were all business, gruff and pointed.

"I guess you'd better bring me this damn dog already," he said.

She was unable to keep the surprise from showing on her face.

He saw it, of course, and directed a wry, twisted grimace inward. "I warned you. Believe me when I say it's for the best that we get this thing started. The sooner she learns how to tolerate me and save my life, the sooner I can get back to work." He paused a beat and added, "And the sooner you can get back to a life without me in it."

About the Author

Lucy Gilmore is a contemporary romance author with a love of puppies, rainbows, and happily ever afters. She began her reading (and writing) career as an English literature major and ended as a die-hard fan of romance in all forms. When she's not rolling around with her two Akitas, she can be found hiking, biking, or with her nose buried in a book. Visit her online at lucygilmore.com.